10⁰⁰
(BOSO)

Baen Books by David Drake

Hammer's Slammers
The Sharp End
The Tank Lords
Caught in the Crossfire
The Butcher's Bill
(forthcoming)

Independent Novels and Collections
Redliners
With the Lightnings
Starliner
Ranks of Bronze
Lacey and His Friends
Old Nathan
Mark II: The Military Dimension
All the Way to the Gallows

The General series
(with S. M. Stirling)
The Forge
The Hammer
The Anvil
The Steel
The Sword
The Chosen

An Honorable Defense: Crisis of Empire
(with Thomas T. Thomas)
Enemy of My Enemy: Nova Terra
(with Ben Ohlander)
The Undesired Princess and the Enchanted Bunny
(with L. Sprague de Camp)
Lest Darkness Fall and To Bring the Light
(with L. Sprague de Camp)
Armageddon
(ed. with Billie Sue Mosiman)

WITH THE LIGHTNINGS

DAVID DRAKE

WITH THE LIGHTNINGS

This is a work of fiction. All the characters and events portrayed in this book are fictional, and any resemblance to real people or incidents is purely coincidental.

A Baen Books Original

Baen Publishing Enterprises
P.O. Box 1403
Riverdale, NY 10471

ISBN: 0-671-87881-6

Cover art by David Mattingly

First printing, July 1998

Distributed by Simon & Schuster
1230 Avenue of the Americas
New York, NY 10020

Library of Congress Cataloging-in-Publication Data

Drake, David.
    With the lightnings / David Drake.
        p.   cm.
    ISBN 0-671-87881-6
    I. Title.
    PS3554.R196W58   1998   98-6745
    813'.54—dc21   CIP

Typeset by Windhaven Press, Auburn, NH
Printed in the United States of America

DEDICATION

To A[rielle] Heather Wood
More widely known as *The* Heather Wood

ACKNOWLEDGMENTS

I'm afraid that I use both machines and people very hard when I'm focused on a project. The machines tend to break; the people, my friends, do not. Sincere thanks to Dan Breen; Jim Baen and Toni Weisskopf; Mark L Van Name and Allyn Vogel; Sandra and John Miesel; and my wife Jo.

A NOTE ON WEIGHT AND MEASURES

As most of my fiction is set either in the far past or the distant future, I regularly face the question of whether to use weights and measures familiar to the reader or instead to reflect the differences that time brings. In this particular case I've decided to use English and metric measurements rather than inventing different but comparable systems.

In my opinion the weights and measures of thousands of years in the future will differ as strikingly from those of today as the latter do from the talents and stades familiar to classical Greeks. Those future systems may well vary among themselves as confusingly as the Euboic and Aeginetic standards did. But while I hope a reader may learn something from this novel as well as being entertained, the state of the world isn't going to be improved by me inventing phony measurement systems.

Me that 'ave followed my trade
In the place where the Lightnin's are made . . .

—Kipling

BOOK ONE

Lieutenant Daniel Leary ambled through the streets of Kostroma City in the black-piped gray 2nd Class uniform of the Republic of Cinnabar Navy. He was on his way to the Elector's Palace, but there was no hurry and really nothing more important for Daniel to do than to savor the fact that he'd realized one of his childhood dreams: to walk a far world and see its wonders first hand.

His other dream, to command a starship himself, would come (if at all) in the far future; a future as distant in Daniel's mind as childhood seemed from his present age of twenty-two Terran years.

For now, he had Kostroma and that was wonder enough. He whistled a snatch of a tune the band had played at the supper club he'd visited the night before.

Daniel smiled, an expression so naturally warm that strangers on the street smiled back at him. The Kostroman lady he'd met there was named Silena. The honor both of a Leary of Bantry and the RCN required that Daniel offer his help when the lady's young escort drank himself into babbling incapacity. Silena had been very appreciative; and after the first few minutes back at her lodgings, pique at her original escort was no longer her primary focus.

Cassian was only a little above average height with a tendency toward fleshiness that showed itself particularly in his florid face. His roundness and open expression caused strangers sometimes to dismiss Daniel Leary as soft. That was a mistake.

A canal ran down the center of the broad street. During daylight it carried only small craft, water taxis and light delivery vehicles, but at night barges loaded with construction materials edged between the stone banks with loud arguments over right-of-way. The pavements to either side seethed with a mixture of pedestrians and three-wheeled motorized jitneys, though like the canals they would fill with heavy traffic after dark.

The Kostroman economy was booming on the profits of interstellar trade, and much of that wealth was being invested here in the capital. Rich merchants built townhouses, and the older nobility added to the palaces of their clans so as not to be outdone.

Folk at a lower social level—clerks in the trading houses, the spacers who crewed Kostroma's trading fleet, and the laborers staffing the factories and fisheries that filled those starships, all had gained in some degree. They wanted improved lodgings as well, and they were willing to pay for them.

Daniel walked along whistling, delighted with the pageant. People wore colorful clothing in unfamiliar styles. Many of them chattered in local dialects: Kostroma was a watery planet from whose islands had sprung a hundred distinct tongues during the long Hiatus in star travel. Even those speaking Universal, now the common language of the planet as well as that of interstellar trade, did so in an accent strange to Cinnabar ears.

Civilization hadn't vanished on Kostroma as it had on so many worlds colonized during the first period of human star travel, but Kostroman society had fragmented without the lure of the stars to unify it. The centuries since Kostroma returned to space hadn't fully healed the social fabric: the present Elector, Walter III of the Hajas clan, had seized power in a coup only six months before.

Nobody doubted that Walter intended to retain Kostroma's traditional friendship with the Republic of Cinnabar, but the new Elector needed money. At the present state of the war between Cinnabar and the Alliance of Free Stars, Walter's hint that he might not renew the Reciprocity Agreement when it came due in three months had been enough to bring a high-level delegation from Cinnabar.

Daniel sighed. A high-level delegation, with one junior lieutenant thrown in as a makeweight. Daniel had almost certainly been sent because he was the son of the politically powerful Corder Leary, former Speaker of the Cinnabar Senate. Daniel's—bad—

relationship with his father was no secret in the RCN, but the ins and outs of Cinnabar families wouldn't be common knowledge on Kostroma.

A man came out of a doorway, pushing himself onto the crowded pavement while calling final instructions to someone within the building. Daniel would have avoided the fellow if there'd been room. There wasn't, so he set his shoulder instead and it was the larger Kostroman who bounced back with a surprised grunt.

No one took notice of what was merely a normal hazard of city life. Daniel walked on, eyeing with interest the carven swags and volutes that decorated unpretentious four-story apartment buildings.

Kostromans didn't duel the way members of Cinnabar's wealthy families sometimes did. On the other hand, feuds and assassination were accepted features of Kostroman social life. Daniel supposed it was whatever you were used to.

In Xenos, Cinnabar's capital, real magnates like Corder Leary moved through the streets with an entourage of fifty or more clients, some of whom might be senators themselves. You stepped aside or the liveried toughs leading the procession knocked you aside. The free citizens of the galaxy's proudest republic accepted—indeed, expected—that their leaders would behave in such fashion. Who would obey a man who lacked a strong sense of his own honor?

Birds fluted as they spun in tight curves from roof coping to roof coping overhead. They were avian in the same sense as the scaly "birds" of Cinnabar, the winged amphibians of Sadastor, or the flyers of a thousand other worlds that humans had visited and described. The details were for scientists to chart and for quick-eyed amateurs like Daniel Leary to notice with delight.

During the final quarrel Daniel had said he'd take nothing from his father; but the Leary name had brought Daniel to Kostroma. Well, the name was his by right, not his father's gift. Daniel didn't have a shipboard appointment, and he really had no duties even as part of Admiral Dame Martina Lasowski's delegation; but he'd reached the stars.

The Kostroman navy was small compared to the fleets of Cinnabar and the Alliance, and even so it was larger than it was efficient. Kostroma's captains and sailors were of excellent quality, but the merchant fleet took the greater—and the better—part of the personnel. Ratings in the Kostroman navy were largely foreigners; officers were generally men who preferred the high life in Kostroma City to hard voyaging; and the ships spent most of their time laid up with their ports sealed and their movable equipment warehoused, floating in a dammed lagoon south of the capital called the Navy Pool.

A starship was landing in the Floating Harbor. Daniel turned to watch, sliding the naval goggles down from his cap brim against the glare.

Starships took off and landed on water both because of the damage their plasma motors would do to solid ground and because water was an ideal reaction mass to be converted to plasma. Once out of a planet's atmosphere ships used their High Drive, a matter/anti-matter conversion process and far more efficient, but to switch to High Drive too early was to court disaster.

At one time Kostroma Harbor had served all traffic, but for the past generation only surface vessels used the city wharfs. The Floating Harbor built of hollow concrete pontoons accommodated the starships a half mile offshore.

The pontoons were joined in hexagons that damped the waves generated by takeoffs and landings, isolating individual ships like larvae in the cells of a beehive. Seagoing lighters docked on the outer sides of the floats to deliver and receive cargo.

The ship landing just now was a small one of three hundred tons or so; a yacht, or more probably a government dispatch vessel. The masts folded along the hull indicated the plane on which Cassini Radiation drove the ship through sponge space was very large compared to the vessel's displacement.

The hull shape and the way two of the four High Drive nozzles were mounted on outriggers identified the ship as a product of the Pleasaunce system, the capital of the deceptively named Alliance of Free Stars. That was perfectly proper since the vessel was unarmed. Kostroma was neutral, trading with both parties to the conflict.

Kostroma's real value to combatants lay not with her navy but in her merchant fleet and extensive trading network to regions of the human diaspora where neither Cinnabar nor the Alliance had significant direct contact. Formally the Reciprocity Agreement granted Cinnabar only the right to land warships on Kostroma instead of staying ten light-minutes out like those of other nations.

As a matter of unofficial policy, however, neutral Kostroman vessels carried cargoes to Cinnabar but not to worlds of the Alliance. That was an advantage for which General Porra, Guarantor of the Alliance, would have given his left nut.

The dispatch vessel touched down in a vast gout of steam; the roar of landing arrived several seconds later as the cloud was already beginning to dissipate. Daniel raised his goggles and continued walking. A graceful bridge humped over a major canal; from the top of the arch Daniel glimpsed the roof of the Elector's Palace.

An Alliance dispatch vessel might mean Porra or his bureaucrats believed there was a realistic chance of detaching Kostroma from Cinnabar. Alternatively, the Alliance could simply be trying to raise the price Admiral Lasowski would finally agree to pay. Walter III would have invited an Alliance delegation as a bargaining chip even if Porra hadn't planned to send one on his own account.

Well, that was only technically a concern for Lt. Daniel Leary. As a practical matter, he was a tourist visiting a planet which provided a range of unfamiliar culture, architecture, and wildlife.

Whistling again, he strolled off the bridge and along the broad avenue leading toward the palace.

Adele Mundy stood in the doorway, fingering a lock of her short brown hair as she surveyed what was only in name the Library of the Elector of Kostroma. Adele was an organized person; she would organize even this. The difficulty was in knowing where to start.

The room was large and attractive in its way; ways, really, because whichever Elector had been responsible for the decoration had been catholic in his taste. Time had darkened the wood paneling from its original bleached pallor. The enormous stone hood of the fireplace was carved with a scene of hunting in forests that looked nothing like Kostroman vegetation, and blue-figured tiles formed the hearth itself. The knees supporting the coffered ceiling imitated gargoyles.

The last were a singularly inappropriate choice for the interior of a library. The notion of figures gaping to gargle rainwater onto Adele's collections made her shudder.

The chamber had probably been intended as a drawing room for Electoral gatherings smaller and more private than those in the enormous Grand Salon below on the second floor. There was quite a lot of space in terms of cubic feet since the ceiling was thirty feet above, but there would have to be a great deal of modification to make it usable for shelving books.

The modification was one of the problems Adele had been trying to surmount in the three weeks since she had arrived in Kostroma City to take up her appointment as the Electoral Librarian. One of many problems.

"Pardon, pardon!" a workman growled to Adele's back in a nasal Kostroman accent. She stepped sideways into the room, feeling her abdominal muscles tense in anger.

The man hadn't been impolite, technically: Adele was standing in the doorway through which he and his mate needed to carry a plank. But there was no hint in his tone that the off-planet librarian was his superior or, for that matter, anything but a pain in the neck.

A six-foot board wasn't much of a load for two people to carry, but even that wasn't why Adele became dizzy with frustration. That was a result of seeing the material, polished hardwood with a rich, swirling grain. It was probably as pretty a piece of lumber as she'd ever seen in her life.

Elector Jonathan Ignatius, Walter III's immediate predecessor, was a member of the Delfi clan and an enthusiastic hunter. Jonathan's absence on a six-month, multi-planet safari had permitted rivals in the Hajas and Zojira clans to prepare the coup that unseated him the night of his return.

Walter by contrast wanted to be remembered as a patron of learning, possibly because he had no more formal education than the Emperor Charlemagne. He'd decided to found an electoral library under the carefully neutral direction of a Cinnabar scholar living in exile on the Alliance world of Bryce. He'd assembled the contents of the library by the simple expedient of stripping books, papers, and electronic storage media from Delfi households and those of their collateral clans.

The loot—Adele couldn't think of another word to describe it—was piled here in a variety of boxes and crates. Most of them weren't marked, and she didn't trust the labels on those which had them. The only order in the library was the view out the north windows, onto the formal gardens.

What Adele needed to start—what she had requested as many times and in as many ways as she could imagine—was three thousand feet of rough shelving. What she was getting from the carpenters Walter's chamberlain had assigned to the project was cabinetry of a standard that would grace a formal dining room. At the present rate of progress, the job would be done sometime in the next century.

There was no doubt about the skill of the carpenters, these two journeymen and the master cabinetmaker who never left her shop on the ground floor and never touched a tool with her own hands that Adele had seen. They were simply the wrong people for the job. The twenty Kostroman library assistants whom Adele was to train to the standards of Cinnabar or the central worlds of the Alliance—these were with only a few exceptions the wrong people for *any* job.

Laughter boomed in the hallway. Adele sidled another step away from the door and put her straight back against the wall. The band of tile at neck level felt cool and helped keep her calm. Bracey, one of her assistants, entered with two other men whom Adele didn't recognize.

That didn't mean they weren't library assistants: the positions had been granted as political favors to relatives who needed jobs. The only blessing was that most of them, lazy scuts with neither ability nor interest in library work, didn't bother to show up. Those who did pilfered and damaged materials through careless disregard.

Bracey, a Zojira collateral, was one of those who often came to the library. Unfortunately.

The trio entered the room, passing a bottle among them. From the smell of their breath as they strode past Adele she was surprised they were still able to move, let alone climb the lovely helical staircase to the third floor.

Three other assistants were in the library. Two were fondling one another in a corner. Their lives were at risk if in passion they managed to dislodge the boxes stacked to either side. The third assistant was Vanness, who was actually trying to organize a crate of what were probably logbooks. Alone of her "assistants," Vanness had the interest that was a necessary precondition to becoming useful. The Kostroman wasn't any real help now, but Adele could cure his ignorance if she just got some room to *work* in.

"Hey, save me seconds!" Bracey called to the couple in the corner. Adele's presence hadn't concerned them, but now they sprang apart.

One of Bracey's companions tugged his arm, nodding toward

Adele behind them. Bracey waved the bottle to her and said, "Hey, chiefie! Want a drink?"

Bracey burped loudly; his companions lapsed into giggles. Adele looked through the Kostroman as if he didn't exist, then walked to the data console she'd spent most of the past two weeks getting in order because *that* was within her capacity to achieve without the help of anyone else . . . and she didn't have the help of anyone else.

The console was of high-quality Cinnabar manufacture and so new that it was still crated in the vestibule of the palace when Walter's supporters took stock after the coup. It came loaded with a broad-ranging database which could, now that Adele had completed her labors, access information from any of the computers in the government network; better and faster than the computers could reach their own data, in most cases.

Adele rested her forehead against the console's smooth coolness and wondered whether starving on Bryce would have been a better idea than accepting the Kostroman offer. But it had seemed so wonderful at the time. She'd even told Mistress Boileau, "It's too good to be true!"

Adele smiled. At least in hindsight she could credit herself with a flawlessly accurate analysis.

Adele was a Mundy of Chatsworth, one of Cinnabar's most politically powerful families while she was growing up, though the Mundys' populist tendencies meant they were generally on the outs with their fellow magnates. Adele hadn't been interested in politics. When she was sixteen she'd left Xenos for the Bryce Academy. Her choice was made as much to avoid the alarms and street protests escalating into riots as for the opportunity to study the premier collections of the human galaxy under Mistress Boileau.

That was fifteen terrestrial years ago. Three days after Adele Mundy reached Bryce, the Speaker of the Cinnabar Senate announced that he'd uncovered an Alliance plot to overthrow the government of Cinnabar through native agents—primarily members of the Mundy family. The Senate proscribed the traitors. Their property was confiscated by the state or turned over to those who informed against them, and those proscribed were hunted down under emergency regulations that were a license to kill.

Adele had a bank account on Bryce, but it was intended to provide her first quarter's allowance rather than an inheritance.

Mistress Boileau herself replaced the support which had vanished with the Mundys of Chatsworth. Her charity was partly from kindness, because the old scholar's heart was as gentle as a lamb's on any subject outside her specialty: the collection and organization of knowledge.

But beyond kindness Mistress Boileau realized Adele was a student with abilities exceeding those of anyone else she had trained in her long career. They worked on terms of increasing equality, Adele's quickness balanced by the breadth of information within Mistress Boileau's crystalline mind. Nothing was said, but both of them expected Adele to take Mistress Boileau's place when the older woman died at her post—retirement was as unlikely a possibility as the immediate end of the universe.

Maybe without the war . . .

Cinnabar and the Alliance had fought three wars in the past century. This fourth outbreak had less to do with the so-called Three Circles Conspiracy than it did with the same trade, pride, and paranoia which had led to the earlier conflicts. Those were politicians' reasons and fools' reasons; nothing that touched a scholar like Adele Mundy.

But the decree that came out of the Alliance capital on Pleasaunce touched her, for all that it was framed by politicians and fools. The Academic Collections on Bryce were a national resource. Access to them by citizens of the Republic of Cinnabar was to be strictly controlled.

Mistress Boileau suggested a way out of the crisis. She had friends on Pleasaunce. They couldn't exempt Adele from the ruling, but they could make Adele an Alliance citizen as soon as she renounced Cinnabar nationality.

A moment earlier Adele would have described herself as a citizen of learning and the galaxy, not of any national boundary that tried to limit mankind. Cinnabar was a memory of the riots she saw in person and the slaughter she missed by hours.

But she was a Mundy of Chatsworth, and she would be *damned* before any politician on Pleasaunce made her say otherwise.

Then the Elector of Kostroma asked Mistress Boileau, Director of the Academic Collections on Bryce, to recommend someone to run his new library. The request had seemed a godsend at the time. Now . . .

Bracey cried in alarm. Adele raised her head.

Bracey sprang backward, bumping into the boxed remains of several electronic data units that might antedate the palace. One of his companion drunks vomited. Most of the yellowish gout cascaded onto a gunnysack filled with loose paper of some kind, but splatters landed on Bracey's boots.

"Bracey," Adele said, her voice a handclap, "get out, and take your fellows with you. And stay out!"

"Aw, don't knot your panties, chiefie," the assistant said. His boots were red suede; he tentatively rubbed the toe of one against a pasteboard carton, smearing but not removing the splash of vomit. "I'll get one of the maids to—"

"Get out, by God!" Adele said.

Bracey's face clouded. The friend who still stood had been watching Adele and had seen more than a short, slim female in nondescript clothing. As Bracey opened his mouth to snarl a curse, the friend tugged his arm and muttered.

Bracey shook himself free, then dragged the sick man up by the collar. "Come on, Kirkwall," he said. "If you've ruined these boots, I'll flay another pair from your backside, damned if I won't!"

Two men supporting the third, the Kostromans shuffled out of the library. Adele remained by the data console, following them with her eyes. When she looked around the room again, the other assistants and the two carpenters were staring at her. All of them turned their heads instantly.

"I'll take care of this, mistress," Vanness said as he trotted toward the mess of vomit. He waved the bag which had held the log-books, to use as a wiping rag.

The bag itself might identify where the contents had come from—

But Adele caught her objection unvoiced. There was nothing she'd gain from speaking that would justify the seeming rebuke of a man who was trying to do his job.

"Yes, very well," she said instead. She turned her hawk glance onto the carpenters. They'd resumed measuring their plank against the brackets they'd yesterday fastened to the paneling and the frames mortised into the brick fabric of the wall.

"You two!" Adele Mundy ordered. "Come along with me to see your mistress, and bring that silly piece of veneer stock with you. I need proper shelving *now*, and I don't mean enough for a medicine chest!"

She was a Mundy of Chatsworth. She might very well fail, but she wasn't going to quit. With her face hard, she set off for the cabinet shop in the arches supporting the causeway to the palace gardens.

"I believe there's only one more matter to be considered at this time, sirs and madame," said the Secretary to the Navy Board. She was a woman at the latter end of middle age, utterly colorless in tone and appearance. Her name was Klemsch, but two of the five board members couldn't have called her anything beyond "Mistress Secretary" without thinking longer than they were accustomed to do.

With absolute rectitude and self-effacement Klemsch had served Admiral Anston for over thirty years. Because of that she was herself one of the most powerful individuals in the Republic of Cinnabar.

"Oh, for God's sake, Anston," Guiliani grumbled. "Does it have to be today? I have an engagement."

"It shouldn't take long," Admiral Anston said, politely but without any hint that his mind might be changed. He nodded to Klemsch. "Invite Mistress Sand to join us, please."

"I knew I should have stayed in bed today," the Third Member muttered, scowling at the table's onyx surface.

Three of the junior board members were senators; Guiliani was not, but the present Speaker was her first cousin. She and La Foche had naval rank themselves, but Admiral Anston was the only serving officer. He had earned both his rank and his considerable private fortune waging war successfully against Cinnabar's enemies.

No Chairman of the Navy Board could be described as apolitical, but it was accepted by all who knew Anston that his whole loyalty was to the RCN itself. At this time of present crisis, even the most rabid party politician preferred the office to be in Anston's hands rather than those of someone more malleable but less competent.

Mistress Sand entered the conference room without an obvious summons. She was a bulky woman, well if unobtrusively dressed. "Harry," she said, nodding. "Gene, Tom, it's good to see you. Bate, my husband was just asking after you. Will we see you next week at the Music Society meeting?"

"We're planning to attend," the Third Member replied. "At least if my granddaughter's marriage negotiations wrap up in time."

All the political members of the board knew Mistress Sand socially; none of them wanted to have professional contact with the genial, cultured woman.

"I told my fellows that this wouldn't take long, Bernis," Admiral Anston said. "Why don't you lay out just the heads of the business rather than going into detail as you did with me?"

Sand nodded pleasantly and opened her ivory snuffbox. She placed a pinch in the hollow formed by her thumb and the back of her hand, then snorted it into her left nostril.

There was a chair open for her at Anston's right. She remained standing.

"The Alliance is planning some devilment on Kostroma," Sand said. Admiral Anston wore a slight smile; the four junior board members were frowningly silent. "I'm afraid that the risks are such that we need to take action ourselves."

"There's already trouble with the new Elector, isn't there?" the Fourth Member said. "Time we took the place over ourselves and cut the subsidy budget, *I* say."

"The reasons we decided Kostroma was more valuable as a friend than as a possession," Anston said, "appear to me to remain valid. But we can't permit the Alliance to capture Kostroma, and the Kostromans are unlikely to halt a really serious Alliance invasion. Their fleet is laid up and their satellite defense system hasn't been upgraded in a generation."

"Walter Hajas isn't going to like us interfering," Guiliani said in a gloomy tone. Her family had invested heavily in the Kostroma trade, so the probable disruption had personal as well as national importance to her. "Let alone us basing a fleet on Kostroma. A few ships refitting at a time, sure, but the harbor's already near capacity with the merchant trade. If we reduce that, a lot of people lose money and the new Elector gets unpopular fast."

She shook her head in dismay. "As do we."

"We don't have a battle fleet to send!" the Second Member said. He looked up at Anston in sudden concern. "Do we, Josh? I understood we were too stretched for proper patrolling against privateers."

Three ships in which the Second Member was a partner had been taken by Alliance raiders in the past year. That was partly bad luck and partly a result of the member spreading his investments over nearly a hundred vessels . . . but it was also true that closer patrolling of systems known to outfit privateers might have helped.

As little as the political members liked what they were hearing, none of them had questioned the seriousness of the threat. Mistress Sand wouldn't have come before the full board this way if she'd thought the matter could be handled through normal channels.

"I don't foresee the need of a fleet if we act promptly," Mistress Sand said. "Or for a permanent presence. We can fulfill our requirements with an improvement to Kostroma's satellite defense system and perhaps some experts to maintain and control it. The personnel wouldn't have to wear Cinnabar uniforms."

She rotated the snuffbox between her thumb and forefinger. It was cone-shaped and the carvings on its surface had been worn to tawny shadows.

"We were planning to upgrade the defenses of Pelleas Base," Anston said to his fellow members. "The new constellation is already being loaded on transports. While I'm not comfortable in my mind about Pelleas, the Kostroma situation appears to be more immediately critical."

The political members nodded. Guiliani muttered, "You could buy a battleship for what one of those damned satellite constellations cost, but I suppose we'll find the money somewhere. I'll have a word with my cousin."

"We'll need an escort," said the Fourth Member. "All it'd take is for illiterate pirates from Rouilly to grab that load!"

"I think we can scare up a few destroyers for a cargo of such importance," Anston said without cracking a smile. "And it occurred to me that guardships get too little out-of-system time to be at peak performance if they should be needed. The *Rene Descartes* isn't as fast as a newer battleship, but she can keep up with a transport."

"Walter Hajas can be made to understand that the squadron's presence is temporary," Ms. Sand said. "Merely a training exercise."

"A guardship?" the Third Member said. "What are we leaving unguarded, then?"

"Admiral Koffe's heavy cruiser squadron arrived at Harbor Three yesterday for refit," Anston said, skirting the nub of the question. "That can wait while . . . Admiral Ingreit, I think I'd recommend . . . returns from Kostroma with the *Rene Descartes*."

"Christ," the Third Member muttered. "Well, if you're sure, Anston."

"None of us can be sure of anything except our ultimate demise, Harry," Mistress Sand said, smiling as she returned the snuffbox to a pocket in the front of her silk jumper. "But I think we can reasonably expect a good result—"

Her words lost the overtone of good humor, though a stranger wouldn't have thought the stocky woman sounded worried as she concluded, "—so long as the squadron arrives at Kostroma in time. I'm afraid there may be very little time."

There was a fountain in the plaza fronting the Elector's palace: a fish-tailed Triton sat on a shell and blew water vertically from a conch. The stream splashed onto the shell and finally drained into the passing canal.

Though the fountain was twenty feet high and therefore imposing, Daniel didn't find it in any way attractive. He felt much the same way about the palace itself.

Well, unlike the other three members of the delegation, Daniel didn't even live there. Admiral Martina Lasowski and her senior aides doubtless had more serious concerns than the fact they were housed in a three-story pile of beige brick with pillared arches in the center and windows of many different styles on the wings.

Daniel frowned as he walked over the final narrow pedestrian bridge. Because Daniel was a supernumerary, the admiral had permitted him to find his own accommodation—a harborside apartment. Being billeted in the palace at government expense would have saved money, but at a cost to the freedom of his personal life.

Still, the money would have been nice. Daniel's spending had exceeded his combined income—naval pay and a small annuity settled on him at his mother's death—ever since he broke with his father. He'd gotten considerable credit simply because he was a Leary of Bantry, but even that had stretched close to the breaking point.

If not beyond it. Maybe his sister would see her way clear to a loan.

Daniel no longer told himself that he'd cut back his expenditures in the near future. That hadn't happened in six years, so it wasn't probable now. It cost a good deal to keep up the show required of an officer worthy of promotion, and besides, he'd gotten a taste for high life in his early years.

The palace entrance was a rank of eight archways, with six more in the row immediately behind the first and four final arches giving onto three broad steps to the tall doors. The pillared court stretched sixty-five feet back from the plaza, and the amount of greenish stone in the columns was staggering.

Daniel's mother had raised him at Bantry, the country estate claimed—in legend, at any rate—by the Leary family when the first colony ship arrived on Cinnabar. His sister Deirdre was the elder by two years. She, Corder Leary' pride and presumptive heir, spent most of her time in the family townhouse in Xenos under the care of nurses and other hirelings.

Deirdre had emerged from the capital milieu of vice, pomp, and riot as a sober, pragmatic woman who drank as a duty, ate to fuel her body, and had no vices rumored even by political enemies. Daniel, the product of mother love and rural sport, was . . . less of a paragon.

Well, Deirdre's virtues weren't those of the Republic of Cinnabar Navy. The RCN was a place for hot courage, quick initiative, and the willingness to follow a fixed course when orders required it. Daniel thought he might someday be an RCN officer whom others spoke of, if he survived.

And if he ever got a command. Talent could help an officer to a command, and luck was useful in the RCN as well as all the rest of life. But the best way to a command was through interest: the help of wealthy and politically powerful citizens. People like Speaker Leary, who would have preferred to see his son in Hell rather than in the navy.

Which was why Daniel had joined, of course. One of the reasons. He'd been drawn also by his Uncle Stacey Bergen's tales of far worlds. Those were some of Daniel's warmest and earliest memories.

The vast entrance alcove was lighted only by the sun shining onto the plaza in front of it. That should have been sufficient now at midmorning, but Daniel's eyes took a moment to readapt from full day to these shadowed stones. In bad weather the hawkers, idlers, and thieves thronging the plaza came here for protection. Their trash remained to eddy disconsolately among the pillars.

The great wooden doors into the palace were open. A squad

of guards whose berets were quartered in the Hajas colors, silver and violet, stood nearby. Their weapons, slung or leaning against the wall, were mostly sub-machine guns which accelerated pellets to high velocity by electromagnetic pulses. One guard had an impeller that threw slugs of greater weight and penetration.

A line of scars, filled with plastic but visible because of their lighter hue, crossed the right-hand doorpanel at waist height. Somebody'd raked the doorway with an automatic impeller, probably on the night Walter Hajas became Elector. Maybe one of the present guards had been at the grips of the big weapon then. . . .

Daniel climbed the steps to the entrance, feeling fire in his shins each time he raised his leg. Kostroma City was as flat as the lagoon from which it'd been reclaimed, but the many arched bridges between Daniel's apartment and the palace had taken their toll.

Hogg, Daniel's manservant, had offered to drive him in a three-wheeled jitney of the type that was universal in the city. Daniel had walked instead as the best way to see the city. In hindsight, he thought that perhaps he could've seen enough of Kostroma from the jitney's back seat.

A Cinnabar naval officer was expected to have servants. A wealthy lieutenant, the sort of fellow Daniel would have been had not he and his father disowned one another, might have a dozen servants in port and several even on shipboard during war service (though all but one of the latter would be ratings paid from the officer's pocket for additional services).

Hogg was neither fish nor fowl: no rich man's sophisticated valet, but not a sailor either. Hogg was a countryman in his early fifties, balding and cherubic to look at. He'd been Daniel's watcher as an infant and his servant in later years.

Hogg had taught Daniel the history and legends of the Leary family; had guided him through every copse and ravine of the vast Bantry estate; and had spanked the boy with a hand hard enough to drive nails the day Daniel struck his mother in a six-year-old's tantrum.

Mistress Leary had never known about the spanking. She'd have dismissed Hogg in a heartbeat if she'd learned, despite Hogg's long service with the family. Daniel had been aware of that; but there were matters for mothers, and other matters that men settled among themselves.

Daniel apologized to both of them, mother and servant, for

behaving in an unworthy fashion. Looking back on it, he thought that afternoon had been his making as a man.

Hoggs had been retainers of the Leary of Bantry for as far back as the parish records ran. Mostly Hoggs appeared in those records as smugglers and poachers; in that, too, Daniel's servant ran true to type. Daniel hadn't asked how Hogg came by the jitney, because he was pretty sure he didn't want to know.

The Hajas guards ignored the Cinnabar lieutenant while they argued about a professional handball match. Daniel didn't suppose he looked like an assassin, but the guards' lackadaisical attitude disturbed him as a military professional. The folk guarding the Senate House in Xenos were polite, but strangers didn't enter the building without someone to vouch for them.

The Elector's Palace was the seat of government as well as a residence and function hall. Inevitably there were more bureaucrats than space for them. A dozen desks were set against the inside of the staircases sweeping up both sides of a vast oval entryway. Clerks—very junior clerks if their cheap clothing was anything to go by—hunched there over papers or, in a few cases, electronic data terminals.

The vestibule was a bedlam of strange dialects and Universal spoken with a Kostroman accent. Folk passed up and down the stairs, talking in voices that echoed from the domed ceiling two flights above. Daniel had been raised in a great household, had lived in a dormitory at Navy School, and had served in warships whose large crews meant each rating shared a bunk with a rating of the other division. This cacophony had a feel of home; he smiled broadly again.

One of the desks in the vestibule faced outward so the man seated at the terminal there could also keep an eye on his fellows. He was gray and thin; pinned at his throat was a short satin shoulder wrap in the Hajas colors. Daniel doubted the fellow's title was anything so exalted as "office manager," but he clearly had authority over this assemblage of clerks mostly half his age.

Daniel slipped a coin from a purse that was extremely flat already and held it in his palm as he approached the senior clerk's desk. The fellow was keying in numbers with his right hand while his left tilted a sheet of handwritten paper to catch light from the electric sconce attached to the balustrade above him.

"Sir!" Daniel said cheerfully, noting the surprise in the eyes of a man who probably hadn't been addressed by a stranger at any time in the past week. "I wonder if one of your underlings can guide me to where I want to go? I could wander all day in a building so impressive as this."

He brought the coin out in a trick Hogg had taught him, walking it between his knuckles without ever touching it with a fingertip. It was Cinnabar money, a five-florin piece: clear plastic with a gold inner layer that danced and winked in the ill-lit vestibule. In the country five florins was a day's wage; in Xenos it would buy a meal without wine. A Kostroman would lose part of the value in changing it, but Cinnabar coinage was flashier and more impressive than the local scrip.

"What?" said the clerk. "Well, an usher . . ."

It took a moment for his eyes to focus on the coin; then they grew wider. "On the other hand," he continued, "I suppose Russo could—"

He looked at the young woman at the desk beside him; all the clerks were now staring at their senior and the uniformed stranger. In sudden decision the man stood up himself. "No!" he said. "I'll guide you myself, good sir. You'd like to find the apartments of the Cinnabar citizens staying here, I suppose?"

"Not at all," said Daniel, passing the coin to the Kostroman with a sweep of his hand. "My uncle was a great explorer himself, and I hope to follow his example. I came here to see what information may be in the Electoral library."

He beamed at the blinking clerk.

If Adele Mundy had spent the past hour talking to the wall of the cabinet shop, she wouldn't now feel a burning desire to flay the wall with a riding whip. That was the only difference she could see between that and her discussion with Master Carpenter Bozeman.

If she heard the phrase "I'm sorry, mistress, but we do things different here on Kostroma" just one more time, she'd scream.

There were four people in the library: the two lovers, who were ignoring the stranger deliberately instead of merely being concerned with their own activity; Vanness, who because he couldn't ignore the stranger but wasn't sure he ought to approach the fellow, was bouncing like a child who needs a toilet; and the stranger himself.

The stranger was a man wearing a gray suit with closer tailoring than the Kostroman fashion. His back was to the door, and he was leafing through a folio volume that dated from before the Hiatus.

"Sir!" Adele said. "I'm the Electoral Librarian. May I ask who you are?"

If he dropped the book or tore a page, she'd—

The fellow turned. The gray suit was a uniform. He was a little on the plump side, with sandy hair and a smile that made him look even more of a boy than he clearly was.

"Honored to meet you, mistress," he said. "I'm Lieutenant Daniel Leary, Republic of Cinnabar Navy. Sorry I can't shake hands with you but—"

He waggled the folio slightly. He had a hand under either board. To turn pages he'd apparently rested a corner on the stack of deed boxes beside him in lieu of a proper reading table.

"—a book like this takes precedence over courtesy. Did you realize this is a *first* edition of Moschelitz's *Zoomorphology of the Three Systems*? I can't read the Russiche, but I recognize the plates from Ditmars's translation. This original color is so much better!"

"Yes, I do recognize Moschelitz," Adele said drily; though she might not have, and it was a wonder equal to a western sunrise than anybody else on Kostroma did. "You're an information specialist yourself, sir?"

Leary closed the huge volume with the care its size and age required. He'd taken it from the middle of a stack. It was a knife to Adele's heart that somebody who understood books should know that she'd allowed it to lie with that weight on it simply because the task of organizing this mire of information had daunted her.

"No, not me," Leary said. His engaging grin slipped a trifle as he—and Adele, from where she stood—looked for a place he could safely put Moschelitz down. "I'm a bit of an amateur naturalist, though. My uncle, Commander Stacey Bergen—perhaps you've heard of him?"

"No, I'm afraid the name's new to me," Adele said. "Here, I'll take that. Perhaps I can store it. . . ."

"At my lodgings," she'd been about to say, but her room was apt to be broken into at any time. If the concierge, Ms. Frick, wasn't a scout for burglars, then her face sadly belied her.

The only safety for the folio was that nobody knew how valuable it was. To that end, leaving it as part of the undifferentiated mass of the library was the best chance of safety.

"I think maybe on that stack there," Leary said, nodding toward three wooden boxes that Adele hadn't gotten around to opening. They might be filled with business ledgers for all she knew. He didn't hand over the book. "I know it's a little high, but it seems a solid base."

"Yes, all right," Adele said. She couldn't lift the folio down herself without a ladder, but she wasn't likely to need to. Vanness could reach it. . . .

Leary walked to the piled boxes, stepping over and around other stacks with an ease that Adele envied. Part of being in the navy, she supposed. Certainly the starships on which she'd travelled, even the luxury liner that took her from Cinnabar to Blythe, had been cramped. Warships were probably worse.

Leary raised the folio over his head, holding it at the balance. He put the book squarely on top of the pile without rubbing the cover on the wood as she'd feared.

"The reason I asked if you'd heard of my uncle," he said as he concentrated on his task, "is that you've a Cinnabar accent yourself. Uncle Stacey had a dozen species named after him by the academics who described specimens he brought back home."

Adele felt her lips tighten. She'd known there was a Cinnabar naval delegation on Kostroma. One of Mistress Bozeman's excuses for delay was her need to refit the wardrobes in the suite assigned to the guests.

In an even tone Adele said, "I was born on Cinnabar, but I haven't lived there in a very long time. I prefer to think of myself as a citizen of the galaxy."

Leary nodded pleasantly and stepped back from the boxes. "That was my Uncle Stacey too," he said. "Not that he isn't a patriot, and no one ever mistook him for a coward either. He didn't push to get a combat posting, even though he knew as well as anybody that a few battle stars are the surest route to promotion."

He shook his head and laughed. "If I'm ever half the astrogator my uncle is, I'll be proud," he continued. "But this—"

He pinched the breast of his gray uniform, beneath the single drab medal ribbon.

"—is the Republic of Cinnabar *Navy*, after all. I guess I'm as fit to fight my country's enemies as the next fellow, and if I get promoted for it—"

His smile lit the room.

"—well, that's fine with me too."

Adele didn't laugh with Leary, but she felt her lips twisting in a grin. He seemed *very* young. The chances were his attitude would seem young to a person like Adele Mundy even if he were fifty years her senior. Leary's enthusiasm was infectious, though, and he knew something about books.

She squirmed to the logbooks Vanness had unpacked earlier in the morning. "You might be interested in these," she said, lifting the top one and opening the metal cover. The sheets within were handwritten and for the most part limited to dates and numbers. "They're hardcopy logs of pre-Hiatus vessels. So far as I know—"

And no one but Mistress Boileau herself might know better.

"—no electronic media as old as them survive. Because this ship's officers backed up their computer logs with old-fashioned holograph, we still have a record of the voyages."

Leary took the log with a reverence due its age—though in fact the nickel-steel case by which he handled it was about as sturdy as the palace's walls. He turned the first page at an angle to the light and read, "*San Juan de Ulloa*, out of Montevideo. A vessel from Earth herself, mistress, and here we hold it in our hands."

His grin broadened. "Space *will* teach you something about not trusting equipment no matter how often you've checked it, that's the truth," he added. "If you survive, that is."

"I apologize for the condition of the collection," Adele said bitterly as Leary scanned sheets one at a time. They'd been filled out loose, then clamped between the covers. "I only arrived three weeks ago, but frankly unless I find a way to get real workmen instead of artists too good to throw up simple shelves, I don't see that the situation will have changed in three years."

A sort of smile—not a pleasant sort—quirked the corner of Adele's tight mouth. "Though of course I won't be here myself," she said. "I'll probably have been executed for murdering a master carpenter, or whatever they do to murderers here."

"They were using the Hjalstrom notational system . . ." Leary said. "Or a precursor of it, at least. That was supposed to have come from Spraggsund University near the end of the Hiatus."

He closed the metal covers, then looked directly at Adele. "I don't mean to intrude in another citizen's business, mistress," he said, "but sometimes going outside a bureaucracy is easier than going through it. My manservant Hogg is very good at finding people who can do things. If you'd like him to locate some common carpenters . . . ?"

Adele snorted. The library budget, if there was one, wasn't under her control. On Bryce, Walter's envoys had given her a travel honorarium. By stretching it Adele had managed to survive since her arrival, but no member of the Elector's staff had flatly admitted it was even their responsibility to arrange for the librarian's future pay. At the end of the week her concierge would be looking for the rent, and Adele would very likely be trying to find room for a bedroll here in the chaos.

"I appreciate the offer," she said, "but I regret that I'm not in a position to take advantage of it. Unless your man could find the carpenters' wages as well as the carpenters themselves."

Leary grinned, but there was a serious undertone in his voice as he said, "I really don't dare suggest that, mistress. While I don't think Hogg would be caught, I'm afraid his methods would bring spiritual discredit on a Leary of Bantry. What Hogg does on his own account is his own business, but if I set him a task . . ."

He laughed again, in good humor but apology.

The world had gone gray around Adele. "You said, 'a Leary of Bantry,' sir," she said. Her voice too was without color. "You'd be related to Speaker Leary, then?"

Leary grimaced. "Oh, yes," he said. "Corder Leary is my father, though we'd both be willing to deny it. If you mean, 'Will I inherit Bantry,' though, no—I certainly will not."

He tried to smile, but the expression that formed was a mixture of emotions too uncertain to identify. "In the first place, Father looked healthy enough to live another fifty years when I last saw him six years ago. My elder sister is the proper heir anyway— the Learyes don't divide their estates, which is why Bantry is still Bantry. And finally, my father and I are not on terms of intimacy. Or any terms at all."

"I see," Adele said. Her voice came from another place, another time; from the past that had led to this present. If there was a deity, which Adele very much doubted, it had a sense of humor.

She crossed her hands behind her back. "Lieutenant Leary," she said, "I have a great deal of work to do before this collection is ready for visiting laymen like yourself. You're a Cinnabar citizen and I will presume a gentleman. I therefore request that you cease to trouble me and my staff until such time as the Electoral Library is opened to the public."

Vanness had been standing nearby, listening to the discussion of books and media. His mouth opened in amazement as he turned quickly away. His cheeks were already showing a flush.

Daniel Leary reddened also. He replaced the logbook on the pile and made a stiff half-bow. "Good morning, mistress," he said. "No doubt we'll meet again."

Leary strode from the library by a circuitous route to avoid passing close to Adele on his way. He moved with a caged grace.

An interesting fellow, Adele thought as she watched him leave. Bright, knowledgeable, and she'd be the first to admit it had been pleasant to hear a Cinnabar accent again. There hadn't been many on Bryce, not since the war restarted.

And the son of Speaker Corder Leary.

Daniel Leary sat on a bench in a terraced formal garden that was probably half a mile from the Elector's Palace. He wasn't sure of the distance or even the direction; he'd simply walked till the adrenaline burned off and he needed to sit.

He hadn't been so angry since the afternoon he broke with his father.

Well-dressed Kostromans, mostly in couples, leaned on railings or sauntered along promenades of limestone figured with white inclusions. The plantings were of exotic species—which meant that Daniel absently recognized several common varieties from Cinnabar as well as other ornamentals which human taste had spread beyond their original worlds. The gardens hadn't been well maintained in at least a decade, but the present ragged profusion had a certain charm.

He'd have to challenge her, of course. The insult had been too deliberate to ignore. He'd take care of that in the next few days. Lieutenant Weisshampl of the *Aglaia*, the communications vessel that had brought the delegation to Kostroma, would probably act as his second. Weisshampl had served under Uncle Stacey. . . .

The whole business was a black pit that had opened without warning. The librarian's cold insults were as unexpected as a section of cornice falling on Daniel's head. He didn't even know her name!

Well, Weisshampl could probably make do with "Electoral Librarian."

The gardens sloped up from the gate at street level, but a tunnel led down to a grotto within the terraces. Green tile rippled on the tunnel walls and the statuary Daniel could dimly glimpse was of a marine character.

He should have tipped the gatekeeper as he entered the gardens. That official, a real battleaxe of a woman, had stretched out her hand to Daniel—and stepped aside when she looked at his face.

He'd been too angry to spare thought to the gatekeeper's presence or her silent request. God only knew what she'd thought of his scowl. He could pay her when he left, but . . . his purse was very light.

Daniel's mother had died when he was sixteen Terran years old. Corder Leary had attended her several times during her final lingering illness, though he'd been in Xenos on political business when she died.

Speaker Leary remarried the day after his first wife's funeral. The bride was Anise, his secretary; a pleasant woman in her forties and very different from the succession of young mistresses whom Daniel had glimpsed wafting in languid beauty through the Leary townhouse in past years.

Daniel had taken an aircar to Xenos when he heard. He'd had the Devil's own luck not to wreck on the way, and the Devil in his heart in all truth when he confronted his father. He'd called Anise a whore, though she'd mothered him the times he'd come to Xenos and he felt as much affection for her as he did for anybody but his mother and Hogg. He called his father worse, and his father hadn't minced words either. For all the difference in their interests, the Leary men had the same volcanic temper.

Had Corder and Daniel been any relation but parent and child, there'd have been a duel in the back garden that afternoon. As it was, Daniel left to join the navy as his father behind him bellowed for his attorney.

Four Kostroman laborers were carefully wheeling a handcart holding a Fleyderling in its atmosphere tank down the ramp to the grotto. Humans were in contact with three non-human races which had developed indigenous stardrives. There had never been a conflict between different species: the metabolic requirements were varied enough to make trade difficult and tourism hugely expensive. This Fleyderling must be the equivalent of royalty on its own ammonia world.

There was no shortage of interstellar conflicts within species, of course.

Daniel had never fought a duel. It wasn't the done thing in the country. Oh, there were fellows who were duelists just as there were fellows whose relations with livestock went beyond the normal meaning of animal husbandry. Neither sort were invited to the homes of their neighbors.

Young people entering the Navy School in Xenos were as prickly about their honor as any set of people on the planet. Cinnabar naval officers—cadets were classed as officers for this purpose— needed their commanding officer's approval to fight a duel, and as a matter of rigid policy the Commandant of the Navy School refused all such requests. Cadets could resign their appointments, but those who did so were forever debarred from the service.

That hadn't been a concern for Daniel. He'd gotten along well with his classmates and later with his fellow officers. He hurt no one by choice and helped those he could; not as a matter of calculation as his sister did, but because it was the way of life Daniel Leary found natural.

He supposed he needed Admiral Lasowski's permission to challenge this *librarian*. The admiral might not want to grant it for diplomatic reasons. If she didn't, Daniel would have the problem of finding his way back to Cinnabar as a private citizen with no funds and no prospects.

Assuming he survived the encounter, of course.

Birds with red throat-sacs trilled as they spun vertical caracoles in the air. At the bottom of their circles they clipped the foliage with their wings. The quick rapping was like rain.

Like a vast black pit, gaping in front of him. He couldn't *believe* this had happened.

Daniel's flat pocket chronometer binged at him. He looked at the sun with a sigh. Kostroma's days were shorter than Cinnabar's; this one was nearly spent. He was giving a dinner for the *Aglaia's* junior officers in an hour and a half.

Daniel stood up, feeling a trembling weakness in the long muscles of his thighs. That was reaction to the hormones he hadn't been able to burn off by instant battle in the Electoral Library. He wasn't sure where this garden was. He didn't have a good sense of direction on land despite—or perhaps because of—being a natural astrogator.

He didn't have enough money to pay a jitney driver to take him to his apartment, but Hogg could probably find the amount. Perhaps he'd do that.

Daniel Leary walked toward the gate and the boulevard beyond. Like a vast black pit . . .

Adele Mundy walked to the data console and seated herself. Her three assistants were whispering among themselves. It was the first time she could remember that the lovers had paid real attention to anything beyond one another's bodies.

The console felt cool beneath her fingertips. She saw it only as a blur. Nothing of this world was in focus, and there was a ball of compressed ice somewhere beneath her rib cage.

The Elector was giving a dinner for dignitaries tonight. Adele was invited. Her electoral office, her high birth, and the fact she was a foreign intellectual all caused her to be added to the guest list.

She'd be at the lowest table in the hall, where the food was likely to be leftovers from the previous day though arranged on an engraved dinner service. Even so, earlier this morning she couldn't have imagined that she'd want to turn down a free meal. No doubt the cold shock would wear off sufficiently for her to eat nonetheless; and she wasn't fool enough to think that her attendance was optional.

The young lieutenant had seemed as open as a garret in summertime. Leary was a common name on Cinnabar—as was Mundy, for that matter. It hadn't occurred to her to connect the fellow with Speaker Leary, who'd linked undoubted political unrest to fanciful Alliance plots and funding, then had drowned his fiction in the blood of the Mundys of Chatsworth.

Daniel Leary might be just as guileless as he seemed. The Leary family hadn't made its political name so much by subtlety as by the ruthlessness with which its members acted if threatened. Speaker Leary brooked no half-measures: his proscription covered every Mundy of Chatsworth over the age of twelve. When inevitably a number of younger children were killed as well, the Speaker added their names to the original list.

Adele hadn't been close to her parents, but she knew they were Cinnabar patriots. They were no more likely to take Alliance money than they were to sacrifice infants to Satan!

And yet . . .

Adele's eyes hurt. She'd sat in a brown study, unseeing but not blinking to wipe her corneas with the necessary moisture and lubricant either. She closed her eyes and rubbed them, then looked grim-faced around the library.

The assistants had gone back to their affairs; literally, in the case of the couple. Vanness was industriously digging out volumes of bound broadsheets from the past century, works which had nothing but size in common with Moschelitz. A good-hearted soul; probably too stupid ever to handle research questions, but the perfect man to shelve works properly when they were returned.

And yet . . .

Adele's parents would never have accepted Alliance help, but some of the others proscribed with the Mundys wouldn't have been so scrupulous. Samir Chandra Das was a high-living lecher whose only choices were bankruptcy or an immediate change in the political establishment and the cancellation of debts. Adele had known that even at sixteen; and had known Chandra Das as well, because he was a frequent visitor to Chatsworth.

The Parvennys; Rhadymantus of Selbourne; the Marcomann brothers, shipping magnates who'd been hit hard by bad investments—all of them proscribed as members of the Three Circles Conspiracy, all of them intimates of Adele's parents and elder kin.

Adele slammed the heel of her right hand against the console. The tough casing bonged without injury. Vanness hunched his shoulders; the lovers' whispering paused, then resumed.

There was a pistol in Adele Mundy's pocket, a flat weapon of Cinnabar manufacture. She carried it on Kostroma as a sensible precaution for a woman who because of poverty walked home alone at night to lodgings in a bad district.

But the reason she owned the gun and could blow the head off a rat at fifty meters with it was because of her training as a child. Her parents had been determined that every Mundy of Chatsworth would be able to take a place at the barricades on the day the people gained power and the reactionaries came to take it away from them.

Marksmanship hadn't helped her parents when an armored vehicle crushed through the front wall of the Mundy townhouse. Marksmanship hadn't helped Adele's ten-year-old sister Agatha either, though what happened to her was later, and slower, and much worse. *Nothing* could justify what had happened to Agatha.

Adele closed her eyes. She couldn't remember ever crying as an adult. People said crying was healthy, that it made them feel better. Perhaps. Personally Adele thought the folk who talked that way were fuzzy-minded weaklings, just as likely to advocate prayer to nature spirits or a diet of bark infusions as a route to health, but perhaps they were right.

It didn't affect Adele Mundy, though. She didn't cry, any more than she took her clothes off to dance on tables. What she did do, what she must do, was prepare this collection for . . .

The door opened. Adele opened her eyes and turned.

The two journeyman carpenters and Master Carpenter Bozeman entered the library. Ms. Bozeman wore a green velvet robe and carried a meterstick plated with one of the noble metals to give it a dull, eternal sheen. Her juniors carried two shelves, this time. The material was veneer-quality hardwood which had been polished as smooth as the meterstick.

"Good afternoon, mistress librarian," Bozeman said in a rasping bellow. She was a big woman with a florid face and hair in ringlets beneath her beret. She'd put on the formal garb of her status before coming to ram her point of view down the foreigner's throat. "We've come to set the first pair of shelves for you."

Adele got up and walked toward the trio. She should be getting into formal wear for the dinner herself, but first things first.

The journeymen had entered in front of their superior. Now they moved to Ms. Bozeman's other side.

"I believe we've had this discussion before, master carpenter," Adele said in a pleasant tone. She owed Leary a good deal for reminding her of who she was.

"I hope you've come to your—" Mistress Bozeman said.

Adele gripped the meterstick and pulled it from the carpenter's hand. She turned and flung the symbol of rank through a window. The sash exploded in shards of glass and splintered wood. More work for the carpenters, Adele supposed.

"We aren't going to go over the subject again," she said. "We're going to go to your shop now, and then we're going to take all this lovely and unsuitable wood to a supplier who can provide what I need to do my job. Do you understand, Ms. Bozeman?"

Adele was approximately half the size of the carpenter. Her smile was genuine because at last she'd seen that the obvious path out of her dilemma was to assert her authority—in the certainty that she had *no* authority if she didn't assert it.

Bozeman's mouth worked; it was surprisingly small and bow-shaped in a face that otherwise resembled a pie. No words came out. She wiped her empty hands on her robe, crushing splotches in the velvet. She turned in sudden fury on her journeymen and snarled, "Come along, you damned fools! Do you expect me to carry lumber?"

Adele turned to her own staff. "And you lot come as well," she said. "Donkey work is probably all you're good for, but that's what's required today."

"That's not our job!" one of the lovers protested.

Adele felt her face change with the suddenness of ice slipping from a sunlit roof. "Am I not a Mundy of Chatsworth?" she shouted. "If I hear any more insolence, the one who speaks will take the field with me if they've any blood to be worth my bullet! And if not, I'll find a whip that works as well on two-legged beasts as any other. I swear it!"

The carpenters had already scuttled from the disordered room. Vanness opened his mouth. Adele pointed her finger at his face. He swallowed and padded out of the library with the other two assistants.

Adele closed the door behind her. "This work is a matter touching my honor," she said to the Kostromans' backs. "I advise you to remember that. If to put it right I must shoot the whole lot of you and start over with a staff that knows what it's doing, then I'll do just that. Depend on it!"

One of the lovers had started to whimper. The other moved away so as not to be caught in any thunderbolt that resulted.

There should be time to transfer the lumber before the dinner, Adele thought; and if not, well, she'd be late. That was a prerogative of a Mundy.

Daniel Leary stood and raised his glass. "Fellow officers," he said, "I give you the *Aglaia*. May she always rejoice in good officers!"

Hogg watched beaming from the hallway. He'd taken over the landlord's kitchen to prepare dinner for the *Aglaia's* four junior commissioned officers—Captain Le Golif was at the Elector's dinner in Daniel's place.

Daniel couldn't afford red meat at Kostroman prices and Hogg was, truth to tell, no more than a passable cook, but matters had gone well. The pilaf had been adequate, and Bantry was a coastal estate. Nothing could have better trained Hogg to prepare a meal on Kostroma, a planet where fish was the staple and there was almost no land more than fifty miles from the sea.

Besides, the wine was excellent.

"And may Admiral Martina bloody Lasowski leave the ship's officers to do their jobs on the voyage home!" muttered Lt. Mon. His steward had filled about three glasses to every two for the other officers dining.

They all drank. Wonderful wine, absolutely wonderful.

Three hours in the company of the *Aglaia's* two lieutenants and two midshipmen had returned Daniel's normal sunny disposition. The wine hadn't hurt his mood either. No sir, not in the least.

Lt. Weisshampl belched, stared at her empty glass for a moment, and thought to pat her lips with her napkin.

"Maybe we could lock down the blast door in the corridor to the passenger suites?" said Midshipman Cassanos, a fresh-faced youth of eighteen on his first commission.

Midshipman Whelkine was female, a year older, and had never given Daniel a real smile in the three weeks he'd known her on shipboard. Her hands clenched on her glass when Cassanos spoke, but that wasn't necessarily a response to the words. Whelkine's skills were well above the norm for officers at her level of experience, but Daniel had never before met anyone as fearful of putting a foot wrong.

"Midshipmen with interest," Mon said, fixing Cassanos with eyes like two obsidian knives, "should have sense enough not to insult admirals who can spike any chance of command assignment for those midshipmen in future years. Do you understand me, Cassanos?"

Cassanos stiffened in his seat, flushing with embarrassment. "Sir," he said. "I spoke out of turn. I humbly ask the pardon of our host and the assembly."

"Did you say something, Cassanos?" Daniel said as he sat down carefully. "Nobody here heard you, I'm sure."

Mon's reaction was kindness, not hypocrisy. He was the second lieutenant of RCS *Aglaia*, a communications vessel with a light cruiser's hull and masts but the armament of only a corvette. Space normally given over to weapons and magazines provided passenger suites comparable to an admiral's accommodation on a First-Class battleship. The delegates to Kostroma travelled swiftly and in the luxury befitting their rank, but without tying up an important naval asset and putting the nose of Elector Walter III out of joint.

Mon's skills as an officer were respected or he wouldn't have a berth on a showpiece like the *Aglaia*; but he *didn't* have interest, and he hadn't had either the flair or the good fortune to get a command slot in other ways. Mon would be promoted, slowly but steadily, through a series of staff and ground positions till he retired . . . unless drink and bitterness led him to say something that the RCN couldn't overlook.

Cassanos had a chance. Mon didn't want the boy to lose it through the misfortune of aping a loser like himself.

A steward filled Daniel's glass. The servants were from the *Aglaia*'s staff, attending this dinner through some arrangement Hogg had made with the purser. Hogg had provided the wine also. As usual he hadn't volunteered information about his source of supply and Daniel had determinedly refused to ask. Daniel was scrupulous about the provenance of his normal fare, but this dinner was a matter of honor. If he *knew* that Hogg had raided Admiral Lasowski's private stock, he'd have to do something about it.

"I served under Lasowski when she was captain of the *Thunderer*," Lt. Weisshampl said. The wine in her refilled glass was the rusty color of a dried cherry; she stared with solemn intensity at the highlights on its surface. "A cautious officer. Not a person to trust a subordinate to do her job—but fair, wouldn't invent a problem if there wasn't one. Just cautious."

Technically the *Aglaia*'s crew weren't subordinate to Admiral Lasowski in the chain of command. The admiral and her staff were passengers on the RCS *Aglaia*, a vessel under the command of Captain Le Golif. Nobody who'd ever met an admiral believed that would be the reality, but Daniel knew the *Aglaia*'s situation was worse than most.

As Weisshampl said, Admiral Lasowski was a cautious officer—
but she was also a person who used minutiae to settle her mind
from the pressures of her real duties. Lasowski had the responsibility of satisfying Walter III with arrangements on which her
honor would ride, but she knew also that the Cinnabar Senate
would repudiate those arrangements if a majority if its members
believed that was best for the Republic.

The Elector of Kostroma, an autocrat (albeit one who faced recall
at gunpoint at any moment), would know only that Martina
Lasowski had made untrue statements to him. Officers of the RCN,
also an autocracy, were likely in their heart of hearts to view matters
much the same way. Admiral Lasowski would have to resign,
disgraced at the climax of a previously successful—if cautious—
career.

"Being between the Senate and a dictator who needs money,"
Daniel said aloud, "would make anybody pace the decks. They
just don't happen to be her decks, is all."

The admiral was no particular friend of his. She'd made it clear
that Lt. Leary had replaced her godson in the delegation by the
decision of persons with whom she disagreed. For all that, she'd
ignored Daniel rather than working at making his life hell. Daniel
liked most people, and Lasowski hadn't given him reason to add
her to the short list of those he didn't.

"The way to make that tinpot Kostroman see reason," Lt. Mon
said, "is to park a battleship in orbit over the palace until he decides
there's nothing he'd rather do than kiss our bum. God and all
His saints! How long does Walter think there'd be a Kostroman
merchant fleet if we declared him an enemy?"

"Now *that*," Cassanos said, coming to life again, "would mean
serious prize money!"

Daniel felt his eyes glaze with the thought of the sudden wealth
that could accrue to even a junior lieutenant if hundreds of rich
transports became fair targets before they could reach neutral ports.
That was dream wealth, though; there'd never been any doubt that
the Reciprocity Agreement would be renewed. Even if it weren't,
Kostroma wouldn't become a hostile power.

"I was posted from the *Hemphill* to the inspections department
at Harbor Three," Mon recalled with morose savagery. "I hadn't
been off the books three days when the *Hemphill* took a transport trying to run four thousand tons of fullerenes into Pleasaunce.

And then, instead of a combat tour I'm sent to squire around Admiral Pain-In-the-Ass Lasowski!"

"I understood you to be discussing your hemorrhoids, Mon," Weisshampl said to her junior. "If that isn't what you said, you might want to think about sleeping off the cargo you've taken on board tonight."

"I'm all right," Mon muttered to his glass. "I'll watch my tongue."

The *Aglaia* had an unusual number of officers for a complement of 180 ratings. A corvette of that crew would be under the command of a lieutenant who might be the only commissioned officer aboard. On some small vessels the missileer stood watches, even though that warrant officer wasn't a spacer like the Chief of Ship and Chief of Rig.

Even so, meddling by an admiral passenger, which might be bearable on a battleship with a crew of a thousand, would stretch a saint's patience on the *Aglaia*. Lasowski had inspected the ratings' quarters not once but twice on the voyage out. The only way to escape her was to climb one of the masts which drove the vessel through sponge space. Daniel had frequently done just that, but the option wasn't open to the officers standing watch.

A ship preparing to enter sponge space with its masts extended in all directions looked like a sea urchin. The mast tips formed the points determining the size and shape of the field against which Cassini energy pressed. The plasma motors were shut down as soon as the ship left the atmosphere; the High Drive was at low output to provide maneuvering way. The masts weren't stressed for anything approaching 1g acceleration when spread.

When the charge and alignment of the masts was correct, the vessel slipped into the fourth-dimensional Matrix in which the cells of sponge space coexisted. Rather than enter another universe, the ship itself became a separate universe. Its progress in respect to the sidereal universe was again a matter of the masts' alignment and charge.

Navigational tables provided a starship's commander with basic instructions, but the Matrix through which she guided her bubble universe could not be directly sensed. An astrogator used the minute rise and fall in mast charges to plot variations in the Matrix and the corresponding change in the ship's relation to the sidereal universe.

A really successful astrogator had a sense that, like perfect pitch, went beyond skill and training. That astrogator's mind saw into the matrix. His runs were faster, her planetfalls more precise, and when he voyaged beyond the existing charts she brought her ship back.

Commander Stacey Bergen was an astrogator whose reputation inspired deserved awe in others, his nephew included. But with a quiet and never-spoken assurance very different from the pride that also was a part of his character, Daniel Leary felt he was as able an astrogator as anyone he'd ever met *except* his Uncle Stacey.

Lt. Weisshampl got to her feet with a slow grace that belied the amount she'd had to drink. She was a tall woman with the features of someone more petite. Her parents had some status but no money; an aunt, however, had married wealth and provided Weisshampl with the support an officer needed beyond RCN pay.

She raised her glass. "Fellow officers," she said, "I give you Command. May she come to all of us, and may we prove worthy of her!"

"By God, yes!" Cassanos said and gulped his wine. Daniel blinked, for the midshipman's words were those he'd caught before they reached his own lips.

Lt. Mon drank with a face like a raincloud. He lowered his empty glass and gripped it in both hands as if to strangle it and himself as well.

"Would the master like me to bring in the brandy?" Hogg murmured in Daniel's ear.

"Brandy?" Daniel repeated. The unexpected word dragged him from a fantasy in which Admiral Daniel Leary stood on the steps of the Senate House to receive the acclaim of an adoring nation.

"I thought it'd go well now, sir," Hogg said with a satisfied grin. He wore clean clothes, a loose green shirt over blue trousers with a red cummerbund to tie the ensemble together. Shaving had been neglected in his care to prepare the dinner. Hogg looked like a cheerful pirate at the moment, which was pretty much the reality as well.

"It'll go very well indeed, Hogg," Daniel said. "Bring on the brandy!"

He leaned back in his chair, a heavy thing of plush and dark wood borrowed from the landlord. He was at peace with the world.

Some time in the distant past a librarian having a bad day had said something that Daniel must have misinterpreted. Who could be angry about such things when life was a wonderful thing, shadowed only by the absence of command?

Command would come, as surely as good fellowship and good wine and the stars themselves had come to Daniel Leary!

The Grand Salon where the Elector held formal dinners rose the full height of the Palace's second and third stories, with a rebated clerestory above that. The ceiling was a single enormous fresco, but the light wasn't good enough for Adele Mundy to see more than a hint of bare limbs and flowing drapery.

She'd have liked a better view, but since she hadn't bothered to visit the salon in daylight she didn't suppose that her interest could be as great as all that. Primarily she was feeling the utter boredom of the gathering.

"Now . . ." said the man to her left, a provisions merchant from Kostroma City and the only person seated below Adele at the fourth and lowest table of the dinner. "This is egg salad, of course—"

He wiggled a dab of vaguely peach-colored matter on his fork; Adele wasn't sure that "of course" would have been a phrase she used in the identification.

"—but what *kind* of egg, I ask you? Not hen as you might think, but domesticated Kostroman Diamondtail!"

"Pardon me, mistress," said the member of the Alliance delegation on Adele's right. He was a husky, dark-haired fellow in his forties who'd said his name was Markos. He spoke Academy-grade Universal with a rasping undertone of the Pleasaunce slums. "I believe I've been seated higher than my proper precedence should have allowed. Please accept my apology and change places with me."

"I'm sure—" Adele began, then caught herself. "Ah."

Even if Markos were a junior clerk as he'd claimed, he should have been higher as a simple matter of diplomatic checkers. At the head table Admiral Lasowski sat to the Elector's right while the Alliance chief of mission was on the left of Walter's mistress, looking sour. Not only had the Cinnabar envoy been given precedence, an admiral's dress uniform with six full rows of medals and a gorget of honor at the throat completely upstaged the robes of the Alliance civilian.

The order at the two middle tables was reversed. A grandnephew of Guarantor Porra, a peacock in full plumage, sat at the top while

the Cinnabar civil head was two places below him; likewise the
two naval captains at table three, an Alliance delegate sitting above
Le Golif of the *Aglaia*—not properly a member of the Cinnabar
mission, but present in Lt. Leary's place.

It was proper that at table four the mid-ranking functionary from
the Cinnabar Navy Office restore balance by being seated higher
than Markos; but no member of the delegations for whom the
banquet was arranged should have been *so* low. The notion that
Markos should really have been below the Electoral Librarian was
ludicrous, a piece of gallantry which Adele knew her looks didn't
justify and nothing else *could* justify.

"Yes, thank you for your courtesy, sir," she said as she rose
with Markos to trade places. She could deal with whatever lay
beneath the surface of the fellow's offer when it appeared. For
now, the important thing was that Adele no longer sat next
to the merchant, whose invitation had evidently been bartered
for the food. Adele had begun to doubt that even a free meal
would be worth another five minutes of the Kostroman's ram-
bling boredom.

Adele sat down. Servants were already removing the settings
for this course, so there was no need for her and Markos even
to trade flatware.

She heard her former neighbor address a question in his inevitable nasal whine. "I'm sorry, sir," Markos said in a loud voice.
"I'm deaf in my left ear and I can't hear a word you say."

When Adele had gotten the new data console running three
days before, she'd tested its connection to the palace net by
accessing the guest list for the banquet to which she'd just received an invitation. The information was protected, but what passed
for protection on Kostroma was child's play for Adele with an
extremely powerful processor at her service. She had a talent for
information retrieval and training at the most advanced center for
the purpose in the human universe.

Markos was not an invited guest at the time she'd checked the
list. The Alliance delegate at table four was supposed to be Captain
Crowell, a female ground-forces officer; and she should have been
two seats down from the Cinnabar bureaucrat.

An ensemble of Kostroman flautists playing both straight and
transverse instruments stood on an internal balcony at second-floor
level. Their music echoed as a high, insectile overtone in the huge

room. Adele found the effect surprisingly pleasant when mixed
with conversation and the clink of the dinner service.

A light-skinned, tow-haired servant, a native of one of the
impoverished northern islands, set the next course in front of Adele.
It was minced *something* on a bed of lettuce. Kostroman lizard was
her best guess, but some of the planet's insect equivalents got very
large also.

Beggars can't be choosers, and the tiny portions hadn't yet
managed to slake the fires of three weeks of hunger. Adele took
a bite and found the meat tasteless but the sauce intriguingly spicy.

"Do you keep in touch with Mistress Boileau, mistress?" Markos
asked pleasantly.

Adele's head jerked sideways. Markos took another forkful of
food, his attention apparently focused on his meal. He glanced
toward her with her a bland smile.

Aloud Adele said, "I haven't as yet. When I settle in"—she
suppressed a grim smile—"I'll let her know how things are going."

She cut a wedge from the mince, noting with pleasure that the
fork didn't tremble in her fingers. "You haven't been on Kostroma
long, Mr. Markos?" she added. She turned to look at him again,
her lips wearing the muted smile of strangers talking at a dinner
party.

Markos's expression didn't change, but shutters closed behind
his eyes. Adele chewed with tiny movements of her jaw. The food
was sawdust now.

*He's deciding what to say. Whether to tell the truth or to lie, and if
a lie—which one.*

Oh, she knew the type very well. They came to the Collections
not infrequently—and trembled since they couldn't use a system
so complex without help, but they feared to ask for help because
their questions could become weapons to use against them. They
were folk to whom the truth was always a thing to be determined
on the basis of advantage, never spoken for its own sake.

"Only a matter of hours, mistress," Markos said with a tinge
of grudging approval in his tone. "I arrived on the *Goetz von
Berlichingen* this afternoon. Perhaps you saw us land? The dispatch
vessel."

"I was busy in the palace all day," Adele said truthfully. "I have
no interest in anything that takes place beyond the library. Not
that I could tell one ship from another anyway."

She went back to her meal, wishing that she could taste it. Markos had proved he knew her background to see how she'd react; she'd reacted by showing that she knew things about him also. Because of the sort of person he was, Markos would twist like a worm on the hook of *how much* Adele Mundy knew about him. It should keep him from picking at her during the remainder of the dinner.

In fact Adele knew almost nothing, and certainly she didn't know the answer that mattered most to her. It was inevitable that the Alliance delegation would include a high-level intelligence agent.

What Adele really wanted to know was why the agent had arranged to be seated next to *her*.

The latrine was in the apartment building's courtyard, adjacent to the kitchen facilities. Daniel opened the latrine door and stepped out, feeling a great deal easier than he had a few moments before. He'd had a strong temptation to walk onto his suite's minuscule balcony to save himself a trip down the unlighted stairs.

He wouldn't have been the first, of that he was sure, but naval training had held. Personal hygiene was a matter of greater concern in a starship's close quarters than anyone raised on a country estate could imagine.

Hogg was in the kitchen, removing another bottle of brandy from the locked pantry. He grinned at Daniel, bobbed his head in salute, and said, "The arrangements're to your taste, I hope, sir?"

"Hogg, you're the wonder of the universe," Daniel said. He bowed to the servant in drunken formality. *A naval officer was never too drunk to carry out his duties. . . .*

Though that raised a question that Daniel supposed he had to address sometime. "But say, Hogg," he said. There was enough still to drink upstairs that his guests weren't going to miss him— or the fresh bottle—for a minute longer. "I don't mean to complain, but are there going to be questions raised about . . . ?"

He dipped his chin in what could be read as a gesture toward the brandy bottle.

"Oh, don't worry yourself, sir," Hogg said. He eyed the bottle with critical pride. "They'll all be filled, resealed so's the vineyard couldn't tell, and put back neat as you please. The local slosh is plenty good for a jumped-up grocer like Admiral Lasowski anyhow."

Daniel grimaced. He thought of saying something about the unopened bottle, but he decided that would be too much like refusing to kiss the girl goodbye in the morning.

"Ah, not to pry . . . ?" he said instead, prying. Compliance of the purser and stewards in something this blatant couldn't simply have been bought.

"One of the stewards thought she could play poker," said Hogg with a reminiscent smile. "She and her buddies fleeced me all the way out from Cinnabar in florin-limit games, they did. When we got here, I told them I'd gotten into my master's private funds and could play for real money."

Daniel snorted. "My private funds would just about stretch to a florin-limit game, that's so," he said.

"Ah, but they didn't know," Hogg said. "Take my word for it, sir: the best investment you can make is convincing some snooty bastard that he knows what really he don't know. The stewards got the purser to back them with the big money, so that made things a good deal simpler."

Oh, yes. A purser dipping into his ship's accounts could spend the rest of his life on a prison asteroid. That was much more of a problem than questions about a dozen bottles of wine souring on a long voyage.

Daniel laughed loudly. He eyed the stairs, then said, "Go on ahead, Hogg. I'm going to wait a minute to let my head clear before I navigate my way up."

Hogg bobbed again obsequiously and shuffled away on the narrow treads. The servant had probably drunk as much as any member of the dinner party, but he had a lifetime of training besides his barrel-shaped body with plenty of mass to stabilize the alcohol. Daniel drank like a naval officer, but Hogg drank like an admiral.

Two women came out of the landlord's apartments, talking quickly in a local dialect. They were heavily muffled; in the darkness Daniel wasn't sure whether they were sisters, nieces, or some combination. He walked farther into the courtyard so as not to be loitering at the door of the latrine.

Kostroma City had no street lighting, and the citizens shuttered their windows at night. The stars shone as bright as they did in Bantry, but they weren't the stars of Daniel's childhood. The "bird" flitting around the eaves tracked its prey by heat-sensitive pits in its snout, not echo location like its equivalent nightflyers on Cinnabar and Earth.

Even Kostroma's seawater tasted strange on Daniel's tongue. It was tinged with a different mixture of salts and less of them in total than the fluid that lapped the shore of Bantry.

Anger and Uncle Stacey's stories had taken Daniel Leary far from home. Standing here in the night, though, he knew he'd found another home: the stars in all their wonderful profusion.

Adele nibbled through the dozen thin slices of meats and vegetables set before her on a wooden skewer with charred tips. The provisions merchant had listed the ingredients in a voice pitched to be heard by the aristocrat from a minor island seated across from him. If Adele heard correctly—gathering information was instinctive for her, both a blessing and a curse—one of the slices was "poisonous love-apple."

She smiled despite herself. "Poisonous" would cover most of the love affairs she'd seen played out; though that was a subject of which she had only academic knowledge or interest.

They'd consumed twenty-two of the menu's thirty dishes. Because Adele had never attended a Kostroman banquet before, she hadn't realized each dish would be a separate course. At this rate it would be well after midnight before the gathering concluded.

Most of the guests were accompanied by an aide who stood near the main doorway, chatting with others in the same boring circumstances. If a message came for the guest, a palace servant informed the aide, who in turn passed the information on to his or her principal. Occasionally a diner rose after such a consultation and left the salon to deal with the crisis.

Much more frequently a guest staggered out to the temporary toilet facilities curtained off in the hallway. Kostroman society was very advanced in many respects, but Adele considered the sanitary arrangements of even the ruling class to be barely minimal.

The menu hadn't listed the ocean of wines, beers, and distilled liquor that flowed with the food, probably because that went without saying on Kostroma. Adele had neither a taste nor the head for alcohol; she would have drunk with great care even if this function were not a matter of her duty as a member of the Elector's staff.

Part of the reason for the banquet was to honor the two

delegations bidding for Kostroma's friendship—and to put them on their mettle by bringing them face to face in public. Equally important from the Elector's point of view was to display his power to the politically important folk of Kostroma. Most of the two hundred guests were Kostromans being shown to be subservient to Walter III.

Because collating information was Adele's life as well as her vocation, she found the actual order of precedence at the tables to differ strikingly from that planned in the original guest list. Something had gone seriously wrong within the ruling coalition.

Kostroman political life was a shuffling of clans which were more or less congruent with individual islands. Kostroma Island was a melting pot where virtually all the politicians lived, but those worthies had their power bases elsewhere on the planet.

Walter III had come to power through an alliance of his Hajas clan with the chief personages of the Zojiras, another large clan. Both major parties had collaterals, minor clans that looked to them for leadership and protection and which in turn could supply support and manpower.

The winning coalition had shared out offices following Walter's victory. Adele's staff was a typical mixture of folk owing allegiance to either Hajas or Zojira, granted their places for reasons that had nothing to do with their enthusiasms or their ability to make a library function.

Adele didn't know the banquet guests by sight—she knew almost no one on the planet—but all of them wore their clan colors as collar flashes or in their headgear. The Zojiras and their collaterals were consistently three places below where they'd been seated in the original plan. The change was minor in one sense—the food was the same, whichever chair the diner sat in. In context the change was comparable to shifting a decimal point in an equation.

The woman to Adele's immediate right was a Zojira collateral; her beret was quartered orange and horizon blue, but the pompon topping it was Zojira black and yellow to indicate affiliation. She was well dressed and had put more emphasis on style than on cost, but Adele knew nothing else about her. The woman had sat with rage mottling her complexion throughout the meal. At a guess, she should have been sitting above the Hajas supporter now two places to her right.

Between the silently contemplative Markos and the silently furious woman on the other side, Adele was having a quiet meal. Her lips quirked in a tiny smile. She couldn't complain about being bored during dinner either. Boredom was one of those things that improved with absence.

"Now, many of my competitors make the sauce from any fish at all," whined the provisions merchant. "Fish *parts* I suspect in—"

Leonidas Zojira, the head of the clan, leaped to his feet at the high table. The servant behind him prevented his chair from hitting the floor with a crash. Not to be balked of a scene, Leonidas picked up his plate and hurled it into the serving tray. He stalked toward the hallway doors.

As though Leonidas had snagged a line, scores of other diners got up. All wore black and gold either as their primary colors or as quarterings. The woman beside Adele stood, leaned forward deliberately, and spat in the dish of her Hajas rival before she joined the exodus from the Grand Salon.

"Rather to be expected," Markos said to Adele in tones of suave amusement. The trouble appeared to have restored his good humor. "The whole history of Kostroma indicates that no alliance lasts much longer than the common enemy. A mercurial folk, the Kostromans."

The table decorations were stemless flowers floating in silver bowls. In reflection, Adele saw the Alliance spy waggle a finger toward the main doors. A youngish woman came toward him from the gaggle of aides there. She wore Kostroman business dress, out of place to a degree among the bright livery of those with whom she'd been waiting.

The woman bent over Markos and whispered in his ear. He nodded solemnly and said to Adele, "You'll have to excuse me, Mistress Mundy. My secretary tells me I have an urgent call. Perhaps we'll meet again."

"Good day," Adele said without inflection. She watched Markos leave the hall with a lengthening stride.

The Cinnabar "Navy Office" functionary was already out the door because he hadn't bothered with the fiction of being summoned by an aide. If Adele hadn't seen Markos's gesture, even she might have accepted his charade at face value.

The Alliance and Cinnabar delegates were frantically signaling for their aides. Le Golif of the *Aglaia* looked startled and concerned. He wasn't a diplomat, and he had no idea what had happened.

Adele went back to the dish which had been put before her at the instant of the Zojira exodus. It was sliced vegetables in a very spicy red sauce; she wouldn't have guessed the sauce had anything to do with fish were it not for the merchant's description.

She didn't suppose the fuss would affect her task one way or the other. Vanness, the only assistant she'd have made an effort to keep, was a Hajas; by the same token, Bracey was a Zojira collateral and she'd already dismissed him herself.

Kostroman politics were a concern for foreign intelligence agents, not for librarians. . . .

Aircars were common enough on Kostroma that the sound of one approaching probably wouldn't have interrupted the drinking if Lt. Mon hadn't recognized the fan note. "That's one of ours, by God!" he said.

The midshipmen sat at the end of the table nearer the balcony, but they'd drunk themselves almost legless. The three lieutenants proved their greater capacity, professional as well as alcoholic, by getting onto the balcony almost simultaneously despite the litter of chairs, glasses, and Midshipman Cassanos on the floor behind them.

The *Aglaia* carried a quartet of ducted-fan aircars, an unusually high number for a naval vessel but in keeping with the expected mission of a communications ship. The duty car, 73 on the bulbous forward fan nacelle, idled up the street while a rating checked building fronts with a spotlight.

"Here we are!" Mon bellowed. The balcony flexed; Daniel hadn't thought more than two people would fit on it, but that had been when he was sober. "*Aglaia!*"

The spotlight swept them at leg level, illuminating but not blinding the officers. The car angled closer, keeping slightly above second-floor level.

"Sir!" called the petty officer behind the light. He bellowed to be heard over the fans' whooshing intake. "Lieutenant Mon is to take a cutter up and launch a message cell. The middies are to round up crewmen on leave, and Lieutenant Weisshampl will hold the ship in readiness for the captain's return!"

Daniel relaxed—as much as anyone could, squeezed so tight that the railing creaked. Something had happened, but it couldn't have been too serious if Le Golif himself hadn't reported back. This was diplomatic excitement, not the kind of emergency in which lives or the very ship herself depend on fast action. It was more important to finish a formal dinner.

"Bring the boat close," Weisshampl ordered with the decisiveness expected of a naval officer. "We'll board from here."

The aircar dipped toward them. If the crewmen aboard had an opinion of the idea, it wasn't theirs to question.

Weisshampl put her right foot on the low railing. The railing toppled with her into the street ten feet below. Weisshampl rotated a perfect 270 degrees in the air, landing flat on her back on the stone pavement.

The aircar bobbled back and dropped to the street. "Cancel that order!" Weisshampl roared. She started to get up, then turned to vomit so that the street's slight camber would carry the ejecta away from her uniform.

Daniel nodded approvingly as he clung to the transom. Weisshampl was a real professional, no question about it.

He turned. The stewards were shepherding Cassanos and Whelkine down the stairs. The gentleness of the process was a positive commentary on the way the *Aglaid*'s ratings regarded the midshipmen. Lt. Mon walked behind them alone. He had a sort of funereal grace, holding a glass of brandy with the dignity owed a communion chalice.

Hogg eyed the debris of the party. There was no breakage except for the railing, some glasses, and a chair. The latter hadn't been in good shape even before Daniel trampled it on his way to the balcony. "In twenty minutes we'll have it clean as your mother's parlor, sir," he said judiciously. "That's if we have a clear field, I mean."

He quirked an eyebrow at Daniel to drive home the point that the master would be very much in the way of the clean-up.

The aircar's crew had loaded Lt. Weisshampl onto the open vehicle's middle seat. The midshipmen entered the street under their own power, though stewards were hovering nearby. Cassanos raised his foot to step over the car's low side. He lost his balance, pirouetted on one foot, and fell backward into the rearmost section. Whelkine toppled directly on top of him.

Mon entered the middle section. His drink sloshed as he eased Weisshampl to the side. "Whee!" cried Midshipman Whelkine. "I've got brandy on my butt!"

The dinner might have loosened Whelkine up to a useful extent, Daniel thought. Assuming she didn't hang herself out of embarrassment when she sobered in the morning.

"Home, James!" Weisshampl commanded from where she lay. The aircar skidded forward on surface effect, then rose in a turn with the fans screaming.

Petty officers would have to coddle the midshipmen who'd be nominally in command of the parties calling in leave-men, but that wouldn't be either a problem or the first time. Daniel could remember the night only the grip of a husky rating on each elbow had kept him navigating the Strip outside Harbor #3, searching for no-shows who were a great deal less drunk than he was.

He returned his attention to the waiting servant. "I'm going to take a stroll down to the docks, Hogg," he said. "I'll watch the cutter lift, and then I'll see if I can find some other entertainment. You needn't wait up for me."

Hogg pursed his lips in whiskery concern. "You'll be alone, then, sir?" he asked. "One of the stewards here—"

"I'll be alone," Daniel said, just as firmly as Weisshampl had spoken before she toppled into the street, "until I find that other entertainment. Carry on, Hogg!"

He strode toward the staircase with a martial stride; and, because Hogg snatched the remains of the chair out of the way, Daniel didn't trip and plunge down those stairs nose first.

The gardens behind the Electoral Place were unlighted except for the lamp hanging in front of the shelter where a dozen guards chewed tobacco and complained of being bored. They watched Adele pass without concern. If she'd been trying to enter the palace they might have challenged her; and again, they might not. Boredom created apathy, and apathy swallowed first initiative and then life itself.

Adele smiled. She'd always found whatever she was doing to be extremely interesting. Her experience didn't include standing in one place and expecting nothing to happen, but there was no lack of other ways to spend one's existence. The guards would probably say that their duties were better than having a real job, but Adele was by no means sure they were correct.

First initiative, then life . . .

The vast black mass of the palace was between her and the vehicles arriving for the other guests, but even so she had a hint of the pomp of the leavetaking. Most of the foreigners and a good third of the Kostromans at the banquet came and left in aircars, either personally owned or hired for the event. Their lights swam across the sky in temporary constellations, multicolored and blinking. Even the guests who used ground vehicles or canal boats appointed like yachts made the air waver with searchlight beams to advertise their importance.

Adele wove past the construction vehicles and locked equipment trailers parked along the rear driveway. The clutter must have complicated deliveries of food for the banquet. The whole area reminded her of the floor of the library.

Walter III was renovating portions of the palace and changing the garden layout as well. Were his other projects as ill-conceived as his creation of an Electoral Library?

An aircar cruised by a thousand feet overhead. Its klaxon grunted over the howl of its drive fans. The racket was unpleasant at ground level and must be downright hideous for the occupants of the car, but pride would be served. The owner could have gained even more attention by painting himself—or herself!—blue and dancing nude in the Grand Salon; though as fat as the banquet guests tended to be, the result might have been even more unaesthetic than the klaxon.

She reached the back of the gardens. The right half of the wrought iron gate was missing, a casualty of the night Walter Hajas became Elector. "Hey!" called one of the guards as Adele walked by.

She threw up her right hand so that the light aimed at her face didn't leach away all of her night vision. "I'm a guest going home," she said and resumed her brisk pace in the direction of her lodgings.

"Don't you have a lantern?" a guard called.

"No," she said without slowing or turning her head.

A light would make her a target. By walking close to the darkened buildings she would be past muggers before they were aware of her presence. If they chose to come after her, then, well . . . her left hand was in her pocket, and it wasn't empty.

The carpenters were sorted out, though she'd revisit the cabinet shop in the morning to make sure Mistress Bozeman hadn't had second thoughts. The crew had the proper materials, now; enough for a start at least.

Three workmen—two, in all likelihood; the Master Carpenter still wasn't going to get shavings on her robes—weren't enough to accomplish anything quickly, and the journeymen weren't trained for *this* job however good their intentions now were. Still, one step at a time. Adele was further forward than she had been at this time yesterday.

Rainbow light flared several seconds before the roar of plasma motors reached her. A starship was lifting from the sea. The wavering torch of its exhaust continued to climb even after the beat of the motors muted to a throb that was felt rather than heard.

One step at a time.

Daniel stood beside the timber piling at the end of a pier in the natural harbor, now used only by surface traffic. Half a mile to the west, the tide rocked starships in the Floating Harbor.

When Daniel was younger he'd have sat cross-legged on top of the piling instead of resting his palm on the wood as he did now. The staff at Bantry used to joke that the boy thought he was a seabird, though it wasn't anything so simple as that. The pose required a degree of agility, an awareness of the wind's strength and direction.

And yes, it set Daniel Leary a little apart. He relished the feet-on-the-ground human world, but he hadn't been willing to be limited to it even as a boy.

Daniel snorted. He'd be on the piling now if he weren't wearing his only 2nd Class uniform. The damp wood would stain the cloth, and he had further use for the uniform tonight. Women noticed a uniform, oh yes they did. A uniform meant the wearer was committed and disciplined. You didn't have to be much of a naturalist to know that females of most species were hardwired to value those traits.

The surface harbor was active even at this hour. The larger vessels that fed the people and industries of Kostroma City generally docked during daylight hours, but loading and unloading proceeded around the clock. Several big freighters sat in floodlit pools across which their irregular outlines threw wedges of shadow. A derrick squealed; whistles called, and once a voice boomed in tones of unintelligible anger from a distant ship.

Lighters served the starships in the Floating Harbor, transferring cargo in both directions. One was even now nosing toward a quay to the right, its diesel engine chuffing an ill-tempered rhythm. Tarpaulins covered three pieces of heavy equipment on the open deck. Tokamaks for fusion power generation, Daniel thought, but he couldn't be sure even when he dialed his goggles' magnification and light-gathering features full on.

There was more than human activity going on in the harbor. Ripples crossed the water in faintly starlit V's. By switching to thermal imaging Daniel could see the fish that cruised beneath the surface, browsing the microorganisms which bloomed in the nutrient-rich sewage borne here by the city's canals.

Daniel was focused on a fish longer than his arm. A leatherfin, he thought, though the *Aglaia*'s natural history database hadn't been specific to Kostroma.

A shadow flicked in and out of the goggles' present narrow focus. The water exploded in foam.

Daniel reflexively switched back to a normal field of view while remaining in the infrared spectrum. A whiptail had been sitting on a bollard not far from him. It had just glided out over the water and snagged the fish with a stroke of its barbed, prehensile tail.

"Bravo!" Daniel shouted. A perfectly executed attack on a worthy opponent!

Flapping laboriously with the fish snugged close to its belly, the furry-winged "bird" swept in broad circuit around the harbor. The whiptail's vans flared like stage curtains as it landed on a freighter's foremast. Its lower beak stabbed once, severing its victim's notocord at the base of the skull; then it began to feed on strips daintily pincered from the flanks.

Daniel supposed it was a common enough sight to anyone on Kostroma who paid attention to what went on around them; but it wasn't common to *him*. And indeed, how many people on any planet paid attention to anything at all?

The freighters served the city; the lighters served the starships in the Floating Harbor. Smaller vessels yet, bumboats, served the crews of those starships.

Some of them were little more than dinghies. They carried fruit, liquor, and sexual partners to the personnel who had to remain on board. Not infrequently the boats returned to land with drugs and other contraband, but that had been a fact of ports throughout human history.

At this hour most bumboats clustered either along the harbor shore or were tied to concrete floats among the starships. A few of the craft burred slowly over the water, driven by tiny engines. They were probably acting as water taxis, taking officers out to their ships or bringing to shore ratings finally released on leave when they completed their duties.

Officers, even Cinnabar naval officers, allowed the bumboats to attend their ships because they couldn't stop it. A captain who tried to isolate his crew after a voyage through sponge space would lose his personnel to desertion if not his life to mutiny.

Starship crews had to be highly trained and motivated to do their jobs. They understood the need for groundside maintenance and an anchor watch; but a wise captain, a *sane* captain, likewise understood the need for relaxation after touchdown. A disciplined, happy crew kept its on-board partying within bounds; but it *would* party.

Plasma bloomed in the Floating Harbor, casting into relief the starships tethered on the land side of the *Aglaia*. Daniel watched the cutter lift on its single plasma jet.

The little vessel was fitted with High Drive, but it was too small for the masts and crew necessary to enter sponge space. Lt. Mon would carry a message cell above Kostroma's magnetosphere, then launch it toward Cinnabar.

Interstellar messages had to be carried, either by ships or by unmanned message cells. A message cell was programmed to a fixed interdimensional course. Because the Matrix through which it proceeded wasn't fixed, not really, cells were much less trustworthy than a manned vessel.

Their advantage was their relatively small size. The *Aglaia* carried ten 30-foot message cells in a volume that would have been barely sufficient for a single pinnace capable of interstellar travel. A fleet would include dispatch vessels, but a single ship which needed to send a message home used a message cell.

To Daniel's surprise another cutter rose, this time from the opposite end of the Floating Harbor. It had been launched from the *Goetz von Berlichingen*, the Alliance dispatch vessel.

No doubt the Alliance crew was on the same mission as Lt.

Mon, to send home a message of great import. The Alliance delegation must have used shore-to-ship radio despite the risk of inter-
ception, since no courier had flown out to the starship to deliver
the message.

The message was probably about the deep diplomatic significance of somebody farting at the official dinner. People who spent
their lives studying minutiae found crises in events that would be
utterly forgotten in weeks if not days. The stars were eternal, and
there was always something genuinely new among them for humans
to discover.

Daniel laughed with joy at being alive. The pause had brought
his system back close to normal functioning despite the load of
alcohol he'd taken on board. He could navigate without the risk
of falling over.

The supper club where he'd met Silena the other night was only
a few blocks away. It was possible that she'd be there again; and
if not, well, places like that usually had at least one sweet young
thing who'd welcome rescue by an officer of the RCN.

Whistling a gavotte, Lt. Daniel Leary sauntered toward his duty.

Someone was hammering on the street door. Adele heard a man's
voice but no words; only a demanding tone penetrated to her room
at the back of the second floor.

The visitor paused, then resumed rapping with a hard object.
This went on almost a minute before Mistress Frick slid open her
shuttered window onto the entryway and snarled something
querulous. The male voice rumbled. To Adele's surprise, she next
heard triple bolts withdraw and the street door squeal open.

Money must have changed hands. That, or there'd been a threat
sufficient to move a concierge who was threatening enough herself.

Adele got out of bed and dressed with a perfect economy of
motion even though the room's only light came from the stars
beyond the one barred window. She was an organized person who
lived by herself and therefore knew exactly where every garment
and item of apparel was.

The house had six rooms in addition to the concierge's own
tiny hole off the entryway. The visitor didn't have to be for Adele
Mundy. Adele had usually been right to assume bad news, though,
and someone calling at this hour was certainly bad news.

She'd put on her work clothes, a suit of sturdy brown fabric that looked dignified and didn't show dust. Her personal data unit, the only item of value Adele owned, fitted into its special pocket in her trousers. Closed it was only ten inches by four, and a half inch thick, an insignificant bulge to anyone looking at her.

The last thing Adele did was to slip her pistol into the left side pocket of her jacket. The right was her master hand, but she could shoot with either one.

The footsteps of two persons, neither of them the wheezing, clumping Ms. Frick, came up the stairs and down the creaking hallway. The visitors carried a light. It was deep yellow and strikingly bright where it bled around the warped panel into the complete darkness of Adele's room.

The tap on her door was polite but peremptory. She opened it at once.

Markos stood with a small lamp in his left hand and his right still raised to knock. He wore the cloak and wide-brimmed hat of a merchant in middling circumstances. The aide Adele had seen in the Grand Salon accompanied Markos. Both her hands were concealed beneath her cape, so she didn't carry the light as one might have expected.

Markos frowned slightly to see Adele up and dressed. The aide's expression was perfectly blank. She reminded Adele of a snake, dry and emotionless.

"I regret the hour, Ms. Mundy," Markos said in his cultured accent. "I'd appreciate it if you came for a drive with me so that we can discuss matters in greater privacy."

"All right," Adele said. She gestured Markos back with a flick of her fingers, then stepped into the hall and closed the door behind her.

She didn't bother to lock it. It would open to a kick on the latchplate, and Ms. Frick had the key anyway. Only a fool tried to affect things that were clearly out of her control.

The apartment building's street door opened while Daniel was still whistling midway down the block. He waved to Hogg with the filmy garment he'd found in his pocket as he walked home in the predawn hours. He didn't recall how the bit of silk got there, perhaps because his attention had been focused elsewhere at the time.

"Good evening, Hogg, and a *very* good evening it has been," he called.

Daniel's feet got crossed on the threshold; the servant caught him with a skill born of practice. They'd had more to drink at her place. A great deal more to drink.

Hogg pulled one of Daniel's arms over his own shoulders and walked him through the hallway to the courtyard. "I've already drawn a tub for you in the bathhouse, sir," the servant said. "I'd as soon you not sing tonight. The landlord's not best pleased about the broken railing."

"Ho!" Daniel said. Now that he was safely home he felt like a marionette whose strings had been cut. He was running a tab at the supper club—God knew how he'd pay *that*—but he hadn't had a florin in cash for a taxi when he slipped out before the lady's servants stirred.

Hogg more carried than helped Daniel to the bathhouse. It was lighted by a dim electric bulb. The interior tiles formed a garden scene, attractive even beneath a mask of grime. The tub was of enameled metal with a wooden rim: long and deep, but disconcertingly narrow to Daniel. He was used to more space for his shoulders when he leaned back.

Daniel tried to help Hogg undress him, but as usual he found that his best choice was holding still except to raise a limb when requested. The oil-fired geyser in the corner was wreathed in steam; he amused himself by blowing patterns in the warm fog.

"I've been making some inquiries about Cinnabar citizens living here in Kostroma City, sir," Hogg said as he hung Daniel's trousers with the jacket, shirt, and boots in the alcove. Undergarments were piled in a corner.

"Ah?" said Daniel. Hogg would have been scouting for people who might want to smuggle high-value items back to Cinnabar. The *Aglaia* as a naval vessel wasn't subject to search by the civil customs authorities. The RCN conducted its own checks, but naval personnel felt a kinship with their fellows on inbound vessels and could usually be squared by a modest bribe.

Daniel braced his hands on the rim of the tub and started to climb in.

"Sir!" Hogg said. He drew Daniel back, then inserted the hose of the geyser into the bathwater and opened the valve. Live steam bubbled into the water, heating the bath with a roar.

Steam pressure dropped to an asthmatic gurgle. "Now, sir," Hogg said as he replaced the hose and shut off the burner.

His body slid under the surface. The water was blood temperature. It soothed Daniel and almost put him to sleep. Thought dissolved like sand castles in the tide.

"There's a Cinnabar citizen on the Elector's staff," the servant continued as if absently. Hogg was rarely direct when he had anything serious to say. "The librarian, a woman just come here from Bryce. I wouldn't mention it to you, but it seems she's a Mundy of Chatsworth."

Daniel's faculties clanged back into full function despite the curtains of comfort and alcohol. Nothing that had happened during the past twelve hours affected him any longer.

"Just about the last of them, I wouldn't be surprised," Hogg said. He offered a sponge that Daniel ignored. "She was off-planet when it happened or she'd have been stood against a post like most of her kin after your father broke the conspiracy."

"Yes, that's probably the case," Daniel said. He took the sponge and began scrubbing himself with firm, powerful strokes.

"Now maybe this Mundy lady is the sort who forgives and forgets . . ." Hogg said.

"She's not," said Daniel. "I've met her."

"Ah?" said Hogg in surprise. "Well, if she's not, the going rate for an assassination here is two hundred florins. It might run a little more for a Cinnabar naval officer, but I wouldn't bet on that. The gangs don't take much notice of international relations."

"Thank you for bringing the matter to my attention, Hogg," Daniel said. "I'll take care of it."

"I have some friends who'd help if you wanted to, ah . . ." Hogg said diffidently. He was embarrassed to make the suggestion and very rightly concerned about how his master would react to it. "I'd talk to them myself, I mean. You wouldn't have to—"

"Thank you, Hogg," Daniel said. His tone, while perfectly polite, ended the discussion. "I'll deal with the matter myself in the morning."

Later in the morning. Sleep would be the best use for the next few hours.

Markos's nameless aide drove the jitney from the open front seat; the Alliance agent sat with Adele in the enclosed rear. The coachlamps cast a little light into the compartment through oval opera windows; Markos's eyes gleamed.

"The Alliance gave you sanctuary when your own nation would have killed you like a dog, mistress," he said. "Fate has offered you an opportunity to repay that kindness."

The jitney's wheels were high and thin. The elastomer tires dulled but could not eliminate the pavement's vibration.

"I'm not political," Adele said. "I'm a librarian. And my service to the Academic Collections on Bryce was at least equivalent to the food and shelter I was given there by a private citizen."

She deliberately turned and looked out the window. They were driving through a district where wealthy merchants lived. The houses were three stories high, shoulder to shoulder along the street frontage. Roof gardens draped fronds over cornices that were more lushly carved than the real foliage.

An armed guard stood watch in front of a house undergoing repairs. The facade was bullet-marked and the windows of both lower stories were boarded up. Presumably it had been the residence of a supporter of the old regime.

The guard's lantern threw into shadowed relief the dedication on the keystone: I PETER CRIBELLI HAVE BUILT THIS FOR MYSELF AND MY DESCENDANTS.

Scaffolding already in place indicated that workmen planned to chisel out the dedication in the morning. Perhaps they would replace it with another brave hope for the future.

"Yes," Markos said, his tone full of heavy menace. "Ms Boileau. We'll come back to her in a moment. What's of interest to the Alliance now is that you already have a data console capable of accessing any material in the national system. That's correct, isn't it?"

"I wouldn't know," Adele lied. She turned to face Markos. "Tell me what you want and then let me go."

"Your skill is not in question, Mistress Mundy," the spy said. The teeth of his slum upbringing chewed into his cultured accent for a moment. "You can get any information you please with that unit. My determination and my power over you and your friends shouldn't be in question either!"

"Tell me what you want," Adele repeated.

"Take this," Markos said, handing her a plug-in software module. "Your terminal's linked to Kostroma's satellite communications net. This will permit someone of your ability to decrypt any information passing through that net, even if it uses Cinnabar security forms."

She took the module; it was no larger than the last joint of her little finger. "What do you *want?*"

"Information," Markos said. There was a smile again in his voice. He was convinced that he'd won the battle of wills. "Whatever information I ask for, you'll find and deliver to me. Then we don't have to worry about a learned old woman coming to grief in her twilight years."

He laughed.

"Why is the Fifth Bureau enlisting foreign librarians for donkey work, Markos?" Adele asked in measured tones. "There must be a score of Alliance agents in Kostroma City. The ship you came on has equipment at least equal to mine and personnel trained to use it. Why are you putting yourself in the hands of an amateur?"

Every department of the Alliance bureaucracy had its own intelligence section. It was more than a guess, though, that a man who'd been provided with his own dispatch vessel was a member of the organization which reported directly to Guarantor Porra.

Markos's face tightened over his cheekbones. "My reasons are just that, mistress," he said. "Mine. But don't denigrate your own abilities. We could comb the Alliance without finding anyone better suited to our needs."

Adele put the module in her belt purse and leaned against the back cushion with a sigh. "Take me home, Markos," she said.

How had Peter Cribelli and his family envisaged the future? Adele's parents talked of a day when the people ruled—guided, of course, by the wisest and most far-seeing members of the state.

"I thought you'd see reason," Markos said with a chuckle. He tapped twice on the panel which shut them off from the aide. The jitney swung, jolting and rocking as the right wheel bumped into and out of a joint in the paving blocks.

Adele sat with her eyes closed. Markos thought she'd agreed with him.

And perhaps she had. It was hard to convince herself that it made any difference what she did. Life was chaos, and individual decisions mattered not at all.

The bumboat carrying Daniel to the Floating Harbor was a family affair involving nine people and three or possibly four generations, depending on which of the women was the mother of the infant. The motor burned crude naphtha and sputtered except for the moments a swell lifted the propellor out of the water; then it screamed like an enraged wildcat.

An air-cushion vehicle drove off one of the concrete floats, hit the waves, and howled shoreward at a high rate of speed. The cloud of its drifting spray enveloped Daniel's boat. The family shrieked curses at their wealthy fellows. One of the ACV crewmen thumbed her nose in response, but the neatly uniformed merchant officers being ferried to shore in comfort paid no attention.

The ACV was a proper water taxi. The boat in whose bow Daniel sat was loaded with fruit and bottles till the gunwales were within a hand's breadth of the water. The younger members of the family, two girls and a handsome boy wearing earrings and a silver-bordered tunic, probably sold more than merchandise to the starship personnel.

Riding as extra cargo on a bumboat was a lot cheaper than a real taxi, though Daniel had to remind himself of his reasoning whenever the motor coughed for what could be the last time. He *would* have money again, as soon as he'd seen the duty officer.

It was hard to appreciate the vastness of the Floating Harbor while approaching it at virtually the surface of the water. When the boat nosed down the back side of a swell, nothing was visible but the next rise of the water. Even at the peak of a wave where scud blew off the curl, one saw only the wet gray masses of the floats and the lighter, even greater, masses of the dozen or so nearest starships.

On a normal day there were at least thirty ships in the Floating Harbor. Today there were forty-seven: Daniel had surveyed the layout from the quay and memorized it. If the boat landed him in the wrong location, he wanted to be able to find his way to the *Aglaia* without depending on the help of other vessels. Several of the latter were transports registered on Alliance worlds, and even the crewmen of a Cinnabar ship might think it funny to send a naval officer the wrong way around a harbor miles in circumference.

Daniel grinned. He'd have thought it was funny himself back when he was a midshipman. Not so very long ago.

The *Aglaia* was in the first rank, easily visible, but Daniel's boat was angling to the north. If they reached the harbor at the point they were aiming at, he'd have a dozen pontoons to cross and the wire-mesh catwalks swinging between them besides. Daniel turned, rose to a high crouch that let him keep a hand on the gunwale—it was at best an even chance whether the boat would come back for him if he fell overboard—and cried, "This way!"

His free arm stabbed in the direction of the *Aglaia*. "The navy ship! *Aglaia!*"

The boy at the tiller of the outboard motor looked to be eight years old or a little less. He stared at Daniel with worried eyes. The old woman beside him waggled the embroidery she was working on at Daniel. She screamed, "The harbor! The harbor! You walk!"

"The *Aglaia!*" Daniel repeated. He took out the hundred-florin piece. Multilevel diffraction gratings within the transparent coin turned it into a rainbow between his thumb and forefinger. He dropped the coin back into his purse.

The family argued shrilly among itself, the eight grown members shouting while the infant added its wordless cries. The boatmen of Kostroma harbor spoke their own patois. It was based on Universal but Daniel caught no more than a third of the words. Some of the vocabulary no doubt came from local Kostroman dialects, but the languages of many other planets played a part as well.

A middle-aged man stepped in front of the old woman and snarled an order to the steersman. The boy adjusted the tiller, pointing the bow toward the *Aglaia* after all.

The old woman screamed at the man; the man slapped her, knocking her against the stern transom. She picked up her embroidery hoop and resumed work, muttering to herself.

A sphere was the best shape for a vessel operating in the Matrix, but spherical ships were dangerously unstable on water unless they had long outriggers. Besides, though a sphere was the most efficient volume to enclose, it presented severe problems for loading and unloading on the surface of a planet. The only spherical ships were small ones and vessels purpose-built for exploration.

All the ships in the Floating Harbor today were shaped like fat cigars. They floated a little above midpoint, and the hull proper was paralleled by an outrigger on either side. The antennae that drove the vessels through sponge space were either folded along the hull or extended for maintenance like the legs of a crushed insect.

The *Aglaia* looked very similar to most of the transports docked nearby. She was 613 feet long with a 65-foot beam. The nominal weight of her hull and fittings was 10,000 tons, though the in-service weight including crew, consumables, and reaction mass was a good 4,000 tons more.

She was built of steel. There were stronger metals and lighter metals, but none that really matched the corrosion and fatigue resistance of steel and its relative ease of machining and welding during repair. Weight was of no significance in sponge space and not very important even when the ship was using High Drive or her plasma motors.

The harbor was formed of multicelled concrete pontoons, individually several hundred feet long. The pontoons were anchored to the sea bottom on cables that adjusted to the height of the tide, and tethered to one another by underwater cables. Pedestrian catwalks dangled just above the waves. Surface lighters were tied to the sides of pontoons opposite most of the docked starships, but the bumboats clung anywhere: to pontoons, to the starships themselves, or to one another. They clumped like duckweed on a pond. Easily moved shelters of multicolored fabric on light frames sprouted on many pontoons for a degree of privacy.

The *Aglaia* was linked to a pontoon by three pivoting steel arms which allowed ship and float to ride the swells without rubbing. Many of the transports used fenders, but an RCN vessel—particularly one that carried the high and mighty of the Republic—had to be careful of its finish.

Ports were open all over the *Aglaia*'s hull for ventilation and easy access to the bumboats. A docking platform extended from the center of the hull to the outrigger. Guards waited there, but only formal traffic passed by that route.

Daniel ducked as his boat passed under the catwalk between two pontoons. The concrete was stained with three horizontal bands of algae—red, blue, and yellow closest to the water, stratified by the plants' relative need to be kept damp. Visible as blisters on the yellow band were fixed invertebrates; filtering gills streamed like smoke whenever a wave dipped the animal's shell back in the water.

The steersman was heading for the power room port, big enough to allow the Tokamak to be removed. "No, no," Daniel shouted, waving toward the landing stage on which three ratings under a petty officer watched his progress. "Put me there! Put me there!"

The boy shrugged and nosed up to the stage. The old woman glared at Daniel and spit into the water.

The boy threw the motor into reverse, killing their forward motion within an inch of the platform. Daniel hopped onto the steel deck without risk or need for the hand a rating was ready to offer. The boy handled his craft with the skill of someone born on the water. He was likely to live all his life there, too, as surely as the fish under the surface.

"Lieutenant Daniel Leary," Daniel said. "Requesting to see the duty officer."

"Welcome aboard, sir," the armed petty officer said. He raised his belt radio. "I'll tell Ms. Weisshampl you're coming."

Formality ended with a broad smile. "You look a lot better than she does, sir. Sure you were at the same party?"

Daniel laughed, glad of a way to break the tension. He sauntered across the wet decking, slippery for all its nonskid pattern. He wasn't worried about seeing Weisshampl or really doubtful about getting her agreement.

He was very nervous about what would come next. Well, the Republic of Cinnabar expected her naval officers to carry on no matter what the circumstances.

The decks of a cylindrical starship ran the long way. The *Aglaia* had five decks, but the lowest two, Decks A and B, were under water when the ship floated normally. They contained bulk storage for consumables and reaction mass, plus the magazines of missiles and message cells.

On the *Aglaia*, unusually for a ship of her size, the ratings' quarters took up most of the volume of Deck B. Normally the crew would have been accommodated on Deck D, but that region on the *Aglaia* was given over to passenger suites.

Daniel entered the central rotunda of Deck C. Armored staircases stood at the four ordinal points. Corridors fore and aft ran along both sides of the hull, but the regions immediately flanking the rotunda on this deck held the *Aglaia's* two Tokamak generators. Their mass had to be kept close to the vessel's center or the ship would be impossible to maneuver if the computer went down or control trunks were damaged in action.

Naval computer systems were many-times redundant and almost

never failed. The space officers who survived to hold high rank were those who planned for unlikely disasters, and they saw to it that naval architects were of the same cautious frame of mind. The *Aglaia* could dance on a pin under manual control.

Deck C contained the machinery spaces and armament: the offensive missile systems and most of the anti-missile plasma cannon. The *Aglaia* had a light cruiser's normal defensive suite: six barbette turrets, each holding a pair of 4" plasma cannon. The turrets were retracted and sealed beneath a hull fairing when the ship was under way, but here at rest on the surface five of the six were extended to increase the interior room. The exception was the turret on Deck A, twenty feet under water.

The *Aglaia* had four missile launchers and only three reloads per tube. That weakness was a nagging irritation to every fighting officer in her complement, but the communications vessel wasn't *meant* to fight. Her missile battery was sufficient to see off any pirate she chanced into; and a commander who risked passengers' lives in needless heroics would face a court-martial and certain conviction if he survived.

By tradition the odd-numbered stairs were up and the even numbers down. Daniel strode across the rotunda and through the open hatch of Stair 1. A grizzled petty officer who looked twice her probable age of forty stood on the landing holding hands with a local girl with a demure expression and nothing on above the waist. They looked startled.

"Carry on, Haynes," Daniel called over his shoulder as he skipped up the stair tower two treads at a time.

"Give up on high life and come back to the working navy, Mr. Leary?" Haynes replied with echoing laughter.

The RCN was a disciplined force—and her enemies would be the last to deny it. Discipline didn't mean spiritless, though, nor was there any attempt to instill the kind of top-down terror that the Alliance seemed to consider an ideal.

An unpopular officer was the butt of "accidents" that made her look ridiculous. An unpopular captain found himself without a crew after his next landfall: the merchant service paid well and didn't ask employment histories in wartime when there weren't enough trained ratings by half.

The crews followed officers they respected from ship to ship, and they didn't respect weakness. By the same token, an officer who couldn't be approached by ratings and wouldn't share a laugh with them had no business and no future in the RCN.

The hatch to Deck D was open. An accordion played music of a style that Daniel had heard at the supper club. There was laughter as well, and the clink of bottles. The delegation wasn't using the fancy compartments at the moment, but that didn't mean the suites were going to waste.

Deck E was officers' country and the *Aglaia*'s command and control area. The turret mounted over the rotunda was extended so Daniel didn't have to walk around it as he'd done during the voyage. The turret hatches were raised as well; fresh air and a skirl of birdsong filled the corridor as he walked to the dayroom.

The clerk's desk was empty, but the door to the Officer of the Day's office was open. Lt. Weisshampl sat upright behind the console, looking morose. Daniel grinned and threw her a sharp salute from the doorway.

"Leary," she said, "if you screw around saluting, I swear I'll lock you in the lower turret and not let you out till we're back on Cinnabar. How the hell do you look so fresh?"

She frowned like a thunderhead. "And *don't* tell me it's youth!"

"Not all of us spent the evening practicing assault drops onto concrete, Maisie," Daniel said. Weisshampl was 28 Terran years old, quite young to be XO of a parade ship like the *Aglaia*.

Weisshampl laughed, then rubbed the back of her neck with a groan. "Yeah, you might have something there," she admitted. "But for God's sake sit, so I don't have to look up at you."

Daniel took the indicated chair. The deck's resilient surfacing was pierced in what looked to an untrained eye like a pattern of tucks. The holes were threaded into the plating beneath. Cinnabar naval furniture was built to multiples of the same pattern so that any piece could be bolted in place within a few inches of where the user wanted it. There were no large objects unsecured on a ship that was under way.

"I came for a favor, Maisie," Daniel said. "I'd like you to release a detail of twenty ratings to me under a solid petty officer. You can log it as building a positive relationship between the nations of Cinnabar and Kostroma. So far as you're concerned, it'll keep some people out of trouble while you're on the surface and there isn't enough to do."

Weisshampl looked at him with an appraising frown. They both knew that Daniel wasn't one of the *Aglaia*'s officers and didn't have command authority over her crew, so she didn't bother to mention the fact.

"You know," she said, "that'll look like some kind of fiddle, officers using ratings to make money on the side. And if it was plenty of other officers, that's what it'd be."

She grinned in a combination of humor and cynicism. "I don't say I wouldn't agree, you understand. But that's not what you're after."

Daniel shrugged. He wasn't sure how he could describe the situation, and he didn't intend to try.

"I served under your Uncle Stacey when I was a midshipman," Weisshampl said as if changing the subject. She picked up the object she used for a paperknife. It was a feather whose vanes were fused into a sharp, glassy membrane. It came from a bird that spent its life swimming in a sea whose high salt content didn't freeze above -4 degrees Celsius, but which nonetheless was frozen over for half the year.

"He had a nose for shifts in the Matrix," she went on, rolling the feather between her paired index fingers. "I was amazed at the time, and the more I see of other astrogators—"

She smiled coldly at Daniel.

"—the more amazed I am. You're good, Leary. Better than me. But you'll never be what your uncle was."

"No," Daniel said, "I won't."

Weisshampl touched a button on her console. "Chief of Rig to the dayroom," she ordered. Her voice rang from the speakers in every compartment and corridor on the *Aglaia*.

Domenico, the bosun, must have been in his quarters just down the corridor. He was at the door of Weisshampl's office before the echoes of her voice had ceased. "Yes sir?" he said, his voice slightly muffled as he pulled his tunic on over his head while he was speaking.

"I want you to round up a detail of twenty under . . . Woetjans, I think," Weisshampl said. "They'll be on detached duty under Mr. Leary, here. For choice pick them from people who've spent their pay advance already."

Domenico grinned like an earthquake in a rocky cliff. "That won't be much of a cull," he said. "Riggers, or . . . ?"

"Riggers if you've got them, but take them from the hullside if you need to," Weisshampl said. "I'll clear it with the Chief of Ship."

"Aye aye, sir," the bosun said. He tapped his forehead in salute and walked out of the office. His voice was booming names even before he reached the stairs.

"I'll lay on an aircar to ferry you to shore," Weisshampl said to Daniel. "Any particular spot?"

"We'll pick up Hogg at my quarters," Daniel said. "Then the Elector's Palace. Before I forget, could you break this out of petty cash?"

He brought out the hundred-florin piece and handed it to the duty officer.

Weisshampl looked at the coin in surprise. "This is a special minting," she said.

"It's legal tender," Daniel said defensively. "It's, well, it was minted the day of my birth. I was given it to, well, carry, you know. Right now I'm a little short of ready cash and—"

"I'll break it for you myself," Weisshampl said, taking out her purse. "If it got into ship's funds, it might be harder to find when you wanted it back."

She put the lucky piece in an inner pocket of the purse, then shoved ordinary coins across the desk in three neat stacks. "I really respect Commander Bergen," Weisshampl said. "The only thing he needed was the willingness to go for the throat."

"I love my uncle," Daniel said as he rose. "I really appreciate your help, Maisie."

He turned and started out the door. Domenico had probably assembled the detail by now.

"You must have gotten the killer instinct from your father," Lt. Weisshampl said to his back.

"For proper proportions over that span . . ." said Mistress Bozeman, looking at the sketch Adele had made, "the shelves have to be seven-eighths of an inch higher. Now, we could get the same effect by reducing the length by about four inches."

The library bustled. It hadn't been this busy since the day Adele arrived and half the palace staff had wandered in for a look at the foreign intellectual. At least half of the assistants assigned to her were here today and many of them seemed willing to work, at least in a desultory fashion.

"Work" for the moment meant carrying boards up three flights of helical stairs that were architecturally breathtaking. They were also about as badly suited to transporting long shelves as any design Adele could imagine, so she was both pleased and surprised that so many of her staff stuck with the task.

"Now you see . . ." the master carpenter said. She put the end of a fabric measuring tape against the masonry of the outer wall and handed the reel with its spring tensioner to the only journeyman present; the other was down in the cabinet shop, directing library assistants to the boards they were to carry.

Ms. Bozeman wasn't being obstructive. For perhaps the first time in a decade she wore a real working costume, a many-pocketed apron over sturdy clothing. The trouble was that she simply couldn't understand that aesthetic design had to give way to efficient use of space in the present circumstances.

Adele needed shelves that would hold the maximum number of logbooks, routing directions, and similar works in 20-centimeter size that had been standard aboard starships since before the Hiatus. She didn't need an inch and a half of clearance above the volumes, and she *certainly* didn't want banks of shelves separated by a four-inch gap that would be absolutely useless for any purpose she could imagine.

Mistress Bozeman didn't understand. If Adele had been asking her to set the shelves without vertical supports, the words would have made equal sense to the master carpenter.

Adele drew a deep breath as she considered which different words to use in what increasingly seemed to be a fruitless attempt to get her ideas across. "Excuse me, Ms. Mundy," said a voice behind her. "I must request that you grant me a brief private interview."

"Go a—" Adele began. She recognized the voice. She turned, the shelving forgotten for the moment.

"Lieutenant Leary," she said. She was more surprised than angry, but not a little angry as well. "I thought I'd made my desires clear at our previous meeting. Quite apart from that, I'm more busy than you can possibly imagine!"

He was wearing the same uniform he'd had on the day before: it had a resewn seam joining the right sleeve to the bodice, a neat job but not one that had escaped Adele's notice. Part of her wondered at the son of one of the richest men on Cinnabar wearing a repaired garment.

"I'm very sorry," Leary said with quiet formality, "but your duties to the Elector don't take precedence to obligations of honor between Cinnabar citizens."

"Ah," Adele said. "I see."

She supposed she should have expected this. Thinking back on their interaction the previous day, it should have been obvious that it would end in a duel. That hadn't been her intention, but . . .

That hadn't been her conscious intention.

"There's an empty balcony down the hall," Leary said, nodding in the direction of the palace's central structure. The building's wings were relatively unadorned, boxes for the staff to work in. The central mass had a triple colonnade on the front and loggias on the second and third levels to overlook the gardens to the rear. "We can talk there."

"All right," Adele said. She looked around to find Vanness and tell him to take charge temporarily. Everyone in the library was staring at her, including the two carpenters. Staring at her and Leary.

"Don't any of you have work?" she shouted. "By God that'll change when I come back, see if it doesn't! Carry on, damn you!"

She returned her attention to Leary. His expression hadn't changed; it was as neutral as the surface of an oil bath. He bowed her toward the door.

"After you," she snapped. The library was her domain. No outsider was going to patronize her here.

The third-floor halls were surfaced in hard-fired hexagonal tiles laid to form patterns in three shades of gray. The effect was nothing like as lush as the varicolored mosaics on the lower floors, but it was attractive and far more to Adele's taste.

She'd fought a duel not long after she found herself in exile on Bryce. An Academy classmate from Trimshaw's End, one of the most rural of the worlds of the Alliance, chose to find insult in an innocent comment of hers. He offered a challenge.

The duel should never have been permitted to go ahead, but the housemaster was lax and the dormitory monitor immature. Both Adele and the boy were outsiders; their classmates viewed the matter more as a cockfight than as a conflict between humans.

Even at the time Adele had known that she should end the farce by an apology. The boy was frightened, in over his head, and more afraid to draw back than go on.

David Drake

Adele wasn't afraid, but she'd learned of her parents' death only two days before. She didn't care about her responsibility for those who weren't able to act responsibly themselves. She didn't care very much about anything else, either.

She'd fought perhaps a thousand duels against holographic trainers at Chatsworth and in the basement of the Mundy townhouse: the Mundys were a hot-blooded lot, very punctilious about their honor. Because she was so thoroughly prepared, her strongest recollections of the real event were the ways in which it differed from what training had led her to expect.

The single-shot electromotive pistols were a set manufactured on Pleasaunce and lent by a friend of the dormitory monitor. Their long barrels threw a heavy slug at moderate velocity, whereas Adele had trained with Cinnabar-style weapons whose pinhead-sized pellets left the muzzle at the speed of a meteor.

Perhaps the barrel's weight caused her to overcompensate when she swung onto her target. She'd aimed at the top of his breastbone; instead, she hit the boy between the eyes. The pinhead would have disintegrated, converting its slight mass to kinetic energy. The heavy projectile went on through and splashed trees twenty yards back with liquified brains.

Somebody screamed. There were at least a hundred people watching, members of the duelists' house and friends from elsewhere in the Academy.

The boy rotated and fell to the ground. His back was bent in an arch. His heels drummed so wildly on the ground that one of his slippers flew off into the leaves. The doctor somebody'd hired for the event didn't bother to go to the victim; instead, she knelt and began to tell the beads of her rosary.

The dormitory monitor was acting as Adele's second. His mouth opened as he stared at the thrashing corpse. She walked over to him, reversed the empty pistol, and presented it.

"Here," she said. The coils in its barrel were warm even from the single discharge.

The monitor looked at her. For the first time Adele had realized that he was little more than a boy himself. He took the pistol's grip reflexively, realized what he held, and let it drop from his fingers. Adele stepped clear as the monitor began to vomit over the ground, the pistol, and his own silken trousers.

Nobody spoke to Adele as she walked back toward the house.

None of her classmates spoke to her for weeks thereafter. Servants packed the monitor's belongings that evening, but he never reentered the house or attended another lecture at the Academy. A long time ago . . .

The third-story loggia bayed out from the wall directly over the ramp leading from the palace into the terraced garden. Two servants had gone out to eat lunch while Leary was in the library. They were seated on the stone rail. One of them gestured with a handful of mince stuffed in a wrapper of large leaves as he told a story, wobbling on what seemed to Adele to be a dangerous perch.

She smiled at the thought. Less dangerous, perhaps, than a duel.

Leary opened the glass doors onto the loggia. The servants looked at him with surprise and a degree of belligerence.

"I'm sorry but we need this location," Leary said with a peremptory gesture. "I'll let you know when you can return."

The male servant who'd been telling the story snarled a reply in a northern dialect; Lupanan, Adele thought, but she didn't have to understand the exact words to get the meaning. Status on Kostroma was generally indicated by bright colors. Leary's uniform was gray with black piping and, to a rube from Lupana, looked like a pot boy's garb.

Leary grabbed the servant's loose collar and tossed him through the doorway. The Kostroman hit the far wall of the corridor. His companion squealed and scurried after him.

Leary closed the glass doors, faced Adele, and crossed his hands behind his back. "Mistress," he said in a clipped voice, "I know nothing about politics except that they exist. My father and sister take care of that end of family affairs."

Adele said nothing; she hadn't been asked a question. Leary wasn't a large man, neither as tall nor as bulky as the servant he'd thrown into the corridor. For a moment she'd thought he was going to pitch the fellow down into the gardens, and even now she suspected the choice had been a near thing.

"When I was just turned seven, there was all kinds of excitement at Bantry," Leary continued. "My father had gotten information from an Alliance agent; tortured it out of him, I suppose, but all I knew at the time was a conspiracy to murder us in our beds with Alliance help. Father flew off to Xenos with most of the guards. The rest of us stood watch all night in case the Alliance attacked."

He shook his head in wry marvel. "Hogg gave me a shotgun," he said. "I'd never been so excited in my life. Now, well, I wonder what a bunch of house servants and groundskeepers were going to do if a squad of Alliance marines in battle armor dropped on Bantry in an assault boat. But that's all I knew or know about the Three Circles Conspiracy, and I care even less."

Adele said nothing. *And I care even less. . . .* Did she care? She certainly hadn't cared about the *issues* at the time. That's why she'd gone to Bryce where the proscriptions had passed her by as surely as they had passed by Speaker Leary's young son.

"While I'm on Kostroma," Leary continued in a tone as emotionless as that of an accountant making a report of expenditures, "I intend to avail myself of the privilege of using the Electoral Library, granted all members of the delegation by his Excellency Walter III. I understand that might be a problem for you, Ms. Mundy. I therefore—"

He took a small case from his purse and opened it. His fingers moved with assurance though he continued to meet Adele's eyes.

"—offer you my card with the address of my present lodgings written on the back. If you choose to have a friend call on me, my landlord will take the message even if I'm absent and we can proceed with arrangements."

Shouted confusion rattled windows in the north wing. The noise might well be coming from the library, but for the moment that wasn't the most important situation Adele Mundy had to deal with.

She looked at the card of bi-surfaced plastic. The front read:

DANIEL OLIVER LEARY
LIEUTENANT, RCN

The finish was slick and hard enough to turn a knifepoint. She flipped the card over to read the address written on the porous back in a neat hand. The street was somewhere down by the harbor, she thought, but she hadn't made an effort to learn the geography of Kostroma City.

As she weighed her response, knuckles tapped and the glass doors opened. She and Leary looked around, Adele in surprise and the lieutenant with obvious irritation.

The woman who'd intruded was big and had close-cropped black hair. She was around thirty and would have had an attractive face if it weren't for the scar across her lower left cheek, ear-tip to chin.

In the woman's right hand was a hammer gripped by the head. She slapped the handle into her left palm idly. The hammer looked very similar to the one the journeyman carpenter in the library had carried.

"Yes, Woetjans?" Leary said in a thin tone.

"Sorry to intrude, sir," the woman replied; she didn't sound particularly sorry. "There was a bit of difficulty when we asked the wogs where the shelving was supposed to go up. If the officer-in-charge here—"

Woetjans nodded toward Adele.

"—will come set us straight, we'll get started."

She smiled with satisfaction. "Doesn't look like much more than a couple weeks' work to get shipshape, though that depends on your man Hogg finding the materials like he says he can."

"What in God's name is going on?" Adele asked mildly.

Leary cleared his throat. In some embarrassment he said, "It appears to me that since you're in charge here, Ms. Mundy, the library project is a matter of Cinnabar's national pride. I've therefore taken the liberty of enlisting a detachment of sailors to show the locals how it's done. Ah . . ."

He looked away, grimaced, and turned to face Adele squarely again. "This business is irrespective of any matters of honor that may take place between two Cinnabar citizens, of course."

Adele tapped the card on her opposite thumbnail. "I see," she said. "An admirably succinct explanation."

She tucked the card into her purse and looked at the lieutenant again. He stood in a loose brace, waiting for her decision. He wasn't nearly as young as she'd first judged him.

"I won't have a friend call on you, Lieutenant Leary," Adele said, "because I don't have a friend on this planet. Few enough anywhere else, though Mistress Boileau no doubt qualifies."

Leary smiled. For an instant he was a boy again, or a friendly puppy.

"I'd appreciate it if you'd come with me now," Adele continued, "to give me your viewpoint on how the library should be organized. I'm always willing to learn from those whose knowledge and ability I respect. And I'm afraid that if the rest of the navy is like you—"

She gave Woetjans a glance of appraisal only slightly softened by a smile.

"—we'll probably find the room completely finished if we delay more than a few minutes."

Leary bowed her toward the doorway. They walked down the corridor side by side. Woetjans strode ahead of them bellowing, "Clear way, you lot!" and gesturing with the hammer to emphasize her point.

Book Two

Daniel Leary eased his way around a group of Kostroman citizens, most of them arrayed like peacocks, already gathered in the third-floor hallway hours before the Founder's Day activities would begin. The procession would wind through all the districts of Kostroma City, but the best place to view it for those who weren't in the grandstands immediately below was from the upper portico of the palace facade.

In contrast to the crush at the front of the building, the hall at the back of the north wing was empty except for a pair of men arguing about freight rates and, at the end, the Electoral Librarian with her hand on the padlocked library door. The staple and the lock itself were new since when Daniel last visited the palace.

"Good morning, Mundy!" Daniel called, waving the loose ball of his handkerchief containing the insect he'd brought. "I'm glad I caught you before you got your seat for the celebrations. Though if you want to leave now . . . ?"

The reserved expression on Mundy's thin face broke into sudden recognition. "Good morning indeed, Lieutenant," she said. "Without your uniform I wasn't sure who it was."

She pressed the thumb and index finger of her right hand against the lock's identification plates. The hasp popped open. "I was arriving, not leaving. You're more than welcome. In fact I was regretting I hadn't come to thank you already. I suppose you've been occupied with your duties, but I should have made the effort."

Holding the lock in one hand, she swung the door open and gestured Daniel into the library. "I cleared up some cataloging matters this morning in my apartment before coming in. I have a personal terminal."

She gestured toward the flat bulge along her thigh.

"I should have checked on the work earlier," Daniel said in apology. "Not that I was concerned about Woetjans."

Shelving already rose floor to ceiling to cover a quarter of the library's area. The room was noticeably dimmer as a result, even now near midday, but conduit snaked across the ceiling decorations in obvious preparation for artificial lighting.

"As for my duties," he added with a tinge of bitterness he didn't like to hear in his voice, "no doubt I'll be informed when any are assigned me. I expected to be sent on a round of diplomatic parties, but Admiral Lasowski's secretary takes care of that."

Daniel cleared his throat, swallowing his next intended comment with the phlegm. The justification for Lasowski's behavior was that "young Leary is a hothead who can't hold his tongue." No point in providing supporting evidence.

"The secretary's a Martino of Ulm," he said instead. "A very cultured fellow and handsome in his way. But not RCN."

Mundy ignored the implications either out of uninterest or because she thought the discussion would be painful to her visitor. She walked down an aisle of quite practical width, gesturing to the new shelves.

"Leary," she said, "I wouldn't have believed it was possible in this length of time. I've cleared a third of the boxes off the floor. I truly believe that in a few days I'll be able to start the rough sorting. I thought . . . I didn't think . . ."

She turned to face him. "Lieutenant Leary," she said, stiff as a statue with the light of the north windows behind her, "when we first met my behavior was unworthy of a citizen of Cinnabar, let alone a Mundy of Chatsworth. I offer you my sincere apologies—and my hand, if you'll take it."

She held out her hand. Daniel reached for it with both of his, then realized he held the handkerchief with his prize in his left.

They shook right-handed. Mundy's flesh felt like ivory, dry and firm. "I saw nothing in your behavior that in any way discredited one of the great houses of the Republic," he said. "And, ah . . . When I was growing up on Bantry I was Mister Leary to my tutors, but always Daniel to the other children on the estate. My friends."

Mundy smiled without humor. "Mistress Boileau calls me Adele," she said. "I've always called her 'Mistress Boileau' or 'professor.' I'm not used to first names for other people."

She gave Daniel a glance that he thought was wistful. "I'm willing to try, though," she added.

"Good, good," Daniel said warmly. They'd covered the subject to an adequate degree. In a conscious effort to sheer away from embarrassment he went on, "And now you can help me, if you will. The natural history database aboard the *Aglaia* is regional and only hits the high points of individual worlds, so to speak. I want to know what this is."

He set the handkerchief on a box and opened the corners, darting his thumb and finger in to catch a leg of the trapped creature before he completely uncovered it. It was the size of his thumb and had four legs like all Kostroman insects. Briefly it unfurled dull wings, then folded them back onto its carapace. The creature's only touches of color were the violet beads pulsing to either side of the neck.

"They live under water on tidal flats," Daniel explained. "The purple color is gills that they spread out on the mud. They lure sucker fish in for dinner by looking like patches of algae."

He grinned broadly. "Supplying dinner, not eating, that is. But when the pools dry, they fly into trees and wait for the tide to come in again. They're *tri*phibious, and I've never seen the like before."

Adele seated herself at the working data console. "Give me keywords," she said as she typed. "Insect, water and air living, fish-eating—what?"

"Family Barchidae," Daniel said. "That's a guess but reasonable from the wing structure."

"If you told me the thing's name was Thomas . . ." Adele said with a faint smile. She continued to adjust her controls. "I wouldn't question it. The only interest I have in bugs is when I find them in my apartment; which, I regret to say, is more often than not."

As she worked, Daniel cleared his throat. He hadn't any good reason to be upset, but . . .

"I *am* wearing a uniform," he said, returning to Adele's first comment in the corridor. "This is a utility uniform, perfectly proper for an officer who's not expected to formally represent the RCN to civilians or members of other military forces."

He plucked the loose, gray fabric. It probably did look like pajamas, but he had only one 2nd Class uniform—and the Full Dress, which wasn't paid for, God knew how he'd do that, and which he'd had tailored for him because he was sure he'd need it for formal receptions on Kostroma.

Daniel cleared his throat. "I've been chasing life at the harbor's edge and I thought these were more suitable. . . ."

Lasowski would skin him alive if she knew he'd been wearing utilities in public whatever the technical wording of the regulations. There wasn't much chance the admiral *would* learn since she seemed barely conscious that Daniel was alive, but . . . In any case, Adele hadn't had any intention of probing a sore point with her remark.

"Huh," she said. "That's odd. From the address this should be a sermon file in the headquarters of the Established Church."

Daniel leaned over her shoulder. The air-formed holographic display was visible only over a narrow angle; all Daniel could see from behind her was a quiver of color with no more substance than an image of the aurora borealis.

"'As the hydropter wallows in the greatest foulness but nonetheless ascends into the upper air,'" Adele said. It was a moment before Daniel realized she was quoting. "'So a man may hope, no matter how great his sin, to achieve the portals of heaven so long as he turn his face upward.'"

She touched her controls again. "I think," she said drily, "that if we search a zoology database under 'hydropter' we may find a more useful—*there*, I think."

She rose, turning the console's chair over to Daniel. He slid into it gratefully. At the top of the display area was the image of a creature identical to the one he'd bundled again into the folds of his handkerchief.

Daniel brought up the text. He could use the data unit—there was nothing unfamiliar about its controls—but he suspected he could have spent days at the terminal without getting the results the librarian had achieved in a minute or two.

"I gave your men the day off," Adele said behind him. "The locals have a holiday. Quite apart from fairness, they wouldn't be able to get into the warehouses for the stores they need."

"Fairness is important," Daniel said as he scanned the description of the hydropter; indeed, a member of the Barchidae. "A Cinnabar rating won't complain about hardship, but God help the officer he thinks is unfair. As for the stores—if Hogg couldn't get through the lock, Woetjans is quite capable of blasting the door down."

He rotated images of adult and juvenile hydropters. The display was so sharp the creatures looked solid. This was a naval-quality system, a light-year more advanced than anything he'd thought to find in Kostroma City.

"I can't get over the amount of work your sailors have done," Adele repeated. Her voice had moved away; she was beside one of the new cases, filled now with books arranged only by size. "And they took time to clear living quarters for themselves in the subbasement here."

She paused. "Ah, I hope that was all right? Ms. Woetjans said it'd save transit time and have other advantages."

"Quite all right," Daniel said. "She checked with me and I informed Maisie—that's Lieutenant Weisshampl. It keeps the detachment closer to its work, and I gather makes it easier to gather the necessary materials outside duty hours."

"Ah, I meant to ask about that," the librarian said in a tone that implied she wouldn't have raised the subject if Daniel hadn't brought it up. "Ah, I trust the wood and other materials aren't coming from navy stores?"

"No," Daniel said, "and the arrangement is quite legal."

He grinned broadly and continued, "Which is why I was informed about the details. You have a warrant from the Elector to receive goods and services for the library operation?"

"That's right," Adele said in puzzlement, "but it's worthless because all expenditures have to be approved by the Chancellor. Her approval hasn't been forthcoming even to the extent of my outstanding pay."

Daniel swiveled out of the console and stood; he didn't like to be seated while talking to a person who was standing.

"There's quite a lot of construction and reconstruction in Kostroma City," he explained. The idea had been his, though it couldn't have gone anywhere without Hogg's local contacts. "In the palace, but elsewhere as well."

"That's right," Adele agreed. She took in information the way a mudhole drank stones, a mild *plop* to indicate receipt and then a blank surface again.

"Quite a lot of what's being torn out or covered over would

be considered valuable art back in Xenos," Daniel said. "Mosaics, frescoes, ornamental railings. Your warrant gives Hogg the right to collect that sort of thing and arrange with the officers of Cinnabar transports to carry them home. The difference in what Hogg pays local workmen for scrap and what he's getting for works of art from the officers covers the cost of shelving very nicely."

He coughed delicately. "With something left over, I assume, which is no more than proper. Ratings who do work beyond their normal duties are paid extra, and my personal finances are such that I'd really prefer those charges not come from my purse."

His chuckle had a hollow sound in his own ears.

Adele laughed merrily for the first time since Daniel had met her. "I've always claimed information was the most valuable resource there was," she said. "I'm glad to see you and your manservant have been able to achieve more tangible results from the theory than I ever did."

Daniel walked over to the west wall, following what were now straight aisles between neat stacks of boxes in place of the jumble things had been in the first time he saw the room. Three panes of a window had been smashed out. The laths, putty, and glass for the repairs were piled beside the casement but at the moment a sheet of clear plastic was taped over the hole.

He pulled up a corner of the plastic, stuck his handkerchief through, and shook the hydropter out into freedom. It dropped several feet, then rose again on membranous wings to whir slowly toward the harbor.

"They're strong flyers," he said as he watched the shimmering flight. "They colonized islands over hundreds of miles of open water even before they started hitching rides with the early colonists. Saves me carrying it back myself."

There was no shortage of hydropters on the tidal flats. If he'd had use for a speciman he'd have killed this one without a qualm. Daniel didn't care to do harm out of sheer laziness, though; not even to a bug.

The hydropter was out of sight. Daniel turned and smiled a trifle wanly. It hadn't been likely that he'd find an unknown species in Kostroma Harbor. "A very common insect, it appears; interesting only to me."

A popping sound rippled from outside the building. That would be fireworks signaling the start of the Founder's Day activities, though he'd be surprised if anything significant happened in the next half hour.

The buzz and shuffle of conversation in the front corridor grew louder as Kostromans moved toward the portico. The spectators here were middling merchants from Kostroma City or nobles from islands at a distance from the capital. The very rich and powerful sat with Walter III on the grandstand in the plaza, but those who'd gained entry to the palace were the next stage in local importance.

"I'm concerned about the conditions your sailors are living in," Adele said with a frown. "I know it was their choice, but they've simply emptied an alcove that was used to store decades of junk. It's clean, now—I looked in on them. But there isn't nearly enough space for twenty people to live in."

Daniel laughed. "I'll take you aboard the *Aglaia*," he said. "That'll show you cramped—and a communications ship has an enormous amount of room compared to a corvette with an equal crew. Besides—"

His tone changed slightly. "Most of the detachment are riggers, you see. Folk who spend their duty hours at the edge of the universe. The Matrix is a glow they can touch and there's nobody nearer than the rigger on the next antenna. They *like* to have their living quarters cramped."

Another salvo of fireworks sounded. The display would lose a great deal at midday, but the Elector had wanted sunlight for the floats and tableaux of the procession.

"Look," Daniel said, "the other reason I came to see you now was because this is a perfect place to see the parade. I'll share my goggles—"

He tapped the band squeezing down the soft brim of his fatigue cap.

"—and you can tell me what's going on."

"Fighting that crowd?" Adele said, looking doubtfully toward the door. She couldn't see the Kostroman spectators from this angle, but their noise had risen to a sullen roar.

"Oh, no!" Daniel said. "I've found us a much better place than that."

He offered the librarian his hand. "I hope," he added with a grin of anticipation, "that you've got a good head for heights."

✧   ✧   ✧

"My God," Adele said as she faced the peach-colored expanse of roofing tiles. The 30 degree downslope was bad enough but the way it stopped ten feet away, straight as a knife-edge, at the gutter—that was terrifying.

The spectators below in Fountain Street cheered. The sound had seemed louder when she was in the library; either the palace hallways had channeled the noise, or her own fear was numbing her ears. Seabirds wheeled above and keened like lost souls.

"See?" Daniel called cheerfully over his shoulder as he walked—not crawled, *walked*—toward the gutter. "I told you it'd be easy once we were up the ladder."

"Yes," Adele said. "You did tell me that."

To her the most amusing part of the whole business was the fact that an hour before she'd have truthfully said that she wasn't afraid to die. It appeared that she was, however, afraid to mash herself to a pulp as the climax to a hundred-foot fall. She supposed it was vanity.

The ladder onto the roof was in an alcove off the south stairwell; the hatch was the front of a small glazed cupola. Adele hadn't known the route existed until Daniel led her to it. The iron ladder was bolted against the brick wall. It was absolutely vertical. Water leaking from the hatch slicked the iron and covered it with flaking rust.

Adele squirmed out onto the tiles. Sunlight had warmed them, but the glaze was smooth. She started down, realizing immediately that she should have backed instead of proceeding nose-first.

Daniel squatted at the edge of the roof. He turned and smiled at her, looking like a friendly gargoyle. "Ah?" he said. "Would you like a hand?"

"I'm all right," Adele snapped. "I'm just not used to this."

Daniel nodded and returned his attention to the crowd below, slipping his goggles over his eyes. She wasn't sure whether he was being polite or if he simply took her statement at face value. Daniel Leary wasn't, quite clearly, a man who did things by indirection.

"An RCN officer has to be able to rig the antennas," Daniel said musingly as he looked at the street. "Has to be able to do all the jobs on a warship, actually, but the one that's likely to wash out a midshipman is rigging. 'Young gentleman' you may be on the ship's books, but you're trained the same as a rating recruited straight off a farm."

Adele concentrated on crawling, moving one limb at a time. The tiles were half-round sections of ceramic pipe laid each over the end of the next tile below. The ridged surface was hard on her knees but there was no way she'd have been able to walk down the way Daniel had, as calm as if he were at ground level.

All she'd have to do was roll forward dizzily and she *would* be at ground level, no question.

"The antenna controls are hydraulic," Daniel continued. "Mechanical on some ships, but that's rare. You can't use electrical power to shift the rig. Can't use radio when you're in the Matrix because even a tiny signal distorts the field and the ship goes God knows where. There's no more alone than that."

Adele's fingers touched the lip of the stone gutter. Verdigrised copper downspouts thrust out every twenty feet of its length. The only gargoyles on the Elector's Palace were those in its internal decoration.

Daniel put his hand beside hers on the gutter though his eyes remained fixed on the crowd. "Use my arm as a brace as you get yourself turned around," he said.

"Thank you," Adele said. She gripped his wrist with her left hand and rotated her legs under her. She didn't need the help, but it would have been impolite to refuse—and it *was* a help.

His arm felt as firm as a piece of structural tubing.

"They say 'One hand for the ship and the other for yourself,'" Daniel said, "but you can't always do that. If a joint's frozen or a valve is bleeding fluid, you need both hands for the job . . . and you use them, even though if you drift and the ship leaves you behind it'll be like you never existed."

Adele put her heels in the gutter but deliberately crossed her hands in her lap instead of bracing them behind her. She took deep breaths and forced herself to look down on Fountain Street. Crews were rolling a float up the palace's entrance drive to the waiting grandstands. It was supposed to be a spherical starship.

"I love standing at the top of an antenna, watching the universe throb," Daniel said softly. "It's like being a part of everything that ever was or ever will be.

"Here," he said. He seemed embarrassed to have been so talkative. He took off his goggles and offered them to Adele. "The sign says this was the first landing on Kostroma, by slowboat. I'd thought Kostroma dated from after sponge-space astrogation."

"Umm," Adele said. She held the goggles to her eyes instead of strapping them on. The image was bright and perfectly clear despite being magnified by something on the order of forty times. A pair of servants carried a banner between them on poles. When the angle was right she could read the legend: CAPTAIN WANG'S COLONY—2706 ANNO HEJIRA.

The servants' skin-tight suits looked like no garb Adele had ever seen before. She supposed it was somebody's idea of what people wore in the days mankind was limited to the Solar System.

Adele returned the goggles and slid her personal data unit from its pocket. She sniffed in amusement at the qualm she'd felt at bringing it out: she was even more afraid of dropping the computer than she was of falling herself.

Using the wands that she preferred to the virtual keyboard, she linked to the base unit in the library below and went searching. The bright sun made her think she should have worn a hat, but she wasn't sure she owned one that would have stayed on in the breeze here on the tiles.

Martial music began to play, its strains severely attenuated by the time they reached Adele's ears. "The float's in front of the grandstand now," Daniel explained with the goggles over his eyes again. He didn't ask what she was doing. "Eight people have gotten out—they can't have had much more room than they would've in a real starship. Especially a slowboat. One of them's claiming the planet, I gather."

"Just as I thought!" Adele said in triumph. All her fear had vanished since she got to work with the data unit. "The first reference to Captain Wang is in a post-Hiatus history of the Swartzenhild clan. That claims that Adria Swartzenhild was Wang's navigator and responsible for bringing the ship safely to Kostroma when the original calculations would have taken them past the system and into the eternal dark."

"Huh!" Daniel said, turning his head toward her. She supposed the goggles adjusted for nearby objects—otherwise he was staring into one of her nasal pores—but it still made him look like a frog. "So that means there was an early colony after all."

"No, it means there wasn't," Adele said in satisfaction. "If the earliest reference is only three hundred years back and in a self-serving source, there's no evidence whatever. All the later references repeat the Swartzenhild account with embellishments and sometimes name changes."

She smiled. "Changes to the name of whoever's telling the story, that is."

A frown furrowed Daniel's forehead as he turned back to the tableau. "Simone Hajas is saving Captain Wang from a mutiny," he reported as figures shifted in front of the grandstand. "Look—"

He raised his goggles to meet Adele's eyes. "So you mean the story couldn't be true because it happened to the person telling it? Her family, I mean."

"No," Adele said. "I mean that if there's no record of the story for sixteen hundred years, and if the person who discovers the information is employed by the Swartzenhilds, who have risen from obscurity to trading wealth in less than a generation—both of which are the case—then the balance of the probabilities are that the story is an invention."

Her smile was cold. A finger-high plant grew from a joint in the roof tiles where windblown dirt had given it lodgment. Adele twisted off the dry head.

"The probability of it being false," she continued, "is about the same that this seed will fall if I throw it over the side."

She leaned over the gutter and dropped the bit of plant. It fluttered away toward the ground.

In sudden embarrassment she added, "I'm sorry. I shouldn't—"

Daniel broke into bellowing laughter. He slapped her on the back and cried, "Fair enough! You won't tell me how to rig a ship for the Matrix and I won't argue with you about history!"

"Well, it's not so much history as information," Adele muttered. "The first question is always whether the person who says something *can* know the truth. This time the answer was, 'Not really.'"

Daniel passed her the goggles again. Though the image through the electronic amplifier was sharp, Adele couldn't hold it steady enough to be of much use. For politeness's sake she watched the end of the skit before she handed them back.

The actors climbed back into the globular float. It rolled down Fountain Street in a haze of recorded music.

The next event was a group of people in checked robes, led by a lyre-shaped metal standard from which ribbons dangled. The legend stamped on the bars of the lyre couldn't be read from this angle, but they were obviously some guild or other.

"No Leary on record joined the RCN," Daniel said as he watched. "Till me. The Bergens, though, my mother's family—they were spacers as far back as the end of the Hiatus. And never a greater one than my Uncle Stacey, either."

Additional bodies of marchers followed the first. Some of them played musical instruments; all wore finery and carried banners or symbols of their craft. A cylindrical float, colored silver in contrast to the gold of the slowboat, was being wheeled toward the stands where it would be introduced into the line of march.

"My father made Uncle Stacey manager of the repair yards at Bantry when he retired," Daniel said. "Stacey brought some of his retired warrant officers to run the hands-on work and the business side, but he did the testing himself. Every spacer's heard of Commander Stacey Bergen, even the ones who never got out of the Cinnabar system. The yard does three times the business under Uncle Stacey than it had before him."

Adele wondered whether this personable young man had known anyone he could talk to since he joined the navy. There were more ways to lose your family than in the slaughter of a proscription.

The cylindrical "starship" was moving into place before the grandstand. "The Second Landing," Daniel read. "3381 Anno Hejira."

Then he added in the same tone of cool reportage, "Mind you, father never ceases to say that only his charity saves his wife's brother from begging on the street. There could be some truth to that. Uncle Stacey isn't much of a businessman."

"This is quite real," Adele said, scrolling up her display. "A secondary colonization from Topaz, under the Princess Cecile Alpen-Morshach. And there was a Hajas . . ."

Daniel touched a control on the frame of his goggles. "Emilius Hajas, Commander of the Royal Bodyguard," he said. "Who it appears is personally laying out the site of Kostroma City. How did there chance to be a Hajas in both the first and second colonies, do you suppose?"

"According to the list of crew and colonists," Adele said drily, "Emilius Hajas was a rigger with a series of disciplinary charges pending. He apparently deserted on Kostroma."

"To the great relief of his watch commander, I shouldn't wonder," Daniel said. "A colony ship must be hell on crew discipline. A training ship's bad enough, full of recruits who don't know one hand from the other."

He raised his goggles again to look at her. "That's all in your little handset?" he said, nodding to the data unit on Adele's lap.

"I'm linked to the library unit," she explained. "And through that to the whole net. There's a transmission lag since signals in both directions have to go through the satellite constellation, but I'm so used to this . . ."

She smiled at the little computer. She knew the expression was warmer than anything living had seen on her face for many years.

" . . . that I almost prefer it to using the big unit directly."

A band of children in Hajas silver-and-violet followed the second float. They were graduated by height. Adele wasn't sure she'd be able to judge how old they were even with the goggles' magnification, but those in the back looked extremely small.

Each child clung to a rope twined with flowers running from front to back of the file. The last few rows were tied to the rope, not just holding it. Stern-faced adult minders in livery marched at the corners of the group, carrying batons.

"You know," said Daniel in a tone of gentle musing, "it's as well that I'm up here and not down on the street. I guess they'll be using those sticks by the end of the procession when the little tykes are tired."

"It's a charity home for orphans," Adele said, reading off her display. They'd been scheduled for earlier in the line of march; she supposed there'd been difficulty getting such small children into position. "I think that's what they are, anyway."

Daniel took off his goggles and put them in his lap. He rubbed his eyes. "Colder than space, charity can be," he said in the same soft voice.

He looked at Adele. "Well, I don't suppose it's the business of a naval officer to tell other people how to live their lives," he said.

"I don't suppose it is," Adele said mildly. She was searching files so that she had a reason to keep her eyes focused in front of her. Any data would do for the purpose.

Daniel sighed and relaxed. "Maybe Admiral Lasowski's right about my temper," he said apologetically. "Sorry."

Adele looked at the mortality statistics for inmates of the Electoral Home for Orphans and Foundlings. The information didn't surprise her—after all, why assume that aspect of Electoral whim would be better organized than the library was? It was amazing, though, that so many of the children were able to walk at all, given the rate at which inmates died after admission to the home.

"Look," Daniel said, smiling but quite clearly not looking at the procession while the orphans were still in sight. "There's parties all over the city tonight. I've made friends with a few of the Kostroman naval officers, a decent enough lot, and I've got an invitation to the Admiral's Ball."

The roof began to tremble at a very low frequency. Adele felt the vibration more as a queasiness than a sound, but the roof tiles clicked together at a gathering rate.

"Ah!" Daniel said. "That'll be the *Princess Cecile* lifting from the Navy Pool. Don't—"

He handed Adele his goggles again. "Here, it's best to use these if you're going to look straight at it, even this far away. They'll adjust for the glare."

He frowned and added, "I hope they're not going to overfly below three thousand meters."

Adele could hear the sound of a starship's motors through the air now. She held the goggles to her eyes, but it was gentle pressure of Daniel's hand that turned her to look south instead of west toward the Floating Harbor. A ship was rising on a plume of plasma.

"The navy uses a lagoon with a barrage across the mouth," he explained as she watched the vessel rise. It wasn't particularly large. "The navy warehouses are there too; that's where the ball tonight's going to be. Mostly the ships are in storage, but they activated the *Princess Cecile* for the celebration."

"I see," Adele said as she returned the goggles. The *Princess Cecile* had leveled out at what seemed to her a reasonable altitude and was cruising north toward the city.

"She's a corvette," Daniel said as he watched the ship. "Quite a nice little vessel, really. Kostroma built, but with most of her electronics bought from Cinnabar and her armament from Pleasaunce."

Plumes of colored smoke streamed from the corvette's outriggers, white on the right and purple from the other. The smoke mixed with the plasma exhaust into glittering, no-colored swirls like mica flakes strewn on mud.

"What I was going to say . . ." Daniel resumed. He offered the goggles; she refused them. "Is that I suppose you've got parties to go to yourself—"

Adele sniffed. He didn't suppose anything of the sort, and he was quite right.

The *Princess Cecile* began to launch fireworks to either side. Sparks of color purer than anything in nature rained from the airbursts. The boom of the charges was dull and arrived many seconds after the light of the display it ignited.

"Anyway," Daniel said, "if you'd like to see how the navy does it, I'm to bring a guest and—"

He paused in momentary horror. "That is," he resumed with formal caution, "if you'd care to attend the Admiral's Ball as a *colleague* of mine, Ms. Mundy, I would be very, ah . . ."

Adele chuckled. It wasn't a sound she often made. "I appreciate the offer, Daniel," she said. "But I think . . ."

She in turn paused. What did she think? That shutting herself in her shabby room was a better way to spend the evening?

And there was Markos, the man and his intentions . . . but she really didn't want to think about that.

"I think," she said, "that while I've never been interested in mating rituals in either the abstract or the particular, it might be interesting to attend the ball, yes. As I've found this event—"

She nodded toward the street.

"—interesting as a window on my new environment. Yes, I'll go with you if you'd care to have me."

Daniel grinned in what she judged was both pleasure and relief. "Good, good," he said, bobbing his head as he spoke. "Now, I've got a jitney and there's Hogg to drive. Shall I pick you up at your lodgings at, say, the ninth hour local time?"

His lips pursed in consideration before Adele could speak. "Hogg has the jitney, actually. But he'll drive us."

Adele thought about her apartment and the narrow, trash-strewn street the building stood on. Not that she needed to apologize for them to a lieutenant in debt to his servant, but . . . "No," she said aloud. "Why don't we meet at the back entrance to the palace gardens? At the guardpost?"

"My hand on it!" said Daniel Leary.

As they shook, the *Princess Cecile* loosed another salvo of fireworks. The explosions sounded like a distant battle.

Adele Mundy sat at the library data console. The information she'd accessed shone in holographic letters in the air before her, all the brighter because the sky beyond the windows ranged from deep azure to deep magenta in the northwest. For the moment her eyes were closed.

A cleaning crew worked in the hallway, calling to one another in the high singsong dialect of one of the northern islands. Bottles clinked together under the thrust of brooms. The palace was the site of the Elector's Cotillion, the most prestigious of the scores of Founder's Day events. There was no holiday for the cleaners who had to sweep up the leavings of the crowds who'd been watching the parade from here.

Daniel had gone off to dress. Adele needed to do the same thing very shortly. As for the information on the air-formed display . . .

She'd told Daniel that she preferred her personal unit to the large console. That was true, but in this case she'd deliberately transferred data to the library computer to keep from subconsciously associating the words with her own equipment.

Adele opened her eyes and read the account for the first time in more than a decade. A Terran trade commissioner on Cinnabar at the time of the Three Circles Conspiracy had made a report on the events. The Academic Collections had received it in the normal course of accessions. Adele had stumbled across it by accident.

> One of the most touching tragedies was that of a ten-year-old child, Agatha Mundy. She was at the home of a playfellow, a cousin on her mother's side, on the afternoon the proscriptions were announced. Her aunt, the younger sister of Agatha's mother, immediately rushed the child onto the street and told her to run away. The girl's attendant and guards abandoned her, to seek their own safety in flight.
>
> The house from which Agatha was expelled was on the outskirts of Xenos but near a main road. The child appears to have wandered along the road for hours, perhaps as much as a day, before she was picked up by a trucker of bad reputation. This man sold the girl to a tavern and brothel near the main civil spaceport. There she remained for a week.
>
> In misery and desperation the child finally accosted a pair of sergeants in the Land Forces of the Republic who frequented the tavern, explaining who she was. One of the soldiers throttled her and then cut the child's head off with

a knife borrowed from the tavern's kitchen. The sergeants turned the head in to the Public Safety Office, claiming the bounty. The Office paid only half the usual amount because the child was well below the minimum age set in the Decree of Proscription.

Adele rubbed her temples, then deliberately overwrote the file so that no one on Kostroma would ever be able to read it again. Not that anyone would care. In all the human universe, Adele Mundy might be the only person to whom those were more than words.

She often told herself that she didn't care. Life would be so much easier if that were true. Caring didn't change the past, nor did it chart a course for the future. Only a fool could think that she understood all the side effects of her actions.

Adele stood and walked to the door. She would attend the Admiral's Ball tonight; and after that, who knew?

Warehouse 17 was one of nearly eighty in the fenced naval compound. The walls were brick with wooden trusses supporting a tile roof. The bunting and strings of colored glowlamps along the walls couldn't hide the big building's origins, but at any rate it was sufficiently large for the crowd of officers and their consorts.

Besides, the acoustics were good. The seven-piece string band playing from a dais opposite the buffet was pleasantly audible without amplifiers, despite conversations and the dancers' feet.

"I think I'll find a vantage point," Adele Mundy said. She bowed to Daniel and moved off toward a corner. He watched her leave with mixed emotions. Part of him felt that he needed to protect the librarian in what passed on Kostroma for a sophisticated social setting.

Another part of him was certain that unsophisticated or not, Adele could take care of herself. Daniel had no evidence to support his belief, but he'd have bet any amount of money that folk who touched her unasked would be lucky to get their hands back.

In any case, she'd promised Daniel that she wouldn't get in the way of his hunting tonight and she was showing herself as good as her word. He squared his shoulders beneath the slightly-too-tight tunic of his Full Dress uniform and looked around the gathering.

The Kostroman navy was of considerable size, but many of its ships were a century old. Some hadn't lifted to orbit in a decade, and a few were in danger of sinking in the Navy Pool where they were anchored.

While the ships were laid up, their stores and equipment were transferred to warehouses and the vessels themselves were sealed. As surely in the Kostroman navy as in any other body, public or private, the amount of material in storage had increased to overflow the available volume. Ancient records, damaged and obsolete equipment, and containers whose contents were unknown to any living being, stuffed the thick brick walls.

Walter III was giving particular emphasis to these Founder's Day celebrations, the first under his electorship. One good result had been the clearance of Naval Warehouse 17. Equipment and stores for the *Princess Cecile* were reloaded when the corvette was commissioned, and Grand Admiral Sanaus ordered enough of a housecleaning in the rest of the complex to clear one warehouse completely as a site for his ball. The material removed had gone to the estates of naval officers if it appeared to have value, and straight into the sea if it didn't. Most of it went into the sea.

"Daniel, my man!" called Lt. Candace from near the buffet. "Come have a drink and tell these cretins how a properly handled corvette like our *Princess* can do a better job of defense than a dozen overage battleships like the *Erebus* and *Terror*!"

Candace was one of the Kostroman navy's brighter lights. He had an active-service appointment as second lieutenant of the *Princess Cecile*, had a good grasp of astrogation theory, and had made several voyages in his family's trading vessels before he received a commission.

Despite those virtues, Daniel found Candace more a personable companion than a naval officer as the term would be understood on Cinnabar. For the past fifty years of increasing prosperity and trade, the Kostroman navy had been the choice of young men of good family who either lacked a talent for commerce or had an overweening desire for the comforts of Kostroma City. Candace was perhaps the best of the lot, but it was a bad lot.

"Now, I didn't say that," said Welcome, one of the other two lieutenants present. The taller one was Parzifal. "What I said is that we need real battleships. If we had a navy in proportion to our merchant fleet, we'd have twenty battleships in commission.

Walter Hajas knows the navy—he's a commander himself in the reserve. I shouldn't wonder if he makes defense a priority."

He coughed. "Expansion will mean promotion for trained officers, you know. It stands to reason."

All the officers in the warehouse were in uniform, but again the word meant something different in Kostroman terms. Daniel was wearing the full dress uniform of the RCN: white silk with gold braid on every seam. It made a dazzling array in most gatherings, but here it seemed as dull as the building's brick walls.

Candace wore a magenta tunic over blue breeches and high boots; Welcome was in orange with trousers of vertical black and gold stripes; and Parzifal's ensemble was a candy-striped green and yellow jumpsuit with a shoulder cape of lustrous white fur. All three men had enough medals to stock a jeweler and a ribbon counter besides. Each could point to a regulation permitting their choice of garb—not that any of their superiors were likely to object.

"Look, Leary," Candace said earnestly as Parzifal pressed a pinkish drink into Daniel's hand. "Let me tell you my idea. You lot on Cinnabar ought to build up our navy yourselves, transfer battleships to us. You see?"

"Umm," Daniel said as he swigged from the glass cup. He'd heard this notion before. Every time Candace got outside a couple drinks, as a matter of fact.

"Now, Kostroma's a friend of Cinnabar, we've always been a friend of Cinnabar," Candace continued. He tossed off the rest of his drink, looking flushed. It wasn't exactly punch. The base was plum brandy, the usual tipple of the Kostroman navy, with a dash of bitters that gave the fluid color. The mixture was at least 60 percent alcohol by volume. "Ships in our navy are just the same as in your own, only you won't have to find officers for them. You see the beauty of it?"

"You'd want to transfer them with crews, though," Welcome said. "There's the devil's own time finding ordinary spacers here. They're all lazy and don't want to work."

Daniel rolled brandy around in his mouth to avoid having to speak; though another "umm" would probably have been sufficient. Kostroman merchant captains paid good wages—and paid them on time, as well. Naval ratings were rarely so fortunate.

"Say . . ." said Candace, his head swiveling. Daniel followed the Kostroman's eyes to a blonde woman in a backless dress.

"Not a lot of front either," Welcome noted approvingly. He snagged another cup of brandy from the buffet table. "To the dress, I mean."

"She's not for us, though," Welcome added. "I saw her come in on the arm of Admiral Sanaus. Rank hath its privileges."

"I didn't think I'd better bring my friend tonight," Candace said regretfully. "Her husband's offplanet, but you know, still . . ."

"It's important that your Admiral Lasowski knows how valuable we can be to your cause if Cinnabar just gives us the help we need," said Parzifal, the most focused of the three lieutenants. "I don't think those politicians in the palace really understand."

"Not that Hajas isn't a first-rate man and a real supporter of the navy," Candace put in. "The advisors he's got around him, though, I don't think a one of them's been aboard a warship."

He sounded to Daniel as if he was giving an honest opinion, not suddenly concerned that somebody would take his friends' opinions as treasonous. The Kostroman navy—like the RCN—was nonpolitical. On Cinnabar the power of the navy was greater than that of any faction that might want to use it; here on Kostroma it was more a matter of the navy being of so little importance that those looking for power didn't bother with it.

"It's a mistake to rely on orbital defenses," Welcome said as he passed Daniel a fresh drink. "They can't do a thing for our ships beyond Kostroma proper. Not even for the mining and manufacturing at Port Starway in the asteroid belt!"

Daniel opened his mouth to argue, then took a sip of his drink instead. The clear brandy was a taste he'd had to acquire since he arrived on Kostroma. Acquisition was complete by the end of his first night of partying with local officers.

Arguing with these men about Kostroman defense policy was as useless as trying to convince somebody that the world wasn't really flat. They were going to believe what it suited their own needs to believe, and argument otherwise would only damage friendships.

In fact Kostroma's defenses were lamentably poor, but building up the fleet to the relative strength it had two generations before wasn't a practical alternative. Kostroma couldn't crew both the warships and her trading vessels, and she couldn't at this point take political control of independent worlds in place of her age-old practice of reciprocal trading links.

Both the Alliance and Cinnabar controlled multiworld empires which were by now held together by self-interest. The star systems of Cinnabar's protectorate had no external political authority, but the local magnates could move to Cinnabar and gain a degree of influence over the affairs of the whole Republic. Protected worlds were in a position clearly inferior to that of Cinnabar itself, but with equal clarity they were better off than they would have been if fully independent.

The situation with the Alliance of Free Stars was even simpler: planets that revolted against the Guarantor's authority were nuked to subsistence level or below. Chief Planetary Administrators were always foreigners, and no warship of any size had a crew with a majority of members from any single planet.

Neither Cinnabar nor the Alliance could be described as a universal democracy, but both systems worked to provide a manpower base sufficient to a large fleet. Kostroma had proceeded in a different fashion in the years immediately following the Hiatus, when those worlds with the ability to navigate the stars had enormous advantages over the neighboring systems they contacted. It was too late to change now.

"Now, we know you can't talk about the negotiations," Parzifal said, bending closer than Daniel liked. "Still, you'll drop a word in your admiral's ear, won't you? Imagine a whole Kostroman squadron with you when you engage the Alliance fleet!"

"When I'm next alone with Admiral Lasowski . . ." Daniel said. That would be sometime in her next incarnation if Lasowski had anything to say about it. "I'll see that the point is stressed."

In fact, neither Walter III or any responsible Elector of Kostroma would accept a gift of warships which required the vessels to be used against the Alliance. That would be equivalent to dropping Kostroma and its trade into a meat grinder. Kostroma couldn't be made strong enough to resist all-out Alliance attack, and taking sides in the conflict would guarantee such attack.

What Kostroma needed was exactly what Welcome had sneered at a moment before: a significant upgrade to its orbital defense system. If the Alliance captured Kostroma, most of its ships, even those off-planet, would come as well because the owners were in Alliance hands.

An orbital minefield prevented a quick capture, since a properly laid one took weeks or even months to reduce. No Alliance fleet could remain so long in a hostile system without a base, knowing that Cinnabar would respond with even greater force before the Alliance could capture the planet.

Well, Kostroma's defenses weren't ideal but they were probably good enough. And they weren't the concern of Lt. Daniel Leary, either.

He finished his cup of punch and said, "I see what you mean," as he prepared to cut himself clear of the trio.

"Say, Leary," Candace said, putting an arm around Daniel's shoulders to move him aside. Welcome and Parzifal turned their backs, obviously by prearrangement.

In a conspiratorial tone Candace went on, "Do you think you can get some time clear tomorrow?"

"Umm," said Daniel. This didn't sound like an offer to address a prayer breakfast, but he'd learned to be cautious about what he was agreeing to. "That might be possible, yes."

"My family's got a fishing lodge on a little island not too far from here," the Kostroman lieutenant explained. "I was going to visit it tomorrow. The accommodations aren't palatial, but there are compensations—privacy, for example. Now, it occurs to me that my Margrethe has a friend who might really like to meet a visiting naval officer. Interested?"

He knuckled Daniel's ribs with the hand that wasn't around his shoulders.

Daniel pursed his lips. He was able to make his own arrangements, but if circumstances wanted to drop opportunities in his lap—that was all right as well. He grinned. "I'd be delighted to see more of your interesting planet," he said truthfully.

"I'll bet you would!" Candace said, punching Daniel again. "At midday I'll be at your lodgings in my aircar. And you'll give good *hard* thought to building up the Kostroman navy, right?"

"I sure will!" Daniel said brightly as he moved away.

It was hard to imagine anything at all good in the idea, but he didn't need to say that. After all, Candace was a friend. And getting to be a very good friend, in his way.

The young officer who'd just danced a gavotte with Adele wore a costume including at least six major color elements, most of which clashed with those nearest them in the ensemble. Apparently Kostroma's *Homo militaris* was even less restrained in his notions of attractive garb than was his civilian counterpart.

The Kostroman stepped back, made a full formal bow, and said, "You have given me a great honor, Ms. Mundy. You dance divinely."

He was quite serious. The pack of his gaily dressed fellows poising to beg her company for the next dance proved that beyond even Adele's doubt. She couldn't have been more surprised if someone informed her she'd been chosen to replace Guarantor Porra.

"No more for a moment," she called loudly to forestall the rush of insistent Kostromans. "I really need to stand for a moment and have something to drink."

That was the wrong thing to have said: she hadn't specified water and the herd of naval officers was already thundering toward the buffet. She'd have twenty-odd glasses of punch pressed on her in a moment. The sip she'd taken earlier convinced her that the fluid would make a satisfactory paint stripper but had no other proper human purpose.

"Your escort is a lucky man, Ms. Mundy," said the boy who'd just danced with her. She wished she'd caught his name. He'd apparently decided that he didn't have a chance at another dance so he might as well keep her company until the punch arrived. "Who is he, may I ask?"

"Lieutenant Leary of the Cinnabar navy," Adele said. Her eyes automatically searched for Daniel as she spoke his name, but the chance of finding someone dressed normally in this assemblage of peacocks was vanishingly slight.

Her own Bryce-style party costume was a beige bodystocking with ruffs at the neck, wrists and ankles. She'd thought it might be extreme for Kostroma. She couldn't have been more wrong.

Of course, she'd also thought she'd be a wallflower here as she'd invariably been when she attended the frequent social functions at the Academy. Wrong again.

"Ah, of course," said the young officer. His fellows were bearing down on him and Adele again, elbowing one another in universal determination to be the first to offer her liquor that she wouldn't touch her lips to. "We provincials can't compete with you sophisticates from the great empires, can we?"

The crowd of Kostroman officers arrived, pushing with increasing enthusiasm as each shouted his particular merits. It was as bad as the mob of water taxis that had greeted Adele when she stepped off the transport that brought her to Kostroma.

"Gentlemen!" she cried in a tone like that her mother used to correct sluggish servants; democracy wasn't an ideal the Mundys pursued within their own home. "Step back, if you will!"

Several of them jostled her, pushed by others behind them, and Adele's former dancing partner had a glass of punch emptied over his back. Still, she hadn't been crushed against the wall behind her. That was the most likely result had she not started acting like a Mundy of Chatsworth.

"Please!" she continued in the same ringing voice. "I wish to continue my conversation with my friend here. Everyone who accepts the social conventions held on Cinnabar and Pleasaunce will permit us to do so."

She was taking a cue from the youth's comment about sophistication. It worked like a charm. The circle around them couldn't have widened faster if she'd announced she had leprosy.

The reason that Adele had this unwonted and utterly unexpected popularity was the fact she came from Bryce, one of the core worlds of the Alliance, and she knew the dance steps current there. That made her very nearly unique in this gathering. Though one of the more prestigious Founder's Day parties, the Admiral's Ball didn't attract recent visitors from "the greater empires" as her partner had put it.

A number of the officers' consorts were attractive—and probably highly paid—imports from Cinnabar and the Alliance, but none of them had been on their home worlds as recently as Adele. They looked daggers at her as they memorized her movements.

Adele smiled coldly. While she'd learned the steps as a necessary part of her academic routine, she lacked the interest to have become skillful at them. In this assemblage she literally couldn't put a foot wrong: her mistakes were assumed to be subtle variations. A dozen whores were already determinedly trying to copy her errors.

An overweight man beyond middle age stepped onto the dais with the help of an aide. His uniform was relatively simple; there seemed to be an inverse relationship between rank and the degree of florid dress.

Having said that, this fellow wore a gold sash as well as gold piping on his blue trousers and tailcoat. His chest was a clinking mass of medals.

"That's Grand Admiral Sanaus," Adele's sole companion explained in a respectful whisper. "Chief of the navy."

Sanaus spoke to the bandleader, then offered his hand to a doll-like blonde woman who clearly believed less was more when dressing to gain attention. Adele sniffed, but she had to admit the girl—she was no more than 25 standard years old—was impressive. Real muscles rippled beneath the smooth skin of her thighs and shoulders, too.

The band hit a low chord and sustained it while the assembly quieted. "My officers and honored guests!" Admiral Sanaus said in the relative silence. "It's my pleasure to greet you in the name of the navy of the Commonwealth."

Sanaus wheezed between words and the puffiness around his eyes was a sign of ill-health Adele wouldn't have wanted to see on anyone she cared about. That was few enough people, of course.

"It's my even greater pleasure to ask for a few words from the lovely lady who's deigned to accompany me tonight," the admiral continued.

He bowed to the blonde. The room broke into good-natured cheers. "Ms. Mirella Casque, the scion of Casque Trading and the representative of that famous house here on Kostroma!"

"He's bragging," Adele's companion whispered. They were only twenty feet from the dais. "But he surely has reason to, doesn't he?"

"He does if he survives the night," Adele said.

"Even more if he doesn't!" the Kostroman replied. He was too young to know how to fake gallantry.

Casque Trading was one of the oldest and largest firms of its sort in the Alliance. This girl seemed young to represent the Casques on so important a trading system as Kostroma, but her being a daughter of the house explained the choice.

The girl bowed, then smiled as she ran her blue eyes across the assemblage. Adele felt their touch. The intelligence within that pretty package was just as real—and as hard—as the thigh muscles.

"I want to thank you and to thank your entire planet for the kindness and hospitality you continue to show me," she said. Her voice was clear and perfectly modulated; perhaps a trifle studied for the ingenue she looked like, but quite in keeping for the local head of an important trading company. "The settlement of Kostroma was a happy day for me and for Casque Trading, as well as for all you wonderful people."

She gripped Grand Admiral Sanaus's hand, bowed again—so deeply that Adele suspected the fabric of her top was glued—and hopped off the dais. She handed Admiral Sanaus down herself, ignoring the aide's attempt to get involved.

"She's really something, isn't she?" Adele's companion said. Conversation had picked up so he was able to speak in a normal voice without fearing the admiral would overhear. "And very wealthy, from what I hear."

"The Casques are old money," Adele said. Her words weren't the agreement the boy probably thought they were. "The founder of the family was a member of the original colony on Pleasaunce, and because the Casques are close to government circles they've grown wealthier as the Alliance has expanded."

"Remarkable," the Kostroman said, watching the woman who called herself Mirella Casque walk away on the arm of his superior.

Remarkable indeed. The woman had a Bryce accent: she was no more a Casque than Adele herself was. The family was a useful cover to explain the amounts of money "Mirella" was almost certainly spending to cultivate the leaders of the Kostroman navy.

Adele didn't know who the woman really was, but she had a good idea of who the woman worked for. Not the Fifth Bureau, though. More likely one of the aspects of Alliance military intelligence.

From what Adele had seen while she worked at the Academic Collections, spies of rival branches of the same nation didn't get along any better than professors at the same university were likely to.

Candace drove the aircar well and fast. The women weren't professionals; so long as the car was in Kostroma City they sat on the two seats in the vehicle's closed back where they couldn't be seen. Margrethe, Candace's "special friend," had a nipped-in waist between a remarkable bosom and lush hips; Bet, Daniel's date for the afternoon and evening, wasn't so much petite as egg-shaped. Her face, framed with lustrous black ringlets, was extraordinarily pretty.

"Benno"—Candace to Daniel—"tells us Cinnabar has the greatest navy there ever was, Lieutenant Leary," Margrethe said. She gave

Daniel a smile that showed her dimples. "You certainly have lovely uniforms."

Bet giggled behind her hand and whispered something in her friend's ear. She winked at Daniel and giggled again.

Daniel was wearing his 2nd Class uniform as the best compromise between his needs and his means. Although Bet was already hooked, so to speak, Daniel was too good a craftsman to wear civilian clothes and miss the effect the uniform could have on the girl he was meeting. On the other hand, he wasn't going to risk his full-dress Whites at a run-down fishing lodge.

"We're fortunate to have allies like Kostroma," Daniel said cheerfully. Candace didn't look best pleased at the way both women were fawning over the exotic stranger. He'd been very well aware when Margrethe leaned forward to point out her parents' townhouse to Daniel—and flopped a breast on his shoulder in the process.

The car was over open sea by now. The water was shallow. Knobs rose from the sea floor, their crests fringed with coral and sponges in colored bands varied by depth. Fish swam among the fixed life-forms. They were as brilliant as daubs of light flung from diffraction gratings.

Daniel looked over the side, wishing that he'd brought an identification chart. The *Aglaia*'s database wasn't complete on Kostroman sea life, but he was sure that Adele could have downloaded something suitable if he'd thought to ask her.

"What do you think of Kostroman girls, Lieutenant Leary?" Margrethe asked. "I'm afraid we must seem very provincial to someone who's travelled the way you have."

"Madame Margrethe," Daniel said; the girls resolutely refused either to call him "Daniel" or to give him their last names. It was a piece of coquetry that he didn't understand, not a concern for their security. "I can honestly say that no female company has impressed me as favorably as that by which I now am honored."

That wasn't true, of course, but it wasn't any greater a lie than failing to correct the impression that he was well-travelled. Besides, the girls were quite adequately pretty and Daniel shared with most men of his acquaintance the feeling that availability enhanced a woman's attractiveness. He knew there were other philosophies on the question, but he didn't hold them.

Bet giggled again. *That* could get old; but not in the length of time Daniel expected to know the lady.

Candace cleared his throat. "Why don't you switch places with Daniel now, Margrethe?" he said, his tone smoothing as the sentence continued. "That'll let Bet and our guest get to know each other better. And some wine wouldn't be amiss."

"Ooh, yes!" Bet said, perhaps the longest sentence Daniel had thus far heard from her lips. She turned and knelt on the seat to lean into the luggage space. "I brought the special white from Herrick's own vineyard!"

Bet wore a thin dress that shone either orange or golden depending on how the light struck it. The fabric was opaque but very clinging. From this angle, Daniel was willing to say that Bet's face wasn't her most attractive feature after all.

"Here, you come back and then I can take your seat, lieutenant," Margrethe said as she half-rose and smiled at him.

It was going to be close quarters to trade seats like this. Daniel could only hope that Candace wouldn't turn to watch the inevitable contact between the moving parties. Daniel doubted the Kostroman lieutenant would abandon him on a deserted island, but jealousy was an emotion Daniel had enough second-hand experience with to respect.

He rose; something in the sea thirty feet below caught his eye. "Say!" he said. "Circle here! Candace, can you circle here?"

"What?" said Candace. He banked the car slightly but he didn't throw it in the tight circle Daniel had wanted. It didn't matter; there was no longer anything to see.

"It was a sweep," Daniel said, giving the others a smile of glum embarrassment. "I'm pretty sure it was a sweep, I mean. It's a predator in your seas here."

The seascape they overflew had remained much the same for the past fifty kilometers. Reefs neared the surface and shelved away into valleys that were rarely more than a few hundred feet deep. In this clear water, bottom life even in those relative depths was visible as movement and shadow.

Daniel had noticed coral standing unusually high and vivid in an oval area which sprawled up the side of an approaching reef. Fish in their striped and flickering brilliance were relatively sparse against the lush background. The beaks of the reef fish hadn't browsed the sessile life of this patch to the same degree as they had neighboring regions.

Only because he was already focused on the unusual region did

Daniel see the paired tentacles lash swiftly over the top of the coral and withdraw into the cave from which they'd so briefly extended. The coral shuddered: all the animalcules went limp in their self-secreted lime caverns, changing the look of the setting without any individual movement great enough to be visible from where Daniel watched.

Simultaneously all the fish in the water through which the tentacles passed rolled onto their backs and began to sink, stunned by the electrical charge the sweep had released into the water. A few fins wobbled randomly.

The coral animals would recover from the shock. Most of the fish would not have time to do so, because when the sweep was sure it was safe from retaliation the tentacles would project again from the pit in which the creature hid. This time they would pick over the reef, searching for the slight electrical charge that all life-forms generated.

The hooked teeth on the tentacles would draw the fish, quivering and still alive, back to the sweep's lair. Its beak would complete the job the electric shock had begun.

"Oh, it must be wonderful to know so many things, Lieutenant Leary," Margrethe said.

Daniel wondered if he could've gotten the same response by saying, "The sun is shining."

"My uncle is a great naturalist," he said aloud. "For a serving naval officer, that is."

On the other hand, Margrethe was trying to communicate something beyond her interest in Kostroman natural history. From the way Candace hunched over the steering yoke, Daniel wasn't the only one getting that message.

Margrethe too must have decided she was being overly obvious. She joined Daniel in an attempt to minimize contact as they squeezed in turn through the narrow center aisle between the front seats.

Bet patted the cushion beside her. She poured wine into a single glass, sipped it, and gave the glass to Daniel. Only then did she pass the bottle and another pair of glasses to the couple in front.

It was good wine. Daniel wondered if Herrick was her husband.

The sea had darkened to a uniform green. The water was deeper here, but there were also scores of islands rising above its smooth surface. None were large and some were little more than rocks. Vegetation waved above the tide line of even the smallest, however.

Bet closed her fingers over Daniel's to retrieve the glass. He squeezed them with his left hand and smiled at her. He felt a little sheepish about his lack of concern for the girl, but this was the first time he'd been off Kostroma Island.

"Has the lodge been in your family for long, Candace?" he said, letting his fingertips lie on Bet's arm as she poured wine from another bottle.

"For nearly a hundred years," Candace said. Margrethe was snuggling him as he drove and his tone was more relaxed. "We've always been a navy family. That means living on Kostroma most of the time. A great grand-uncle who loved to fish bought it to have a place nearby that wasn't on the big island. There's a path and steps down to the water that must go back to the Founding, though."

He turned and grinned through Margrethe's mist of reddish hair at Daniel. "It doesn't get used much anymore, but occasionally it comes in handy."

"I'll say it does," Daniel said. His enthusiasm was real, but not quite as real as he tried to project in his voice.

He let his hand trail down Bet's bare shoulder until she giggled again and pressed his fingers firmly around the stem of the refilled glass. Daniel traded sips, wondering if on another day Candace would loan him the aircar to run out to this wonderful region on his own.

Adele Mundy made a point of reaching the library at precisely the second hour of daylight, half an hour before the time she'd set for her Kostroman staff to arrive. She doubted whether any of the locals would appear today—any who did would be too hung over to work—but she wasn't surprised to hear the whine of saws and glue guns from inside as she approached the open door.

"Sun, are you blind?" Bosun's Mate Woetjans demanded as Adele entered. The petty officer didn't sound angry so much as marvelling at Sun's misalignment. "Bring the left end up! The marks set the *bottom* of the crosspieces, not the tops."

As if part of the same discussion, Woetjans turned and tipped her soft cap to Adele; she must have seen the librarian's reflection in a windowpane. Woetjans didn't miss much of what went on around her.

"Good morning, Ms. Mundy," she said. "Sometimes I think this lot hasn't any more sense than my daft old mother, but you needn't worry: the job'll be done and done right before we leave it."

"I wouldn't dream of doubting you, Woetjans," Adele said as she surveyed the work thus far.

The day before the sailors had switched to using sheets of structural plastic in place of wooden boards. Hogg had found a different supplier, Adele supposed.

The plastic was stronger, thinner, and more stable than the wood shelving of the earlier portion of the work. Some might quarrel with the orange cast of the material, but Adele's priority remained getting the books up from the floor and spine out so that she could organize them. If she lived long enough she might let Master Carpenter Bozeman replace the plastic with high-quality cabinetwork . . . but then again, there wasn't any possibility that she *would* live long enough for Bozeman to complete that job.

"We oughta have the lights working by noon," Woetjans said, rubbing her hands together absently as she looked upward. Six sailors worked on scaffolding glued temporarily to shelf supports, hopping about twenty feet in the air with an apparent lack of concern as to what would happen if they missed their footing. "I've been talking to Hogg about ways to hide the conduits. D'you have any particular feelings about the way we rig that, mistress?"

"I honestly don't care if you leave the wires bare, so long as there's no safety hazard," Adele said. "The room is a space to contain information in a usable form, that's all. Aesthetics are someone else's province."

Woetjans glanced toward the doorway. Adele turned also, expecting Vanness or perhaps a stranger who was curious about the noise.

Markos's female aide stood there. Her smile was thin, meaningless; as empty as her eyes. "Might I have a few minutes of your time in the gardens, mistress?" she said.

"Yes, all right," Adele said. "Carry on, Woetjans."

She walked out behind the aide. The pale young woman reminded Adele a great deal of the roof perch from which she'd watched the procession the day before: nothing whatever for a hundred feet, then a stone pavement.

The aide led down the helical stairs. They might have been strangers to one another for all the palace staffers they met on the staircase could tell. At the bottom Adele caught up with her guide and said, "I notice you're a Kostroman yourself. Have you known your employer long?"

The aide stopped and looked at her. "I'm a messenger, mistress," she said. "I do what I'm told, and only what I'm told. If you have questions, you'll have to ask somebody else."

Adele nodded curt assent. She was angry and frustrated, but it would be wrong to take it out on the aide. To prod the woman verbally would be pointless cruelty—safe enough because the aide was a flunky and unable to respond, just as a big carnivore behind bars can be teased. The aide was as much a victim of Markos, and of life, as Adele herself was.

They went up the ramp from the palace entryway and out into the gardens beyond. Litter remaining from the night's celebrations lay on the paths or was thrust into the hedges' netted branches. A pair of red brocade breeches, probably a man's, perched on the head of a statue.

There weren't any strollers this early the morning after the festival. To Adele's surprise there was work going on, however.

A crew had broken up some brick planters and appeared to be digging a pond in their place. A truck backed toward the workers, its transmission whining. The foreman shouted directions to the driver while other workmen leaned on their tools and talked among themselves.

The area to the right of the central walk was laid out in hedged squares. The aide led Adele down one of the bricked side paths and finally bowed her into an enclosure. The aide remained behind at the single entrance.

Markos was waiting there, as she'd expected. He sat on a stone bench with his back to the dense hedge. Though the top floor of the palace overlooked the garden, no one watching from there could see even the top of his head.

Markos looked at her with cool appraisal. He nodded but didn't speak, apparently to emphasize his control of the situation.

A worm from the Pleasaunce slums does not control a Mundy of Chatsworth. . . .

"I saw a colleague of yours last night," Adele said in her normal voice. "Somebody should tell her to work on her Pleasaunce accent if she's going to pretend to be a Casque."

"No one of that name is a colleague of mine," Markos said. His anger showed in the way his own real origins rasped in his voice. "Let me assure you, mistress—the fact that persons may be sloppy in the way they prepare for a task shouldn't be taken to mean that they won't correct errors in a terminal fashion. Quite the contrary."

"What do you want?" Adele said.

Markos patted the bench beside him. She shook her head minusculely and crossed her arms in refusal.

"Sit down," he said. "I don't choose to raise my voice, mistress. And don't play games with me or third parties will regret it! That's a personal promise, not a professional one."

Adele seated herself beside him. A man like Markos would sooner lie than tell the truth, but she didn't think that particular threat had been a lie. She'd made him angry by refusing to be cowed.

"I want an electronic copy of the palace guard rosters for the next month," he said, calm again. "Names and addresses, and any other information on record about the persons on duty. I believe some of the guards are billeted in the palace proper while others are off-premises except while they're on duty. And of course I want their pay records as well."

"Where do you expect me to find that sort of thing?" Adele snapped.

"I really don't care, Ms. Mundy," Markos replied. "Fuck the chamberlain if you choose. But I suspect you'll turn it up quickly enough through a data search of the sort you're uniquely qualified to perform."

"All right," Adele said coldly. She stood up. "I'll see what I can find. Contact me in a week."

"You will come back here before you leave the palace grounds," Markos said, his tone heavy with the menace that was natural to him. "You will have the information complete. You will deliver the information to my secretary."

Adele looked toward the opening in the hedge. The aide was watching them sidelong; her thin mouth smiled very faintly.

Markos wouldn't have been sent to Kostroma without expert staff and equipment comparable to anything Adele could provide— but the experts and particularly the equipment might not be solely committed to the Fifth Bureau. The *Goetz von Berlichingen* needed a powerful data processor simply for navigation purposes, but Markos couldn't be certain that the uses he made of the computer wouldn't be analyzed by the likes of "Mirella Casque" or agents of other rival organizations.

An impecunious librarian whose only friend was a hostage within the Alliance was a much more trustworthy tool than Alliance naval officers protected by their own organization from the wrath even of a member of the Fifth Bureau. Besides, it was the sort of game that would appeal to the sort of person Markos was.

"I'll see what I can do," Adele repeated. She stepped out of the enclosure.

The information should be easy to find, though it was an even question whether she'd find it in the Hajas database or that of the palace itself. She'd deliver it as soon as she could. Part of her wanted to keep Markos waiting, but that was childish, and it would mean that the business was hanging over Adele Mundy as well.

She strode down the bricked pathway, drawing glances from the workmen for the hard set of her face. She'd take care of this and wash her hands of the business. It didn't matter to her what Markos and other slugs in what they called intelligence did with the information then.

"Here's the island, Leary," Candace said as he adjusted the aircar's fans, slowing the vehicle toward a mushy hover. "I suppose it ought to have a name by now, but we just call it the lodge."

Ten miles back Bet had permitted Daniel to put an arm about her waist; now he had to disentangle himself to look forward between the front seats. Bet leaned against him from behind, proving that she had rather more top than he would have guessed.

The island was only a few hundred meters long and rather narrow. It rose thirty sheer feet from the water, however, and was of some hard black rock rather than the coral limestone of other islets Daniel had seen dotting this stretch of sea.

A line of steps slanted up the cliff from the base where men had blasted a landing place in the stone. Wrist-thick staples were set in the rock for tying up boats. Foliage of the bright green typical to Kostroma covered the islet's top. Its growth was so lush that the lodge's structural plastic roof was hidden almost until the aircar hovered overhead. There'd once been a cleared area beside the building but feather-leafed plants now sprouted there waist high.

"I'll have to get a crew in here to clear things off," Candace said in irritation. "Maybe I can get the CO to detail me some ratings."

He lowered the aircar slowly, using the downdraft to flatten the vegetation so that it didn't get tangled in the fans. Swarms of small insects spun out of the greenery like jewels. Many of them lighted on the upper surfaces of the car and on its occupants.

Bet said, "Ooh!" in irritation as she brushed a sparkling bug off her forehead. They were species native to Kostroma, however, with no taste for human blood.

Candace shut off the motors. "A bit primitive, but I think we'll find everything here we need," he said as he unlatched the sidewall into a ramp. He laughed coarsely. "And after we've found what we need, I've had the servants pack us a bit of lunch. Eh, Leary?"

Bet giggled.

"First-rate plan, Candace!" Daniel said as he walked to the back of the aircar to open the storage compartment. He hoped he spoke with enough enthusiasm to cover the way he'd winced when he heard the giggle again.

The luggage was a picnic hamper and two inflatable mattresses. There was a basket of wine also, but Bet had brought that out with her by reaching over the seat.

Candace pushed open the lodge door which had been ajar. Drifted fronds on the floor had already started to decay to humus.

Small birds went into paroxysms of chirping terror inside. Daniel held the women back a moment to permit the panicked creatures to fly out. He didn't mind carrying the gear, though he'd noticed the Kostroman officer's presumption that it wasn't his own job.

Candace began opening the window shutters. One of them fell off in his hand. The main room had a fireplace and stone benches along the walls; a table and two chairs of extruded plastic provided the only other furnishings. There was a curtained opening at the end with sleeping quarters beyond. The bunks, an upper and lower, were narrow plastic berths on stone supports cantilevered out from the back wall.

"Do you have a well here?" Daniel asked.

"There's a cistern," Candace said. "Though . . ."

Though, thought Daniel to complete the unspoken idea, any cistern here would have been the grave for the legion of creatures which had managed to crawl into it in the years since the lodge was last used. Well, they had the wine.

Candace pursed his lips. Daniel suspected the Kostroman had forgotten just how much a fishing lodge this really was, though the reality was more than sufficient for Daniel himself.

"I'll tell you what, Leary," Candace said. "If you go down the steps to the landing, there's a path off to the left that leads to a cave. Since you're the naturalist . . . ?"

"I'll show him," Bet said unexpectedly. "I've been here, you know."

Her expression was perfectly innocent. Only a cynic would speculate that her comment—her admission—had something to do with watching Margrethe flirt with Daniel during the flight.

Daniel kept one of the mattresses; Bet had a bottle and a glass. He didn't need a guide once they'd forced their way through the feathery undergrowth to the steps at the cliff's edge. Land animals on Kostroma tended to be small, so the vegetation hadn't developed the spikes and knife-edged leaves that made the jungles of many planets hell for humans who had to pass through them.

The steps had been formed by drilling a line of vertical holes to the desired depth, then cracking the overburden away. The treads themselves hadn't been leveled, but passing feet had worn them smooth. Given that this islet must always have been remote from major traffic, Candace was right about the construction being very old.

Bet paused at the head of the stairway, turned her face up unexpectedly to kiss Daniel, and skipped down the steps giggling. The glasses winked in the sunlight.

Daniel followed at a more leisurely pace. In part that was the caution of a man who rigged antennae in sponge space, where a misstep could mean not only death but separation from the sidereal universe. In addition he was intrigued by thimble-sized cones of lichen growing out from the rock. They showed narrow bands of bright color, one laid over the other all the way from peak to base. He'd never seen anything like them before.

Bet stuck her head back around the curve of the cliff. "Are you coming, Daniel?" she called. She hadn't used his first name before. Daniel stepped more quickly.

The steps wound clockwise down the cliff face. Midway they crossed a counterclockwise path. It was a ramp and had been melted, not cut, into the rock. Above the intersection the second path had been blasted away when the staircase was created. What remained, weathered but not especially worn, was a left-hand branch to the steps below the junction.

The remnant of the older path was almost level; at no time had it continued down to sea level. Unless sea level had dropped ten feet since the path was made . . .

"See?" Bet called, standing on the other side of a giant version of the lichens Daniel had been noticing. The cones were more frequent here than nearer the top, but this one was almost a meter high. "It's just this way."

Then she added, "Ooh!" and batted at the insect that had hopped onto her thigh. It was only the size of a fingernail, but its black and blue stripes were in sharp contrast with the fire-hot fabric of her dress.

"Coming, love," Daniel said absently. "But we don't want to lose this, do we?"

He waggled the rolled mattress. There were quite a lot of similar insects here. They were flightless and appeared to browse the lichen.

"We could make do," Bet called with a giggle.

Daniel stepped over the giant cone. Bet vanished into the cliff face just ahead. A tunnel had been burned into the rock. The surface was vitrified like that of the ramp. Daniel walked inside and pulled down his goggles to get a better view of the interior.

Bet had gone to the end, thirty feet or so from the opening. There were niches about five feet long and a foot or so deep burned into the sidewalls all the way to the back. He, Bet, and a slight scattering of dead leaves from the vegetation above were the only other contents of the tunnel.

Bet had set the wine on the end niche. She swayed her dress from side to side, lifting it slowly. "Come *on*, Daniel," she said insistently. As he'd suspected, she wore nothing whatever beneath the clinging folds.

"Just savoring the moment, love," Daniel lied He pulled the inflation mechanism of the pad, then lifted off his cap and goggles.

He had quite a lot of questions about this location, but first things first. The questions could wait.

If he was right, they'd waited for a very long time already.

✧   ✧   ✧

Adele rose from the data console and noticed the bustle of construction around her for the first time in several hours. The Cinnabar sailors used adhesive guns which spit glue with a high whine that Adele found more irritating than the bang of a hammer—when she was aware of it. She wasn't aware of that or much of anything else when she was working.

Compiling the rosters had taken longer than she expected. The people in charge of the palace guard seemed to have entered only fragments of the data necessary to see that their personnel were fed and paid on time. By cross-checking Adele had become certain that about 30 percent of even what was in the various databases was wrong.

The fault was hers. She should have allowed for the guard officers being semiliterate incompetents. God knew they weren't alone in that, on Kostroma or in the wider universe either.

"Looking pretty well, don't you think?" somebody said behind her. Adele whirled.

Bosun's Mate Woetjans's smile became neutral when she saw Adele's expression. "Coming along, at any rate," the sailor said. "In my opinion."

"It's looking wonderful, Woetjans," Adele said with real enthusiasm. She was embarrassed at her seeming harsh response to the petty officer's friendly sally. "If there was one other part of my life that was looking as good, I'd be the Elector of Kostroma."

Woetjans's smile returned. "I guess a citizen of Cinnabar is better than any wog from around here, mistress," she said, apparently oblivious of the library assistants who might be in earshot. "Even the chief wog. Mind, they're fine as spacers. But I'm glad my crew's a bright spot, yeah."

Adele started to speak, then froze with her mouth open because she didn't know which of her two objections to begin with. She closed her mouth again because she realized she'd be wrong to address either of them. "Yes," she said instead. "A very bright spot."

She leaned over the console and ejected the chip onto which she'd copied the data. It had taken hours of work, sifting and correlating files on distant machines whose software was quirky, ancient, and glacially slow. She could have sent Markos the first list she'd found, ignoring the fact that it covered only two of the palace's seven entrances. She didn't like Markos and the task was one that she didn't dare consider very deeply. Even under these circumstances she couldn't let herself do a bad job.

"Hafard!" Woetjans bellowed toward a high scaffold. "Polin! You two keep fucking around and you *won't* like the duty roster after we lift planet, I promise you!"

She gave Adele a sheepish glance. "I better get back to keeping an eye on these lot, sir," she said.

Adele nodded crisply. "I need to get to work also," she said. "Vanness? I'll be gone for about fifteen minutes. If there are any inquiries for me, I'll answer them when I return."

She strode from the library. She'd been offended when Woetjans referred to the Kostromans as wogs. If the petty officer were a pupil of hers at the Academy, she'd have torn a strip off her the first time it happened and dismissed her in ignominy on a repetition.

But Woetjans wasn't a pupil. She was a naval bosun's mate raised to different standards. Woetjans's standards were wrong, of that Adele was sure; but nobody'd appointed Adele Mundy as Lord Corrector of the Universe, either.

She'd had colleagues at the Academy, even after she became deputy director of the Collections in all but name, who took it upon themselves to educate Adele on the ways in which her dress failed the test of fashion. She didn't expect Woetjans would greet a lecture on demeaning language with any more patience—or reason for patience—than Adele had shown for that well-meant advice on her clothes.

Adele started down the spiral stairs at a brisk pace. She slowed when she reached a pair of clerks descending in leisure as they talked. Kostromans were a cheerfully voluble people, who made broad arm gestures in conversation. Adele wasn't in so great a hurry that she needed to make a point of getting around these two.

She'd almost objected to Woetjans calling her a Cinnabar citizen. On reflection, Woetjans's assumption was probably true. The Edict of Reconciliation had restored citizenship rights to survivors of those proscribed, and Adele had never been listed by name anyway. As an adult member of the Mundys of Chatsworth she would have been fair game, but no one could honestly claim Adele had any involvement in general politics let alone with the Three Circles Conspiracy.

She went around the clerks at the bottom of the stairs and picked her way through the loungers and passersby in the main entryway. Kostroman tempers were as noisily enthusiastic as their expressions of undying friendship. Neither could be expected to last. Very different from Cinnabar, where emotions were weapons as unyielding as steel.

She'd heard the Kostromans described as flighty, mercurial. True enough, she supposed. Until humans became saints, though, the alternative was cold, murderous ruthlessness of the sort that had wiped the Mundys from the face of Cinnabar.

Woetjans said the Kostromans were good spacers. In that at least they and the folk of Cinnabar had matters in common.

Adele entered the garden. The sunlight was a subconscious surprise. The ranks of shelves, now filling with roughly sorted books, reduced light from the library windows to a fraction of what was needed. To install the new lighting the sailors had run an additional line from the power room in the palace subbasement. Woetjans had explained that though the fusion plant had sufficient capacity, the building's wiring would fry like bacon.

Citizen of the Republic of Cinnabar . . .

A starship was landing in the harbor. Quite a large one. A transport, she supposed. Daniel Leary would be able to identify the vessel by class and perhaps by name.

A nurse pushed a stroller down the path. Two more children were tied to her waist by leashes; the older of them was no more than four. They tugged in opposite directions, shouting to call the nurse's attention to individual birds or flowers. A male minder with a metal-shod baton and swirling mustaches swaggered behind the group, puffing out his chest and bowing to every woman he passed.

Adele had never returned to Cinnabar. At first her presence would merely have added another name to the roster of victims. After the Edict of Reconciliation was passed, disgust kept her away.

Besides, it was bad enough to be poor in a foreign land. She had no intention of starving before the eyes of those who would have called her a friend in the days before the Proscriptions. The Senate had confirmed a cousin on her mother's side as owner of Chatsworth, she'd heard.

Adele entered the hedged enclosure. It was empty. She heard the sound of a man playing a guitar and singing nearby.

"Good morning, mistress," said Markos's aide behind her. Adele turned. The pale woman had her usual half-smile; not so much superior, as Adele had first thought, but appraising.

"Here," Adele said, holding out the data chip in the middle of her right palm. She didn't care who saw her. She wasn't a spy; they couldn't force her to act like one.

Fingertips brushed her hand, lifting away the chip. "Good day, mistress," the aide said.

The aide walked toward the garden's rear entrance, passing other strollers without seeming to be moving quickly. She was nondescript even in her bright clothing; a person whose presence and absence were equally unremarkable. A person who didn't seem to exist as a human being.

Adele Mundy returned to the palace. She wondered whether she herself had any more existence than a data console did.

Daniel Leary, whistling snatches of the contredanse which had ended the Admiral's Ball, entered the library and stared in pleased astonishment. "Say!" he said. "They *are* coming along. And the lighting's up, I see."

"Yes, or you wouldn't see," Adele said, coming from the half of the big room which wasn't already filled with shelving. She held a pair of loose-leaf binders covered in the hide of something scaly. "Your crew has been indispensable, Daniel. Which is not to denigrate the contribution—"

She turned and nodded to a young man wearing a green cummerbund and holding a tape measure, one of the several Kostromans who'd come forward with her when Daniel arrived.

"—which Master Carpenter Bozeman and the journeymen of her staff have been making toward the project's aesthetics."

"We're veneering the edges of the shelving and supports," the fellow with the measure said. "When we're done, you won't be able to tell the result from prime cabinetry. Even the plastic!"

He frowned and added, "When there's books on them, that is. We can't do much about it otherwise."

Daniel, swinging a knotted handkerchief in his left hand, walked along the end of the stacks and peered into a bay. The racks rose nearly to the room's high ceiling. There were no books or bound papers above head height, and the shelves in use were only partially full. Wooden blocks formed bookends to keep the end volumes from falling over.

"Are the higher ones . . . ?" Daniel said, nodding toward the bare ranks of shelves above him.

"They may be useful at a later date," said Adele who'd fallen into stride with him. The three Kostromans watched with a respect that had been notably missing the day Daniel first visited the library. "Woetjans says she'll rig rolling ladders on each stack. I'm inclined to leave that part of the job for the time at which it's needed. An intermediate floor might be preferable for staff members who aren't—"

She smiled.

"—starship riggers. On the other hand, the future won't have Woetjans and her crew as a part of it. I'm undecided."

"Ah, how are these . . . ?" Daniel asked. "That is, the arrangement."

He waggled his handkerchief toward the shelves. One of those nearest him was a rank of cookbooks. Standard volumes on astrogation—including many obvious duplicates—filled the two shelves immediately below.

Adele smiled wryly. "By number," she said. "I open the boxes of material and assign a number to each volume I find. Mostly I scribble it on a scrap of paper. These—"

She flicked open the leather covers of the binders in her hand, one and then the other.

"—would be one-forty-seven, both of them. They're profit and loss statements from Teichnor Clan trading ventures of the past century."

Daniel nodded. The accounts were nothing that would ever interest him, but he knew how valuable they'd be to someone who understood the context in which they were created.

He'd read Uncle Stacey's logs. They were merely dry listings like, "Antenna 41 sheared under acceleration. Stepped replacement and entered Matrix as calculated." That would mean nothing except to someone who'd listened avidly to Commander Bergen talk to the friends from the old days who'd come to Bantry to see him.

"I'll take them, mistress!" said one of the Kostromans brightly.

If you knew the language—which meant more than grammar and vocabulary—there was no useless information.

"Thank you, Vanness," Adele said, handing the binders over with a smile visible only to Daniel. She continued, "My assistants take the item to the numbered shelf while I dig out the next one. Vanness and Prester agreed to stay late tonight because I need to clear more floorspace for the next stack. Before the morning."

"Amazing!" Daniel said honestly. He'd have guessed it would take the better part of a lifetime to convert the chaos he'd first seen here into order. A couple weeks would be sufficient. Though—

"I don't quite understand the numbering system though, mis— that is, Adele," he went on. "These . . ."

He indicated the cookbooks and stellar directions cheek by jowl.

"Yes, sections sixteen and seventeen," Adele said. Her grave expression dissolved into a smile. "The sixteenth item I pulled from the crate with which I started was *Easy Recipes for Frontier Worlds* by Cyprian. You'll not be surprised to learn that the volume underneath it was the *Star Sector 30 Pilot*."

"Oh," said Daniel. It sounded like an absolutely terrible system, scarcely better than putting the books up at random. "Well, with a proper index . . ." he added.

The librarian smiled broadly—broadly for her, at least. "Right up here," she said, tapping her temple with an index finger. She laughed aloud at his expression. "Daniel, this is a *rough* sort. I'll arrange the holdings according to the standards of the Academic Collections as soon as I've got them out of boxes. Until then you've got to depend on me to find anything."

"Oh," he said in relief. At least he hadn't said anything aloud.

"Ms. Mundy is a genius," Vanness said with a belligerence that was unnecessary, given Daniel's complete agreement. "She's better than any system."

"Thank you for the thought, Vanness," she said dryly. "I'm confident that I'm not immortal, however. Certainly the rest of my family wasn't. I hope to leave my successor a monument to my skill, not my arrogance."

"Ah," said Daniel. He hadn't missed the reference to the Proscriptions. "As a matter of fact, I had Candace drop me here rather than back at my lodgings because I had another question for you."

He waggled the handkerchief. "But if you're busy . . . ?"

"Prester, Vanness," Adele said. "Take a break. As a matter of fact, why don't you both go on home. I think we've cleared enough room, at least with a little judicious restacking of the piles."

"I'll wait, mistress," Vanness said.

"I'll wait too," said the other assistant, a young woman whom Daniel would have described as plain if he'd had any reason to describe her. "It's not as though I need to get home, after all."

"I've got my measurements, Ms. Mundy," the journeyman carpenter said. "I'll be off now, if you don't mind."

"Of course, Reckwith," Adele said formally. "Give my regards to Master Carpenter Bozeman when you see her. I'm delighted with her work and yours."

In an aside that Daniel could barely hear and was only sibilance to the Kostromans, she added, "Contact with sailors who take pride in hard work has instilled a spirit of emulation in the better segment of my staff. I'm as pleased by this result as I'm surprised."

From what Hogg had told Daniel, half the staff was in awe of the Electoral Librarian and the other half was terrified. "The wogs were lucky none of them took Ms. Mundy up on her offer to shoot them," Hogg believed. Daniel didn't disagree.

"I'm glad to hear that," Daniel said. He unknotted the handkerchief.

"Another bug?" Adele asked with a smile. She walked over to the data console now half-hidden behind a wall of older electronics. Most of that equipment didn't seem to be in working order or even complete, but with time and skill it might be possible to retrieve data from the wrecks.

"A beetle, yes," he said. He displayed the lichen-eater that he'd scooped up as he left the tunnel behind Bet. "Hexapod, wingless, longitudinal blue and black stripes. Fused cephalothorax and soft abdomen, but the crucial thing is the six legs."

"I thought bugs on Kostroma had four legs," Adele said as holograms shimmered in the air before her. "Well, I suppose nothing's absolute."

"In biology," Daniel replied, "I'd have said absolutes are pretty nearly universal."

Adele manipulated her console with wands she held like a pair of writing styluses. Daniel knew the technique offered much greater speed and flexibility than the virtual keyboard he used himself, but a minuscule variation in a wand's angle or rotation could introduce huge database errors.

He didn't imagine that was a problem that Adele faced very often.

"I'm sorry," Adele said as she scowled at her display. "I'm not finding anything. As a matter of fact, the information I can access doesn't show any native Kostroman animals with six legs. The information may be in error, but . . ."

She looked up Daniel. "Surely the most likely cause is that the bug is from offplanet. I don't have records for all the possibilities or even most of them, I'm afraid."

"Try Earth," said Daniel. He grinned at the bug whose leg he pinched between thumb and forefinger. With a feeling of rising triumph he added, "It's just possible that I've found evidence of a slowboat landing on Kostroma after all, Adele. That's not as good as a new species, perhaps, but it'd be a nice profit on my afternoon."

He winced to hear himself. Bet was a nice girl; he'd had a very good time in her company. But the Bets of this life weren't as rare as real discovery.

The console purred as it sorted files in its own database. The display was only colored diffraction from the side where Daniel stood.

"I haven't found any hardcopy Kostroman natural histories," Adele said idly as she waited. "The files I've accessed are all work by offplanet observers as well."

Astrogation had revived on Kostroma almost as early as on Cinnabar and Pleasaunce, but Kostromans had remained isolated from other star-traveling worlds for another century and a half. Kostroma hadn't advanced as quickly in some ways without the rivalry of peers, but the culture's very uniqueness was a benefit in itself.

"Kostromans view the universe as a place to get rich," Daniel said. He nodded to the assistants to make it clear that he was offering his opinion to everyone, not treating the locals as furniture. "Which they've been extremely good at."

The waterfall of quivering light stabilized. "There," Adele said with satisfaction. She offered the console's seat to Daniel. "Six-legged and wingless, though not all your other parameters. See what you think."

He flopped the handkerchief loosely over the insect to hold it as he sat. Lichen-eaters don't have to move fast and this one showed no signs of wanting to escape. Daniel viewed the images with growing puzzlement, fingering the virtual keyboard to add and delete parameters.

"It isn't Terran," he said in wonder. "It can't be Terran. The three membranous antennae are like nothing on Earth, quite apart from the other distinctions!"

"Well, Kostroma has been in contact with many hundreds of planets other than Earth," Adele said. Daniel heard in her voice the same cautiously neutral tones which he'd used when asking about the cataloguing system. "Earth was a likely possibility, but . . ."

Daniel laughed as he rose from the console. "Ah, contact, but not contact before the Founding itself!" he said. "A slowboat colony from Earth was just possible, but not a slowboat bringing bugs and lichen from a non-Earth planet. This site's really old, Adele. Much older than the Founding. I think from the weathering on the fused rock . . ."

He grimaced. He wished he'd taken a camera on the jaunt, but he'd had no idea of the degree to which his attention would be on the scenery. The scenery besides Bet, that was. Well, the island hadn't gone anywhere in—

"Thousands of years old. Maybe tens of thousands of years."

Adele didn't speak for a moment. The Kostroman assistants looked at one another with the frowns of people who know they've missed the point of what they just heard.

"Star-travelling aliens with human physiology," Adele said.

"Or human star travel, probably through sponge space," Daniel said. "Probably before recorded history."

"Before the records to which we have access," the librarian corrected with a self-mocking smile.

She reverted to her normal working expression, a tautness like that of a cat waiting for the moment she'll leap on her prey. "Locating the source of the bugs would be my first step, but I don't have extensive natural history files except for the Cinnabar sphere and Earth. Those two came loaded in the database."

Daniel gave three quick nods as a placeholder while he settled plans in his mind. "The *Aglaia* does," he said. "A broad sweep for the whole region. Not deep, but we don't need to identify the species. When we find a world where the biota run in these directions—"

He spun the handkerchief like a magician's wand, holding the corners. He'd have to lay in a supply of lichen for the little creature. There was no way of telling how long they lived.

"—then we can search for details!"

Adele sat at the console. "I can access . . ." she said. She paused with her wands lifted.

Daniel grinned. "No, the *Aglaia* has blocks you won't be able to get through even with your little toy here," he said, patting the frame of the console. "She's an RCN warship, after all. I'll go aboard right now and see what I can find, though."

"Yes," Adele said in an odd voice. She stood, laying her wands neatly in the tray built on the top of the console. "I should have remembered that information on the *Aglaia* would be protected. As would that of the Alliance vessels in harbor also, I suppose."

"Well, I don't think any Alliance captain would let me come aboard to search his database," Daniel said, amused at the absurdity of the notion. "But I'll bet we can get what we need from the *Aglaia*."

He started for the door. "I'll let you know," he threw over his shoulder.

"Yes, I'll be interested," Adele replied in the same washed-out voice she'd used a moment before.

Daniel whistled as he strode down the dimly lit corridor. Adele was probably embarrassed not to have been able to get the information herself. It would upset an artist of her quality to be reminded that there were files even she couldn't access.

Daniel's taxi driver pulled to the curb half a block from the waterfront and stopped. "Here," he said. "You get out."

The driver had kept his left leg stiffly across a pad on the jitney's front panel ever since Daniel hailed him outside the palace. Those words were the first he'd spoken since he set a price for the run. Daniel could've walked, but the implications of the beetle excited him and there were still fragments of the 100-florin piece in his purse.

"Say!" Daniel said. "Take me to the quay like we agreed. What's the matter with you?"

"Fagh!" snarled the driver. He spoke Universal with a guttural slurring that was more likely his own than a regional accent. He hauled hard on his steering wheel and began to turn in the street.

"Hey!" said Daniel. He grabbed the driver's shoulder and rose from the bench seat. "By God you'll let me off or you'll be on the pavement yourself!"

The driver struggled momentarily, then turned his head away

as Daniel slid to the boarding step without losing his grip. Daniel hopped down to the street. He reached for his purse, half inclined to short the driver for his bizarre behavior. Still, the fellow had brought him most of the—

To Daniel's amazement the driver jerked the hand throttle as soon as he was free of Daniel's hold. The jitney jumped ahead with a puff of foul smoke from its little diesel engine. The driver didn't look over his shoulder as his vehicle rattled back the way he'd come.

Daniel watched the taxi leave in wonderment. If this were an alley he'd have suspected the driver was in collusion with bandits, but the taxi had left him on a boulevard in a middle-class district. Well, maybe the fellow's dinner had given him the runs.

Main street or not, Kostroma City was dark. Daniel pulled down his goggles to brighten the night.

Looking past the head of the street to the horizon, the Floating Harbor was its usual dazzling brilliance. Daniel noticed again the big Alliance transport which had landed while he was at the fishing lodge. It was in the first rank like the *Aglaia*, but the two vessels were at opposite ends of the harbor.

That was perfectly proper, of course: Kostroma was neutral, dealing with Alliance traders as readily as it did with those from Cinnabar and her dependencies. It made Daniel think about the implications of Kostroma joining the war on Cinnabar's side as Candace and his friends wanted, though.

If Walter III declared war on the Alliance, a freighter like that one would be fair game. The officer who led the *Aglaia*'s boarding party—even an officer who accompanied the boarding party despite not being technically on the roster of the communications vessel—would be in line for a great deal of prize money. . . .

As the jitney driver had said, fagh! That was a fantasy and a foolish one besides. Cinnabar was probably better off having Kostroma as a friendly neutral than as an active combatant. But it *would* be nice not to have to worry about his debts for the first time since he stormed out of Corder Leary's townhouse.

A foolish fantasy, but Daniel began whistling—

And stopped abruptly as he realized how very odd the waterfront was tonight. The surface freighters that would normally be loading and unloading in the harbor were silent, showing only a few lights for the watch. The bumboats and water taxis weren't running, but Daniel was close enough to the seawall now to see that there was an unusual number of people on the quay.

The harbor was never well-lit, but tonight the handful of pole-mounted floodlights were out. Daniel knew there was nothing unusual about power failures in Kostroma City; anyone looking inshore from the *Aglaia* would know that too. Nothing to cause concern. . . .

Daniel stepped close to the front wall of a building on Water Street. The two lower floors held a ship chandler's shop, closed as normal at this hour. The windows on the third floor where the owner and his family lived were heavily shuttered as well; no light shone through the cracks.

A jitney passed with six people aboard, two of them hanging on the sides. They were armed. The jitney drove down the ramp onto a quay and parked with the vehicles already there. The gunmen got out, cursing the darkness until someone snarled a sharp order at them.

There were about a hundred figures, mostly young men, gathered on the quay and boarding the boats tied up there. Most carried sub-machine guns, but Daniel saw a leavening of shoulder-stocked impellers. The gunmen wore two-tone armbands as a uniform, but the light on the quay wasn't good enough to tell what the colors were.

Daniel himself would have been in plain sight if there'd been better illumination, but in the starlight his gray uniform blended well with the weathered stone building. He raised his eyes to the Floating Harbor and increased his goggles' magnification.

The *Aglaia* looked as she had when he was last aboard her a few days earlier. The guards in the main hatchway were relaxed, but they kept their weapons slung or resting on their laps. The petty officer in charge spit into the sea; because of the magnification he looked close enough to touch.

Daniel didn't have a radio. There were underwater telephone cables from shore to the Floating Harbor, but he wasn't sure any of the locals would let him use their phone. He could go walk back to the palace, or he could—

Vapor spewed from all the *Aglaia's* open hatches. Daniel thought the ship had blown up, but the thumps that reached the shore several seconds later were muted. As the mist cleared, he could see that the *Aglaia's* lights were still on and her hull was unharmed. Gas bombs . . .

Three of the guards were down. The petty officer had been a few meters from the hatch. He had time to unsling his sub-machine gun and start for the pontoon, but the puff of gas caught him. He ran two steps more and collapsed.

The fellow must have been a rigger: even unconscious, he managed to land on the narrow catwalk. Only his weapon splashed into the water to sink the thousand feet or more to the bottom.

The boats full of armed Kostromans roared from the quay, several of them wallowing from the overloads they carried. Some idiot in the lead boat fired a full magazine from his sub-machine gun. Daniel couldn't imagine what he thought he was shooting at.

Even before the sound of the gas bombs reached Daniel, he saw cargo hatches open in the side of the just-landed Alliance transport. A vehicle flew from the starship with an echoing roar. An aircar, Daniel thought, but as the car swung in silhouette against the lights of a Kostroman starship he saw that it was really an armored personnel carrier.

Though lifted and propelled by ducted fans like those of an ordinary aircar, the APC could carry twenty troops behind ceramic armor thick enough to stop small-arms projectiles. The small turret above the bow held a plasma weapon.

The APC turned toward the *Aglaia*, flying just above the water. Its downdraft blew a trough into the foam. A second APC followed the first. The transport continued to disgorge similar armored vehicles from several hatches, but the later ones headed for Kostroma City itself at low level. To unaided eyesight on the seawall their approach would look like great Vees of starlit spray.

Daniel went back down the street by which he'd approached the waterfront. He walked at a steady pace rather than calling attention to himself by running, and he stayed as close the building fronts as projecting porches allowed.

It wouldn't have been difficult to smuggle gas bombs aboard the *Aglaia* along with the whores and the hawkers. All the hatches were open and half the crew was on liberty or drunk at any given time. After all, Kostroma was the next thing to an ally.

Not all Kostromans were allies, though. More to the point, Kostroman clans that were out of power might be willing to deal with Satan himself to change their status. Guarantor Porra was at least the next thing to a devil, but that might not be as obvious in Kostroma City as it was to an officer of the RCN.

Kostroma City would learn how free the stars of the Alliance really were. Of that Daniel was certain.

He turned left at the first corner. His own apartment was only a few blocks away, but going there would mean flipping a coin for his life. This coup had been planned with obvious attention to detail. There was an even chance that those in charge had included in their calculations Cinnabar personnel billeted in the city.

Daniel doubted that any faction on Kostroma could have carried off this operation by itself. The APCs full of Alliance commandoes were a less important factor than the Alliance intelligence officers who must have done the planning.

A pair of jitneys drove past at top speed, bouncing and squealing on irregularities in the pavement. Daniel swept off his cap and goggles, thrusting them into opposite side pockets of his jacket. He hated to lose the vision aids in the goggle lenses, but they marked him as unusual to anyone he met.

Daniel continued walking at his measured pace. He hoped he could locate Candace's townhouse; he'd only been there twice before and both times was being driven by someone else.

He needed clothing and a place to hide. If Candace could provide him with a weapon and an aircar also, that would be even better. If.

Gunfire crackled in the distant night. Small arms only, a spiteful sound that dissipated quickly among the streets and ornate facades. Candace was a very slim reed for a foreign fugitive to lean on, but he was the best Daniel Leary could think of right now.

"Five ninety-four!" Adele said decisively as she handed the monograph on garden gnomes to Prester. She might have grouped the volume either with gardens, 127, or statuary, 201, but she was at the end of a long day and feeling good at the amount she'd gotten done. "The first new category in the past hour, and a good time to stop and go home."

"Thank you, mistress!" Prester said in a tone of weary relief. She scurried off with the book. Her hands—the hands of all three of them; this hadn't been Adele's work alone—were black with the grime and mold that were inevitable results of a job like this.

Adele heard fireworks and shouting nearby. She sniffed and said, "I'd hoped that people would have worked off their Founder's Day high spirits by now, but this isn't the first time I overestimated human nature."

Prester was pasting a numbered scrap of paper to the end of a shelf. She looked over her shoulder. Adele gave her a quirky smile. Prester was adequately smart and had a dogged willingness that made up for her total inability to understand why anyone would want to store information. Her present labors deserved more reward than they were likely to get unless somebody helped.

"Vanness?" Adele said. The fellow brightened to be addressed directly. "There's obviously some partying going on. The streets may not be safe, so I want you to escort Prester to her lodgings."

She reached into her belt purse. "Here," she added. "I'll give you something in case you find a taxi."

Adele wasn't sure precisely what Hogg had said to the Chancellor, but that worthy had released the Electoral Librarian's first-quarter honorarium. Presumably this had involved a commission to the Chancellor, but by now Adele had enough contact with Daniel's servant to know that there were other possibilities. Hogg might have warned that a gang of Cinnabar sailors would smash up the Chancellor's residence if the honorarium weren't paid.

And while Bosun's Mate Woetjans and her crew couldn't have been more friendly and respectful to Adele herself, the threat might not have been empty. The casual violence with which the sailors cleared gawking locals from their path when they were working suggested they were ready to take the shortest way to accomplishing a task.

Adele noted dispassionately that when Prester smiled, her face was genuinely pretty. "But Ms. Mundy," Vanness protested. "You're at risk—"

Booted feet stamped through the door behind Adele. She turned in surprise. Armed guards wearing black and yellow berets spilled into the library. There were six or eight of them.

Markos's pale aide was one of the group. Instead of a beret she wore Zojira colors on ribbons around her upper arms. Her short cape was clasped at her throat, but the wings were slung back over her shoulders. She held a communicator in one hand and a center-grip sub-machine gun in the other.

"Zojiras!" Vanness shouted. He stepped forward, thrusting out his hands. God knew what he intended—to put his body between Adele and the gunmen, she supposed.

A Zojira fired, hitting Vanness in the chest and shoulder, though even at point-blank range half the burst blew splintered craters in shelving. Confetti exploded from a rank of genealogies. Kostroman weaponry was bulkier than its Cinnabar equivalent, and perhaps it wasn't as reliable, but there was nothing trivial about its effect.

Vanness spun backward, hit the floor, and bounced face up again. The sub-machine gun's bullets were too light to have any significant inertia. The victim's own spasming muscles flung him as though he'd been struck by lightning. Each projectile released its kinetic energy like a miniature bomb on the first solid object it struck.

Vanness's left side was a mass of blood and chips of exposed bone, but Adele doubted any of his vital organs were punctured. He had a very good chance to survive if they could bandage him before he bled out through the gaping surface wounds.

Vanness didn't cry out when he was hit. Prester screamed on a rising note, pressing her hands against her temples as if to hold her brain in.

"Put that gun up!" Adele said. She knelt beside Vanness, wondering what to use for a bandage. His own trousers were filthy from the hundreds of books he'd handled today.

The air was fanged with the smell of ozone and burned metal. The sub-machine gun's barrel generated a magnetic flux so dense that it ionized each pellet's light-metal driving skirt during the run up the bore.

The Zojira shooter pushed Adele away and put the muzzle of his gun against Vanness's forehead. Adele grabbed the barrel and jerked it aside. The sheathing of temperature-stable plastic burned her fingers. Somebody clubbed her from behind with a gun butt.

Adele fell sideways. The Zojira fired. Vanness's head erupted in a volcano of blood and solid matter. Each of the sub-machine gun's discharges was as sharp as stone snapping.

Vanness's back arched and his arms flung wide. His palms were black.

Adele lay face up. Her left side was numb, though the fiery tingling in her toes and fingertips meant she would have normal feeling back soon—if she lived.

The gunman who'd killed Vanness swung his sub-machine gun toward Adele. Its bore was a tiny tunnel glowing from the long bursts. Another Zojira, probably the one who'd slugged her from behind, was aiming at her head from the other side. Maybe they'd let recoil raise the gun muzzles when they fired so that they killed each other as well as her. . . .

Markos's aide shouted an order as crisp as the gunshots. She spoke in a Kostroman dialect, not Universal. That angry word was the first time Adele had heard emotion in the aide's voice.

The shooter straightened and snarled back at her. The aide socketed her sub-machine gun in the Zojira's navel. In Universal as precise as the directions in a gazetteer she said, "Step back and only speak when I tell you to speak. I won't warn you again."

Adele saw that she wasn't alone in thinking the aide was as deadly as a spider. The gunman turned and fired his sub-machine gun into a window to let out his frustrations.

The projectiles' high velocity meant that they punched neat circles the size of fifty-florin coins in the glass instead of breaking it. The plasma puffing from the muzzle flickered in reflection from the undamaged panes.

"Search and see who else is here," the aide said calmly to the Zojiras she led. She raised the communicator and spoke into it.

"Nobody else is here," Adele said in a husky voice. "Just the three of us."

There were six thugs, all of them male. They prowled the short rank of stacks, holding their guns out at arm's length as though to fend off any figure leaping from among the books. Two of them opened cartons and peered at the contents.

Adele got to her feet. Her right temple throbbed, but the momentary dizziness had passed. She stretched her left arm to the side and twisted it, making sure that it moved normally again.

Prester knelt on the floor with her forehead pressed against a bookcase. She was sobbing and her hands still squeezed her temples. Blood from the ruin of Vanness's head had dribbled to her bare toes, but she didn't seem to be aware of that.

The aide lowered the communicator and smiled faintly at Adele. "I'm to escort you to the Grand Salon, mistress," she said. Two of the gunmen looked at her. She nodded to them and added, "You two come with me. You others, take the woman there to the cage in the gardens. Report to whoever's in charge for reassignment."

"She's just an assistant," Adele said softly. "She isn't even a Hajas. Just the niece of a cousin of the Chancellor."

The aide shrugged. "Not my department," she said. "Maybe nothing will happen to her."

Two of the gunmen lifted Prester by the elbows. She hung as a dead weight, her feet drawing smears of blood on the tile floor.

"Shall we go, mistress?" the aide said. She waggled the submachine gun. That wasn't a threat; the weapon simply happened to be in her hand. Adele doubted that the woman ever threatened in the usual blustering sense of the word.

Without speaking, Adele Mundy walked into the hall and turned toward the staircase. If she delayed she'd find herself stepping in the trail of tacky blood Prester left on the floor.

The arched windows of Candace's four-story townhouse were shuttered, and there were no lights on in the front rooms to glimmer through the cracks. Candace lived with a retinue of twenty servants, so even if he himself had left the city there was certain to be somebody still in the house.

Daniel stepped into the shallow door alcove and knocked with the pads of his fingertips. The slapping sound of flesh on steel was enough to be heard inside without rousing the whole street. The panel was armored to resist battering rams.

Each of the tiles covering the facade was divided diagonally, half blue and half white; figured friezes separated the floors. The pattern seemed to strobe in direct sunlight because the rods and cones of the human eye didn't register at quite the same point on the retina. Now Daniel's only reaction was to wish the background was a neutral gray that his uniform would blend with. He felt as exposed as an infant in a hog pen.

There wasn't much traffic in Kostroma City tonight. You couldn't really call the situation quiet, though, because every few minutes there were gunshots somewhere in the darkness. Occasionally a firefight spread its lingering roar, and twice Daniel heard plasma cannon in use. The beams of ions had a hissing snarl that distance quickly muffled, but stone or concrete in their path fractured loudly.

Metal burned. A door like this one would expand in a bellowing white inferno, rising to the fourth story and scouring tiles from the wall in shattered fragments.

An eyehole opened at the side of the alcove. There was no

illumination within, but Daniel caught the movement as a lighter shadow appearing among darker ones.

"It's Lieutenant Daniel Leary," he hissed. "Quick, let me in before somebody comes by."

The eyehole closed. Daniel waited a moment for bolts to draw back. He heard nothing. He patted the panel again with his fingertips.

Ducted fans thrummed through the sky. The vehicle was too low over the housetops for Daniel to see it, but he could tell from its powerful note that the motors supported not an ordinary aircar but the twenty-odd tons of an APC. Window sashes rattled.

The Alliance vehicle passed on, still invisible. There was no sound within the house.

Daniel hammered on the door panel with his balled fist, making the steel ring. "Candace!" he shouted. "Let me in! Now! It's Daniel Leary!"

There was argument inside. Daniel couldn't hear the words, but the rhythm of angry voices penetrated the metal. Daniel slammed his fist once more into the door. Making this much noise might get him killed, but by God! he wouldn't go alone.

It was a tall door and had three separate bolts. They clashed back: top, bottom and finally the heavy crossbar in the center. The door swung outward for safety: an attacker would have to break down the heavy leaf, not simply bash the bolts out of their sockets. Daniel stepped back as the panel opened enough for him to slip through, barely, into the anteroom.

He stumbled as he entered. At some point the original floor had been replaced by a mosaic showing sea life battling in gaudy colors. The new floor had been laid directly over the old one, raising the level by more than an inch. The incongruity of Daniel's misstep made him giggle.

Candace was white-faced and furious. He wore his service pistol in a gilt-leather holster. With him in the anteroom were five servants. Two carried sporting shotguns, two had clubs—legs wrenched off a heavy table; and the last, a wizened little man, held a chef's knife with a blade as long as his forearm.

Daniel thought of the night the Three Circles Conspiracy broke; thought also of the plasma cannon in the APCs cruising the city. The door would burn like the white heart of a sun. . . .

"What in God's name do you think you're doing here?" Candace shouted. "I have half a mind to hold you for a patrol to pick up! I swear to God, if I weren't afraid of getting involved that's *just* what I'd do!"

Four of the servants were as frightened as their master. The little man with the knife was another matter entirely. If it came down to cases, Daniel would try to kick him in the crotch and pray for a better result than he expected.

"I need some help, Candace," Daniel said in a calm voice. "You know why. Some clothes, a gun, and the loan of your aircar. Then I'll be out of your life."

There was a doorway to either side of the anteroom. Directly in front of Daniel a hall led to the courtyard and, on the right, a staircase to the upper floors. One of the men with clubs carried a yellow glowlamp, the only light.

"Good God, man, are you insane?" Candace said. "Listen, the Candaces aren't political. Don't you understand what that means? This house has been in our family for four hundred years. I'm not going to throw it away by getting involved in matters that are no business of mine!"

Daniel looked at the Kostroman. He tried to imagine life as Benno Candace. He smiled.

"Can't you even pretend you're a man?" Daniel asked pleasantly. "No? Well, I suppose it'd be too much of a stretch."

He nodded toward the servants. "If one of you dogs will open the door," he said, "I'll be on my way. A Leary doesn't stay where he's not wanted."

The man with the knife grinned. Daniel grinned back. He doubted the fellow was as clever as Hogg, but there was an undoubted resemblance.

A servant handed his shotgun to a fellow. He stepped past Daniel and put his weight against the door.

"Look, Leary," Candace said, spreading his hands. "When this blows over we'll have a drink and laugh about tonight. But it may *not* blow over, don't you see? This isn't like a normal coup. This is—everything's different. Everything!"

The servant had opened the panel no wider than it was when Daniel entered. Daniel put his left palm flat against the embossed leather padding on the door's inner side and straightened his arm.

The door swung slowly, but it didn't stop until it banged against the stops on the outer jamb. "Good night, Lieutenant," Daniel said. "I wish you the fortune your sense of honor deserves."

He stepped into the street, deliberately pausing to dust his uniform with his hands. No point in letting Candace know which direction the fugitive had gone.

The fugitive didn't have the least idea where he ought to go. His apartment, he supposed. In the unlikely event there weren't Alliance soldiers there by now, he could grab some civilian clothes.

The door thumped shut behind him. Instantly, as though there'd been a switch in the doorjamb, light fanned across the street from a third-story window. In the present darkness it had the glare of a searchlight.

Daniel looked up. One of the shutter leaves had been thrown back. From this angle, nearly vertical, he saw only a wedge of pale pink ceiling.

Margrethe leaned over the window sill with a bundle in her arms. The light from behind flowed through her russet hair. She pitched the bundle outward. She'd snatched the shutter closed again before Daniel caught her gift.

He'd braced himself but the bundle turned out to be cloth, bulk without weight. He carried it into the narrow gap between Candace's house and its neighbor to the right. He immediately understood what he was holding.

The jacket was dark, dark blue if the light had been better. The trousers were of the same material with a stripe down the seam that would be red. They were rolled around a peaked blue cap with a frontal of embossed brass.

He sighed. With this, there was just a chance that he could brazen his way into the palace where he hoped Woetjans's crew was hiding. So far as Daniel knew, their billet wasn't listed in any records.

Daniel Leary stripped off his Cinnabar uniform. Trousers first, he donned the service uniform of a naval lieutenant of the Commonwealth of Kostroma.

Well over a hundred people milled in the Grand Salon, which was being used as both coup headquarters and a holding cell for the dozen or so top prisoners taken thus far. Walter III—properly Walter Hajas again, Adele presumed—was present but his mistress wasn't. The Chancellor, barefoot in her fur-trimmed nightdress, babbled to a Zojira who ignored her as he spoke into his hand-held communicator.

Adele smiled faintly at the Chancellor's discomfort. She tried not to dislike people, merely their actions. The Chancellor's combination of graft, pompousness, and bullying came close to making her an exception.

The guards included both troops of the Zojira clan and Alliance soldiers whose battle dress looked as though drab paint had been dripped over the fabric. The Zojiras were possibly a cut above the armed thugs who'd burst into the library; these would be the personal bodyguard of the clan chief and new Elector, Leonidas Zojira.

She wondered whether there'd been a previous Elector of the name or if Zojira was Leonidas I. Given the direct involvement of Alliance forces in the coup, the question was probably meaningless. The real ruler of Kostroma would be the Alliance advisor, if not a planetary administrator appointed from Pleasaunce.

Adele was no expert on the military, but the Alliance troops looked very tough and competent. They wore body armor with bandoliers of weapons and munitions besides the sub-machine guns that were their primary armament. The Alliance planners had naturally chosen shock troops for the initial assault.

Markos's aide paused just inside the doorway, scanning the room for the figure she wanted. "Wait here, please, mistress," she said, as unfailingly polite as she was colorless. She left Adele with the two Zojiras and moved through the crowd with her usual swift grace.

One of the Zojiras let out his breath in a sigh of relief. Adele smiled again, still faintly.

Leonidas stood in the center of the great room, surrounded by aides who like him wore court dress in black and yellow. They looked like so many hornets, a Terran insect tough enough to stow away and become an unpleasant feature of almost as many worlds as had cockroaches.

In the group with the Zojira grandees were several Alliance officers. One of them wore battle dress like the troops on guard, but the khaki uniforms of the other two looked like a simpler version of what the naval members of the Alliance delegation wore to the Elector's dinner a few nights before.

None of those negotiators was in the Grand Salon tonight.

Markos was here, however, standing like the axis around which the world moved. He smiled in black triumph.

A loud explosion sounded in the near distance. The palace shook. The Alliance officers in the central group all spoke into their communicators, while the Kostromans with them froze and looked apprehensive. One of the naval officers lowered her communicator and said something nonchalant to those around her. General conversation resumed.

Markos saw his aide approaching. They must have exchanged signals that not even Adele saw. The aide returned to Adele and said, "He'll see you now, mistress."

She looked at the Zojiras who'd come from the library with her and added, "You're dismissed. Report to whoever's in charge in the garden."

The Kostromans whirled and left the salon. They were moving so fast that the sub-machine gun one carried clanged into the doorpost.

Adele followed the aide to the center of the room. The crowd grew thicker as she went inward, but it wasn't a solid mass.

The assembly was formed of elements ranging from two people to a dozen, talking and gesturing among themselves. Individuals would break off and join other groups in an air of nervous dynamism.

It was like watching the interactions within a rookery of seabirds. The chaos was of overwhelming importance to the people making it, but from Adele's detached viewpoint it was merely empty noise.

Of course, it was noise that had ended her librarianship and might cost her life besides. Walter Hajas stood with a drawn face in a group of prisoners. The others kept their backs to him as though meeting the former Elector's eyes might contaminate them.

Markos moved a few steps away from the central group. The only potential eavesdroppers were a covey of second-rank Kostromans; Markos's aide moved them on with curt whispers and a tap from the muzzle of her sub-machine gun.

"Ms. Mundy," Markos said. "I wanted to thank you immediately in person. You'll be taken care of, don't worry."

"What does that mean?" Adele said.

"Well, we don't know yet, do we?" Markos said with vague humor. "Something commensurate with your deserts, however."

Despite his placid demeanor, the Alliance agent was as keyed up as anyone else in the room. It struck Adele that she and Markos's aide were perhaps the only calm people present—and the aide was a sociopath.

Markos looked around him and sniffed in scorn. "Listen to them," he said. "Every one of them claiming that what he did was crucial, that the coup couldn't have succeeded without him. *I* was the only one who was really necessary."

Adele wondered if the spy recognized the humor in what he'd just said.

He fixed Adele with his eyes. It was like looking into obsidian that has just cooled to black but still throbs with heat. "And after me, mistress," Markos said, "you are the one who mattered. Success couldn't have been so complete without you."

"No," Adele said, but she wasn't sure the word pulsing in her mind actually reached her tongue. Her mouth was dry, and for the first time this night she felt real fear.

There was commotion at the hallway door. A squad of Alliance troops entered the salon with three members of the Cinnabar embassy. The prisoners' wrists were tied behind their backs. Wire leashes around their necks connected them in single file.

Admiral Lasowski was in the lead. She limped, and blood from a bandaged shoulder wound soaked to the elbow of her pajamas. Her lip curled as she surveyed the crowd.

Adele waited, her eyes on the doorway. After nearly a minute she let her breath out again. There wasn't a fourth Cinnabar prisoner being dragged in with his seniors. Daniel Leary was still free.

If he was alive.

The troops brought their Cinnabar captives directly to the command group in the center. Anyone who pressed close for a look or simply didn't clear their path in time was prodded back with a gun butt or gun muzzle. Markos and his aide left Adele as abruptly as a page turns.

Adele thought about what she'd done, and why. Any one of a hundred people could have found the information she'd gathered for Markos. All she'd added to the process was speed and reliability. But because she couldn't lie to herself, she had to admit that speed and reliability might have been enormously important factors in a plan so complex and suddenly executed.

Why *had* she helped Markos? Adele didn't really believe Mistress Boileau had been in danger. Not only was the professor well connected with members of the power structure on Pleasaunce, her knowledge made her a national treasure. The Fifth Bureau knew that better than most.

Beyond question, Adele and her family had been ill-treated by the Republic of Cinnabar. She couldn't claim that she'd acted out of anger, though. The massacre of her family had stunned her, but she wasn't angry now and probably hadn't ever been angry. Hot emotions like love and hate weren't a major part of Adele Mundy's personality.

She had done what Markos demanded because that was the simplest choice. She did it to be finished, so that she could get back to the important work of cataloguing a library.

Adele Mundy had betrayed the Kostroman state that employed her and the Cinnabar state whose citizen she was because she was lazy. She hadn't wanted to be bothered by a man she loathed but who might have the power to harass her.

Markos stood facing the Cinnabar delegates. Alliance soldiers held either end of the leash binding the three together. The civilian member of the Navy Board spoke angrily about the law of nations, but Lasowski and the man from the finance office were coldly silent as they met Markos's eyes.

The room quieted. "Kneel down," Markos ordered pleasantly.

"I'll be damned first," Admiral Lasowski said. Her voice was thin with pain from her wound.

"Force them to kneel," Markos said to the soldier on one end.

The soldier frowned and looked toward the officer in battle dress. "Make them kneel," the officer said. He didn't sound comfortable. "Mr. Markos is in command."

The soldiers stepped back to tension the leash, then used their weight to drag the prisoners down. The Navy Board functionary cried out as he lost his footing and slipped headlong. The Alliance officers watched with obvious distaste.

"You see," Markos said, "it's possible that our Zojira friends here think that in the future they might be able to invite Cinnabar to return and nonetheless keep their ruling positions on Kostroma. That can't be permitted."

Leonidas Zojira shook his head nervously. He was a dapper little man with a mustache as sharp as paired stilettos. "I assure you that our treaty with the Alliance of Free Stars is sacrosanct, good sir. You need not—"

"As sacrosanct as your pledge of eternal alliance with Walter Hajas here, no doubt," Markos said with catlike amusement. "Well, never fear. You'll stay loyal to the Alliance."

He crooked a finger toward one of the soldiers standing in back of the prostrate Cinnabar delegates. "Shoot them," he said.

"You can't do that!" said an Alliance naval officer. "They're prisoners of war. We don't shoot prisoners!"

"I'll remind you of what Colonel Dorrien just noted," Markos said. "The Guarantor has put *me* in charge."

He nodded to his aide. She stepped past him, aimed her submachine gun one-handed, and fired a single shot. Admiral Lasowksi thrashed like a pithed frog.

"Oh good Christ," said the Alliance naval officer who'd protested. He turned his back. The colonel in battle dress was expressionless, and the other naval officer looked white with rage. "Oh good Christ!"

The aide fired twice more. The snapping discharges weren't loud in the big room, but they echoed in the eyes of all those watching.

The Navy Board member was flailing and crying out. When the pellet hit him, his voice rose to a high-pitched whimper. The aide grimaced and put a second round into the back of his skull.

"I suppose it's better that the executions be carried out by a Kostroman citizen anyway," Markos said. "Don't you think so, Elector Leonidas?"

He laughed and added, "Anyway, now we can get back to deciding the future shape of the government of Kostroma."

Adele Mundy turned and walked out of the Grand Salon. No one paid any attention to her.

Not that she cared.

Somebody'd put a burst of shots into the head of the Triton. Water streamed from a dozen ragged bronze holes, but only a little dribbled out of the conch itself.

Three Hajas guards lay in a short row in the entryway. They'd been riddled too, but they'd long since stopped leaking fluids. Splotches of blood remained beside the pillars where they'd fallen.

Water had been sluiced over the mess, but it still looked as though buckets of maroon paint had burst on the dark stone.

Daniel strode toward the entrance, looking grim. The expression was appropriate for his persona as a Kostroman staff officer, and it was certainly easy to arrange.

Two jitneys and a three-axle truck, all of them mounting automatic impellers, were drawn up in front of the palace. Daniel was sure that long bursts from such powerful weapons would flip the jitneys over on their backs, and he suspected that if the gun on the truck fired broadside rather than in line with the wheels the same would happen.

That didn't much matter because the Alliance APC on the other side of the entranceway would carry the real weight of further fighting. Its plasma cannon could hose the square in iridescent hellfire, vaporizing any conceivable counterattack the Hajas clan could mount. The Alliance commandoes standing at the bow and stern of the big vehicle looked as though they were begging for an excuse to shoot somebody.

Daniel imagined he was Candace in the same situation. He lowered his eyes, twisted his face to the side, and let his course curve away from the bow of the APC as though the two of them were magnets of the same polarity.

The nearest commando snorted, then spit near Daniel's feet. Daniel scuttled a little faster without looking up.

He knew he wasn't being entirely fair to Candace. The Kostroman's proven cowardice was moral, not physical. But Daniel didn't feel like giving Candace the benefit of the doubt, and it was the sort of behavior that the Alliance commando would like to see. Wogs whimpering at the feet of the tough Alliance soldiers. . . .

Spectators watched from the roofs of buildings across Palace Square. Small clumps of civilians gathered on the pavement itself, talking in muted voices and jumping whenever a vehicle rumbled by in the street behind them. They carried pennants of black and gold divided in a variety of fashions—whatever they'd been able to sew together quickly.

Prostitutes were already working the plaza. Daniel saw a statuesque blond man approach a commando in the door arch. He left laughing, but without doing business at least for the moment.

An APC ran its fans up in the gardens to the rear of the palace. The vehicle lifted just high enough to be seen as movement beyond the building's mass, then curved south in the direction of the Navy Pool. Sporadic gunfire continued across the city, and a red glow to the west hinted of fire.

A squad of guards with Zojira armbands stood in front and to the left of the main door; there were three Alliance commandoes to the right. The Kostromans talked loudly to one another, waving their weapons and passing a bottle of plum brandy. Empty bottles lay nearby in the entrance alcove, some of them smashed.

The Zojiras were in a reasonably good mood: they were alive, and the flaccid bodies of their Hajas predecessors were an immediate reminder of the alternative. Nonetheless they were drunk and too excited to be safe with automatic weapons.

That was another reason Daniel stepped directly to the sergeant in charge of the trio of Alliance commandoes to say in a calm, quiet, voice, "I'm Lieutenant Benno Candace, signals lieutenant on the staff of Grand Admiral Sanaus. I'm here to collect written instructions on the navy's employment and bring them to Admiral Sanaus. Can you tell me where the Elector is?"

Just-landed Alliance soldiers wouldn't realize that Daniel spoke Universal with a non-Kostroman accent. If his luck was really bad, though, one of them might recognize a Cinnabar accent.

For that matter, Daniel didn't know the name of the new Elector; he thought he was lucky to recognize Zojira black and gold. It wasn't likely that a commando would ask him the Elector's name. It was even more unlikely the Alliance troops really gave a fuck which fucking wog thought he was in charge of this fucking pisspot planet, but you could never tell.

On the other hand, you could be hit by a meteor while lying in bed. It didn't do to worry about things you couldn't change.

"What're you telling me for?" the sergeant growled. "Do I look like a guide dog? Go ask somebody inside."

"Thank you, sergeant," Daniel said with obsequious politeness. He stepped past the nearest Zojira and entered the vestibule.

None of the local guards had heard the exchange in detail, but they weren't going to interfere with a man the Alliance troops had passed. If they tried, there was a fair chance that the commandoes would back Daniel out of sheer bloody-mindedness and feelings of superiority.

It would only take one thing going wrong for Daniel to become another tacky smear like the one he walked around on the mosaic just inside the doorway. There'd been a half-hearted attempt to mop up the mess, but bits of lung tissue as well as blood still stuck to the patterned stone.

The desks in the anteroom had been smashed either in the fighting or in an orgy of destruction that had more to do with mobs than it did with war. Somebody'd emptied a sub-machine gun across the furniture to the left, blowing out bright yellow splinters of wood and fountains of shredded paper.

The head clerk Daniel remembered from his first visit knelt among the wreckage, trying to piece together torn files. None of his fellows were present. Daniel stepped past quickly to hide himself in a group of noncombatants wearing Zojira colors. It was unlikely that the old clerk could have recognized anyone through his tear-brimming eyes.

Daniel turned to the right and walked purposefully down the corridor past open offices. The lights were on in most, but the people who'd ransacked them had generally passed on.

Occasionally he saw armed Zojiras who drank and broke up furniture. They eyed Daniel, but the only direct challenge he received was from a woman sprawled against the wall facing the doorway. She waved a half bottle of brandy and called, "Hey! I could use what you got, handsome!"

He couldn't imagine circumstances in which he'd be flattered by attention from that particular quarter.

The Zojiras were a major clan, but the coup had required very large forces to cover all the critical locations. The Alliance commandoes provided backbone and heavy weapons, but they didn't know the city and couldn't number more than a battalion even if they and their equipment had been packed into the just-landed transport like sardines.

To get the necessary numbers, the planners had recruited anybody willing to point a gun at fellow-citizens. Real discipline was impossible, and at least half the additional personnel must be criminals. The new regime would find the apparatus of government smashed. They'd be lucky if Kostroma City weren't burned to the ground besides.

The stairs to the basement and subbasement were in an alcove off the corridor, much like the one on the third floor that held the ladder to the roof. At the rear of the palace was a broad flight of steps which was the usual entrance to the dank arches of the basement, but only low-ranking clerks worked there. Daniel thought he'd call less attention on himself by entering the front instead of having people wonder why a naval lieutenant was going down to the basement.

The stairwell door was ajar but unattended. There was a light fixture at the mid-flight landing, but it hadn't worked any of the times Daniel had used the stairs to see Woetjans.

His half-boots rang in the stairwell, but the sound would be lost in the noisy excitement echoing from the masonry cavern below. He didn't have the slippers with small tassels on the toes that were the proper footgear with this uniform. Even if someone noticed, the Kostroman navy wasn't a stickler for detail.

Somebody fired a shoulder-stocked impeller within the basement. The *whack!* of the heavy slug hitting a pillar was followed instantly by pebbles slapping against the walls and floor in all directions. People laughed hysterically.

Even a single round would blast a divot the size of a man's head in this brick. If the idiots weren't careful, they could cut through a pillar. A collapsing ceiling would spoil this party for good and all.

Daniel grinned. The chaotic violence made it less likely that he'd be arrested by the authorities, but there was a pretty good chance some drunk would blow his head off as surely as they'd decapitated the fountain in Palace Square. Well, he'd wanted an adventurous life.

The stairwell's basement-level door was closed. Daniel passed by it and continued down. Ceiling-level windows let enough light into the basement to make the space usable if not comfortable for clerical activities. The line of electric fixtures running down the middle of the central vault was enough to keep somebody down there by night from running into a pillar, but no more than that.

The subbasement had no windows and fewer lights, at least until Woetjans moved her contingent into it. The Kostromans used the space only for storage, the powerplant, and a quartet of huge pumps. The last were intended to lift ground water into a sewer and keep the palace from sinking into the bog from which the land had been reclaimed, but according to Woetjans only one of the pumps still worked.

There was no light at all in the subbasement. Daniel paused to put on his goggles and switch them to thermal imaging. He hadn't wanted to wear an item as out of place with a Kostroman uniform as a brass brassiere, but he had to be able to see.

The pillars on which the entire palace rested were ghostly outlines that belied their massive construction. The archways were filled with broken furniture and machinery, old carpet and wall hangings carried down here to rot in billows of mold, and boxed documents. The junk had been stacked any which way, and decay had caused even that rudimentary organization to sprawl in chaos.

Infrared gave the inch-deep pools of groundwater a bright, even sheen because they were a degree or two cooler than the irregular pavement on which they lay. The only difference between storing material here and dumping it in the harbor was that the subbasement was a shorter distance to carry things.

There should have been *some* light on the vault ceilings. Daniel walked toward the bay which the Cinnabar detail had converted to living quarters. It was marginally higher than most of the region and therefore dry, though the frequent *plink* of condensate falling into pools of seepage reminded Daniel that "dry" was a relative concept.

The pillars were quatrefoil rather than round in cross-section. A man waited in the niche between two lobes, watching Daniel. His body heat made him stand out against the brick like a floodlight. Though the human form was clear, thermal imaging blurred the face into oval sexlessness.

"You there!" Daniel said. "Identify yourself!"

"Goddam good to see you, Master Daniel," Hogg said. "I was about ready to turn into a mushroom or a fish, waiting for you."

He switched on a tiny deep-yellow light he wore as a thumb ring. It was intended for reading maps at night, but in the present darkness it made an adequate area light. "Now let's get out of here, shall we, sir?"

Daniel gratefully removed his goggles as Hogg led the way back to the inside staircase. "How did you know I'd come here?" he said. He didn't bother asking about Woetjans's detail since they were obviously safe without his help.

"Well, I figured you'd have better sense than to go to the apartment," Hogg said. He moved soundlessly through the clutter

like the old poacher he was. "There wasn't any place I could hide
and catch you if you did anyway. There's a squad at both ends
of the street waiting for you. Best bet was you'd come here to
find Woetjans. If you didn't, well, we'd deal with that."

Hogg stopped at the foot of the narrow staircase. "Sir," he said,
"I should've known about it sooner. When I learned what was
going down, you were long gone with that ponce Candace and
the girls. If something had happened . . ."

The pudgy little man shook his head. "I don't remember praying
since I was in diapers. Maybe there's a God after all."

Daniel snorted. This wasn't a time to show feelings, if there
ever was one. "Did you think I was going to let this lot run
me down?" he said with carefully modulated scorn. "You raised
me better than that, Hogg. Now, let's get on about our business."

They started up the stairs. Hogg stopped dead; Daniel froze
behind him. All the reflexes he'd learned in the Bantry wood-
lands had returned full force.

Someone was coming down the staircase toward them.

The light around the bend of the stairs was so faint that Adele
was conscious of it only when it vanished. She stopped on the
step above the landing. "Woetjans," she said, "this is Adele Mundy.
I'm alone."

She folded her hands in front of her. Nobody had bothered
to search her, but neither had she found herself tonight in a place
that she thought the pistol in her left pocket could improve.

"Good God, it's Adele!" cried Daniel Leary. She couldn't have
been more surprised to hear Markos, whom she'd left behind her
in the Grand Salon. "Hogg, we've got to take her with us. They'll
figure out sooner or later that she's really a Cinnabar citizen."

Daniel stepped onto the landing. "Show a light, man!" he
demanded. He groped for Adele, caught her hand, and shook it
enthusiastically.

The tiny glow returned. Hogg stood behind his master, looking as grimly displeased as could be implied by a complete lack
of expression.

"I came to warn the sailors," Adele said. Warn them to do what?
she wondered. She couldn't have gotten Woetjans and the others out of the palace, nor could she have hidden them in her tiny

room if they did get clear. But she'd felt she had to do something after watching the executions in the Grand Salon.

"Sir, I think it might be best if the Ms. Mundy went her own way," Hogg said, looking off at an angle as if he were surveying the stairwell in preparation to bid on repainting it. "And I think we all—"

"Nonsense!" said Daniel, the good humor gone from his tone. This was an odd place to hold a discussion, but quite obviously the three of them weren't going to go anywhere until the discussion had been held. "We're not going to abandon a Cinnabar citizen in a bloody shambles like this! That wouldn't be honorable."

"Lieutenant," Adele said. Daniel's explicit confidence in her as a fellow citizen was a knife to her heart. "I think Hogg is correct. I'll be all right, but upstairs they just murdered the rest of your delegation. That may have been a one-time warning through terror, but you can't take the risk."

She turned and started up the stairs.

"Nonsense!" Daniel said and caught her right wrist. He didn't squeeze, but she could as well have pulled free from handcuffs as she could the lieutenant's grip. "We're all together now. Hogg, you're leading."

"Sir—" Hogg pleaded.

"I think what your servant means but doesn't care to say," Adele said with cool dispassion, "is that the Three Circles Conspiracy proved Cinnabar citizens, even members of the best families, were quite willing to turn their friends over to butchers to save their own necks. He has logic on his side. If you'll release me, Lieutenant Leary, I'll return to my own affairs."

"A moment please, Adele," Daniel said. He didn't loose her hand completely, but he reduced the contact to minimal pressure from his thumb and forefinger.

"Hogg," he said, "Ms. Mundy is a friend of mine; I won't stand for any suggestion that she might behave dishonorably. On the other hand I can appreciate your concern for your own safety in conditions so involved. I therefore release you to do as you please. Adele and I will find our own way without burdening you further."

"Don't be a fool!" Adele said. She snatched her hand away but she didn't take a step upward.

"And I might add, Hogg," Daniel added as though he hadn't heard her, "that it was the Alliance paymaster who provided the evidence on the Three Circles Conspiracy, not its citizen members!"

"What it pleases me to do, sir," Hogg said with gravel-voiced dignity, "is to go on serving the young master the best way I know how, just as I've been doing the past twenty-two years. For all that the little fellow acts the right stiff-necked prick now and again."

The ground shuddered violently; dust and fragments chipped from the brick walls danced in the stairwell. Several seconds later arrived the airborne shockwave, a sound as prolonged as distant thunder.

"For *God's* sake!" Adele said. "Let's get out of here before they blow the palace down around our ears!"

"After you, Hogg," Daniel said, bowing his servant forward. "After all, you know where we're going."

Hogg gave Adele a sheepish smile and tapped his forehead in salute as he squeezed past. Adele followed as Daniel waved her ahead on the narrow stairs. She heard him humming behind her, secure in his hopes for the future and his confidence in his friends.

Adele thought of the information she had provided to Markos. She'd rather anything than that she'd given in to the Alliance spy.

And she'd rather that she lay dead in the Grand Salon beside Admiral Lasowski than that she be here and alive beside a man who trusted her implicitly.

The woman screaming as they passed the door to the basement made it easier for Daniel to recompose his face in appropriately stern lines. He *supposed* the sound came from a woman. If he'd heard it on Bantry he'd have assumed an animal was being slaughtered, but in Kostroma City tonight the smart money would bet that the victim was human.

Hogg paused at the stairhead to don a black and gold beret. He opened the door with a flourish and swaggered into the corridor ahead of Adele and Daniel.

The regular palace lighting seemed bright after Daniel's plunge into the vaults below. Adele Mundy was as coldly aloof as she'd seemed when Daniel first met her in the library. She gave no sign of being perturbed by this disruption of her normal scholarly routine.

Corder Leary, ever the aristocrat, would have said, "Blood will tell." Watching the librarian made his son feel proud to be a citizen of Cinnabar; the same thing, perhaps, but in a more generalized form.

The corridor was much as Daniel had seen it before, but three Zojira officials were trying to halt the destruction. One of them, a man in full court dress, was arguing with the drunk who'd been shooting out window panes one at a time.

The official kept patting at the flap-covered pistol holster he wore for show. His companions, who wore only shoulder cockades to proclaim their Zojira affiliations, watched their fellow's gestures with obvious apprehension.

Daniel thought they were right to be worried. The drunk was perfectly capable of blowing the first man's head off and killing the other two as well if he had any ammunition left.

The woman of the trio stared at Daniel, who'd just appeared from a doorway she didn't know existed. "What are you doing?" she demanded. Daniel suspected her real purpose was to distance herself from the colleague who appeared to be provoking a gunfight.

Daniel stared at her coldly. If he spoke—

"We're carrying out our orders," Adele said in a cold voice. She made the statement in Universal with an upper-class Alliance accent, obvious to anybody who noticed dialectical differences. "I suggest you do the same, or you'll have reason to regret it."

Hogg spat a few inches from the questioner's foot and sauntered on. The three Zojiras grouped a little closer together, saying nothing. The drunk started shooting at the ceiling decorations.

The new rulers were trying to bring order to the crowd in the big anteroom. Two Alliance civilians bellowed into bullhorns. Neither would have been much good alone; in combination they merely raised the volume of cacophony. Commandoes in battle dress watched the scene with expressions like those of visitors to the zoo.

The commandoes were on guard at the ramped exit to the gardens, but they weren't attempting to control traffic in either direction. Their helmets contained full communications suites; in open air they could even use the planetary comsats directly. If the Alliance planners wanted them to stop a Hajas counterattack they'd be ready, but they watched Daniel and his companions pass without concern or even interest.

If their superiors wanted every Kostroman in the anteroom killed, the commandoes might be ready for that as well. Daniel thought about what Adele had said: Admiral Lasowski murdered with the other two members of the delegation. Even with half the Zojira force made up of thugs, that seemed incredible.

Somebody would pay for it. With a little luck, Daniel Leary would collect the first installment.

Half the garden's considerable expanse was partitioned off by woven-wire fencing on temporary poles. Hundreds of Kostromans inside sat or stood disconsolately among the plantings. A few were crying.

The makeshift prison would have been easy enough to break out of: twenty people running together at a section of fence would flatten it. Zojira guards stationed around the perimeter would probably open fire if that happened; the commando watching from the open cupola hatch of her armored personnel carrier certainly would. The Zojiras standing between the plasma cannon's muzzle and the escapees who were the intended target wouldn't slow the commando in the least.

Hogg walked past the APC and through a group of Zojira officials carrying clipboards with lists of names. They were talking among themselves and glancing from their lists to the faces on the other side of the wire.

The cage was being used as a general impoundment rather than serving only captives from the palace itself. Trucks and jitneys pulled in from the street and wound around the construction equipment parked in the drive. They were delivering more prisoners: men and women in their nightclothes, children wailing in terror that their elders were too frightened to dispel.

Daniel wondered if it had been like this on Cinnabar during the proscriptions. He'd been kept in Bantry with his mother.

The most exciting thing that had happened to Daniel Leary during the period was seeing a migratory roc that rested on a high outcrop during the night. Hogg had carried Daniel near the cliff base. An hour after dawn the great flyer had spread its forty-meters vans and launched itself into the swelling updraft. The roc's scaly underbelly was almost close enough for a boy to touch when lift mastered gravity and the huge creature mounted skyward again on the next stage of its ten-thousand-mile flight.

Daniel wondered what Adele Mundy remembered about the proscriptions. She'd have heard about them much later, of course.

Banks of floodlights glared across the garden, throwing hard shadows and dazzling reflections that were more confusing than more muted illumination could have achieved. The mobile fusion powerplant that drove the lighting must have come from the Alliance transport.

The cage blocked one arm of the circle from street to street, so the vehicles carrying prisoners had to leave the same way they arrived. The remaining driveway into the gardens was a snarling traffic jam. Normally the route would have been tight but possible, but the construction equipment along the drive made movement a matter of skill and patience—both of which were in short supply.

Hogg walked to the back of a one-ton van marked GEDROSIAN AND DAUGHTERS. A Kostroman thug with a Zojira beret and his hands in his pockets stood nearby. He sauntered away whistling when he saw Hogg; neither man spoke.

The van's concertina rear door appeared to be padlocked, but Hogg slid it a few inches to the side by simple pressure. Daniel realized that the hasp was sawn through so that the door could be opened from inside or out.

"Some local friends of mine found this for me," Hogg muttered. "It won't be reported missing for the next two days."

The back of the van was full of Cinnabar ratings. "Sir!" said the figure nearest the narrow gap. "Bosun's Mate Ellie Woetjans reporting for orders!"

The relief in Woetjans's voice was as obvious as a cement block. Damned if she didn't throw a salute despite the cramped quarters. Daniel almost returned it. There were times reflex could get you killed. . . .

"Stand easy, Woetjans," Daniel said. He felt surprisingly calm. He was too busy to be scared, he supposed. "Now, what equipment do you have?"

"Not a fucking thing but ourselves, sir," Woetjans said. The ratings behind her were a restive mass of people trying not to breath so that they could hear their superiors' low-voiced exchange. "No food, no weapons. Well, hammers and pipes, you know."

Daniel hoped it looked as though he and his two companions were having a conversation a little away from the angry traffic in the drive. They had to plan, and the worst thing they could do was to look furtive. Everyone suspected everyone else tonight, and Daniel's disguise wouldn't stand scrutiny.

"I'd been figuring we could lay up in a warehouse somewhere for a few days till things got sorted out, sir," Hogg said. "That was when I heard about the business. But I didn't know the Alliance was in it so deep. Those bastards're real soldiers, and I don't guess they're planning to leave any time soon."

"Right on both points," Daniel said. With no equipment or safe hiding place, his detachment had very few options. Their best chance would be to seize a starship tonight before the Alliance forces consolidated their hold on Kostroma.

There was almost certainly an Alliance squadron no more than a few hours out from the planet, though. The chance of the escapees being able to lift before the warships arrived was even slighter than the chances of twenty-odd unarmed Cinnabar citizens reaching the Floating Harbor alive, let alone capturing a ship there.

"Thing is, sir," Hogg said in great embarrassment, "I've got friends like I say, but it isn't like we're family or something. Maybe if it was you alone we could hole up for a good while, but if it's a whole army . . ."

"It's certainly the entire naval detachment I command," Daniel said more sharply than he'd intended. Hogg had worded the statement so carefully that it didn't have to be read as a suggestion that Lieutenant Leary abandon the ratings to save his own neck. "First we'll need clothing. Then—"

"I can get the password into the navy warehouses," Adele said. "I'll have to return to the library. My personal data unit got in the way while I was sorting books, so I took it out of its pocket and left it there."

"By God!" Daniel said. He could suddenly imagine a path to the future that didn't end in a flare of plasma or Zojiras laughing as they used swimming Cinnabars for target practice. "With Kostroman naval uniforms we just might pull this off! And there'll be food stores. If we can hide for the next few weeks till normal traffic in the port resumes, there's a damned good chance!"

That wasn't really true. Still, they'd have a chance that could be measured in percents instead of tenths of a percent.

"There'll be weapons in store, I'd guess," Hogg said, "Can we . . . ?"

"No," Daniel said. "Much as I'd like to, I can't imagine any circumstances in which the armory wouldn't have extra guards tonight; and probably Alliance guards. Guns will have to wait."

Hogg shrugged, "My friends put a few little somethings in the cab," he said. "Nothing I want to go fight the Alliance army with, but guess we'll make do."

"I'll check which buildings have what you need." Adele said. She seemed detached rather than nonchalant. Though their lives depended on this, Adele had been more animated when she was searching for an answer to Daniel's zoological question. "I'll be back as soon as I can."

She turned. Hogg stepped back and sideways so that he blocked her path without seeming to. "Maybe I should go along to protect the lady, sir," he said.

"Mr. Hogg," said Daniel. "This is a command decision. Do you understand?"

Hogg grimaced, nodded, and gave Adele another minuscule salute as he stepped aside.

"If I hadn't forgotten my handheld, I could examine the warehouse contents now," Adele said. She half smiled. "There's something else I should do in the library before I leave, though, so I suppose it's just as well."

She walked toward the palace entrance. "I'll see you as soon as I can," she called over her shoulder. Straight-backed and unhurried, she made her way through the nervous crowd as steadily as a drill enters wood.

"Goddam if I don't think I'm going to start praying as a habit," Hogg muttered. He wiped his forehead with his beret.

Daniel sighed. He doubted Hogg was worried about what might happen to Adele, but it wasn't necessary to pursue the question.

Vanness's body had been removed from the library. Judging from the smears on the tile flooring, they'd dragged it onto the loggia overlooking the gardens. Adele grimaced at the thought of her late assistant being tossed over the railing and loaded onto a truck to be disposed of in the harbor with the rest of the city's garbage. Adele hadn't wanted to look at the corpse again, though.

Her mild pleasure at not seeing Vanness was more than counterbalanced by finding Bracey and his two drinking companions in the library with a pair of women. They had bottles, but the men's main present concern seemed to be to coax one of the women into sex with all three of them. She wasn't quite drunk enough, and the other woman seemed to be more competition for the men than an alternative target.

All five displayed Zojira colors in some fashion or other. One of the men had a pistol thrust under his black and yellow sash. Bracey carried a slung sub-machine gun, but the ammo tube that should have been parallel to the barrel was missing.

Adele swept the group with expressionless eyes as she entered; no point in pretending they weren't present. No point in speaking to the scum either. She found her personal data unit on the console where she'd left it. After sliding it into the pocket where she should have left it to begin with, she squatted to open the main console's sideplate.

"Hey!" said Bracey in surprise. He got up from the stacked boxes on which he sat, tumbling the one on top onto the floor beside him. "What the *hell* do you think you're doing, bitch?"

People were dying tonight; Adele shouldn't let herself worry about a carton of what seemed to be service manuals for machinery that had been rust for a hundred years. Even so . . .

She turned and looked at Bracey with the cold loathing of a human for a slug. "Because of the unsettled conditions at the moment, Bracey," she said, "I'm not going to order you out of here. But neither will I have you interfering with the way I carry out my duties. Shut up and mind your own business."

She turned back to the console's internal architecture. When she'd emplaced the decryption module Markos gave her, she'd deliberately reversed its polarity as a minor act of rebellion. She was quite confident that neither Markos nor any Kostroman technician he brought to check the installation would figure out why it didn't work.

In the event, Markos hadn't asked for information from the *Aglaia* which would have told him twenty members of her crew were billeted in the palace. Now Adele wanted that decryption capacity herself: what would work on Cinnabar naval communications would work equally well on their Alliance equivalents.

"What do you mean, *your* duties?" Bracey said. He stepped toward Adele. His fellows looked puzzled; the drunken woman began to croon a lullaby. "I'm the Electoral Librarian, now. You're nothing, bitch! You're dirt!"

Adele seated herself at the console and used the wands to bring

up the operating system. She needed to enable the module now
that it was properly in place, and she also wanted to conceal its
existence from anyone examining the software.

Movement in the doorway . . . Adele's eyes flicked to the right.
Markos's aide had entered the library.

"Turn around or by God I'll use this!" Bracey said. The aide
raised an eyebrow in mild interrogation.

Adele looked over her shoulder. Bracey was pointing the sub-
machine gun at her. She couldn't tell whether he thought she was
too stupid to know the gun was unloaded, or whether the fool
didn't know himself.

"Get him out of here or I'll kill him," Adele said quietly to
the aide. She shifted both control wands into her right hand.

Bracey pulled the trigger, answering Adele's unspoken question.
When nothing happened, he gave a wordless scream and gripped
the weapon by the barrel to use as a club.

Adele drew her pistol. Bracey stepped back; the two men with
him ducked behind piles of boxes. The more sober woman was
cradling her drunken companion's head, smiling in satisfaction as
she ignored whatever else might be going on in the room.

"You won't use that!" Bracey said. Adele grinned faintly.

"I wonder how many men have had that for their last words,"
said the aide, speaking for the first time. She crooked the index
finger of her left hand toward Bracey. The sub-machine gun in
her other hand shifted slightly.

"I'll use this," she added with her insectile smile. "Out of here
now, all of you."

One of the hiding men raised his head to survey the situation.
He and his companion circled their way out of the library, giving both Adele and the aide as wide a berth as possible. Bracey
saw them leaving. He started after them, stumbled on a fallen book,
and hurled the useless sub-machine gun away as he scuttled through
the doorway.

The women were leaving also, wrapped in their own world.
Adele dropped the pistol into her pocket and resumed her task.

"Mr. Markos noticed you weren't in the Grand Salon," the aide
said. "He wanted to be sure that you were all right."

Adele continued working. "Please thank Mr. Markos for his
concern," she said, "but assure him that I'm quite capable of looking
after myself."

"I warned him that you were," the aide said with catlike humor, "but he didn't believe me."

Adele finished the modification. Portions of the console's software and memory could now be accessed *only* through her handheld unit. They no longer existed so far as an operator at the unit's integral controls were concerned.

"Good night, mistress," the aide said in her expressionless voice. "I'm sure we'll have other dealings in time."

She left the library. Her absence was like the coming of spring.

Adele got up from the console and checked to be sure her personal data unit was settled in its pocket. There was still winter in her heart.

Hogg returned from the truck's cab. Something bulged when his loose jacket hung against his beltline the wrong way. Beside them a man was hammering on a jitney's splashboard while screaming at the driver; she screamed back.

"I handed one through the panel into the back," Hogg said. "I figured the guys there, they can't see out and they're going to feel like canned meat unless they've got, you know, a good luck charm. Do you want the other one, sir?"

"No," said Daniel. He leaned against the back of the truck, trying to look as though he belonged here. His eyes scanned the broad, arched doorway into the palace. "A gun would look wrong without the proper belt and holster. You're probably better with it anyway."

Besides, he wasn't sure he'd want the weapon. If he carried a pistol he'd be wondering whether or not to use it every time there was a crisis. Lt. Daniel Leary had to think as a commander, not a gunman, if his detachment was to survive.

Alliance troops had begun to sort out the traffic jam, starting at the street entrance. They weren't trained for the job, but their brute force approach—a gun in the face and a curt order—was beginning to have an effect. Soon it might be possible to pull the van back onto the pavement and leave the gardens.

Adele had left them just under twenty-five minutes ago. Daniel didn't need to check the time: his mental clock was accurate even now when he was waiting for something that was out of his control.

Adele would need a minimum of ten minutes to reach the third-floor library without the sort of haste that would arouse attention.

Ten minutes more to return. Five minutes wasn't much for what-ever it was she needed to do when she got there, not really.

"Didn't sound to me like any of the shooting came from up there," Hogg said morosely, nodding his chin in the direction of the north wing of the palace. They couldn't see the end windows that served the library because the van was parked so close to the main building. "Of course, with so much shit going on it's hard to tell."

Gunfire was omnipresent in Kostroma City tonight, like the cries of nightbirds at Bantry. The sharpness of light weapons didn't travel very far, but neither was it possible even for a poacher like Hogg to be absolutely sure of the direction it came from.

"I've got everything," Adele Mundy said from Daniel's side. "We can leave now so far as I'm concerned."

"Christ *Jesus* son of God our savior!" Hogg snarled. "Where did you come from, woman?"

"Adele, sit beside Hogg in the cab," Daniel said. "He'll be driving. I'll hang on the running board so people see my uniform."

"I'm a librarian," Adele said to Hogg. She walked around the side of the truck toward the cab. "For an answer to that you'll have to ask a priest or a philosopher."

Daniel blinked when he realized she was joking. His eyes hadn't picked up Adele's drab brown clothing as she left the building and strode toward them at a measured pace. In this confusion of light and noise, she'd been merely part of the background.

As an afterthought Daniel slammed the concertina door shut. "Woetjans?" he murmured to the panel. "You can open it after we're out on the street, but we can't afford anybody glancing in while we're stuck here in traffic."

Hogg started the engine, an air-cooled diesel, as Daniel put his feet on the passenger-side running board and reached through the open window. The cab was a tight squeeze for two; the three of them couldn't possibly sit inside.

Although the jam was beginning to clear, Daniel assumed they'd have to wait anything up to an hour before they got into traffic. Instead Hogg leaned out the window and waved frantically at a jitney. The driver, a man who'd have looked villainous even if he'd had both his ears, stopped dead and opened a gap.

The turbocharger howled as Hogg pulled back the throttle, sending the truck into the traffic stream without difficulty. "A guy

I know," Hogg murmured. "He must be laughing his head off to be working with the cops tonight."

Hogg's driving had generally been done on country tracks, but his rough and ready style didn't seem out of place in the present circumstances; at least he was sober. Daniel hung on grimly as they bumped and squealed toward the exit one truck's length at a time.

The commandoes let vehicles pass in opposite directions alternately at the bottlenecks. To avoid seeming furtive Daniel looked at each Alliance soldier that the truck came abreast, but the troops in battle dress weren't interested in wog officers. They just wanted to get the mess cleared up so that they could return to the porch of the palace. Nobody wanted to tell his grandchildren that he'd been crippled by a wog jitney while pretending to be a traffic cop.

"You didn't have any trouble inside?" Daniel asked, speaking with his lips close to Adele's ear.

She turned to look at him. "No," she said. "Nothing worth mention."

The truck reached the exit. A jitney with three screaming women tied together in the back tried to pull through the opening ahead of them. The commando on gate duty fired his sub-machine gun into the jitney's splashboard. Bits of plastic sprayed the driver and the buttocks of his companion, facing backward to keep an eye on the prisoners.

The passenger yelped and jumped out of the vehicle. The driver stalled his engine. Hogg gave the commando a friendly salute and drove through the gateway, slamming the jitney sideways with his fender as he did so.

They swayed into the street in a wracking turn. "Here we go, sir!" Hogg cried cheerfully. "We're really moving now!"

"We'd be moving if we jumped off the palace roof," Adele said calm-faced over the intake howl. "And the result might be very similar."

Before tonight Daniel hadn't considered the librarian to have a sense of humor. He'd been wrong, but on balance he thought he'd prefer that Adele keep her humor to herself for the time being.

The first time Adele Mundy had seen the entrance to the Naval Warehouse Compound, the gateposts were decked with bunting in honor of the Founder's Day celebrations. Tonight a three-bar barrier was swung across the road and the squad of Kostroman sailors on guard aimed stocked impellers at the approaching truck.

Hogg rowed through the gearbox to slow the truck before he actually squeezed the brake lever. Either the brakes needed maintenance or most of his experience had been with vehicles with bad brakes. Riding with Hogg made Adele wonder if the fellow *had* any experience. He'd only grazed objects with the truck's left side, though, so perhaps he was just being especially careful of his master hanging on to the passenger-side window.

The truck ground to a halt six feet from the barricade; the engine ran at a chattering idle. Three sailors were outside the gate. They moved to the sides, out of the fan of light from the headlamp mounted in the center of the truck's hood. Only the first of the four light standards along the entranceway worked, and it was now behind the vehicle.

"I'll take care of this," Daniel muttered into the cab. He dropped from the running board and strode to the sailor who wore a holstered pistol instead of carrying a heavy impeller. "We're here with a delivery for Grand Admiral Sanaus," he said to the Kostroman. "Items for safekeeping during the present awkwardness. The password is Greatorix."

"The password's canceled," the Kostroman said. "We've got orders not to let anybody in tonight. Go on back. Maybe in the morning things'll be different."

Hogg leaned out the window on his side so that he could hear better. Adele did the same. The sailors were nervous and looked frequently back the way the truck had come, toward the glow of fires over Kostroma City.

"Dammit, man!" Daniel snapped. "I've given you the password. This is Admiral Sanaus's personal brandy stock. If anything happens to it you'll have him on your necks, not some politician who's here today and gone tomorrow!"

The pistol-armed Kostroman shook his head in a combination of concern and denial. "Look, I can't open up. If you want to park here till morning—"

"If you can't carry out the admiral's orders," Daniel said, "then get an officer out here who can. Your obstructionism means the ass of everybody in your chain of command, don't you see?"

"Where do you suppose he comes from?" said a bearded sailor leaning against the gate from the inside. He was ostensibly talking to the petty officer in charge, but his loud voice was meant for everybody in the guard detachment. "He sounds funny to me."

Hogg swore softly as he twitched away the wiping rag covering the bulky electromotive pistol in his lap. He leaned back in his seat and muttered, "Get ready for trouble!" to the small open panel between the driver's compartment and the back of the van.

Daniel Leary took two strides to the gate and grabbed the sailor by the throat with his right hand. His fingers choked the man's yelp before it reached his lips.

"Scum don't normally criticize the accent of a gentleman of L'ven!" Daniel said. "Do you understand that, scum, or shall I use your mouth for a latrine?"

The Kostroman sailor held an impeller at the balance. Daniel shook him violently, banging the man's chest against the barrier's crossbars. The weapon rattled until the sailor dropped it.

None of the others interfered, though two half-raised their impellers without pointing the muzzles anywhere. Daniel looked around the detachment with fierce scorn, then hurled his victim back into the compound. The sailor's face had started to turn blue.

Fixing his glare on the Kostroman petty officer, Daniel said, "Hogg, we're going to drive through this gate if the scum don't open it for us. And if they shoot, they'll learn what Hell is like *before* they reach it!"

He strode back to the truck, scowling in utter fury. Adele didn't remember ever having seen a better piece of acting, or a better place for it.

Her hands were on her lap. She relaxed them to her sides, putting her fingers a little farther from the opening to her left pocket.

The petty officer turned toward the compound, his expression troubled. Hogg revved the diesel into a ringing whine. His hand held the brake firmly.

"Open it!" the Kostroman shouted. "Let them in and to hell with them!"

A sailor drew out the thick pin locking one end of the barrier to the brick post. The whole detachment worked together to swing the gate into the compound. It was so heavy that they didn't seem to notice they were also pushing the man whom Daniel had dropped within the gate's arc in wheezing incapacity.

Daniel jumped onto the running board. His face was as distorted as a bomb-burst. Hogg eased the truck forward, just enough to spur the sailors to a final effort.

"I can't believe that scum!" Daniel said in a hoarse whisper. "What kind of navy is it when a rating thinks he can be discourteous to a superior officer?"

"But . . ." Adele said. She didn't know how to continue. "You're not a superior officer" was so obvious that she couldn't very well say it.

The way was clear. Hogg drove into the compound, accelerating as hard as the tons of human cargo in the back of the truck permitted. Their headlight swept the buildings. The warehouse facades were decorated with brick pilasters and swags of cut stone despite their utilitarian function.

"We're looking for Building Forty-four," Adele said to Hogg. She set her personal data unit on her lap, although she'd memorized all the necessary information when she called it up the first time. "It's in the third row, according to the plan."

"What *kind* of navy?" Daniel repeated. Adele finally had to admit silently that the Cinnabar lieutenant hadn't been acting after all.

Considering that his fury was directed at a gross lapse of professionalism, Adele found herself inclined to agree.

Daniel punched the last of eight digits into the keypad on the door of Warehouse 12 and stepped back. The lock clicked. Woetjans thrust a short prybar into the door seam instead of struggling with the recessed handle. She pulled and Dasi, the huskiest man in the detachment, shoved on the back of the bar.

The door jerked sideways as though blown along its track. Several ratings grabbed the edge while it still had rolling inertia and slammed it all the way to the stop.

Hogg had the truck angled so that the headlight shone into the warehouse. Miscellaneous junk was piled in the aisle at the front of the building just as it had been at Warehouse 44, but Bell hopped nimbly over the obstruction and cried, "Here's the ration cartons!"

Adele had gotten out of the truck. She walked over and stood beside Daniel as he watched in satisfaction. He grinned at her as he called to the ratings, "Just one layer of boxes to cover the floor. You're packed tight enough already."

The Cinnabars now wore Kostroman utility uniforms, loose red shirts and blue trousers. They were barefoot as well, a problem for feet not hardened to it but necessary if they were to avoid comment. For an officer to wear the wrong kind of shoes meant little or nothing; a rating with any footgear at all was instantly noticeable.

"Is there liquor stored in the compound?" Daniel asked. "Can you find it?"

Adele looked surprised, but she squatted without comment. She leaned her back against the warehouse wall so that she could balance the little computer on her knees.

The gear piled in the doorway was bedding. Instead of simply tossing it aside, the Cinnabars cleared their path by stacking the pads and blankets in a side bay. The result was neater than the situation the Kostromans themselves had left.

Daniel grinned in quiet pleasure. He was an officer of the RCN in command of a naval detachment. Even if he died before he became captain of a starship, he had this.

"Building Fifty," Adele said. "It's listed as paint in the manifest, but it's in a triple-locked warehouse along with high-value electronics, not with the rest of the paint in Thirty-one and Thirty-two."

She looked up at Daniel. With a careful lack of emphasis she added, "Are you sure the liquor's a good idea?"

Daniel chuckled. "Oh, good God, it's not for us," he said. "Not—"

He felt himself sober. Two ratings had jumped into the back of the truck. The remainder of the detachment formed a chain to pass heavy cartons of ration packs, all in metal cans, from the warehouse to the vehicle.

"—that I'd worry about this crew drinking itself incapable while there was a job to be done. I want it for trading material."

Adele switched off her computer and slid the control wands into their recess, but she didn't return the unit to the pocket of her trousers. She straightened, raising an eyebrow to Daniel in further question.

"We need to hide," he explained. "We'll either have to fight or barter our way off the island."

He felt a little diffident about verbalizing his plan. Growing up under Corder Leary instilled a feeling that if you stated an idea, someone in authority would ram it down your throat to prove they *were* in authority. The Navy School had done very little to counteract that impression.

Adele nodded understanding. Daniel grinned. "Being a civilized person," he continued, "I prefer to barter. Not to mention the fact we don't have proper weapons."

"Three more cases!" Woetjans called from where she viewed the loading. "Then lock the place. We don't need to leave tracks."

"L'ven is one of the northern islands, isn't it?" Adele said. Daniel followed the line of her eyes south toward the city. An APC, a bug at this distance, crawled across a backdrop of rosy flame.

"Right, there's an amazing colonial shellfish that lives around the shoreline there," he said. "They're called castle clams. They build towers that actually siphon the tide through the entire colony. The augmented flow means they can live in water as much as five hundred feet deep."

"That's how you were able to mimic a L'ven accent?" Adele asked carefully.

Daniel finally understood her real question. Why didn't people just say what they meant? "Oh, I haven't the faintest notion of what a L'ven accent sounds like," he admitted cheerfully. "I don't even know that the island's inhabited, though I suppose it is. I just happened to think of the place because of the clams. And I thought I'd better say something fast."

"Yes," Adele said in a tone as dry as straw rustling. "I think you were right about that."

"Sir, we're loaded," Woetjans said. The ratings were already jumping aboard the van. The reduced ceiling height meant the taller ones had to bend over. The vehicle already sagged on its springs, but it'd have to do.

"Right!" said Daniel. "Warehouse Fifty and then we can get out of this place for good!"

He hadn't any right to feel cheerful as he hooked himself onto the running board again; but he did.

Adele opened Warehouse 50's three separate locks. Daniel and Hogg were in conversation through the cab window about the next stage of the escape. Woetjans and Dasi had the door in motion almost before Adele's finger left the last key. A dozen more sailors jostled her as they sped the panel fully open. Adele stepped out of the way.

Working around these Cinnabar sailors was like using a powerful machine. You had to be very careful of where you stood when you put them in motion.

Warehouse 50 was at the end of a row. On the farther side was woven-wire fencing and supposedly a minefield. Mines didn't seem practical in the marshy ground beyond the fenceline, but the bog itself was a considerable barrier to anyone trying to break in.

Farther still to the north, the sky over Kostroma City glowed. Occasionally a fleck of greater brightness snapped through the night; projectiles, she supposed, but they could have been reflections from an aircar.

Sounds were lost in the distance. All Adele could hear from where she stood were the cries of seabirds and valves slapping at the mouth of the Navy Pool. The tide was coming in to fill the lagoon.

"Found it, sir!" a sailor called from the mouth of the warehouse. "How much do we take?"

"Four—no, six cases!" Daniel said, stepping from the driver's side running board to look into the building. "And the stronger the better. Brandies, not wine, all right?"

Adele saw a spotlight finger the roof of the warehouse on the other side of this short street. The beam dropped to vanish in the skyglow. "Someone's coming!" she called. "On the main—"

A four-wheeled vehicle pulled across the intersection, blocking the only way for the Cinnabars to get out. The passenger in the vehicle's open cab shone a spotlight down this street as he had the one before. The beam locked on the sailors and Hogg's van with its nose toward the open warehouse.

"Hold where you are!" a woman's voice ordered. "Get your hands up!"

Adele couldn't see well against the beam of the spotlight, but she could make out several figures in the back of the other vehicle. One of them was manning the automatic impeller mounted on a pintle in the middle of the deck.

Daniel stepped forward, twisting his mouth into a smile as the gun truck pulled into the cul-de-sac. The truck's twin headlights lit the van and the Cinnabars around it, so the officer in the passenger's seat turned her spotlight on the warehouse door. There were half a dozen ratings inside, but Woetjans, who had the only pistol, was in plain view.

Four Kostroman sailors were in the back of the truck. On the sleeves of their utility uniforms were broad white armbands with embroidered anchors: this was a detachment of Shore Police. Three carried stocked impellers, while the last was behind the automatic weapon trained on Daniel's navel. A sub-machine gun stood upright in a boot between the driver and passenger so that either could grab it at need.

"It's all right, officer," Daniel called, wondering if his accent was going to be a problem again. "We're authorized to be here. The password's Greatorix, and Admiral Sanaus gave us the door codes, as you see."

He wanted to shade his eyes from the headlight glare, but he decided that would be a bad idea. He was better off showing the police a pleasant smile than looking uncomfortable for any reason whatever.

"Put your damned hands up!" the officer repeated. The gun truck stopped ten feet from Hogg's van; she stood but didn't get out of the vehicle. "How many of you are there, anyway? They told me there was two civilians and a lieutenant."

She sounded peevish. Daniel couldn't see her rank tabs at this distance but she couldn't be more than a lieutenant. There was nothing obviously wrong about Daniel's presence here—he had the codes and password, just as he'd said. He'd never known an RCN shore policeman to cut any slack for personnel in the real navy, though, and he didn't imagine the situation was different on Kostroma.

An unusually loud explosion in Kostroma City made roofing tiles click here in the warehouse compound. The muzzle of the automatic impeller wobbled as the gunner holding the grips flinched. The Shore Police would know just enough about the coup to make them nervous, but that didn't make the Cinnabars' situation easier.

"Nobody's supposed to enter the compound tonight," the officer said. She remained standing in the cab of her vehicle. "I want you all in line against the front of the building. Everybody in the building come out right now or by God I'll blow you out!"

"Sir, there's plenty of liquor here to go around," Hogg called in an ingratiating voice. "Maybe the lady and her friends would like a case to, you know, make their duty easier?"

"Who are you?" the officer said on a rising note. She unhooked her holster flap with one hand and gripped her pistol with the other. "Who do you think—"

The rating standing behind her in the truck bed leaned forward. He clouted the officer across the head with the butt of his impeller.

The impact sounded like an axe on a tree trunk. The officer's arms flapped as she flew out of the gun truck and hit face-first on the brick roadway.

The Kostroman who'd struck her pointed the impeller from his waist at Daniel. "You got a problem with that?" he said.

"Hell, why should we save good booze for rich officers who never did anything for us?" Adele Mundy demanded shrilly. "Let's drink it *all* ourselves, I say!"

"Too damned right!" Hogg seconded. He hopped out of the van and stumped over to Daniel. "All of it!"

"All right, all right," Daniel whined in what he hoped sounded like angry resignation. "We'll say it was hijacked. The way things are tonight, nobody's going to know the difference."

Somebody cheered. The Kostroman who'd hit his officer jumped down and started for the warehouse door. The ratings from both the van and the gun truck surged after him. Woetjans and three of her huskier fellows held back slightly to be sure of entering behind the last of the Shore Police.

Daniel put his hands in his waistband and began to whistle very softly.

Adele stood near the door of the warehouse. If she hadn't known better, she'd have been sure that the activities within were carefully rehearsed.

The van's headlamp threw a fan of light into the building. The sailors' figures cut it into wobbling, distorted shadows.

"Now!" called Woetjans. She grabbed the barrels of two impellers and jerked the weapons upward, out of the hands of the policemen carrying them. Dasi hit one on the head with his prybar; Sun grabbed the other from behind by both elbows and ran him headfirst into a brick pillar.

There wasn't a shot or even a shout in the whole operation. Glass shattered as somebody broke a brandy bottle over a Kostroman's head, but there were plenty more where that one came from. The Shore Police were down before they knew there was anything waiting for them except cases of liquor.

"All shipshape, sir," Woetjans called.

"Five of you put their armbands on," Daniel called. Hogg had gone to the warehouse doorway with his pistol ready, but his master was kneeling over the Kostroman officer. "Adele, come here if you will."

It sounded like an order rather than a request to her; perfectly proper under the circumstances. She went to Daniel's side.

He was unfastening the officer's belt and holster. Now that the victim was lying in the beams of the gun truck's lights Adele could see she was a young woman with tight blonde curls and rat-like features. The right side of her scalp oozed red, but she was breathing normally.

Looking up again, Daniel said, "I think this'll fit you. Get into it fast. We'll have to hope that the gate guards don't pay a lot of attention to you as we leave."

"Oh," said Adele. She saw the logic immediately: the guards had called a squad of Shore Police to check on the van they'd passed into the compound. If the van tried to leave unescorted, the guards were going to wonder what had happened to the squad. It was at least possible that they'd come up with the right answer. None of the female Cinnabar sailors was slim enough to pass for the police commander.

Understanding was one thing. The thought of actually pretending to be a Kostroman officer, *acting*, made Adele queasy with stage fright. She'd never liked being in front of groups or having everyone look at her.

Aloud she said, "Yes, all right."

She shrugged out of her tunic. The Kostroman uniform wouldn't have a pocket for her personal data unit. For now she could bundle her own trousers around it and carry the packet under the seat of the police vehicle.

Daniel finished stripping the Kostroman officer, then walked to the warehouse doorway while Adele dressed. "Tie them but not too tight," he ordered the sailors inside. "I want them to be able to get loose after we're gone."

Adele pulled on the officer's trousers. They fit properly, but the uniform was cut tighter than she liked. Frustration at the rub of the cloth built to momentary fury. She reminded herself that she

was merely transferring her anger at the whole situation to something trivial—and the situation was more her own fault than that
of anyone else around her.

Perhaps that was why she was so *very* angry.

Daniel came back to her. He pulled the pistol from its gilt leather
holster and said, "I don't suppose you've ever used one of these,
Adele?"

"No," she said. It was an electromotive pistol of local manufacture; she'd never fired or even handled one. The weapon was
very bulky, but its projectiles were no bigger or faster than those
of the little Cinnabar weapon in Adele's pocket.

For all that, Kostroman weapons were satisfactory if you didn't
mind their size. Vanness's death was proof of that.

Daniel grimaced as he stood. "Well, I didn't think you would've,"
he said. "Look, this is the safety; push it forward with your thumb
to shoot. But it's probably better if you don't try that. You're likely
to do more harm than good."

Adele opened her mouth in amazement. It took her a moment
to realize that Daniel's question had been meant in a general
nature—"Have you ever fired a gun?"—and she'd answered words
that he'd actually used: "Have you ever used a Kostroman pistol
like this one?"

"I'd like to wear it myself," Daniel added, looking toward the
warehouse from which the sailors were now carrying the brandy
they'd come here for in the first place. "I don't dare, though. The
lieutenant of a detachment of armed Shore Police has to be armed
herself. Oh, well."

He reholstered the pistol and handed it to Adele. She started
to correct the misunderstanding, but the words caught in her throat
from embarrassment and a degree of anger. Who was *he* to assume
a Mundy of Chatsworth didn't know how to shoot?

Before she could decide what to say, Daniel walked over to the
line of Kostromans his sailors had dragged out of the warehouse.
They were bloody and bound with their own tunics, but none
of them seemed as seriously injured as Adele would have assumed.

Daniel looked down at the captives with his hands on his hips.
"You shouldn't find it hard to get free," he said in a pleasant tone.
"What you do then is your own business. We're going to leave the
warehouse open, so if you want to have a good time and make some
money selling what you don't carry away inside you, go right ahead."

The Cinnabar sailors waited in respectful silence, listening to their commander with as much interest as the Kostromans showed. They knew their lives depended on Daniel making the right decisions.

"On the other hand, you may decide to report exactly what happened here," Daniel continued with a smile. "I'm sure your lieutenant will be particularly pleased to give her version of events. It's your choice."

He turned. "Everybody ready?" he said. "Adele? Then let's mount up. Police armbands in the gun truck, the rest of you as before. Hogg leads in the van and our police escort follows."

"Duty stations!" roared Woetjans, who wore a Shore Police brassard herself. She climbed behind the steering yoke of the gun truck.

Adele had barely settled herself on the other seat in the cab before Hogg pulled the laden van past them. Gunning her engine, Woetjans fought the truck through a turn and roared onto the roadway in pursuit.

Adele wondered what a lieutenant was supposed to do. As for what Adele Mundy was supposed to do—her computer was under the seat, ready for use.

And her own pistol was in the side pocket of the borrowed jacket.

Candace's uniform was too tight on Daniel's shoulders and thighs despite being loose at the waist and decidedly baggy in the butt. It might have made Daniel feel as though he was in better shape than he'd given himself credit for; in his present mood, he just felt uncomfortable.

A starship was landing in the Floating Harbor, waking echoes and ghostly reflections from the marshy landscape. Under the circumstances, this was probably an Alliance vessel concerned with the coup: a warship, or another transport loaded with troops and heavy weapons.

Daniel'd almost fallen backward when he climbed into the cab carrying a case of brandy. *That* didn't impress him with what it said about his physical abilities.

Hogg glanced over at the liquor balanced on Daniel's knees. "There was room enough in back, you know, even before the six of them transferred to the cop car."

"This is for our friends at the gate," Daniel said. "I don't want to open the back up when we stop for them."

"Ah," said Hogg. The road ahead wobbled like a topo map where seepage had softened the bedding layer; Hogg slacked the hand throttle slightly. "Seems to me," he went on with his eyes on his driving, "that changing styles after you find one that works isn't generally very smart."

"We could've locked the police patrol in the warehouse," Daniel agreed. "And we could bull our way out the way we got in, more or less."

He smiled to think about that. He'd treated the gate guards as he would have done a gang of recruits too raw to understand discipline of any but the most basic sort. An officer rarely had to use his hands on a properly manned ship, because the experienced personnel hammered insolence out of a cocky recruit during the first "lights out."

"But you know, if the whole complex is looted while the guards are drunk," Daniel continued aloud, "or better still *by* drunken guards, nobody will even know we existed. I prefer that to leaving a trail of bodies and pissed-off survivors behind. You take more flies with honey than vinegar, Hogg."

Hogg snorted. "And what's a fly's pelt worth, young master?" he said. "For the things that *are* worth the trouble of skinning, I find a wire noose generally works best. But I take your meaning, sure."

The three-barred gate, backlit by the pole lamp forty yards down the approach road, was closed again. There was a small light on in the brick guardhouse that formed the east gatepost.

Kostroman ratings moved to either side of the roadway as the vehicles approached. They lifted their impellers but didn't point them.

Hogg downshifted and crawled the last hundred feet to the gate in the van's bottom gear. The cab doors were front-hinged. Daniel unlatched his and let inertia swing it fully open as the van finally halted. He put his foot on the running board, swung the brandy to his shoulder—no problem, thank God—and stepped to the ground.

"Here you go, my friends," Daniel said breezily as he walked toward a Kostroman. He deliberately chose the rating he'd choked unconscious when they arrived. "This case was broken in transit, you know the sort of thing."

He hunched the brandy off his shoulder and swung it to the startled Kostroman. The man tried to take the gift while still holding his impeller. The weight was too much—the case was wood in addition to the glass bottles themselves—so he dropped the weapon to use both hands.

"I wouldn't want you to think a gentleman of L'ven can't be generous," Daniel said avuncularly.

The other ratings converged on their fellow. One of the trio outside started to climb over the gate to get her share, despite the petty officer's angry command.

Daniel put a hand on top of the case as Kostromans jostled for possession. "Let's let me get out of here first, shall we?" he said. He dipped his left index finger toward the gate.

"Right!" bellowed the petty officer. "Open the gate and then we'll see what we see about the other."

"I'll look after the brandy," Daniel said with a paternal smile at the six ratings trying to hold the brandy. "Just set it down here."

The Kostromans looked at one another. The one in the middle knelt and set the case on the brick pavement. Then as one they rushed to the gate, drawing it open with even more verve than they'd shown when they admitted the van in the first place. Daniel wondered idly if the ratings ever obeyed their own officers as well as they did him.

Well, from what he'd seen, there wasn't much reason to obey Kostroman officers. . . .

Hogg revved the engine when he thought there was clearance enough. Daniel waited in seeming leisure until the Kostromans returned, a little winded from their exercise. He nodded to them as he got into the truck.

"Gently, now," he ordered Hogg. "We don't want them to think we've just robbed the bank."

Hogg grimaced, but he pulled through the gateway at a rate that didn't, for a change, seem calculated to tear the transmission out of the van. The gun truck followed.

The ratings had begun trying to pry open the case with their impeller muzzles. Several of them cheered Daniel as he rode away.

The streets of Kostroma City were busier than Adele remembered them being earlier in the evening. Black and yellow bunting or a banner flew from every civilian vehicle she saw, but many of them obviously carried would-be neutrals who were leaving town with the most portable of their valuables.

There were still jitneys full of Zojiras and gangsters who wore Zojira colors for the time being. Some vehicles carried prisoners; others were packed with loot.

"The Alliance's got people up on the rooftops already," Woetjans muttered in obvious disquiet. She drove the gun truck with competence but no flair, gripping the yoke as if to hurl the vehicle into turns by main force. "We should've gone around the city instead of straight back through it."

Adele had seen groups of two and three people watching the street from roofs as they passed, but she'd thought of them as spectators or owners guarding their homes. They were armed, but that was natural enough too. Woetjans's experienced eyes had noted uniforms and equipment that meant something else again.

The Zojira clan was terrorizing its enemies; native-born Kostroman criminals were making fortunes. The Alliance of Free Stars was focused on control of the planet rather than such ephemeral affairs.

"Hogg didn't have any choice," Adele said soothingly. Woetjans was rightly nervous about the situation, but blaming Hogg might cause problems later. "All the roads on the island go through the city, at least here on the south tip. The whole planet was settled from this spot."

"Yeah, well, I guess Mr. Leary knows what he's doing," Woetjans said. "Him being in charge's the only good luck there is in the whole business."

Adele didn't see how Daniel *could* possibly know what he was doing, but she wasn't going to say that now. Daniel seemed to be on top of the situation, that was true.

Perhaps that was all there really was to being a naval officer: you pretended that you knew what you were doing. It didn't work that way in her specialty, information retrieval, though.

Hogg's van slowed. Daniel leaned out of the cab and waved the gun truck forward.

A gang was looting a house, carrying furnishings through the smashed front door to a barge in the canal which ran down the center of this boulevard. Several members acted as traffic wardens, gesturing oncoming vehicles to reverse and cross the humpbacked bridge to the other side of the road.

"Look alive," Woetjans said over her shoulder. The four sailors in the back were already aiming. The automatic impeller clanked as the gunner charged it to fire.

Adele wondered if she should unclip the sub-machine gun. She decided not to: if it came to shooting, she was probably better off with a familiar weapon.

Woetjans started to pull the gun truck around the van. The gangsters scattered to either side. Hogg accelerated again, brushing the end of a couch dropped in the haste of those who'd been carrying it. Inlays of ivory and mother-of-pearl splintered away like butterfly wings. The wheels bumped over a fallen cushion; then they were through.

"How many spaceports are there on Kostroma anyway?" Adele asked, deliberately casual to settle her stomach. A body beneath the wheels would have felt just the same.

"One bloody one if you mean starport," Woetjans said grimly. "There's some trade from other islands to the asteroids. The mining and manufacturing base on the asteroids, that does some direct out-of-system trade. It'll be in Alliance hands too, but I wouldn't be surprised if Mr. Leary figured to slip us up there by one of the provisions ships."

She looked at Adele and added, "I don't guess they'll be expecting somebody to steal a ship from the asteroids, don't you think?"

"That may very well be," Adele said.

She felt hollow. What the exchange proved to her was that Woetjans, far more experienced than she was—or Daniel Leary was, if it came to that—didn't see a way out of this system-wide trap. All they were going to accomplish by running in circles this way was to be shot down instead of simply being interned.

They were approaching a plaza dominated by the palace of a clan that had ruled Kostroma in the era before the Hiatus. The building remained an imposing mass of age-darkened brick, but the rooms were now laborers' apartments. The topmost—third—story had been split by an intermediate floor. The new ceiling ran like a horizontal bar across the banks of high windows.

The plaza's two large fountains were dry. The local residents had converted them to rubbish dumps. Eight streets joined in a circle around the plaza. The van entered and slowed abruptly; because of the traffic, Adele thought, and then realized that an

Alliance APC squatted in the middle of the plaza between the fountains.

Over a hundred armed Zojiras were checking every vehicle that entered the circle. Each local squad had an Alliance officer, and Alliance troops were in force on the rooftops.

The jitney ahead of Hogg's van stopped and tried to back out of the plaza. The nearest Alliance officer spoke into his helmet's integral microphone. At least six marksmen opened fire from the rooftops.

Impeller projectiles moved at the speed of meteors. They punched through the vehicle's flimsy body and everything within, then shattered the pavement on the other side. Shards of brick pavers flew about like grenade fragments, but the projectiles vaporized when they finally hit something hard enough to stop them.

The driver sprawled out of his saddle. There'd been someone inside the back as well; her arm flopped into sight when a projectile severed the door latch. Diesel fuel gurgled in a glistening dark circle beneath the jitney. It didn't ignite, though an oil fire licked sluggishly from the riddled engine.

"Pull ahead of the van," Adele ordered crisply. She stood in her seat, bracing herself with a hand on the top of the folding windshield.

"We can't fight all these—" Woetjans said.

"Do as you're told!" Adele said. She licked her dry lips and added, "We're not going to fight anyone. I'll talk us through."

Woetjans rang the electric bell of the gun truck to warn Hogg she was moving past. Kostroman gunmen were already approaching the van from either side as the Alliance officer looked on. A Zojira leveled his sub-machine gun at Woetjans.

"Stay here," Adele said as she got out and walked toward the troops. "You, sir!" she called to the Alliance officer.

"The navy doesn't cut any weight tonight," said a gunman. He reached for the handle of the van's concertina door.

"Don't touch that vehicle if you hope to see the morning!" Adele said, speaking Universal in an upper-class Bryce accent.

She pushed aside the pistol another Zojira rather diffidently pointed at her torso. Her nose wrinkled with the smell of diesel fuel and the feces the jitney's driver voided when he died.

"I'll handle this," the Alliance officer said. He stepped forward to join Adele at the van's front fender. "Yes, who are you?"

His accent was Pleasaunce, and he quite clearly realized that Adele didn't sound like a local. He was a young man with a trim black mustache and a tic in his left eye.

"My name doesn't matter," Adele said. The officer was uncertain and she was not; she ruled the situation, even though a word from this *boy* could mean her life in an eyeblink. "The Kostromans in both these *vehicles* are operating under my orders. Call your superiors and tell them this is code Blue Chrome. If they find any difficulty in confirming my free passage, they are to ask Mr. Markos. Do you understand?"

The officer scowled at her. His tic was worse. "Step back, please," he said. Adele sneered and stayed where she was.

The officer backed a slight distance himself and spoke into his helmet pickup. Adele couldn't hear the words, but she saw his lips form "blue chrome."

It was the code for securing Kostroma. She'd found it in the Alliance message traffic she'd browsed while she waited in the warehouse complex for the Cinnabars to load the van. Nothing in the messages themselves mattered to the escapees, but Adele's knowledge of the code word gave objective proof of what her accent implied: that she was an Alliance agent working under cover.

Markos's name didn't mean anything to a low-ranking officer overseeing a checkpoint, but it would to his superiors. They would be no more likely to question Markos or delay one of his agents than they would stick their head into a hot furnace.

A hot furnace was, after all, a very possible end for anyone who got in Markos's way.

The officer's mouth opened silently as he listened to the response to his question. "Yes, sir," he said loudly. He gave his head a reflexive nod. "Yes *sir*. Balthasar Three-One out."

"Make sure we're not bothered by any of the rest of this rabble," Adele ordered without waiting for the officer to address her directly. She waved toward the next inspection post along the circle. "And don't log this. Don't even remember it, do you understand?"

"Yes sir," the officer said. "You're free to go, sir."

"Go on ahead," Adele said in a curt voice to the cab of the van. She strode back to the gun truck.

Hogg and Daniel looked as though they were in awe of her. She could trust them both to do a perfect job of acting when it counted.

✧   ✧   ✧

Beyond the northern outskirts of Kostroma City the road became gravel and was in increasingly poor repair. The van was so overloaded that its rear springs were bottomed even before a wheel hit a pothole. Daniel supposed the jolts weren't as bad in the cab as they were in the back, but they were bad enough.

"Okay, there it is," Hogg said as their headlight swept the corner of a building through a screen of vegetation. "Now, I'm not telling you what to do, sir, but these are probably folks *I* know."

"Yes, of course," Daniel said. "You'll handle the negotiation if the situation's as we expect."

The road turned 90 degrees; Hogg slowed. As the van wallowed through the deep rut on the outside of the curve, its headlight painted a sizable waterfront community of two- and three-story buildings.

"Why, these are real houses," Daniel said in surprise. For the past several miles the only dwellings he'd seen along the roadside were shacks with roofs of sheeting and walls of scrap wood. "I hadn't expected . . ."

"Smuggling's a pretty good way to get rich, sir," Hogg said. "A pretty common one, too."

The buildings had shops on the ground floor and housing on the upper stories. The brick used to build them had a rustier shade than the peach and pale yellow general in Kostroma City. The broad pavement between the buildings and the harbor was brick also. Goods were stacked there, sometimes under tarpaulins, but the only permanent structure was an octagonal brick office for the harbormaster.

The harbor sheltered at least a hundred vessels. Small boats were in the majority, many of them racked three and four high in roofed sheds. A number of barges and yachts lay along the quay.

The community built around this little harbor wasn't as abjectly terrified by the coup as Kostroma City. Windows were shuttered, but lights were on inside as the residents waited for the next act in the drama. The harbormaster's office was lighted also. It seemed to be the headquarters for the twenty-strong garrison.

Daniel assessed the guards coldly: thugs, few of whom had taken the trouble to pin on Zojira colors. Much as he and Hogg had expected.

The headlights had warned the garrison of company coming.
Each had a sub-machine gun, and many wore pistols or knives
to look even more threatening. In addition to personal weapons,
there was a six-wheeled flatbed truck with an automatic impeller pointing out over the cab.

The heavy weapon was aimed at Daniel and Hogg. That was
as expected also.

"Okay," Hogg said softly as he slowed the van to a stop twenty
yards from the harbormaster's office. The armed flatbed was parked
alongside, while most of the thugs used the seawall as a trench and
aimed their weapons over it. "It's Ganser's lot, okay. I've done business
with him, but he's not one I'd ever want to turn my back on."

"All right," said Daniel. He and Hogg opened their doors
together, slowly and smoothly. "You deal with him and I'll brief
the detachment."

"You bastards turn around and go back where you come!" a male
voice called from the office. "This is ours, do you hear?"

"It's me, Ganser," Hogg called. He stepped in front of the van
so that the headlight fell across him at an angle. Hogg had a big
Kostroman pistol shoved under his belt, but he kept his hands
clearly in the open. "Time for us to do some trading, that's all."

Hogg sauntered toward the office. Daniel nodded in acknowledgment to the garrison, then walked to the back of the van and
opened it. He didn't need to have seen the jitney riddled to know
what a burst from the automatic impeller would do to everyone
in the back of the van.

He smiled pleasantly to reassure any watching thugs who might
have itchy trigger fingers. "Get some distance between you," he
said to the ratings poised tensely within. Sun now had the pistol Woetjans had given up when she moved to the gun truck. "If
anything happens, run for the marsh."

Whistling, his hands in his trouser pockets as he mimed care-
free innocence, Daniel walked to the gun truck. Woetjans had
stopped twenty yards away. She'd switched off her headlights so
that they didn't silhouette the van if shooting started.

The ratings with stocked impellers had spread out from the
vehicle; one of them watched the road behind in case the garrison'd
had sense enough to set an outpost there. Daniel doubted they
had, but it was a professional concern that spoke well of his
personnel.

Woetjans remained in the driver's seat. Lamsoe, the gunner, had his automatic weapon aimed not at the garrison's truck but at the harbormaster's office. A burst would disintegrate the small brick building. Adele Mundy, looking more like an officer than anyone else Daniel had seen in a Kostroman uniform, stood slim and disdainful beside the gun truck.

Daniel'd been amazed at the way the librarian had breezed them through the checkpoint. He'd been counting on the confusion to get his Cinnabars out of Kostroma City. The Zojiras weren't organized enough to freeze all movement, and Daniel's story of being on a personal mission for Grand Admiral Sanaus was both believable and impossible to check in the present chaos. His accent was a danger, but this wasn't a night they could hope to survive without danger.

"Hogg is going to rent a ship for us if things work out," Daniel said. He didn't want to shout, so the three ratings at a distance probably weren't able to hear him. "He says that the people we're dealing with aren't to be trusted, so keep a particularly close watch until we're out of here."

Adele sniffed. "I wouldn't think anyone on Kostroma tonight is to be trusted," she said. She didn't sound concerned; just analytical.

"Except ourselves," Daniel agreed.

Hogg left the harbormaster's office after a brief conference. Daniel went to meet him, striding more purposefully now. Kostroman gunmen were climbing up to sit on the seawall instead of sheltering beneath it. A shouted summons brought them all into the office, even the trio manning the automatic weapon.

"There's a twenty-meter yacht, the *Ahura*," Hogg said as he met Daniel beside the van's cab. It was a tribute to Cinnabar discipline that the ratings who'd moved away from the vehicle didn't bunch closer to hear what Hogg was discussing with their commander. "Solar powered, electrostatic foils, a real beauty. They'll let us have it for two cases of brandy and the trucks we come in."

"It's stolen?" Daniel said, squinting toward the harbor. He saw what he thought was the vessel, a trim craft tied up at a quay just at the edge of the lighted area. A yacht like Hogg described was at least as expensive as a luxury aircar.

"Next thing to it," Hogg agreed. "The owners were on the wrong side when the Hajas took over, so it got confiscated along with their houses and all. Now that the Hajas are out, the survivors are going to come claiming their stuff. Ganser figures if the *Ahura* goes missing, nobody's going to be able to prove it was his lot responsible."

Daniel looked from the yacht to the office. With his goggles down he'd be able to see through the building's windows, but identifying himself to this gang by using Cinnabar gear probably wouldn't be smart. "It still seems too good a bargain," he said.

"Yeah, I think so too," said Hogg with a sour expression. "But I don't see much choice but to keep our eyes open and go ahead."

Daniel clapped his servant on the shoulder. "When we drive to the quay to unload, we'll be on the back side of their automatic," he said. "Without an edge like that, this sort won't start anything."

He waved to the scattered ratings. "Mount up!" he ordered. "We'll transfer our rations to the ship over there, then we'll take a little vacation."

Daniel believed in planning if you had the time and information to do it; but if you didn't, you acted anyway. There was only one thing worse than trying to imagine every possible occurrence when you were for all practical purposes flying blind: remaining frozen because you *couldn't* imagine every possible occurrence.

"And if they do start something, Hogg," Daniel said as he got into the cab beside his servant, "then we'll deal with it."

Adele had made a half-hearted offer to help load the ship. Woetjans had said, "No, mistress, you're an officer," in a tone that made it sound like, "You'd be more trouble than you're worth."

Adele didn't take the implication as an insult since it was objectively true in her opinion. She stood at the top of the seawall, out of the line of traffic, and observed events.

Hogg had backed the van to where steps led down to the quay, but the distance from there to the *Ahura* was too great for the Cinnabar sailors to form a human chain. They carried the rations, one carton per trip.

Woetjans and three other sailors dismounted the automatic impeller from the police vehicle, then carried it and its case of ammunition to the ship also. The weapon had to be rigidly mounted to be of any use; the truck's pintle was welded to the frame and couldn't be removed. Either Woetjans thought she could jury-rig a mounting on the *Ahura*, or she was just making sure the gun wasn't in Ganser's hands while the Cinnabars were still in range.

The Kostromans hadn't volunteered to help load the *Ahura*. Adele doubted that Daniel would have permitted them to become involved anyway. They stood watching and occasionally talked among themselves in low voices. She knew that she was imputing sinister motives to the gang members because of their appearance, but people who went to so much effort to look sinister probably *were* a scurvy lot.

The armed sailors stayed aboard the *Ahura* while their fellows made multiple trips with the cargo. Daniel must have decided that he wanted his available weapons concentrated aboard the vehicle on which the Cinnabars hoped to escape. He'd called Adele to him; she'd shaken her head and remained where she was.

The back of the flatbed truck was twenty feet away from her. The heavy sheet of armor welded behind the cab protected the gun crew from fire from the front, but because of the way the automatic impeller was mounted, it could only sweep an arc of about 60 degrees to the right or left of the direction the truck was pointing. So long as the truck stayed where it was, the gun didn't threaten the *Ahura*.

Adele might not be any use in carrying boxes to the ship, but she was quite confident that the automatic impeller wasn't a danger to the Cinnabars so long as she survived.

Daniel had vanished within the *Ahura* to check the hull. Only then did he reappear to examine the cockpit. Now that Adele thought about it, there was only a superficial similarity between a spaceship and a marine vessel. Daniel might be the only Cinnabar present who knew anything about craft like the *Ahura*, and that because he was raised on the coast rather than from any sort of training.

Five Kostromans came out of the harbormaster's office and walked in Adele's direction. They were talking among themselves with studied innocence, but the strands of "conversation" didn't interweave: none of the thugs was listening to the others.

They were about to attack.

Three of the Kostromans, all men, went to the truck. The other two, a man and a woman, split off and stood on the seawall to Adele's other side, only six feet away. They faced the harbor, but their eyes flicked sideways toward Adele every few seconds. The man was describing the *Ahura*; the woman talked about the leaking roof that made a pool in her room every time it rained.

Adele turned her back on the pair beside her and watched them as reflections in a window of the office. When the Kostromans thought their target was no longer able to see them, both tensed.

Two of the other group hopped onto the back of the truck and sat there with their legs dangling over the side. The third man got into the cab. The engine ground for a moment, then started.

Adele lifted her right hand and ostentatiously scratched the back of her neck. Her left hand dipped into her tunic pocket and brought out the pistol, hidden in her palm.

The gun vehicle pulled twenty feet forward in a curve, then stopped. Its transmission went into reverse with a clang. The men pretending to relax on the back stood up. A sailor on the *Ahura* shouted a warning.

Adele turned toward the thugs beside her. The man started to point his sub-machine gun. Adele shot him at the top of the chest. The pistol snapped like a mousetrap in her hand, but the sound of the pellet hitting the man's breastbone was as loud as boards slapping. A muscle spasm threw the Kostroman backward over the seawall.

The woman lunged toward Adele instead of trying to use a weapon. Adele shot her in the throat. The pellet's temporary shock cavity gaped as wide as the woman's shoulders, nearly decapitating her. Most of the blood sprayed upward and back, but Adele felt droplets fleck her face. She turned, ignoring the touch of the dead woman's hand as inertia tried to complete the intended movement.

The truck was backing with the steering yoke reversed to bring the automatic impeller to bear on the *Ahura*. Several weapons were firing behind Adele. An impeller projectile hit the truck's armor and blew a glowing trench in the metal without penetrating.

The Kostroman gunners were behind their weapon; only their heads showed. They were thirty yards away from Adele. She aimed at the loader's nose and hit within a finger's breadth of that.

His head spun around as though a horse had kicked him; he went down. The gunner, his hand still on the impeller's charging handle, turned in surprise to look at his partner. Adele shot him in the temple.

Something stung the back of her right calf. She ignored it. She fired at the truck driver. The windshield shattered but she doubted pellets from her little pistol had enough mass to actually penetrate normal glass.

The driver leaped out of the cab, screaming and covering his face with one hand. He held a sub-machine gun in the other. He was moving and the light was bad. She fired twice more with no better target than his upper torso. He went down, but she could hear him still wheezing and gurgling in the darkness.

Adele walked toward the truck; it had stalled when the driver bailed out. The barrel of her pistol glowed red from the rapid fire. Pocket weapons like hers weren't intended for continuous use. The magnetic flux that accelerated pellets to 9,000 feet per second was dissipated as heat, and the light barrel didn't have enough mass to be a good heat sink. In an hour she'd have blisters on the web of her thumb and the side of her index finger where it touched the receiver.

She drew the Kostroman pistol with her right hand and dropped her own weapon into the empty holster. The leather would scorch but it wasn't likely to burn the way her pocket lining would. If she tossed the little pistol onto the bricks it might not be at hand the next time she needed it.

Nobody was paying any attention to her. All *her* opponents were dead. With the truck between her and the office, Adele looked over her shoulder.

Three bodies sprawled on the pavement. A sailor and a Kostroman thug wrestled for the latter's weapon. A Kostroman stepped out of the harbormaster's office and sprayed both indiscriminately with his sub-machine gun. An impeller slug fired from the *Ahura* tore the shooter's left arm off and flung his body sideways to thrash in a widening pool of blood.

The gang members had run into the brick office to join their leader when the shooting started. All the living Cinnabars were on the vessel or hidden beneath the lip of the seawall. The *Ahura* was far enough back that those aboard it could see over the seawall to a degree, but only the upper half of the building was visible to them.

Adele tried twice to climb onto the truck, using a back tire as a step. Finally she laid the service pistol on the truck bed to free both hands. She was still awkward but she got up.

The gunner had rolled off the vehicle. The loader still lay there on his back, his hands clawing spasmodically. Her pellet had cratered the left side of his face, but his right eye remained. It was open.

She'd never used an automatic impeller, but this one had a grip and a trigger like a pistol's. Adele depressed the weapon as far as it would and pulled the trigger.

The gun cycled three times before she could let up. The heavy projectiles cracked like thunderbolts, making the truck shudder violently from recoil.

The rounds blew platter-sized openings in roofing tiles as they hit; on exit they smashed even larger holes through the brick wall on the other side. A cloud of glowing gas slowly dissipated in front of the muzzle. It was the vestiges of the projectiles' aluminum driving skirts, ionized by the dense magnetic flux.

Without backing the truck, she couldn't lower the muzzle enough to hit the people sheltering inside the building. There was nothing more she could do.

"All right, Ganser!" Daniel Leary shouted from the *Ahura*'s bow. "That's your warning! Come out unarmed with your hands up or Lieutenant Mundy will blow you all into a crater in the street. Now!"

Adele retrieved the Kostroman pistol. If the gangsters tried to fight, she could at least use it.

"How do we know you won't just shoot us?" Ganser called from inside the office. He began to cough; a rosy haze of brick dust swirled from the shattered walls.

"You know we *will* shoot you if you don't give up!" Daniel said. He jumped from the ship.

"Master!" Hogg cried. Daniel ignored the servant and walked up the seawall's slope in plain sight of anyone looking out a window of the office. He was still unarmed.

"Last chance, Ganser," Daniel said cheerfully.

Somebody threw a sub-machine gun out the door. More guns followed. Sailors looked over the edge of seawall, some of them aiming weapons they must have taken from Kostromans in the initial confusion.

There was a long pause before the first of the thugs scuttled through the doorway, her hands raised and her eyes closed. Others crept behind her.

Adele felt her muscles relax without her conscious volition. She sat down in the truck bed because otherwise she would have fallen.

Daniel watched as Woetjans and Dasi finished tying the Kostromans with wire stripped from the back garden of one of the nearby houses. Daniel was willing to pay if the owner complained about the ruin of his snap beans, but nobody came from the house.

Daniel wasn't in a mood to volunteer anything.

Munsford and Olechuk were dead. Whitebread's belly looked like a rat had chewed her, but the wounds were superficial. The pellet had hit the carton she was carrying. It sprayed her with terne plate and fish stew instead of disemboweling her as direct impact would have done.

"You said you wouldn't kill us!" said Ganser, desperate to keep the question in his mind out of his voice. He was a fat man and already half bald despite being younger than Adele.

"Yes," said Daniel, thinking of Munsford and Olechuk. "I did say that."

Lamsoe was in line for an armorer's warrant. He and Tairouley were cutting down the *Ahura*'s flagstaff to mount the automatic impeller.

Hogg and the bulk of the detachment were on a scrounging expedition through the harbor's other vessels. The *Ahura* was in generally good condition, but she'd been laid up without maintenance for long enough that there were a few problems. Daniel's quick check had convinced him that the batteries wouldn't hold enough of a charge to keep the vessel under way long by themselves. The last thing they needed was a ship that was a sitting duck except in bright sunlight.

"Sir," said Woetjans quietly. Air-hardening ointment sheathed her right forearm to replace the skin she'd scraped off in diving over the seawall to safety. "They must have some friends at least in the houses here."

She nodded toward the facades. Stray projectiles had blown holes in the bricks; curtains fluttered behind a shattered windowpane. "If we leave them alive, they'll be free before we're out of the harbor. And the right man with an impeller can nail something as big as the boat from here to the horizon."

"You promised!" Ganser cried. "You promised—"

Dasi bent down and slapped the Kostroman with a hand as hard as a boot. Ganser screamed, spraying blood from lips cut against his teeth.

"Shut up," Daniel said in a quiet voice, "or I'll have your mouth taped."

If the tape covered Ganser's nostrils as well, the thug's face would darken until it was almost black; and then he would die. Like Munsford and Olechuk.

It'd be simpler just to tie a boat anchor to Ganser's ankles and those of the ten surviving members of his gang before dropping them into the harbor. There'd be nothing to watch but bubbles in that case, however.

"I didn't promise them anything, sir," Woetjans said. "Come on, Dasi, let's get this lot over the seawall."

Several prisoners began to scream or plead, but to Daniel's surprise most of the Kostromans continued to lie in numb silence. They'd been sure they were going to die from the moment they'd surrendered. It was the only sensible course for their Cinnabar captors to take.

And Daniel couldn't do it.

Woetjans rolled Ganser over on his belly and gripped the wire that bound the prisoner's wrists and ankles behind his back. She walked toward the harbor, hunching as she dragged her burden over the slick, wet bricks.

Adele Mundy walked out of the office. She'd been cleaning the pistol she'd used to end the attack almost before it started.

"No," she said. "Put them down."

Woetjans slacked the wire and looked at Daniel. "Sir?" she said.

Dasi stepped back from the two thugs he'd started to lift. They babbled in high-pitched voices. He kicked them to silence, one and then the other, as he waited for Daniel's response.

"I watched your other delegates executed earlier today," Adele said. "I don't want to see anything like that again. And I'm certainly not going to be a party to it."

She returned the flat pistol to her tunic pocket. She apparently carried it all the time, though Daniel hadn't had the least notion of the weapon's presence. He'd been surprised, but not nearly as surprised as the majority of the Kostromans who'd died here tonight.

"No," said Daniel Leary. "I'm not going to be party to it either."

He stood. "Woetjans," he said, "the *Ahura* isn't particularly spacious but there's room for more ballast. We'll carry this lot in the bilges and off-load them on an island when we're a good ways out."

Daniel smiled. A door in his mind had closed. He was very glad not to be looking at what lay behind it anymore.

"I wonder how well the bilge pumps work?" he added cheerfully.

Adele sat cross-legged on the yacht's bow, out of the bustle of sailors carrying equipment aboard and striding back for more. She tested the system once more, then switched off her data unit with a sigh of relief. She'd hoped she would be finished long before the *Ahura* left harbor. She'd made that personal deadline, but the business had taken nearly an hour longer than she'd expected.

Her expectations had been unrealistic. She should've known that Kostroma's comsat switching protocols would be as ineptly designed as the government data network had been. It was harder to overcome incompetence than it would have been to defeat deliberate protection.

She stood up with the care that her cramped thigh muscles required. She slid the little computer back in its pocket. She'd changed into her own clothes as soon as she'd finished cleaning her pistol. This way she didn't have to worry about the computer falling over the side unless she was going with it; in which case she didn't think she'd care.

The yacht rocked as two sailors boarded carrying a large piece of equipment slung to a pole between them. Adele didn't have any idea what it was. More batteries, perhaps, though she'd have thought the crew had by now stripped every vessel in the harbor that had a compatible electrical system.

Adele stepped around the forward solar sail; its furling mechanism was under discussion by three sailors. The sky was still an hour short of true dawn, but the crew needed to learn how to operate the equipment on which their lives would depend.

She entered the open cockpit just as Hogg left Daniel with a wave and a loud, "Okay, sir, you leave it to me!" Woetjans had been about to speak, but she nodded to Adele in deference.

"Daniel, you said you didn't trust the ship's navigation equipment," Adele said. "The Alliance fleet dropped a geopositioning system in orbit as soon as they arrived. I've tapped it. On a minute's notice I can tell you our location within three meters."

"You can?" Daniel said. "You did? That's wonderful! Woetjans, tell Racine to stop worrying about harmonizing the gyros and go help the team rigging the charging system shunts."

"Right," said the petty officer as she left the cockpit at a gliding run. After a lifetime among academics, it amazed Adele to see people who moved fast as a regular practice.

"I also modified the satellite controller to void all record of our use of the system," Adele added. "There's no risk of anyone tracing us back through our queries."

"What?" Daniel said in a tenser version of his previous surprise. "Is that really possible? I didn't think it was."

Adele sniffed. Her smile mirrored the cold pride within her. "I could do it," she said. "Though since the trace would have to be done through the Kostroman grid, I couldn't do it very easily."

Daniel laughed and clapped her on the shoulder. She blinked. That sort of friendly contact wasn't a part of academe either. "Well, we're getting there," he said. He seemed to relax to a degree as he talked to her. "I want to get under way as soon as the sun's up enough to power the engines, but . . ."

He shrugged, grinning like a little boy. "Until it happens, I won't be sure," he said.

Palfrey walked down the quay toward the yacht with fishing rods over one shoulder and a large case of some sort in the opposite hand. "The material you're taking," Adele said, nodding toward the sailor. "We're taking . . . ?"

She let her voice trail off in question.

"As of earlier today," Daniel said, "Cinnabar is at war with the Commonwealth of Kostroma." His voice now had no more give in it than a stone block does. "I won't countenance looting by any person under my command, but I'll cheerfully seize any material of military value."

His mouth quirked up at one corner; the expression was nothing at all like Daniel's normal friendly smile. "And if it's necessary to destroy civilian property to disrupt the enemy's military objectives," he went on, "I'll do that too. One of their objectives being to neutralize my detachment."

"Ah," said Adele. "Yes, I see that."

She wasn't used to thinking in military terms. She wasn't a

member of the military herself, of course. She wondered if that meant she'd be hanged as a—what, pirate?—if she was captured.

Daniel cleared his throat. He'd turned his head to examine the automatic impeller mounted at the right rear of the cockpit. With his eyes still on the weapon he said, "You know, if that was really the first time you'd used a pistol, you're a very fast learner."

He met her eyes and grinned shyly. "And a good thing for us, too."

"Yes, I'm sorry about that," Adele said. She caught herself turning away and overcame that embarrassed reflex by effort of will. Fiercely she continued, "I'd misunderstood your original question and I didn't correct my statement when I *did* understand. The Mundys of Chatsworth have always been great duelists. That tradition, at least, was one to which my father subscribed."

"He taught you well," Daniel said, nodding approval. "My family wasn't much for duels. I suppose if I'd lived in town I'd have had some training, but in the country it wasn't the thing. I'm a good wing-shot for bird hunting, but it's not the same thing."

"No," said Adele, "it's not. As you say, dueling is a skill of urban life, like eating with ruffed sleeves, that I'd prefer never to need. Never to have needed."

Hogg trotted down the quay, paused, and jumped the narrow gap to the *Ahura*'s stern. He stumbled as he landed but two sailors grabbed him before he fell.

"It's all set, master!" Hogg wheezed. "Transmit on fifteen point five for three seconds, that's all it takes."

"Woetjans?" Daniel called.

The busy confusion of moments before on the yacht's deck was past. Lamsoc took the grip of the automatic impeller and rotated it to point toward the buildings. Dawn was already lighting the roofs of the little community. The tiles were fiery orange, and the topmost windows reflected the sun in opalescent splendor.

"All present and accounted for, sir!" Woetjans said. She stood beside the cockpit, splitting her attention between the vessel and the shore. Sailors held the bow and stern lines, which were looped around posts but no longer tied.

"I have the helm," Daniel said, gripping the *Ahura*'s joystick control. He squeezed the thumb button; the two masts squealed as they rotated, aligning the solar sails with the rising sun.

"Twenty percent," Racine called from the power board read-outs on the left side of the cockpit. "Thirty-two percent."

The sailors had rigged four analog dials in addition to the original light-column display. The *Ahura* was designed for one-man operation if necessary, but Adele wouldn't have wanted to be that single man even without the equipment the Cinnabars had added.

"Cast off," Daniel ordered. Sailors whipped the lines they were holding away from the mooring posts.

Daniel's index finger touched another button on the joystick; a pump began to whir without load. "Fend us away from the dock."

Barnes and Dasi leaned into poles—cut-down jackstaffs. The yacht quivered, then inched sideways into the harbor.

Daniel twisted his joystick slightly and squeezed the throttle lever. The pump throbbed as water entered it and spewed out the rear. The *Ahura* drove forward, her bow swinging to port and Woetjans adding her strength to Dasi's pole to prevent the stern from rubbing.

"Fifty-nine percent!" Racine called.

"All right, Hogg," Daniel said. His servant touched a key of the cockpit radio.

A white flash lit the underside of Ganser's truck, still parked beside the ruined harbormaster's office. The sharp *bang* an instant later was simultaneous with the billow of orange fire enveloping the front of the vehicle. Hogg's small explosive charge had rup-tured the fuel tank and ignited the contents.

The *Ahura* drove toward the harbor entrance at increasing speed. The blaze on the waterfront would hold the attention of those in the houses. Lamsoe kept the automatic impeller trained on the community; other sailors had their weapons ready as well, but the yacht might have been leaving a city of the dead for all the response Adele saw.

The masts adjusted automatically so that the solar panels gathered the maximum available sunlight. Daniel was giving orders and the Cinnabar crew seethed with meaningful activity as the shore receded, but Adele's mind was in a place of its own.

The boy she'd killed had haunted her dreams for fifteen years. Now that accusing corpse would have five fellows for company.

✧   ✧   ✧

"We're at a hundred percent and rising, sir," Racine called. "Shall I bring the charging system on line?"

Racine was a fitter from the *Aglaia's* power room and seemed comfortable with the inside of delicate electronics. The riggers who made up the bulk of Daniel's detachment were resourceful and extremely good with their hands, but they tended to think in terms of breaking strain rather than impedances.

"Not yet," Daniel said. "I want her up on the skids first."

He turned toward Woetjans and said, "Prepare to deploy skids!"

"Grab hold, everybody!" Woetjans bellowed.

Daniel wasn't concerned about the ratings knowing what to do, but he glanced over his shoulder in the other direction to make sure that Adele had obeyed. She held one of the handgrips bolted to the cockpit sides. Her hair, almost as short as that of the naval personnel, ruffled in the twenty mile per hour breeze. This was the best speed of which the *Ahura* was capable with its hull wet.

Daniel grasped the lever in front of him with his left hand. He drew it back firmly.

The two narrow skids made a grinding noise as they rotated out of their housings in the forward hull. Miniature ball lightnings appeared to port and starboard, six feet from the cockpit. Daniel's hair rose on end. He'd been aboard electrofoils a dozen times, but this transition phase always made him wish he'd stayed on shore.

The *Ahura* lurched onto her skids with a crackling roar. Without the drag of her hull the yacht jumped ahead, though for the moment the waterjet continued to provide the propulsion.

The *Ahura* was levitating on static charges induced in the sea beneath her and precisely equal charges in the skids. Unlike a hydrofoil, the electrofoil could hover at a dead stop without any portion of the vessel touching the water.

"No drop in power, sir!" Racine said. "She's clean and the current's still going up. Shall I—"

"Not yet!" Daniel repeated. He set the automatic pilot for 60 mph, then engaged it while watching the bubble level.

The waterjet, the vessel's last contact with the sea over which she floated, retracted into the lower hull.

The *Ahura* surged ahead again, her speed continuing to build. The electrical charges were no longer in balance: the induced field migrated sternward by a matter of a few centimeters. The difference meant that the charges' repulsion thrust the hull forward instead of merely lifting it.

The yacht reached sixty miles an hour and steadied. Windthrust was a serious force, particularly for the ratings on the open deck. Daniel was sure he could increase speed by another twenty miles an hour, perhaps more, but the punishment the crew would take wasn't worth the increment.

The *Ahura* was as sweet a craft as a man could wish. She handled this heavy load with a smooth ride and perfect docility in the controls.

"Engage the charging system, Racine," Daniel ordered. "Cafoldi, come take the helm."

The batteries would charge from the excess of solar power over the needs of the foils. With luck the *Ahura* would be able to continue all night without reducing speed.

Cafoldi squirmed into the cockpit. He'd been a fisherman before he enlisted in the RCN. He placed his hand over Daniel's, then took control as Daniel stepped back.

Daniel relaxed with a great sigh. He hadn't realized how tense he'd been for how long.

They were well out of sight of land. Daniel met Adele's eyes and grinned broadly. "Getting away was the first stage," he said over the wind roar. "Next thing is to get some*where*. Can you find us an uninhabited island at least a thousand miles out, Adele? Say, fifteen hundred miles."

"I can find an island," Adele said. As she spoke she squatted in the back corner of the cockpit and drew out her personal data unit. "I can't guarantee that there won't be anybody on it, but I can find something that doesn't have a permanent population registered. There's probably a thousand possibilities to choose from."

"Wonderful!" Daniel said. "We're heading due east now, but direction doesn't really matter. I want to drop off our prisoners where they won't be found any time soon. Then we'll go somewhere else to wait things out ourselves."

He stepped past Adele and up on deck. Ratings grinned at him, though many had gone to the cabins below. They'd be packed in tight to use sleeping quarters meant for six civilians, but that was the way most of the spacers would like it.

Daniel walked forward to the far bow, bending against the wind of the yacht's passage. He lay flat with his face over the edge of the deck. Because the hull didn't touch the water there was no roostertail of spray lifting to either side, but an occasional wind-blown droplet slapped him with its familiar sting.

Below, the vivid life of Kostroma's seabottom shimmered with a beauty that relaxed him. First, to get away. Second, to plan and prepare.

And finally to come back, bringing the message the RCN had always brought to the Republic's foes. But that could wait until it was time to think about it.

BOOK THREE

A dele sat in the swivel chair that unfolded from the right side of the bow, comparing the atoll before her with the image projected from the little computer in her lap. The seat and the similar one across the deck were intended for sport fishermen; each was fitted with a rail and safety belt. Even now as the *Ahura* slid toward the shore on inertia alone, Adele felt better when she was strapped in.

Daniel was at the controls again. Cafoldi stood in the extreme bow, shading his eyes with an arm as he peered toward the water ahead. The *Ahura* had electronic depth-ranging equipment of the standard to be expected on a luxury yacht, but none of the navy men trusted it.

"Ease her right!" Cafoldi called. The *Ahura* rode a flat, crackling bubble of electricity. At this slow speed, the ozone which the system generated wasn't blown astern. Adele's nostrils wrinkled. "That's it, just a cunt hair!"

Lamsoe stood at the automatic impeller, scanning the shore. Most of the sailors were armed and on deck, some of them aiming toward the vegetation. Adele wasn't sure whether they were really concerned about a threat from the island or if they were just showing off with the armament they'd captured from Kostromans of various stripe. It seemed an empty exercise to her.

According to the satellite image, the atoll was comprised of a ring of eight islands connected by reefs. All Adele saw from the sea was a heavily overgrown hump against the lighter green of the water. Small birds flitted from the twisted shrubbery to the sea and back, dipping among the insects; their larger ocean-coursing brethren circled high overhead.

The *Ahura* glided toward the spill of tawny sand at the island's left end. Still farther left, water frothed in the currents and occasionally showed the teeth of the coral which combed just below its surface. The next island of the chain was a quarter mile beyond, shimmering like a mirage in the sea haze and the noonday sun.

The *Ahura's* static fields collapsed. She slid onto the beach, her hull grinding softly on the coral sand. Daniel threw switches in the cockpit, shutting down all the yacht's driving systems.

Adele felt enormous relief at the removal of the high-frequency tremble that had been a part of her existence for the day and a quarter of high-speed running. She'd become aware of the vibration only now that it stopped, but it had been present all the time—creating discomfort that she'd blamed on psychological factors.

"All right, let's get this cargo off-loaded!" Woetjans ordered. "Port watch, haul them up from the bilge; starboard watch stay on guard."

Adele put her computer away and unstrapped herself. Insects glittered silently in the air, sometimes lighting on her skin with a ghost touch. One brushed her eye; she grimaced and blinked rapidly in an attempt to wash it away.

Daniel came forward to join her. "Lovely, isn't it?" he said. "A real paradise. Of course, I don't suppose our prisoners are going to feel that way about it."

"I'm on their side," Adele said drily. "Thus far it reminds me of the unsorted storage in the subbasement of the Academic Collections building, bugs and all. Mind, the lighting's a lot better."

She waved her hand in front of her to keep more of the minute insects from landing on her face. It was like trying to sweep back the tide.

Cinnabar crewmen were bringing the prisoners up from below. Ganser and his thugs looked sickly and gray. They'd remained trussed like hogs throughout the run with only minimal time on deck for sanitation.

"Of course," Adele added, "some of them may be smart enough to remember what the alternative was. I doubt it. People like that prefer to invent realities in which they're always in the right."

"Not only people like that," Daniel said with a smile.

Four sailors hopped to the sand. Four others on deck took the bound prisoners by the shoulders and ankles and tossed them over the side. Adele blinked in surprise. She'd wondered how the thugs would be landed, but she hadn't expected anything so brutally efficient.

Although . . . it wasn't actually brutal. The Cinnabars treated their captives like so many full duffelbags, but the sailors on the ground caught each flung body and lowered it to the sand brusquely but gently. Most of the sailors would have been willing to put Ganser and his killers over the side in deep water, but needless cruelty wasn't a part of their character.

The sea moved in long swells, licking the shore of the island and surging against the reef. The water of the lagoon stood still and jewel-like, unmarred even by diving seabirds. It was dark blue in contrast to the pale green of the open ocean.

"Where do you want to go now?" Adele asked Daniel quietly. Most of the prisoners had been unloaded; Hogg walked among them with a pair of wire-cutters, snipping the bonds from their wrists and ankles. The Kostromans remained where they lay, perhaps unable as well as unwilling to rise while their captors grinned at them over gunsights.

"We'll get over the horizon before I decide," Daniel said. "Probably on a completely different course. I think we're all right, but I don't care to test our luck needlessly."

Adele nodded. She'd set the base unit in the Elector's Palace to search message traffic, Alliance and Kostroman alike, for any reference to Cinnabar, Daniel Leary, or Adele Mundy. She then used her personal data unit to scroll through the literally thousands of references to Cinnabar. Neither of the individual names had rated a mention.

And no reference to Cinnabar involved Daniel's detachment. He and his companions, Adele included, had dropped out of existence so far as anyone else on this planet was concerned.

The captives were all freed. The sailors reboarded the *Ahura*, grabbing the chromed rail at the deck's edge and hauling themselves up with a quick kick against the side of the hull. Dasi got a hand from his mate Barnes, but only Hogg bothered to use the ladder attached to the vessel's side.

"Woetjans, toss them a carton of rations," Daniel ordered. He faced the Kostroman thugs, his hands on his hips.

"I'm leaving you a little food," he said. "After that, you'll have to make do with what you find. There may not be fresh water here, but there's fruit and several of these plant species excrete salt to store water in their trunks."

He smiled brightly. "I hope you're up on your native biota," he said. "It's a fascinating one."

"You can't just leave us!" Ganser said.

"Oh, I certainly could," Daniel said. "But in fact I'll let people back in Kostroma City know where you are in thirty days or so. Of course, I can't guarantee that any of them will care."

Two sailors pitched a case of rations to the sand at Ganser's feet. The wood broke and steel cans rolled out.

Daniel turned. "Prepare to get under way!" he ordered. "I'll take the helm."

"The nozzle's clear, sir!" called Dasi, leaning over the stern to peer into the crystalline water. With the bow well up on the shore, Daniel preferred to drag the *Ahura* backwards with the waterjet rather than try to tickle a sufficient charge into dry sand.

"Everybody who doesn't have a job move back to the stern!" Woetjans ordered, a sensible command and one Daniel should have thought to give himself. The ratings trotted aft, lowering the stern by their weight and so lightening the portion of the vessel that was aground.

Daniel slowly advanced the throttle. He'd rotated the nozzle. The jet spewed forward, making the hull vibrate as though a hose were playing on the vessel's underside. The *Ahura* slid back in a boil of water, scrunching for the first few feet of her motion and then floating free.

Daniel chopped the throttle, looking over his shoulder to be sure that they were drifting clear and weren't about to hit something. He couldn't see behind because the crew was standing along the stern rail, but somebody would have shouted a warning if there was a problem.

On shore, the Kostromans glared at the vessel with undisguised hate. Adele stood at the rear of the cockpit. Daniel caught her eye and said, "There's plenty of natural food on the island, but I wonder whether that lot isn't more likely to try cannibalism instead?"

Adele sniffed. "For people of their sort," she said, "I suppose cannibalism *is* natural."

The yacht had left the sand at a slight angle. She now floated parallel to the shore and was beginning to curve back on her remaining momentum. "Spread yourselves out," Daniel ordered. "I'm going to bring her up on the skids."

He engaged the electrofoils while the ratings were still spreading forward. They moved with less immediacy than they'd run to the stern. The skids shuddered, but Daniel didn't hear a grinding as he had the first time he'd deployed them. Scale and caked lubricant had loosened with use; the *Ahura* was in better condition than she'd been in some while, probably since she was laid up.

Daniel Leary was in better shape than he'd been in a long while too. There was no worse way to treat tools or men than to leave them to rust.

The yacht lifted. Daniel knew he could trust the mechanism now, so he brought her directly into dynamic balance on the skids instead of waiting until the *Ahura* was under way on the waterjet. They were alone in this sea. They didn't need to adjust their conduct to the comfort of neighboring vessels.

"Clear at the bow, sir!" Cafoldi said; rote, since there was no doubt of the fact. A good crew handled even the most cut-and-dried operations by the book, never cutting corners.

Daniel twisted the joystick slightly to port, then increased the throttle pressure minusculely. The yacht wobbled ahead. The bow angled seaward. They slid past the end of the island.

"Don't forget to write!" Lamsoe called, waving to the stone-faced Kostromans twenty feet away on shore.

Spray exploded toward the *Ahura*. A pair of hundred-foot tentacles arched from the interior of the lagoon. The flattened tips were each the size of Daniel's torso and covered with fine cilia. They crossed the reef and seized the *Ahura's* starboard skid.

The yacht tilted with a wrenching clang. The electrofoils and the giant sweep's own bioelectrical charge interfered with one another. A rainbow nimbus lit the air twenty feet from the vessel's every surface.

The tentacles retracted, pulling the *Ahura* onto her stern. Ratings shouted curses as they went overboard. The sweep was dragging the skids and hull through the coral heads. There were a few shots, their sound almost lost in the vessel's grinding, snapping destruction.

Somebody with a sub-machine gun punched three holes and

a spiderweb of crazing in the windshield. The pellets missed Daniel's head by less than he had time to worry about.

He let go of the joystick because whatever input he had on the yacht's controls just made things worse. Adele was spreadeagled against the cockpit's port bulkhead, gripping two handholds.

The power board shorted in blue fire as salt water reached a conduit whose sheathing had been scraped away on the coral. An instant later a generator blew explosively; foul black smoke spewed up through hatches and the fresh cracks in the decking.

Lamsoe had gone over the side at the first impact, but the automatic impeller was still on its mount. Daniel grabbed its twin spade grips. The deck was no longer down; it sloped at 60 degrees as the sweep's powerful tentacles continued to contract. The creature was tipping the *Ahura* on her back, using the coral reef as a fulcrum.

Daniel braced his feet against a stanchion and one of the cockpit handholds. He thumbed the plate trigger between the impeller's grips.

The gun recoiled violently but the jury-rigged mount held. The first projectiles raked water empty except for the surge and bubbles stirred by the sweep's tentacles. Daniel shot the burst on, adjusting his aim by twisting his whole body and using the gun itself as a support.

The projectiles' kinetic energy blew the lagoon into an instant fog. He continued to walk the impacts toward the memory of his target: the point where the tentacles emerged together from the lagoon.

The *Ahura* was nearly vertical. Men and debris floated about her in the churning sea. Daniel's right leg twisted around the gun mount but his left foot dangled in the air.

Bright yellow blood geysered in the steam at Daniel's point of aim. Chunks of flesh, some of them bigger than a man, spun in all directions. A tentacle writhed across the water like a beheaded snake, both ends free. The other tentacle contracted in its final convulsion as the impeller emptied its magazine.

The *Ahura* tilted over on her back, falling toward the lagoon where bloody, boiling water subsided. The impeller slipped from its mount and tumbled on its own course, taking Daniel with it in the instant before he let go.

He caught a glimpse of Adele in the air. Her face was set and disapproving. One of her hands gripped the computer sheathed along her right thigh; the other was in the left pocket of her tunic.

"Cinnabar!" Daniel shouted as he hit the water.

Adele supposed she ought to be thankful that the water at the edge of the beach was shallow enough that she hadn't drowned. She'd come down on her knees, though, and the shock of the water and then packed sand three feet below the surface had made her nauseated with pain.

Even now, ten minutes after Cafoldi brought her onto dry ground in a packstrap carry, she walked stiff-legged. She'd be surprised if she didn't have bruises to midway on both thighs and shins.

But she'd found her personal data unit worked perfectly despite the ducking. It was at least an open question whether or not she'd prefer to have broken her neck if the alternative was to be stranded on an island without access to civilized knowledge.

Now that Adele had the mental leisure to notice, she saw that the sailors were all at work. Apparently nobody'd been killed or even seriously injured. For the most part they'd rolled into the water before the yacht flipped in the monster's final convulsion.

Daniel stood in the shade of a tree with small leaves and ropy branches. From each tip hung a nut that grew to the size of a clenched fist. While Daniel talked to Woetjans he peeled the flexible shell of a nut with a small knife, popping bits of the white flesh into his mouth at intervals.

He broke off and grinned broadly when he saw Adele approaching. "You ran your data link through its paces?" he called.

"Yes, thank God," she said. "It's supposed to be sealed against worse than a bath in salt water, but until I tried it I wasn't sure."

Daniel flicked off another piece of nut meat. He held it out to her between his thumb and the knife blade. She shook her head; she was still doubtful whether her modest breakfast of crackers and meat paste was going to stay down.

"What I was more worried about than damage," she went on, "was that I'd lose it and not be able to find it under water."

The *Ahura* had fallen entirely within the lagoon. The yacht's stern lay on the reef so several feet of the inverted hull were above water. Sailors diving beside the wreck were coming up with stores and equipment.

The water was a sickly green, a combination of colors leached from vegetation on the surrounding islands and the blood of the creature that had destroyed the yacht. Adele assumed the low, gray mound floating a hundred feet from the shore was the sweep's corpse.

"It's huge," she said, looking from the lagoon to Daniel. She couldn't imagine how he'd been able to aim as the *Ahura* shuddered up on end. She'd barely retained her holds on the bulkhead.

"Yes," Daniel said with a smirk of fully justified pride. "It's not a new species, I suppose, but it still should get my name into the records somewhere, don't you think? Big game hunting if not zoology texts."

He laughed with the easy assurance Adele had come to associate with him. "It was too big to ever leave the lagoon. It certainly wouldn't have had any competition for food inside the ring of the atoll, but I'll be interested to learn just what that food could be."

Barnes sat on the vessel's stern, holding tarpaulins and rope knotted into a pair of saddlebags. They hung to either side of the hull. Cafoldi, one of the divers, came up from the foul water with a shout and a sub-machine gun in his hand. He splashed on three limbs to the vessel and thrust the weapon into the bag on his side.

Ganser and his Kostromans kept their distance, glowering at the Cinnabars. They weren't precisely under guard, but any attempt to rush Daniel would have to get past Dasi holding an impeller by the barrel as a club and Hogg, who was trimming a point on a sapling he'd cut down with a knife much sturdier than the one in his master's hand. As a spear it looked crude, but nobody who knew Hogg would doubt it was lethal.

Lamsoe and Sun sat cross-legged on a mat of leaves cut from a parasol-shaped shrub. They were each stripping a sub-machine gun to its component parts. Adele obviously wasn't alone in doubting that any locally manufactured electronics, electromotive weapons included, could survive immersion in salt water.

She wasn't sure what the sailors could do to refurbish the guns, however. Flushing in fresh water, sun-drying and prayer, she supposed, but she recalled Daniel's question whether there *was* any fresh water on the island.

"Do you want me to call Kostroma City for rescue?" Adele asked quietly.

Daniel looked at her in surprise. "Good heavens, no," he said. "That'd be the same as handing ourselves over to the Alliance."

His concern broke in a smile. "We've invested quite a lot in avoiding that already. I don't think we need to give up just yet."

"I, ah . . ." Adele said. She looked at the web of jungle, then behind her to the open sea. You could sail a thousand miles across that ocean without finding land more promising than this on which she stood.

She knew that. She'd just come that thousand miles and more.

"You think we can live here indefinitely?" she said. "Well, I suppose you're the expert. . . ."

Daniel laughed aloud. "Now, did I say that I'd rather leave us here forever to rot than wait in a camp on Pleasaunce for an eventual prisoner exchange?" he said. "This is a delay, Adele. But we needed to lie low for a time anyway so we're not really losing anything."

He nodded toward the *Ahura*'s stern. Barnes was standing, holding one end of a line over which he'd strung the bags of salvage. A sailor stood in mud to her ankles pulling the bags to the shore. Two others waited nearby to empty the gear; the divers held on to the yacht and chatted while they waited for the bags to return.

"I don't think we'll be able to use the hull," Daniel said. "It's a one-piece casting and very tough, but when the integrity's breached the core of the sandwich starts to fray. Since we can't reheat the edges to three thousand degrees Kelvin, we're better off using wood. I'm pretty sure we can get the waterjet back in operation, though, and at least one of the solar sails."

"I see," Adele said, not that she did. She stared at the jungle, visualizing a boat made of *that*.

"You can access a forestry database from here, can't you?" Daniel said. "I've only got the once-over-lightly from the *Aglaia*'s library. We don't want to learn that we're building the hull of a tree whose sap makes people turn blue and die in a week."

He laughed. In the lagoon the divers were back at work, bringing up objects so disguised by clinging mud that Adele couldn't guess their identity. The atoll's outer face was clean sand and clear water, but the lagoon-side shores were gray-black muck that the ocean currents didn't reach to scour away.

"I can access any electronic information that I could have found for you while we were in Kostroma City," Adele said, feeling disassociated from the cheerful bustle about her. It was as though a thick glass wall encircled her, keeping her apart from her companions despite her presence in their midst. "I suppose there are botanical files as well as the zoological ones we've used in the past."

"You know?" Daniel said, looking out into the lagoon. He'd finished the nut; he tossed the rind into the undergrowth behind him to decay into nutrients like those that stained the still water. "If the *Ahura* hadn't been an electrofoil, we'd never have learned about the sweep. They're quite harmless to humans, you know. Though—"

His grin.

"—I wouldn't care to have gone swimming with that one."

"Yes, that's probably true," Adele said.

The contrast between her dour feelings of defeat and the cheerful optimism Daniel shared with his sailors suddenly amused her. She chuckled also. Daniel was genuinely glad to have observed a creature of previously unknown size. It had almost killed him and his companions; it had almost wrecked his plans to escape Kostroma—

But "almost" was the key word with Daniel Leary. He didn't worry about things that were past; it was at least an open question in Adele's mind whether he worried about the future either. Though she wasn't about to call him a simple man. . . .

Daniel and Woetjans were discussing food and water. Daniel nodded to the sailor's queries and clipped another ripe nut as he listened.

Adele walked past Lamsoe and Sun, stepping carefully so that the wind didn't blow sand particles from her soles over the dismantled weapons. Hogg, cleaning sap from his knife with a fibrous leaf, nodded to her, then grimaced.

Hogg had a bad bruise on the right side of his head. A film of ointment closed the scrapes and the cut above his temple, but Adele was afraid he needed better medical attention than was available here.

She stepped between Hogg and Dasi, facing the group of former prisoners. They stopped their low-voiced conversations and looked at her with a mixture of emotions. A sort of bestial *hunger* was part of the brew she saw now in the thugs' eyes.

Adele smiled. It was her usual version, an expression nobody could mistake for good-humored.

"You'll have noticed that all the guns were soaked when the boat was wrecked," Adele said. "You may believe that they won't work until they're properly cleaned, probably cleaned better than is possible here on this island."

"Mistress!" Dasi blurted in horror behind her. In the corner of her eye Adele saw Hogg move, putting a restraining hand on his companion.

Adele drew her own pistol from her jacket pocket. She fired off-hand. A bell-shaped fruit exploded on a branch twenty feet in the air, spraying pulp and seeds down onto the Kostromans. Ganser shouted and covered his bald scalp with his hands.

"My gun was made on Cinnabar," she said. "It works quite well."

Adele slid the weapon back into her pocket. "And so do I," she added over her shoulder as she returned to Daniel's side.

Sunlight awakened Daniel. It filtered through the shelter of leaves and saplings his ratings must have built around him while he was asleep.

"Why didn't—" Daniel said as he sprang upright. Every muscle in his body, particularly the big ones in his thighs and shoulders, grabbed him simultaneously. It was like being attacked by a platoon of madmen with icepicks.

"Mary Mother of God!" Daniel cried tightly. His mouth would have been content to scream instead.

Overwhelming pain had made his eyes blink closed. Memory painted across the inside of his eyelids an image of himself forty feet in the air, wrapped around the shuddering gun mount.

Daniel Leary had done amazing things yesterday, he'd tell the *world* he had, but exertion like that came with a price tag. He was paying it now.

"We thought you could use your beauty sleep, sir," said Woetjans, seated with her back to the shelter's end post. She stood easily and offered Daniel her hand.

"I'm not proud," he muttered. He took Woetjans's callused grip as a brace to hold him as his legs levered him upright.

After the first instant, it wasn't too bad. The first instant felt like the madmen had exchanged their icepicks for flensing knives.

He laughed at Woetjans's concerned expression. "Remind me

to get into shape before the next time I go out for trapeze," he said. "I'll be all right, I'm just stiff."

Very carefully Daniel stretched, locking his fingers behind his neck and arching his spine backward. He'd moved the detachment into a natural clearing formed by a protrusion of the igneous rock around which the island had grown. The ground cover was low-growing and soft. The hard rock wouldn't support larger vegetation, and the canopies of surrounding trees shaded but didn't cover the sky.

"Ganser's lot buggered off in the night," Woetjans said. "I don't guess that's much loss. They took a case or two of rations, but we had all the guns under guard with us."

"I wonder where they think they're going to go?" Daniel said with a frown. He didn't understand the situation, so it worried him. The Kostroman thugs had scarcely seemed the sort who'd be ashamed to take charity from a Cinnabar contingent which was obviously more competent at living rough.

"I told the crew to make sure they're always two together, even if they're just going around the next tree to take a leak," Woetjans said. "If anybody runs into a problem with the wogs, then I guess we'll finish things the way we could've done back on Kostroma."

Lamsoe and Sun, the detachment's armorer and armorer's mate by necessity, were in the clearing working on the guns. Daniel had seen enough of the pair to respect their competence but, like Adele, he very much doubted that the weapons *could* be safely reconditioned under the present circumstances.

"Where's Ms. Mundy?" he asked. He heard ratings calling from the forest, gathering food from the species he'd indicated before the sudden tropic nightfall of the previous day. They'd begun cutting wood besides. Rhythmic axe blows rang from deeper in the forest.

Hogg lay on a leaf mat, beneath a shelter like the one that had covered Daniel. At intervals Sun leaned over and mopped Hogg's face and mouth with a damp rag. Hogg was breathing hoarsely and, for the first time in Daniel's recollection, looked his age.

"She went back to the beach for a better line to the satellites she's using," Woetjans said, also a little grimmer for viewing Hogg. "There's six ratings there on the salvage detail, so no wog's going to catch her alone."

The big bosun's mate shook her head. "Mind, I'd bet her against the whole lot of them. She surprised the living shit outa me, she did."

"Yeah," said Daniel. "Me too."

He shrugged, loosening his muscles a little more. "I'm going to take her on a tour of the neighborhood," he said. "She can get me details on the wildlife through her computer."

Daniel grinned and added, "And she can be my bodyguard, so don't put on that sour expression, Woetjans. The rest of the detachment has its duties laid out, so I'm the party best spared for scouting."

Whistling and feeling better with every step—he still had a ways better to feel, he admitted—Daniel walked down the path to the beach. It was improved over the simple trackway they'd forced through the undergrowth the day before. The yacht hadn't carried machetes or axes, but the ratings had improvised.

Adele sat at the edge of the beach, her back to a tree with knobby joints in its trunk. Her legs splayed out before her instead of being crossed. As he'd expected, the personal data unit was on her lap and the wands in her hands. She didn't notice Daniel's arrival till Barnes shouted a greeting from the *Ahura's* upturned hull.

"I'm downloading everything I can find on Kostroman botany," she said by way of greeting. Despite the brusque opening, she'd smiled to see him up and about. "The files are an awful tangle. Everything on this planet is an awful tangle."

"That's why they need experts from Cinnabar," Daniel said cheerfully. "Let's take a walk and see if we can't do some untangling."

Adele shut her computer down and transferred it to its sheath with a stringent caution that any spacer could recognize and approve. Only then did she rise, using Daniel's offered arm as an anchor. It was like watching someone stand while wearing stilts. The two of them had stayed aboard the yacht until the instant it went over, so they'd had long dives into the water.

Daniel gestured to the left, past the salvage crew and along the lagoon side of the island. Fresh water was going to be a major concern when they left the atoll's fruit behind in their jury-rigged vessel, and barrel trees couldn't set their free-standing roots in ocean currents.

"A good thing we didn't hit the land," he said. He grinned. "Or the coral."

"When I got up this morning, I didn't think I could hurt any more than I did," Adele said as she fell clumsily into step with him. "My knees were the size of melons. By now some of the swelling's gone down and I'm almost glad that I wasn't killed."

Daniel blinked, then realized she was joking. He chuckled.

He supposed she was joking.

There was no path through the jungle anywhere on the island. Daniel would have been surprised to find it otherwise since large animals were unlikely to reach the atoll except if carried here by humans. It was fairly easy to move through the interior because the shaded undergrowth grew soft-stemmed and sickly, but to find the barrel trees they had to scout the margins.

He took the lead as they entered a thicket. The shrubs had thin, ropy stems with an explosion of green and yellow leaves at the peak fifteen feet in the air. Despite Daniel's weight, the plants resisted him like a human mob.

"How is Hogg?" Adele asked quietly from behind him.

"Not great," Daniel admitted, as he forced his way through to a less obstructive stretch of vegetation. He was sweating and breathing hard as he spread the last of the ropy shrubs for his companion.

"We can use these for fiber if we need to," he said to Adele. "Though there was plenty of spare line aboard the *Ahura*. That'll be simpler unless we can't locate it now."

Tiny insects shimmered about them, tickling as they drank human body oils and sometimes drowned in the droplets they craved. A wedge of lagoon entered the island here. Stalked eyes peered from the water, then vanished in bubbles and swirls of mud.

"They'll do nicely to expand our diet," Daniel said. "Crustaceans of some kind. There ought to be shellfish both here in the mud and on the ocean side."

He met Adele's eyes. "I'm worried about Hogg," he said. "He's got a concussion and there's not a damned thing we can do here except supportive treatment."

Adele gestured to her sheathed computer. "Any time you want . . ." she said.

Daniel shook his head. "No," he said. "I have responsibility for the whole detachment. Things happen in wartime."

Daniel took them inland to where they could step over the notch instead of trying to cross its original ten-foot width, even though that would have saved a hundred yards from their trek. He was sure that no major predator could have shared the lagoon with the giant sweep; but a day ago he'd have sworn that no sweep grew more than twenty feet in total length.

It wasn't as though they had a particular place to get to, after all. Daniel found two barrel trees on this side of the notch and saw another one across it. The squat trunk was hidden in the undergrowth but vast, billowing foliage marked the tree clearly.

Whenever he had a question, Adele squatted and brought out her personal data unit. When she'd come as close as she could from the parameters he gave her, she handed the miniature computer to him to refine the data.

The librarian's face as she parted with the unit was like that of a mother letting a drunken stranger hold her baby. She didn't protest, though, and only the perfect rigidity of her expression indicated the horror she must feel in her heart.

By midday they were only a few hundred yards from the sandy beach where they'd started their trek, but Daniel was even more confident that his plan of escape was practical. He could now point to the elements that would fulfill their needs instead of just being sure that he'd find them somewhere on the atoll.

"Time to head back, I think," he said. Before him was another notch into the island's fabric, this one only about five feet wide at the mouth. "I don't much like that sky."

Cumulus clouds had billowed into a wall across the western heavens. A thunderstorm had caught the *Ahura* on her first afternoon out of Kostroma. It was so violent that Daniel had shut down the foils, furled the solar sails, and ridden the waves for an hour and a half on waterjet alone.

"And besides, I could use some lunch," he added with a grin. "I could catch us each a mudhopper—"

He gestured to the shoreline. Eyes apparently floating on the water vanished in a swirl of mud.

"—but I'm not quite hungry enough to eat one raw."

Adele nodded. "I think I can live on stored body fat for long enough to get to the camp," she said.

She stepped aside to let Daniel lead on the way back as well. He turned—and as he did saw something in the corner of his eye.

"Ho!" Daniel said. "Oh, will you look at that? Yes, we *will* stop here."

He pointed down the narrow waterway to the clump of rough-barked trees some twenty feet away. On their branches grew fungus in stages of ripeness from white pimples all the way up to swollen yellow balls the size of a man's head. When fully ripe they dangled from a narrow umbilicus.

"Soap bubble fungus," Daniel explained. "It infects several species of nut trees. It doesn't seem to injure the tree seriously, so it may be a symbiotic adaptation."

Adele started to pull out her computer. "No, the *Aglaia*'s database covered soap bubble fungus adequately," Daniel said. He spoke softly because of an instinct not to rouse danger, though at this distance he and Adele weren't in danger. "The only really important thing to know about it is that you don't want to come within ten feet of it, or twenty if you're the cautious sort."

"It's poisonous?" Adele said. Even though Daniel had told her not to bother, she was calling up information from the material she'd downloaded this morning.

Daniel grinned. The way Adele turned to her computer was instinctive too: she didn't *own* knowledge unless she'd seen it written. The same words from the same source had more effect written than they did spoken.

"They're delicious when ripe, I'm told," Daniel said as he continued to eye the infected grove. The fullest of the fungus bubbles seemed to quiver with internal life. That was actually possible. "They'd be eaten by every bird or animal within fifty miles before they could open, if it weren't for the beetles that live inside them."

He pointed to the darkest, ripest of the fruiting bodies. "Anything that breaches the rind is set on by a dozen or so insects with bites like red-hot pokers. There's nothing on Kostroma that deliberately opens the fungus, and animals that do so by accident can be bitten to death."

"Even humans?" Adele said, now looking toward the globular fungus. Her control wands were motionless.

"Especially humans," Daniel agreed. "There's a few cases every year, city folk having a picnic and children who haven't been trained to be careful."

He grinned broadly. "I *am* getting a first-hand look at Kostroman natural history, aren't I? Rather fortunate to have been wrecked here, don't you think?"

"I don't know that I'd go that far," Adele said with her dry smile, "but I'm willing to be happy for you."

The rain hit when they were halfway back. At least, Daniel noted, it did something toward washing the caked sweat from their clothing.

By the time Adele and Daniel staggered into sight of the salvage crew on the *Ahura* she was dizzy with . . . well, she wasn't sure where to assign causation. The pain in her arm and shoulder muscles from hanging on while the yacht thrashed in the monster's grip was a factor. Exhaustion from walking through a landscape that fought her, carrying at the same time several pounds of mud clinging to either foot, was certainly a factor also.

And she assumed that the oppressive heat and humidity were working on her as well. She'd never before been in a climate where sweat beaded and rolled down her skin because the air was too saturated to accept even the least further increment.

Adele hoped that fear of the unknown wasn't weighing on her also. She was lost in a wilderness of the mind, a place where she didn't know any of the rules. Daniel and his sailors seemed perfectly comfortable here. Perhaps they'd been trained for this sort of uncertainty, in which gunmen might walk into a library at any instant or an ugly-looking fruit could disgorge lethal insects.

It wasn't the physical environment that bothered Adele, but rather the randomness of her present life. She was used to the stress of grinding poverty and demanding work, but there'd been a sameness of existence until now. She desperately missed that predictability.

Woetjans was with the salvage crew. The bosun's mate wore a look of relief as she saw Daniel reappear from the jungle. Obviously the cycle of random disaster hadn't ended yet.

"Sir, we got a problem," Woetjans said before Daniel could catch his breath at not having to fight the vegetation for a while. "Last night those wog bastards must've got the lifeboat from the ship."

She nodded toward the *Ahura*. The stern seemed to have settled lower since Adele last saw it, but Barnes still perched there.

"I should've known there'd be one," Woetjans continued. "It's my own damned fault. It was in a compartment under the stern decking, but I'd never thought to wonder why the panel had a

red stripe around it. Hafard found it hanging open when she was
feeling around in the water this morning."

The sailors who'd been nearby on shore came close enough to
listen. The pair who were diving in the lagoon paused, clinging
to floats made from bundled reeds. They and Barnes looked
shoreward, straining also to hear.

Woetjans handed Daniel a thin metal plate with rivet holes on
either end. "This was pinned to the inside of the panel," she said.
"The wogs must've known what was there all the time."

"Well, they can't go far in an inflatable boat," Daniel said. "And
if . . . Oh, I see what you mean."

Adele leaned over Daniel's shoulder to read the legend on the
plate. Its raised letters read:

EMERGENCY EQUIPMENT
RAFT (CAPACITY 10) AND MOTOR
SOLAR STILL
EMERGENCY RADIO
FISHING L . . .

"Oh," said Adele.

She took out her personal data unit and seated herself on the
ground, using a case of rations as a desk. She crossed her legs
reflexively. The jolt of pain from her bruises didn't hit before she'd
started the movement and wasn't severe enough to prevent her
from finishing it. When she was working, nothing short of decap-
itation was going to stop her.

Daniel and his sailors were talking and looking toward the next
island of the atoll, across the line of reefs. Adele dropped into
the universe of her holographic screen. The natural world sloughed
from around her.

She quickly located the first mention of Daniel's detachment.
It was a radioed note from an Alliance liaison officer with the
port authorities in Kostroma City to his superior in the Alliance
military government. Cinnabar pirates had marooned Kostroman
citizens on a barren island but had been stranded on the same
island themselves. The Kostromans would guide troops to destroy
the pirates.

Adele smiled slightly as she noted the time slugs on that and
the first follow-up. There'd been no action on the report for several

hours. It had been received not long after midnight, and if any-body noticed it they'd put it in a class with sightings of angelic visitors.

An officer had probably come in at dawn. Shortly thereafter somebody had refined Ganser's original SOS, though the exchange wasn't recorded anywhere Adele could find it. The follow-up, now reporting Cinnabar naval personnel were operating on Kostroma, had been passed on to Blue Chrome Operations. The invasion force was wholly distinct from the Alliance military government here.

At this point things happened very fast and were fully recorded in electronic files from which Adele could retrieve them. The link to Ganser was still only the *Ahura*'s emergency radio, but it and Kostroma's geopositioning satellites were adequate to the needs of the Alliance.

Adele finished her survey and leaned back with a sigh. She didn't shut down but her eyes were far enough back from the focal point that the display merged into a blur of mutually-interfering beams of coherent light.

Daniel and Woetjans were looking at her. "You've got some-thing, Adele?" Daniel asked.

The whole detachment was now present, Hogg included. The servant looked worn, but the pupils of his eyes were the same size and he walked without help. The whole left side of his face was the livid purple yellow of a decaying bruise.

The sailors were armed, but the few who carried impellers held them by the barrel as clubs. Knives, spears, and clubs of the native wood predominated.

"Ganser is in radio contact with the Alliance military authori-ties," Adele said. She laid the information out as flatly and sim-ply as possible so that she wouldn't be misunderstood. "The Kostromans are on the adjacent island, about three hundred meters from the shore nearest to this island. A platoon of Alliance com-mandoes in an armored personnel carrier will arrive at local midnight to kill or capture the Cinnabar naval personnel and to capture the Kostromans."

"Why so long?" Dasi asked. "An APC could make it here from Kostroma City by dusk, even if they just started."

"They want us to be asleep," Daniel guessed.

"Yes," Adele said. "Ganser warned them that we were armed. He said they should shoot us on sight and not take any chances."

"Wish we were armed," said Lamsoe. "Wish to *fuck* we were armed."

He looked wistfully at his impeller. A piece of flexible plastic dangled from the battery compartment. Lamsoe had disconnected the power pack so that there was no risk of his accidentally pulling the trigger and shorting the mechanism explosively.

Daniel looked at his chronometer, returned it to his pocket, and smiled purposefully to Adele and his sailors. "That gives us seven hours," he said. "Now, the first thing we'll need—"

Daniel swept the opposite shore slowly with his goggles set to maximum magnification on thermal imaging, then swept it again with the magnification backed off to normal. There was always the possibility that a glitch in the imaging software would mask a target when two systems were combined and pushed to their limits.

This wasn't a time Daniel could afford a glitch.

He took off the goggles and handed them to Woetjans, beside him in the undergrowth. The remainder of the detachment was a silent presence several feet deeper in the jungle, where the thick foliage would mask their body heat from any detection apparatus Daniel knew of. The Kostromans probably didn't have infrared equipment, but Daniel's margin of error was too slight for him to make things worse by any assumed "certainties."

"I don't see any sign of a guard," he said. "Keep watching, of course."

Daniel stretched to full height, bracing his paired hands on a treetrunk. He'd stripped to a belt, a sheath knife from one of the ratings, and his shorts. Woetjans held a long reel of fishing line whose free end was tied to Daniel's belt.

The shorts weren't for modesty but from a due concern for small swimming things that might nibble or sting in the darkness. A nipped *toe* wouldn't be disabling.

"I'll be off now," he said. He walked toward the water, feeling the gritty soil change to mud between his toes.

"Sir," said Woetjans as she stepped out of the undergrowth beside him. "I wish—"

"I'm the best swimmer in the detachment," Daniel said. "If there's a problem, Cafoldi's my backup. but you *have* to get a strike force to the Kostromans tonight. Now, go back to your duties."

At this moment Daniel wanted only to get on with the task, but he didn't let his nervous fury cause him to lash out at the petty officer. Woetjans was just as worried at being left in charge of a situation without clear orders as Daniel was at swimming the strait separating the islands. It ought to work out for both of them, but only a fool wouldn't wonder.

"Yessir," Woetjans said. She saluted and vanished into the jungle.

Daniel entered the water. It felt warmer than the night air on his naked skin. He began a leisurely breast stroke toward the distant shore, giving the wrecked yacht a wide berth.

Sundown was less than an hour past, but the night was so black that only by the pinpricks of starlight could Daniel separate the sky from the land and sea. Both Kostroma's tiny moons were up but they were scarcely more than bright planets even when full.

The tide was rising and currents flowed strongly through the reef from the ocean beyond. Daniel drifted farther into the lagoon; he changed his angle, stroking at an angle against the current in order to hold his intended landfall.

In a perfect world Daniel would have been making this swim between tides when the water was still; though now that he thought about it, in a perfect world there wouldn't be any need for him to swim at all. At least he didn't have to do it when the tide was going out and the rip pulled him toward the fanged reef closing the interval between islands.

Daniel still would have tried. The task was necessary, and the likelihood that it would be fatal wouldn't make it optional.

Something bumped him. He lost a stroke in frozen surprise. More things nudged him and slid off with rubbery persistence.

Unblinking eyes humped the water. Forms squirmed past Daniel into the lagoon like a bubble slick. The contacts were mindless, harmless; mere collisions in the night. An enormous shoal of soft-bodied creatures was entering the lagoon with the tide and darkness to feed.

All Daniel could see were the eyes. He couldn't guess the creatures' body shape from their boneless touch, but the largest were at least the length of his forearm.

Daniel continued to stroke, hindered by the creatures' presence. More serious were the jerks and tugs from behind as the shoal snagged the fishline as well. If the line broke, he'd have to do this all over again.

So be it. He'd take the process one stroke at a time, as he always did. At least he'd learned how the sweep had been able to feed itself to such monstrous size.

He swam with his head out of water so that he could see the shore at all times. There was nothing *to* see, and no likelihood that Daniel would be able to tell in this darkness if Ganser's whole band was waiting to spear him like a fish caught in the shallows.

His thigh muscles were hurting very badly. He felt an incipient cramp as he bunched for another frog kick; instantly he relaxed and lay in a dead man's float while he prayed that he'd been in time.

He had. The big muscles of his right thigh didn't wind themselves into a furious knot as they'd been on the verge of doing, but Daniel didn't dare risk them further tonight.

He swam on, using only arm strokes. His legs dangled behind him like those of a broken-backed dog.

Daniel had overstressed his thighs when he clung to the impeller mount, and he was out of shape. No point in lying to himself: Daniel Leary wasn't as fit as an RCN officer needed to be. If anything happened to the ratings he commanded, it was his fault in all truth as well as by regulation.

Daniel's shoulders weren't in any better condition than his thighs, but the back muscles were less likely to cramp from an inability to dispose of waste products. He was losing strength, though. He needed to reach land soon or he was going to find himself with no option but to float until somebody noticed him at daybreak.

Daniel Leary, floating with the corpse of a sweep the size of a yacht. Well, he hadn't let himself get so fat that there'd be doubt about which was which.

He chuckled, a mistake in that it put off his timing and he breathed water. Maybe a good thing anyway; humor was never out of place in a tight situation.

Besides, he was close to his goal. He could smell the mud, though the toe he dabbed down didn't find bottom. A few feet more—

Something whacked him in the chest. This was a real blow, not the squirming touch of a creature riding the currents. Daniel's head went under water before he could close his mouth.

Fear of someone on shore watching for a disturbance didn't check Daniel's deep lizard-brain fear of drowning. He rose, flailing and spluttering.

He couldn't see anything on the surface. Had he struck a submerged treetrunk? It'd felt solid enough.

Treading water carefully in hope that his thighs wouldn't pack up on him now, Daniel felt in front of him with his outstretched left hand. He didn't touch anything.

He stroked forward again. Something punched him on the left side. As he lurched, he took another underwater blow to the center of his chest.

Daniel knew what the problem was now, and he knew what to do about it. He just wasn't sure that he'd be able to do what was necessary in his present physical condition.

There was a colony of giant tube-worms on his side of the channel, harmless filter-feeders. They rose from their tunnels after dark to sweep the water about them with feathery gills which they withdrew into their bodies every few minutes to ingest the micro-organisms trapped in the gills' netlike structure.

The problem was that though the worms lived in colonies, each protected its immediate hunting ground by butting away rivals which tried to tunnel into the mud too close. These worms thought Daniel was one of their own kind, and they didn't intend to let him settle in the territory they'd already claimed.

Daniel turned and paddled feebly parallel to the shore. He'd used a good deal of his strength fighting the tide when it tried to push him in this direction; now when he could use some help he was in quiet water.

He could really use some help. Well, so could his detachment. What Adele and the ratings had was Daniel Leary, and on his *honor* that would be enough.

Twice he turned toward shore again. Twice the clamped gill covers of an outraged worm prodded him back. He giggled: Kostroman tube worms had a sense of honor very similar to that of Cinnabar nobles. All this time he'd thought society on the two planets was very different.

He supposed the pain in his lungs and shoulders was giving him hallucinations. Well, his present reality had very little to recommend it.

Daniel wasn't fully aware that his fourth attempt to reach shore had succeeded until his left hand dug into mud. He collapsed, still in the water, and dragged sobbing breaths into his lungs. It was nearly a minute before he managed to crawl out of the lagoon and stand upright.

A bush rubbed him; its leaves felt like sandpaper. He ignored them and waved toward the shore he'd left a lifetime ago. Woetjans would be watching through the goggles.

Daniel tested the fishline. It still had the tension of its own full length. Slowly, careful not to snap it now against an unseen snag, Daniel began to hand in the line and the heavier cord that his ratings would by now have fastened to its end.

A bird whose wings were a meter across swooped over the lagoon with a *coo-o-o*, then vanished again in the overhanging trees. Adele jumped; the Kostromans across the twenty feet of water from her bellowed and sprang away from their campfire. One of them got to his feet and hurled a stone into the night when he was sure that the creature was gone.

The thugs settled again. One of them tried to build up the fire, but the wood he added was damp. The flames sank to a hissing glow and the rest of the gang snarled curses at him. They were very nervous.

They had even better reason to be than they knew.

Adele shivered. The air, though warm in any normal sense, cooled her by evaporation as it dried the salt water from her skin. She'd been too exhausted to eat when she and Daniel returned from scouting, and she hadn't eaten later because tension and the flurry of activity had masked her hunger.

Now she was cold and wet and alone in the darkness. She liked to think of herself as a creature of the mind, but her body was reimposing its own reality.

She'd know better the next time. The thought of there being a next time like this made her grin despite herself: Dangerous Adele, the Pistol-Packing Librarian.

She sobered. There probably would be a next time, if she survived this one.

The Kostromans subsided into glum speculation again. They were urban thugs, as unused to these sorts of conditions as Adele herself was, and they didn't have her self-disciplined willingness to deal with a situation as she found it.

Ganser had pulled into a notch midway along the lagoon side of this islet. He hadn't built a real camp. Open ration cans winked orange in the firelight; one floated near where Adele crouched on the opposite shore.

The inflatable liferaft was drawn up on the mud near the fire. Adele wondered if it was tied. The thugs probably didn't think they'd need the boat again, but the Cinnabar sailors certainly did.

She and the Cinnabar sailors. For the first time since the Mundys of Chatsworth were massacred, Adele Mundy belonged to a group.

Something plopped loudly in the lagoon. A thug cried out and turned. The rhythm of night-sounds shifted for a moment after the cry, then resumed at its previous level.

Daniel Leary stepped out of the undergrowth on the other side of the Kostromans' fire. He carried a wooden baton a meter long.

"Good evening," Daniel said. "Surrender quietly right now. You're surrounded."

The thugs bawled and scrambled away from the fire. One of them aimed a sub-machine gun at Daniel. Adele was no longer cold. She shot the gunman in the knee. The gunman screamed in rising pain and fell backward.

Ganser swung at Daniel. Daniel jabbed his baton into the thug's soft belly, then rang the wood off Ganser's scalp as he doubled over.

A Kostroman squatting at the edge of the light had a sub-machine gun also. Adele hadn't noticed it until the thug pulled the trigger. They'd retrieved guns from the lagoon, but unlike the sailors they hadn't even tried to wash the salt out of the circuitry.

The sub-machine gun blew up in a vivid green flash: its battery had shorted through the mechanism. Vaporized metal and globs of burning plastic casing splattered in all directions like the contents of an incendiary grenade.

Daniel shouted, but the thugs themselves caught most of the fireball. Woetjans and Barnes burst from the undergrowth to either side of their commander and joined him in clubbing every Kostroman still standing.

Adele didn't shoot again. She didn't have a safe target, and the three Cinnabars across the inlet didn't need her help.

The only rope the Cinnabars had that was long enough to span the strait between the islands was Kostroma-made and only a quarter-inch diameter. Daniel was unwilling to stress it with more than one person at a time crossing hand over hand to the other side. If there'd been more time the sailors could have braided a bark hawser; but there wasn't time, for that or much of anything else.

Three Cinnabars had crossed to join Daniel. Adele was the first, because of her pistol and her skill with it. Barnes and Dasi were supposed to follow, but Woetjans had come in Dasi's place.

The fight in the Kostroman camp, such as it was, ended. Daniel swayed, panting as he held his club by both ends. He looked across the notch of water and called, "Don't try to come around, Adele. We'll bring you over in the boat as soon as we've got this lot tied."

The four Cinnabars had worked their way up the shore from the island's tip until they found the Kostroman camp on the other side of this inlet. They hadn't been able to make a plan until they saw the location. Adele had been the one to suggest she stay here where she had a better line of fire than she'd have if she worked around with the others.

She'd felt alone as she waited for Daniel to strike. That wasn't a problem; she'd felt alone for most of her life.

A thug keened in a high-pitched voice that cut through the moans and sick-hearted curses of the others. The one she'd shot, perhaps; or the one who'd incinerated herself by pulling the sub-machine gun's trigger.

Adele had a good view of the camp from here, but it hadn't been good enough. If the sub-machine gun had worked, Daniel Leary would be dead. She didn't see any way the group could survive if they lost Daniel.

In rational moments she didn't see how they would survive under Daniel's command either, but it was surprisingly easy in the young lieutenant's presence to suspend disbelief.

Adele looked at the water, then tucked the pistol into the purse she wore on her waistbelt. "I'm coming across," she said. She walked into the inlet.

At midpoint the channel was deep enough that Adele had to splash in an awkward parody of swimming. There was no current; the bottom muck, though unpleasant, slid off her skin like thick oil instead of gripping her. A week ago—a *day* ago—she'd never have considered plunging into water foul with jungle decay, but her standards of acceptability had slipped.

Daniel gave her a hand out. "You shouldn't have done that," he said. "We can't afford to take unnecessary risks."

"Nor can we afford to waste time," Adele said tartly. That wasn't the real reason she'd walked across, though. She was punishing herself for missing the second gunner until it would have been too late.

Woetjans and Barnes were tying the prisoners with the same cord by which Adele and the two sailors had crossed the strait. The campfire had been trampled in the fighting, but it perversely burned brighter than it had under the Kostromans' leisured direction.

Adele took her pistol out of the purse. Daniel looked down at the prisoners. Several were conscious but they waited stolidly to be tied again. Blood still pulsed from where the club had laid open three inches of Ganser's scalp.

"I suppose I need to put a pressure bandage on that," Daniel muttered; but he didn't seem ready to do so quite yet.

Daniel was still breathing hard. A spatter of flaming plastic had blistered his right forearm; he hadn't dressed it yet.

He reached again into the first aid kit Woetjans had brought over. The horribly burned shooter lapsed into slobbering silence. Daniel put the injector back in its clamp in the kit.

"I already gave her three ampules," he said softly to Adele. "It's a waste of drugs, but it was that or knock her head in. I didn't want to do that, but if she hadn't shut up . . ."

"What about the one I shot?" Adele asked. She didn't know which Kostroman it had been. She'd seen the gun and fired, picking her target by instinct rather than design.

"On the end," Daniel said, nodding to the edge of the firelight. "I gave him a shot too, so he wouldn't go into shock. He'll be all right. He'll live, anyway."

"That's the lot, sir," Woetjans said as she straightened.

"Right," said Daniel. "Woetjans, you take the lifeboat back and gather up the others. It'll take two trips, I think, to bring them and the gear we'll need."

He smiled at his surroundings with what Adele thought was anticipation. "The rest of us'll get to work here, readying things for our friends from the Alliance."

The emergency radio was a flat box that hummed softly. Every ten seconds the output display beside the speaker spiked, indicating that the unit continued to send a homing signal.

"I hear 'em coming," whispered Woetjans. "Hear it? Like thunder a hundred miles off, that's the lift fans."

Daniel spread his hand for silence. The radio's integral microphone wasn't very sensitive, but they didn't need to take chances.

Eleven Cinnabars sat around the fire, wearing Kostroman civilian clothing with an addition of Zojira black and yellow. Woetjans was trying to use the excess in her trousers' waistband to make up what was lacking in inseam length; to say Ganser's clothes were a bad fit for her would be putting it mildly. Other ratings weren't much better off.

It probably didn't matter. The Alliance commandoes weren't coming to stage a fashion show. The blood that stiffened the shoulders and right sleeve of Daniel's shirt wouldn't surprise anybody either.

Barnes and Dasi were across the strait, tending the original camp on the other island. It was a dangerous job, but that description would cover most of what was going on tonight.

The eight other ratings guarded the prisoners. They were all neck deep in the water of an inlet eighty yards from the Kostroman camp. Overhanging foliage ought to block the remainder of the human heat signature, at least from a quick-reaction force that was trying to locate known groupings rather than searching for people who *weren't* where they were supposed to be.

"Zojira civilians," a voice rasped from the radio. The person speaking was male, but the single-sideband emergency signal and a degree of professional disdain almost concealed even his sex. "Give us a vector from your camp to the bandit position. Over."

The burned Kostroman had died, so Daniel hadn't been required to decide whether to put her in the water with the others. Both her hands had been charred off, and her heat-shriveled intestines writhed where there was no longer a ribcage to cover them.

Her death had been the best option for all concerned. Daniel supposed it was a failing of his as a man as well as an officer that he'd been unwilling to speed the result himself.

Daniel bent over the microphone. The emergency unit's poor sound quality was a blessing under the circumstances: it'd take a better linguist than most commandoes to notice a problem with his accent.

"Master, the pirates're east of us," he said in tones of breathy nervousness. "Maybe a little south, too, a little southeast. They're not half a mile away!"

Daniel could hear the deep bass note of an APC at speed now. The commandoes were coming in fast, despite the risk that the sound of their ducted fans would alert their quarry.

The power it took to lift and propel twenty-odd tons by thrust alone came at the price of a sonic signature, no matter how much you tried to minimize it. Quick and dirty was probably the better choice, as well as the option that would appeal to members of a strike force.

"On my signal," the radio voice said, "fire a flare straight up. I repeat, straight up. And stay off the radio! Out."

Woetjans smiled lazily and stood, holding the flare gun from the *Ahura's* emergency kit. She was obviously glad to have a task to occupy her while the others could only wait.

Adele sat on an upturned metal bucket. Her attention was seemingly a million miles away. Daniel grinned at her. She raised an eyebrow in question, realized Daniel was just being sociable, and returned to her reverie. Her hands slowly rotated the head-sized object she held between spread fingertips.

Lamsoe and Sun held sub-machine guns; the Kostromans had salvaged guns, so the Cinnabars taking their place had guns too. Lamsoe held his as if it were a bomb. Daniel wouldn't let him disconnect the battery because the APC's sensors might be able to tell the difference, but the safeties of both weapons were on.

The APC's thrum was louder now. A few minues earlier the pulsing note could have been concealed in the night sounds except to ears that were searching for it.

"Zojira civilians," the radio ordered, "fire one flare now! Over!"

Woetjans walked two steps closer to the bank of the inlet, aimed the gun skyward, and sent up a flare as close to vertical as you could tell without a plumb line. Daniel hoped the process hadn't been too expert, but the commandoes would probably figure the wogs had just gotten lucky.

"Good, I'm already stiff from sitting here," said Hogg. He still looked like he'd been exhumed on maybe the third day. Daniel'd planned to leave his servant with the prisoners, but at the last instant he'd lacked the courage to say that.

Hogg would've ignored the order anyway. The fellow who'd changed your diapers wasn't going to kiss your boots just because you had "Lieutenant" before your name now.

The flare's tracer burst a hundred feet up in a brilliant blue dazzle. There was enough wind from the sea to push the sparks away from the campfire; not that the commandoes would've cared.

The APC came *fast* over the trees, heading east toward the first island. The downdraft drove the flare's falling particles into the lagoon as a hundred scattered steam vents. The hiss of quenching sparks was lost in the roar of the fans.

The big vehicle banked left. The plasma cannon in its cupola raked the original Cinnabar camp with a hell of stripped ions.

Steam and fire blew from the jungle. The vegetation was wet, but even stone burned when bathed in radiance as hot as a sun's corona.

A mushroom of soot and vapor erupted from the target area. Daniel heard the chatter of sub-machine guns as well, a sign of ruthlessness and bad fire discipline. Personal weapons had nothing useful to add to the plasma cannon's swath of destruction.

"Those bastards," Hogg said as he stropped his knife on his palm. "Kill us all while we slept, *they* would."

He spat, and smiled, and looked much more his old self.

The APC went into a reverse bank and swept back. The cannon fired again, its dense saffron beam ripping apart the pillar of smoke from the first pass. A glowing rock flew out of the impact area, dimming as it tumbled. It landed in the lagoon and exploded from thermal shock.

Daniel was white with cold rage. This was war: if it claimed Barnes and Dasi, well, that was a hazard they understood when they took their oaths. This Alliance commander wasn't alone in his willingness to shoot sleeping enemies without giving them a chance to surrender.

And it wouldn't change anything about what happened next; nothing except that Daniel Leary would take more pleasure in viewing the Alliance casualties he very much expected to see.

Apparently satisfied with what it had achieved on the neighboring island, the APC idled toward what it believed was the Kostroman camp. The muzzle of the plasma cannon pointed toward them as a white-hot oval, cooling slowly.

Daniel stood and raised his hands to shoulder height. A part of his mind was already composing the letters he'd write to the families of Barnes and Dasi, if that were required and if God preserved him to carry out that duty.

Adele watched the armored vehicle come toward her at a slow pace, thunderously loud and bigger than she'd expected even though she'd seen APCs before. She supposed it was because of the circumstances in which she was watching this one that it seemed to loom so large.

The APC was closed up; its driver and gunner used electronic imaging to view their surroundings. Daniel said that vehicles of this sort had sensor suites that could tell if a gnat farted.

The saving grace of the situation was that this jungle had many, many gnats. As in Adele's own proper job, the difficulty was to sort vast quantities of data for the single item you needed. No ordinary weapon was going to pass the electronic frisking, though.

The APC hesitated in the air, then dropped to the surface of the lagoon. Spray erupted in a screen that would have been rainbowed if there'd been any lights to refract within it. The vehicle resumed its leisurely progress, waddling up the inlet toward the camp. It didn't even show the minimal running lights Adele had seen on APCs in Kostroma City during the coup.

The sailors were all standing. They looked nervous, the attitude the commandoes would expect as well as the way Adele supposed they really felt. She didn't want to stand, but at last she got up awkwardly from the bucket so as not to look out of place.

Daniel spoke; sailors moved forward slightly. Adele, though not concealed, was now in the background.

She wasn't afraid. She was too detached to be afraid. She understood precisely what was required of her; if circumstances permitted, she would execute her task. There was very little uncertainty except about the outcome.

The APC's bluff bow slid out of the water, bulldozing a wedge of root-bound mud ahead of it. Spray doused the campfire and drove the sailors back, cursing and covering their eyes.

Adele turned away. She could scarcely be wetter than she was already, but the deliberate insult set her face coldly. Scorn a Mundy of Chatsworth, would they?

She turned again, smiling internally at her own reaction. She'd have laughed, but that would have been out of keeping with her pose as a small-time crook and smuggler. Instead she let her face muscles relax into a neutral expression. She'd never cringed, so she was afraid of an unsatisfactory result if she tried to fake it now.

The APC swung broadside to the eleven Cinnabars. Its stern

shoved aside undergrowth and nestled there. The cupola rotated so that the plasma cannon stayed trained on the presumed Kostromans. Five sub-machine guns projected from miniature gunports in the armored side.

Realistically, the weapons weren't much danger because those threatened were close enough to the vehicle to duck under the cannon and flatten themselves against the APC's flank between the gunports. The muzzles would have a psychological effect, though, especially on the stupid thugs the commandoes thought they were facing.

The driver shut his fans down. The roar of air through the eight intake ducts stilled, but a high-pitched whine indicated various parts continued to spin in readiness for any need.

The plasma cannon twitched, aiming at Lamsoe's head. "You two with guns!" the Alliance voice shouted, this time through a conformal speaker somewhere on the vehicle's hull. "Throw them in the water now! And the six of you who have knives, you too! Now! We can see you!"

Daniel stood a half step in front of his sailors, waggling his raised hands and smirking in apparent terror. At the command he clawed into his pocket and came out with the little knife he'd used to peel nuts.

Lamsoe and Sun spun their sub-machine guns toward the inlet. Sun's splattered mud on the bank, but Lamsoe got rid of his with the enthusiasm owed a live grenade. It took longer for sailors to fumble folding knives out of their pockets, but they flew toward the water too.

Though Hogg threw his knife, Adele heard it *thunk* into a tree bole in the near distance. If the Alliance officer noticed the slight disobedience, she passed over it for now.

A hatch opened in the vehicle's side, just back of the cupola. The man who got out was barely taller than Adele but strongly built. He held the central grip of a sub-machine gun, a weapon both more compact and more deadly than the Kostroman equivalents the sailors had just thrown away.

"Now listen up!" the officer said. He spoke in an upper-class Pleasaunce accent.

The officer waved the sub-machine gun as though it were a conductor's baton. The hatch behind him was a pale rectangle; the vehicle's interior lights were faint, but they were brighter than the jungle now that the fire was dead.

"You wogs will go back under restraint," he continued, "or you'll stay here till you rot. And you can count yourselves lucky that my colonel has a softer heart than I do, or there'd be another burned patch of jungle and we'd be heading home without the trouble of tying you, do you understand?"

"But master—" Daniel whined. He sounded so much like a crying child that Adele felt her jaw clench.

The officer thrust his gun an inch from Daniel's face. "Shut up or I'll do it my way!" he said.

Daniel whimpered and bent away. Adele tossed her ripe soap-bubble fungus through the open hatch. The officer's eyes flicked sideways at the movement and Daniel caught his gun-wrist in his left hand.

Sailors dived for cover as they'd been warned to do. Screaming chaos broke out within the APC. A sub-machine gun raked the night.

Adele ignored the shots—they weren't aimed at her or, most likely, aimed at anything at all. She bent to tip over the bucket she'd used as a seat. Her pistol was beneath, concealed from sensors by the galvanized iron bucket.

She straightened with the gun in her hand. There wasn't anything she needed to shoot.

The plasma cannon pointed at a crazy angle as the howling gunner tried to free himself from his harness. A commando emptied a sub-machine gun through a port on the opposite side of the APC; pellets lit the jungle like a stream of fireflies, clipping foliage and sending up puffs of splintered wood. Other troops hammered the sides of their vehicle, but even a crash-bar hatch release required a little more coordination than these retained in their present puling agony.

Daniel held the Alliance officer between him and the APC. He had both his wrists, now. The Alliance officer twisted with a grace suggesting he was expert in unarmed combat, but the Cinnabar lieutenant was stronger and very angry.

"The men you squirted over on the other island, master?" Daniel said in a hard, precise voice.

The Alliance officer tried to bite him; Daniel had the leverage and kept the teeth away from his shoulder as his hand continued to grind together the bones of the officer's gun wrist. "They were really warm stones wrapped in blankets to give the right heat signatures. I had two of my ratings tending the fire there, though, and I hope—"

The commando's wrist failed with a sound like that of stones rubbing. His eyes rolled up and he fainted in Daniel's arms.

"I really hope they heard you coming in time to cover up in their dugouts," Daniel concluded, his voice softer. He straightened— he'd spread his legs to brace himself during the struggle—and surveyed the situation, still using the Alliance officer's body as a shield.

"It seems to have worked," Adele said. She stood with her pistol at her left side. Two sub-machine guns still protruded from gunports, but their muzzles were tilted up. Their owners had dropped the weapons as they tried to fight off an enemy more insidious than poison gas.

A gun fired *inside* the vehicle. Sparks, pellets or metal spalled from the inner face of the armor, spun through the hatch.

A commando finally managed to release the latch that dropped the whole side of the troop compartment. Soldiers tumbled out, twisting and moaning. One commando shambled blindly into the undergrowth, clawing the air with her hands. The sailors let her go.

The soap bubble fungus had ruptured into fluffy tendrils on the compartment's deck. A single insect the size of Adele's thumb glittered in the lights, then settled on the neck of a commando.

Daniel took the sub-machine gun from the officer he held, then laid him on the ground and stepped back. There'd been sixteen troops aboard the APC. None of them were upright now. Some thrashed, but Adele could see at least half a dozen others were as still as death.

"I think we'd better get back a little farther," Daniel said in a voice wheezy with recent exertion. "They're not supposed to fly farther than a couple meters from the nest, but I don't want to be the one to prove that was as wrong as the data on how big sweeps get."

Adele put her pistol in her pocket. Together they walked slowly toward the sailors now appearing from the jungle. Hogg joined them.

"The beetles aren't supposed to live longer than ten minutes from when they leave the fungus, either," Daniel added. "But we're going to stay on the safe side there, too."

Behind them, tough Alliance soldiers moaned in mindless pain.

✧   ✧   ✧

"Couldn't we come by boat?" Adele complained. She was acting for the benefit of the prisoner the two sailors were dragging through the jungle behind her and Daniel, but the peevish tone wasn't entirely put on. Feet had worn the trail to a narrow creek with muddy banks.

"Our Alliance friend might try to escape," Daniel explained. His voice was breathy with exertion. "Or drown himself, anyway, especially if he figures out what's waiting for him. Besides, it was your idea to get the information this way."

It actually had been Adele's idea, offered diffidently when Daniel wondered aloud how best to interrogate the prisoners about the *Aglaia* and her crew. Daniel and Hogg were enthusiastically sure that the plan would work, at least after they'd refined it. Adele found that hard to imagine; but her knowledge of what went on in other people's minds was not, she knew, to be trusted.

"I don't know anything," the commando said muzzily. "And if I did, I wouldn't tell you fuckers."

The Alliance prisoners had been stripped—Daniel wanted their uniforms, but Adele knew the psychological effect would be useful as well—tied, and held separately in nooks in the jungle. Any of them who tried to speak had been gagged as well. The interrogation had to wait till daybreak.

Their prisoner was a sergeant whose skin was startlingly white beneath a mat of black chest hair. His wrists were tied in front of him and a pole was thrust between his elbows and his back. Barnes and Dasi held opposite ends of the pole, forcing the sergeant to walk sideways, crab fashion, along the trail.

"Well, I hope you're wrong," Adele said in her usual coolly astringent tone. "The two soldiers we tried this on first didn't talk, and I'm getting tired of tramping through the mud."

"I got nothing to say," the prisoner repeated. His foot caught in a trailing vine, tripping him so that his weight fell on the pole. He gasped at a pain so severe that he staggered again.

Barnes and Dasi paused; they'd have to carry him if he blacked out completely. "Daniel," Adele murmured, halting the lieutenant. Sailors had improved the trail from the first time she and Daniel scouted it, but whoever was in the lead still had to force fresh growth aside.

A fungus beetle had bitten the prisoner on the right shoulder. His arm and the whole side of his chest were still lividly swollen. Pus oozing from the wound trailed a yellow crust as far as his elbow.

"Well, I tell you, sarge," Dasi said with bantering menace, "I'd just as soon you didn't talk. I'd just as soon none of you talked. I was back at the other camp, you see, when you bastards had your fun shooting it up. I got blisters on my butt from that, and I guess I was still luckier than you planned me to be."

Barnes leaned over and pinched the sergeant's cheek. "You be just as tough as you want, boy," he said. "I really like to hear you fellows scream."

The prisoner didn't speak. He had his feet under him again. Dasi twitched the pole.

The party plodded the short remaining distance to the inlet where soap bubble fungus grew. Daniel and Adele stood to the side so that the sailors could bring the prisoner up to where he had a good view.

"Now sergeant," Daniel said with slightly patronizing formality, "this is the situation. We're going to tie you to one of those trees there—"

He gestured to the grove twenty feet away. Two naked commandoes were there already, seated on the ground with their hands tied around the trunks of the trees behind them.

They were dead and their bodies were swollen horribly. A red, two-inch beetle sat motionless on the protruding tongue of one of the corpses. Above each body were the tattered remains of a soap bubble fungus, its core everted from the yellow rind like trails of cotton batting.

"The fungus is quite tasty," Daniel said. He smiled. "Not that you'll have time to appreciate it, I'm afraid. As I said, we're going to tie you near your friends and walk a good distance away before we start asking you questions. If you answer all the questions completely, then we'll untie you and take you back to camp. But it has to be a 'full and frank disclosure,' as they say."

"You can't do this," the sergeant whispered hoarsely.

"That's a remarkably silly thing to say," Adele commented. "Given that you can see we already have done it."

"He's woozy from the sting he got last night," Daniel said soothingly. "Poor man, I've heard that a bite from a fungus beetle hurts worse than being stuffed into a hot furnace."

He smiled at the prisoner. "But you see," he went on, "that's just one bite. If you're sitting under a nest when my friend here blows it open—"

Adele raised the pistol high enough from her pocket for the prisoner to see it, then let the weapon slide back.

"—you'll be bitten many times. And I'm afraid that's invariably fatal."

Daniel walked toward the grove. He moved as though he were stepping on eggs.

"Be careful, for God's sake," Adele snapped. The concern in her voice was real enough. She knew that Daniel didn't take risks he thought were excessive, but she wasn't willing to trust his judgment of "excessive."

With thumb and forefinger, Daniel picked the beetle off the corpse's tongue. He strode back to the others, moving much more quickly.

He offered the insect to the prisoner. Adele looked closely as well; she hadn't seen the creatures by good light before. The bright red wing cases were edged with cream. It was quite attractive in its way.

"They only live a few minutes after they come out of the nest," Daniel said in a friendly, informational tone. "Striking colors, don't you think? These aren't fangs, exactly, they're really modified antennae, but they certainly carry poison the way fangs do. I guess you know that better than me."

Daniel grinned. He wiggled the insect in the direction of the prisoner's swollen shoulder. The prisoner screamed and tried to twist away. Barnes cuffed him back; he screamed again and slumped.

Daniel tossed the insect into the lagoon. "Tie him to the tree between those other two," he ordered. He spit at the floating bug and spun it over in a swirl of bubbles. "And don't bump the fungus yourself, all right?"

"What do you want to know?" mumbled the sergeant. "I swear to God, I'm just a soldier, but I'll tell you what I know."

"Let him sit," Daniel said to Barnes, "but keep hold of the pole."

He looked at the prisoner and said, "Where's the crew of the *Aglaia* being held? The Cinnabar naval vessel that was in harbor when you landed, the *Aglaia*."

The prisoner's eyes were closed. "All those guys are locked up in the ship," he said through thick lips. "Not the officers, though.

I think they're in the palace but I don't know, I never had that duty myself. They'll be taken off-planet as soon as the rest of the squadron lands, I heard."

Adele withdrew her data unit and seated herself cross-legged in the mud. She got out the wands and began to enter the sergeant's information.

"When do you expect the rest of the squadron?" Daniel was asking.

Kostroman birds and insects buzzed warmly in the grove, devouring the luscious fungus which Adele had shot open earlier in the morning. For the most part, the local creatures ignored the human corpses.

The Alliance soldiers were among the six who had been killed by multiple bites inside the APC, unable to escape when Adele flung the nest through the hatchway the night before.

Gambier and Barnes had endorsements on their paybooks indicating the RCN thought they could fly ducted-fan vehicles. Half a dozen other ratings had experience as well, either in civilian life or less officially in the service. Daniel didn't have to worry about who could fly the armored personnel carrier.

There was plenty else to worry about, of course, but right at the moment Daniel Leary was feeling pretty good. Pretty damned good.

The APC revved, then lifted. Gambier was at the controls. The sides were folded down as if for a quick insertion, so the ratings in the troop compartment were clearly visible. They and their fellows on the ground cheered as the big vehicle slid along the inlet. It rose slowly until the downdraft no longer exploded the water away to either side.

"Isn't it dangerous to have passengers aboard when you're testing the equipment?" Adele asked as she watched the APC at his side.

Daniel shrugged. "There might have been a problem getting off the ground," he said, "though it's all pretty automated."

Adele turned her head to look at him. "I suppose if you'd thought it was really dangerous," she said, "you'd have been aboard yourself."

Daniel grinned. "I didn't think it was dangerous," he said, avoiding the direct answer that would have made him sound like he was trying to be a hero. The ratings expected an officer to share their dangers; to avoid doing so would be unprofessional.

Likewise, it would be unprofessional for an officer to involve himself in the common dirtiness of naval life, washing dishes or scrubbing grease from hydraulic control systems. That was where the extreme democrats went wrong. Though . . .

He'd now gotten to know the surviving representative of the Mundys of Chatsworth, the family who according to Corder Leary were the life and breath of radical democracy on Cinnabar. Adele wasn't what Daniel would call a radical democrat.

Perhaps there'd been some misrepresentation on both sides of the question. That was pretty generally true in politics, he supposed.

Daniel glanced higher into the wedge of sky visible past the overhanging trees. "Someday I'd like you to help me with the constellations from here," he said. "The Kostromans do name their constellations, don't they? I guess I was just assuming they do."

"What?" said Adele. "I have no idea, but I'll find out."

She sat on the ground and brought up her little computer. Daniel hadn't meant Adele to dig into the problem immediately. "Someday" meant to him "when things have settled down."

Realistically, things weren't going to settle down while he was on Kostroma. Though for his own sense of well-being he had to pretend this was an aberration in the life of a naval officer, that the normal routine would soon return.

Daniel squatted beside Adele, his arms wrapped around his knees and his buttocks slightly above the ground. Not that he could get much muddier . . .

"The trick would have worked just as well if we'd done it in all truth," he said. "Tying live prisoners under a fungus bubble and letting the beetles kill the first one or two if they didn't talk."

The note of the APC's fans changed from a pulse to a whisper; the ratings had landed on the other island to retrieve items salvaged from the wreck. The APC had more carrying capacity than the little liferaft, and using it provided hands-on experience in a leisured environment.

"Perhaps," said Adele, "but we'll never know."

She put her wands down and looked over at Daniel. "People like us will never know. But *our* way worked."

A hand-sized crustacean scuttled from the muddy bank, extended a pair of tentacles to seize a ration can the Kostromans had flung down, and ran back the way it had come. Each segment of the creature's jointed back had a stalked eye at the midline. They twisted like flowers in a rainstorm to watch the humans.

The crustacean vanished into the water with its prize; the can gave a *plop!* as water filled it. The little creature was probably after a home rather than food, but Daniel didn't know enough about the local biota to be sure.

"There are constellations, yes," Adele said. "They seem to be named for geographical features of Topaz, where the colony originated. Would you like to see the display?"

She offered the data unit. Daniel shook his head, smiling his thanks. "Not right now," he said.

He pointed to the trail the crustacean's many feet had wriggled into the mud. "I was going to put the prisoners on a detail policing up the mess they'd made," he went on. "The local animals seem to be pleased with the chance to take care of it themselves. Besides, it's probably best to keep both lots hogtied until we're ready to leave. I don't want another slip-up."

The prisoners, Ganser's thugs and the surviving Alliance commandoes, lay like so many duffelbags at intervals along the opposite bank of the inlet. They were bound and anchored by the neck to rooted saplings. Two guards were with them, but the prisoners were visible to the Cinnabars on this side of the water also for additional safety.

They were gagged. A prisoner who moved more than a guard thought necessary was kicked, but that was a matter of casually brutal control rather than torture.

"You know," said Daniel, "if we'd dumped the gang off the end of the dock on Kostroma, we wouldn't have the APC and Alliance uniforms now. Funny how things work out, isn't it?"

Adele sniffed. "That had nothing to do with the decision," she said. "It shouldn't have anything to do with any similar decision either. Or are you suggesting that the Lord is with us because our hearts are pure?"

Daniel laughed loudly and got to his feet. "Your heart may be pure," he said, "but for my own part I've just been too busy. One of Ganser's little friends doesn't look half bad in the right light."

Adele rose beside him. He looked at her and, now that he'd defused her suggestion with a joke, said, "Adele, I don't think God will preserve Cinnabar. That's what the Republic has a navy for,

after all. But I do think that the people with least on their con-
sciences sleep better than others do. I like my sleep."

He thought about the little blonde with a snake's tail tattooed
from her neck to reappear on her bare midriff, heading lower.
In a return to his cheery tone, Daniel added, "And if God wants
to throw us a bonus, that's all right with me."

Adele sat with her head out of the cupola as Barnes brought
the overloaded APC down where the Cinnabar camp had been.
Streams of plasma had considerably enlarged the clearing, but all
signs of the shelters and goods salvaged from the yacht were gone.

Water sprayed as the vehicle settled. After the ions had burned
long tracks of soil away, rain and seepage through the porous rock
had filled the ruin.

Adele wondered if Daniel was dropping the Alliance soldiers
here rather than on the beach to make a point. Daniel Leary was
an extremely straightforward man, but she'd realized early after
meeting him that he was quite subtle in his direct fashion—when
he chose to be.

It was hard to remember that she'd met Daniel only a week
before.

Barnes adjusted the drive fans to a whining idle. Without orders,
Hogg and several of the sailors crammed into the troop compartment rolled the prisoners onto the ground. The Alliance troops
were bound individually and roped to one another by their wrists
as well.

Adele lifted herself up to sit on the folded-back cupola hatch.
By leaning forward, she could see the Alliance troops as they
writhed and splashed, cursing.

Daniel stood on the vehicle's side panel folded down into a
ramp. He lifted a prisoner's face from the trench in which she
spluttered and supported her until she squirmed into a position
that was survivable if not necessarily comfortable.

"Shut the motors off for a moment, Barnes," Daniel said. "I want
them to be able to hear what I have to say."

Sixteen of the Cinnabars, Adele included, wore commando
uniforms including the communication helmets. She heard Daniel's
voice clearly over the helmet intercom as well as a faint echo
through the air.

The helmets were fine for now, but they'd have to switch off the radios well before reaching Kostroma City. Even if the Alliance forces were too busy to institute a comprehensive signals watch, chatter in Cinnabar accents over Alliance equipment would raise a red flag.

The rhythmic hum of the engines sank to a quiver. A squad of sailors dragged the prisoners, still linked, a few yards farther so they couldn't grab a landing skid as the APC lifted.

Daniel stepped to the ground and faced the naked prisoners. "There's enough food and water on this atoll to keep you forever," he said. "Also we're leaving most of the rations we brought from the naval stores, here and on the other island. If you don't like the division of supplies I've made between you and Ganser, you can go across and discuss the matter. Or you can join forces, of course."

He smiled at the Alliance lieutenant without humor. Adele knew Daniel well enough by now to recognize that he was angry; surprisingly angry, she thought, until she remembered what the plasma-ripped campsite meant to him.

"The last time I did something like this," Daniel went on, "I told the people I was marooning that I'd send them help in thirty days if they hadn't managed to get off the atoll themselves. I'm not saying that now. All you're getting from me is your lives . . . which is rather better than you were offering, isn't it?"

He stepped up into the troop compartment. "You can't leave us tied!" a soldier said. The one who spoke was the sergeant who'd first told what he knew about the *Aglaia*. "We can't survive unless you cut us loose!"

Daniel grimaced. "Hogg, throw him a knife," he said. "Barnes, take us up to a hundred feet and circle the area."

Hogg smashed a brandy bottle on the side of the hatchway. As the motors began to grunt under load, he tossed the jagged neck in the direction of the sergeant.

The sides of the troop compartment were hinged horizontally. They lifted halfway to form railings on either side while the compartment remained open to light and air. Adele slid back into the cupola seat as the vehicle rose.

Daniel touched her shoulder. "I'll trade places, if you don't mind," he said.

Embarrassed to have usurped his position—he was commander, of course; what had she been thinking of?—Adele squirmed out of the cupola and into the rear compartment. Sailors made way for her with quiet deference. She looked over the side.

At the specified altitude, the APC slowly circled the two islands and the reef joining them. An occasional pop in the helmet's integral headphones told Adele that Daniel was talking to one or more of the sailors on a separate channel. She could listen in if she wanted, but there wasn't any reason to do so.

The *Ahura*'s lifeboat floated in the lagoon, turning slowly in the still water. A slick of pollen and bits of foliage drifted behind the boat. The Alliance soldiers were barely visible past the treetops as they squirmed to free themselves, while on the other island some of the Kostromans were already standing upright.

"Starboard watch," Woetjans ordered over the intercom. "Aim at the liferaft."

Sailors jostled one another in cheerful surprise, thrusting submachine guns captured from the commandoes over the railing. Adele remained at the rail but she didn't bother to draw her pistol. Sailors on the other side of the compartment complained good-naturedly.

"Open fire!"

Water exploded in a spray that completely hid the little boat. The air filled with ozone and ionized aluminum even though the troop compartment was half-open. The crackling gun mechanisms echoed like logs splitting.

"Cease fire!"

The raft was a tatter of flexible red plastic in the center of foam which spread a hundred feet in all directions. The sailors weren't marksmen—some must be amazingly bad shots, judging from where their rounds hit—and the light pellets weren't intended for work at this range. Nonetheless the target had been completely destroyed.

The APC pulled through a figure-8 that reversed its direction. "Port watch," Woetjans ordered, "aim at the yacht."

There were loud cheers. Most of the remaining sailors had already bent over their railing, hunched and squinting in a variety of distorted notions about how to shoot accurately. One of them—inevitably—jerked his trigger an instant before Woetjans said, "Fire!"

The upturned stern didn't vanish, but it began to crumble like a sand castle in the rain. Again Adele saw water spout thirty yards from the intended target, but a sub-machine gun with a 300-round magazine didn't require a crack shot to be effective.

"Cease fire!" Woetjans ordered. "*Cease* fire, Dasi, or I'll take the fucking thing away and feed it to you!"

There was a moment's silence. The plasma cannon roared. What was left of the *Ahura* erupted into an iridescent mushroom cloud. The APC rocked with recoil from the one-second jet of ions, each of infinitesimal mass but accelerated to the speed of light.

Adele heard the cupola hum as it rotated. Nevertheless the second spurt of plasma startled her. Steam and shimmering fire enveloped the remains of the lifeboat.

The lagoon danced briefly with fairy light as ions recombined to their normal atomic state. That passed, but vari-hued fish, scalded by the manmade hellfire, floated to the surface.

Daniel stepped out of the cupola. "Barnes," he ordered on a general channel, "follow the programmed course and speed to Kostroma City. Gambier will spell you two hours out."

He grinned at Adele and said—not using the intercom, "Communications Officer Mundy, take over and make sure we're not getting into something we don't expect. What we do expect is bad enough, right?"

Adele shrugged. "So far," she said, "it appears that it's better to be on our side than against us."

She settled herself on the cupola seat. The vehicle's extensive sensor and communications suites were arrayed in a ring attached to the hull below the cannon in the dome. Adele logged onto the Alliance military net, using the codes of a cutter hanging out of service aboard a destroyer in the Floating Harbor. As soon as she had access, she searched for any sign that the *Aglaid*'s officers had been moved from cells in the basement of the Elector's Palace where she'd located them the night before.

She smiled as she worked, her touch certain despite the unfamiliar system. Communications Officer Mundy.

Adele Mundy. One of *us*.

"Tarnhelm, this is Mike X-ray Five Three Nine," Adele said with the formality of a scholar reading a script. "Over."

She *was* a scholar reading a script, Daniel knew, but he controlled his desire to wince. Adele might not sound like an officer tired after a long, boring mission, but she could put on a Bryce accent that wouldn't set off alarms the way Daniel might if it were him on the radio.

"Go ahead Mike X-ray Five Three Niner," the Alliance harbor control authority replied. *He* sounded bored, which was good.

If the military command had gotten concerned about why its commandoes hadn't reported back from dealing with the reported Cinnabar sailors, it might have careted the APC's number and identification transponder with harbor control. Daniel preferred to be one of the day's several hundred indistinguishable movements through the air about Kostroma City.

"Mike X-ray Five Three Nine requests permission to land at Dock Twenty-Five to pick up a passenger," Adele said. "Over."

She didn't sound worried. She probably wasn't worried, which put her one up on Daniel Leary right at this moment. But he suspected Adele couldn't be less than precise if life depended on it.

It did, but they'd make out one way or another. The Alliance military probably had its share of officers who always sounded like they had a broomstick up their ass.

Daniel doubted that sort very often found themselves commanding special operations troops—or survived very long when they did—but the technician in harbor control might not even know what MX539 was. Unless he had some reason to care, the APC was merely a number and a radar track to be routed away from other numbers and radar tracks.

It was dusk. On the horizon lights moved through the air above Kostroma City and across the water at its margins. Both the Floating Harbor and the surface harbor were much brighter than Daniel had seen them in the past. The Alliance forces had brought in additional lighting, as well as much else.

"Roger, Mike X-ray," the radio voice said. "You're cleared at altitude twenty meters, vector two-three-one, I repeat two-three-one, degrees. Tarnhelm Control out."

Daniel had made sure the commo helmets were shut off so they wouldn't accidentally be used. "Keep the speed down to thirty, Gambier," he shouted toward the driver's compartment.

Gambier flew with his seat high to raise his head through the open hatch, but Barnes was beside him watching the instrument panel. Barnes tugged the driver's leg and repeated the command.

Adele looked down at Daniel. There wasn't room for two people in the cupola ring, so he squatted beside her in the narrow passageway from the troop compartment to the driver's compartment. "Was I all right?" she asked.

She *had* been worried, she just didn't show it. "You were fine," Daniel said. That was true: they'd gotten clearance. This wasn't an acting class where performances were graded on a curve. "If everything else goes as well, we'll be back on Cinnabar before my birthday next month."

That was true too. If Daniel'd been asked if he thought that was a probable result, well, that would have been a different question.

"More ships have landed," Adele said. Unlike Gambier she preferred to view her surroundings through electronic imagery. The vehicle commander's position had a panoramic optical display as well as a combiner screen which echoed all the driver's gauges. "And Alliance forces seem to have taken over most of the government departments, not just traffic control."

Daniel nodded grimly. "Three destroyers and I count six big transports; that's a brigade at least, with full equipment. People who ask for help from Guarantor Porra don't realize what they're really going to get. Though by now they ought to."

"Are you thinking of the Three Circles Conspiracy?" Adele asked without emotion.

Daniel felt his stomach tighten. "No," he said. "I wasn't."

If he'd been thinking about what happened fifteen years ago on Cinnabar he'd have had better sense than to say anything out loud. The last thing he wanted to do was to offend the woman on whom the detachment's survival had depended, and still depended.

Adele sniffed. "I was thinking about it," she said. She appeared to be observing the ships in the Floating Harbor on her display.

Daniel cleared his throat. "Cinnabar and Kostroma are very different," he said, because he was afraid he had to say something.

"Yes," said Adele. "And Corder Leary isn't a complete fool like Walter III."

She shook her head and continued, "My parents were very passionate people. I'm sure passion is a useful characteristic or it wouldn't be so general in the human population, but I've always thought it must get in the way of accurate assessments."

She met Daniel's eyes and offered her pale excuse for a smile. "Of course, my parents had friends," she said. "As I do not."

Daniel tapped her shoulder with his clenched fist. "You've got friends," he said.

And Daniel Leary had one friend more than he'd had when he arrived on Kostroma.

The APC's landing skids grated minusculely as it settled to the *Aglaia*'s concrete dock. Adele, wearing the commando lieutenant's uniform, reached for the hatch mechanism.

Behind her Daniel called into the closed-up troop compartment, "Remember, nobody says a word except Ms. Mundy. Not if there's a gun in your face!"

Adele opened the narrow hatch beside the cupola and stepped out, remembering the Alliance officer doing the same thing the day before. She wondered if she ought to display hectoring anger as the commando had done.

Adele smiled slightly. So long as the guards on the *Aglaia*'s landing stage didn't make the correspondence perfect by throwing a grenade through the hatch.

The ports and panels that had been open when the *Aglaia* was in Cinnabar hands were now clamped shut, except for the main hatch where six soldiers armed with stocked impellers waited. The guards wore tan, not camouflaged, uniforms, so they were sailors rather than soldiers, Adele supposed.

The guards watched with interest just short of concern as Adele and the commando-uniformed Cinnabars exited one by one. Dropping the sides of the troop compartment might have looked provocative, and there was just a chance that a guard would notice that the five Cinnabars still aboard wore Kostroman naval garments.

Adele strode across the unrailed catwalk to the landing stage. Waves lifted the ship and the pontoon in differing rhythms; when the sailors tramped onto the light-metal ramp behind her Adele's balance problem got even worse.

Adele kept her eyes focused on the face of the bearded petty officer commanding the guards. Her own visage was grim, perhaps a more suitable expression than she'd have been able to arrange had she not been afraid of falling into the *damned* ocean.

"We're the relief for Lieutenant Wozzeck's platoon," Adele said coldly as she reached the landing stage. It too rose and fell, but without the twisting vibration. Did dignitaries never fall in the water?

"Wozzeck?" the Alliance sailor said. He'd been born on rural Leon from his dialect; Adele's statement puzzled him, but not her

Bryce accent. "Sir, the navy took over here ten hours ago. This is the prize ship *Aglaia*."

"Of course it's the *Aglaia*," Adele snapped. "Vishnu and his Avatars! Where's Lieutenant Wozzeck?"

The guards looked at one another in worried puzzlement. One of them—speaking toward her petty officer, not Adele—said, "Wozzeck was watch commander on the duty sheet before Glanz took over, but that was last watch."

"All right, where's your damned command post?" Adele said with an angry grimace. She slapped her left thigh to add to the effect. "I'll try to raise somebody who can tell me what's going on."

She looked over her shoulder. Daniel had reached the landing stage. The rest of the Cinnabar sailors were strung out along the walkway or still on the pontoon because Adele hadn't left them room to go farther. They were nonchalant; probably more nonchalant than real soldiers would have been.

"Leary," Adele said, "you come with me. The rest of you stand easy until I get back with some information. And keep your mouths shut! This is supposed to be a non-disclosure mission."

"Non-disclosure mission" didn't mean anything that Adele knew of, but she'd been in and around bureaucracies most of her life. Nobody in a large organization knew everything that was going on, and this hint of mystery gave the sailors an excuse not to betray themselves by their accents.

The petty officer reached for the radio in a belt sheath, then quailed before Adele's stony glare. "Nawroos, take them to the bridge," he ordered abruptly.

An Alliance sailor handed his impeller to one of his fellows, then crooked a finger for Adele and Daniel to follow him into the *Aglaia*. He led them into one of the armored staircases off the entrance lobby.

Adele noticed that Daniel had started for the opposite set of stairs; he caught himself, she thought, before the sailor noticed. Familiarity with the *Aglaia*'s regulations as a Cinnabar ship had almost caused a problem.

"The ship seems pretty big for a sixteen-strong guard detachment," she remarked to the guide ahead of her in the echoing stairwell. "Is that enough for the job?"

They wound past a door open to the next deck. The guide lifted his hands in unconcern. "All the Merks we captured are in Hold

Two, sir," he said. He didn't bother to turn around, so dialect and reverberation blurred his words to the edge of understandability. "No light, no running water, and no fucking trouble for us."

Adele's sub-machine gun hung beneath her right arm on a short-looped sling. Her hand lay on the receiver to keep the gun from swinging, but she didn't really think of it as a weapon.

Her weapon rode, as usual, in the left side pocket of her tunic.

The guide stepped through the next door off the stairwell and turned left. They were in a hallway of some sort, lighted by surface-glow paneling. Daniel was a half step behind Adele, his head swiveling to observe points of distinction in what was to her a featureless landscape.

Offices to either side of the hall had been ransacked messily; drawers had been turned over on the floor. There'd been no attempt to clean up after the search, if it was anything as formal as a search. Looting was, perhaps, more likely.

"Hey, Lieutenant?" the guide called to the open door at the end of the hall. "Here's some soldiers that think they've got the duty here. Blaney sent 'em up to you."

The guide waved Adele and Daniel on and headed for the stairs by which they'd come. Obviously he felt no need to get into a discussion with his commanding officer. Adele strode through the door before any of the occupants decided to come out to meet her.

There were six tan-uniformed people inside a room with a great deal of built-in electronic equipment. None of the Alliance sailors looked particularly interested to have company. Two were playing a board game, not chess; another poured herself a cup of coffee from a carafe on a hotplate, and two watched an erotic recording on a holographic display.

The sixth, an overweight man, put on a cap decorated with gold braid and rose from the swivel chair where he'd been sitting. The console behind him was live. It was of a standard pattern, one that Adele could operate in her sleep.

"Yes?" the Alliance officer said. He wasn't impolite but he wasn't welcoming either. Adele didn't know how their two ranks compared.

"I need to check with my commander," Adele said. She walked past the naval officer as though he were a doorman and sat at the console. The seat was still warm.

"Who the hell do you think you are?" the Alliance officer asked indignantly. "You can't just come barging in here and taking over!"

Adele locked the console and all outgoing communications links, the matter of a few quick commands. There was no certainty of what would happen in the next minute or two, and the guards couldn't be permitted to summon help.

Adele swiveled the chair around. "All right," she said to Daniel.

Daniel looked down the corridor, then closed the door. It was a massive, armored panel and took all his weight to swing it home.

"Hey!" said a sailor.

The door banged against its countersunk jamb. Daniel unslung his sub-machine gun. "All of you against the port bulkhead," he ordered with a nod.

The nearest sailor flung her coffee and jumped at Daniel. He stiff-armed her away with his free hand. Adele shot the sailor in the shoulder.

The sailor's clavicle shattered as the pellet whacked into it. She screamed and spasmed into the wall. The Alliance officer turned as though to grab Adele, saw the pistol aimed at the bridge of his nose, and backed carefully against the wall.

The sailors followed their officer. Two of them helped their injured fellow. She whimpered with pain, but the wound was survivable unless a bone splinter had nicked a major blood vessel.

Adele unlocked the console while Daniel held his sub-machine gun on the bridge crew. When she'd finished, she stood up and said, "There. You'd better take over now."

"I will," Daniel said as he traded duties with her, "but don't sell yourself short." He grinned. "The RCN lost a great officer when you buried yourself in a library."

To the ship's public address system he went on, "Mistress Woetjans, complete the transfer of authority at the landing stage and report to the bridge with two ratings to take charge here. I'm coming to take over the remainder of the detachment."

Daniel looked at Adele. "Are you all right with these until Woetjans gets here?" he said, nodding toward the prisoners. "I want to release our people below right away."

"Oh, yes," said Adele. The captured sailors were looking at her. "There's only six of them, after all, and I've got nineteen more rounds in my pistol magazine."

She smiled without humor, wondering which of these faces might be staring at her in dreams for the rest of her life. Probably none of them, because they seemed to be very frightened of her.

That meant they understood.

As Daniel led ten "Alliance commandoes" down the passageway toward Hold 2, he felt the *Aglaia* quiver in a sequence of constantly changing harmonics. Since her capture, the *Aglaia* had been shut down except for the minimal systems required by the guard detachment. Woetjans was bringing the ship to life again.

Hold 2 held bulk consumables when the ship was fully loaded. The voyage from Cinnabar had run the stocks down, and the quantities remaining had been off-loaded on landing to be surveyed and replaced if they'd deteriorated. The RCN didn't feed its crews spoiled food, and if corners ever had to be cut it wouldn't be on a communications vessel like the *Aglaia*.

Four Alliance ratings were on guard at the inner hatch. The hold opened on the hull side also, but at the moment the exterior hatch was under twenty feet of salt water. Hold 2 made an excellent prison, if you didn't care about the conditions of the captives within.

The guards had gotten up from their card table when they heard Daniel's detachment approaching. They were chewing *kift*, a plant native to Pleasaunce with a mildly narcotic effect on humans. When the stalks were reduced to a tangle of soggy fibers, the guards spat them onto the deck and bulkheads to cling and dry.

"Yeah?" said one of the guards. Impellers leaned against the bulkhead nearby, but the guards didn't even glance toward their weapons.

Lamsoe pointed his sub-machine gun at the guards. "One move and you're all dead," he snarled. "I wouldn't half mind splashing your guts across the passage after the mess you've been making down here!"

"Too fucking right!" Sun agreed. The whole detachment had leveled their weapons. The Alliance ratings couldn't have been more surprised if an archangel had materialized before them.

"Let's nobody get excited, shall we?" said Hogg. Unlike the naval personnel, his master included, he wasn't horrified by the filthy sty into which the guards had transformed the *Aglaia*. "If people start shooting, the ricochets gotta go somewhere."

Hogg gestured the Alliance ratings toward the end of the corridor with the coil of cargo tape he'd brought to secure them. "Sit down and hold your hands out, you dumb bastards, and you'll live through the day, all right?"

As the guards obeyed, Daniel examined the hatch mechanism. The hold could be padlocked, but only a simple rod now blocked the system. Daniel tossed that to the deck and activated the power latch, then backed out of the way.

"All right, Cinnabars," he called to the fetid darkness within Hold 2. "You're free now. Come out without noise or jostling. I want the senior officer to report to me immediately."

"It's Mr. Leary!" a rating called in delighted wonder. Daniel permitted himself the shadow of a smile, despite the tension and his anger at the stench in which his shipmates had been confined.

Discipline held. The first person through the open hatch was Domenico, the bosun. He braced to attention and saluted—an admiral's inspection salute, not the forehead tap of a fighting ship on service. "Sir!" he said.

Ratings poured out of the hold. Some hugged friends among Daniel's detachment or even kissed the deck in delight to be freed, but the process was as orderly as a barracks emptying at a call of General Quarters.

"I don't mind saying I'm *real* glad to see you, Mr. Leary," Domenico added with a smile that involved every millimeter of his craggy face. "The best we were hoping for was passage to Pleasaunce and maybe exchange in a year or two."

"I think we can do better than that, Domenico," Daniel said. "What's our present strength?"

He glanced around to be sure everything was under control, but there was really nothing *to* control: these were veterans, every one of them. The most junior rating could rig, work ship, or handle the armament without a petty officer's attention.

"A hundred and thirty, including me and Chief Baylor," Domenico said. "The rest is ratings. The commissioned officers they took someplace else, and there's forty of the crew killed or sent to hospital when the bastards took us over. Chief of Ship Nantes, she choked on her tongue."

The bosun scowled like a thundercloud. "Talk about catching us with our pants down, sir, they did that for fair!"

"Yes, well, we'll see if we can't surprise our Alliance friends in turn," Daniel said mildly. "We'll ready the *Aglaia* for liftoff while a party frees Captain Le Golif and his officers, then reach orbit and head for home before anyone realizes what's going on."

His stomach twisted to think of the casualties to the *Aglaia*'s crew, though he supposed he should have known. The Alliance had used non-lethal gas in their takeover, but even so there were bound to be people who got an overdose or were allergic to the compound.

"Sir, it won't work," Domenico said miserably. "They didn't want us getting ideas about crawling out through a cable trunk or some damned thing, so they dismantled the High Drive. Had a detail of our own people do it so we'd know for sure that even if we got loose there wasn't any place to go."

"And they cleaned out the arms locker," said Chief Missileer Baylor, who'd joined them from the hold. He was a slight, sharp-featured man who looked as though he'd aged a decade since Daniel saw him a week and a half ago. "Primary and secondary armament's still in place, such as it is, because they didn't have time to offload it."

"Very well," said Daniel. "We'll have to do something else, then."

Learning that they couldn't escape in the *Aglaia* was a shock, but it passed in a few heartbeats. Shocks were always brief for Daniel Leary. His wasn't the sort of personality that thought it could plan for every eventuality. He did think, *feel*, that he could handle any crisis that arose, though. Thus far he'd been pretty successful at that.

The *Aglaia*'s crew was sorting itself by watches and specialties in the corridor, each portion under the command of a petty officer or the senior rating if no petty officer was present. Daniel's detachment threw the four guards, bound with cargo tape, into the hold in place of the Cinnabars. The process was more violent than would have seemed necessary if the conditions for the former prisoners had been a little better.

"I think we'll take the *Princess Cecile*," Daniel said as calmly as though the idea had been at the top of his conscious mind for a week. "I don't imagine any of the Alliance vessels will be so poorly guarded as to give us the opportunity we need, but I've found you can generally count on the Kostromans to let things slide."

Daniel looked at what was his command, by God, until the *Aglaid*'s proper officers came aboard. He gave the crew a pleased, professional smile and said, "Right. Warrant officers to the bridge with me, the rest of you to general quarters and await orders."

"Aye aye *sir*!" over a hundred ratings boomed as they scrambled to obey.

"Em Ex five three niner," said the controller's voice; a different person but as bored as the first one. "You're cleared to leave harbor. Maintain fifty meters altitude until you're three klicks out. Tarnhelm control out."

"Go ahead, Gambier," Daniel called from beside Adele. The APC slid off the pontoon and accelerated across the water's surface for several seconds in a trough of spray before rising to the prescribed altitude.

Daniel nodded approvingly. "Gambier's using surface effect till we build momentum," he said.

Adele started to climb out of the cupola; Daniel waved her back with a grin. "Stay there," he said. "We're more likely to need you on the radio than we are me on the cannon. I hope to God that's true, anyhow."

His grin broadened into his full-dress smile, an expression that made even Adele feel absurdly positive. "Besides," he added, "you could probably use the cannon too."

Adele sniffed. "About as well as you could handle the communications chores," she said. She permitted herself a tiny grin. "Which might be adequate. I've noticed that you have a very good ear."

Kostroma City had shrunk to a smudge on the horizon on Adele's panoramic screen. Gambier was following the programmed course, taking them well out to sea before curving southward toward the Navy Pool. The harbor and warehouse complex had Alliance detachments overseeing the Kostroman naval personnel on duty, but they weren't linked to Tarnhelm control.

Adele had listened to enough of their radio traffic to know that the standards at the Navy Pool were lax. Very nearly as lax as they'd been under Walter III, in fact.

"I'd like to use something less threatening than an APC," Daniel said as he scowled at the receiver of the sub-machine gun that was effectively part of his uniform. Adele had never seen Daniel fire a shot, now that she thought about it. "Our Alliance friends stripped airboats and anything else movable off the *Aglaia* as soon as they took over, it seems. The cutters too, though I wouldn't want to use a cutter."

"An Alliance APC will be an advantage," Adele said. "The Kostromans won't dare question us."

She didn't know whether she was being logical or merely soothing. She rather thought she was trying to be soothing, but that wasn't a familiar experience for her.

A dam crossed the jaws of a bayou to form the Navy Pool. It swelled in Adele's display, looking like a causeway supported by buttresses. The flap valves on the inner side formed a solid wall when the incoming tide no longer held them open.

The APC slowed mushily. Barnes stuck his head back between the drivers' seats to call, "Sir, there's a big aircar right slap in the center of the tender moored to the *Princess Cecile*. What do you want us to do?"

Adele glanced at the display before she remembered Daniel was the person who had to be able to see what was going on. She started to squeeze out of the way, then realized Daniel didn't need the display. He'd already echoed the image through his helmet's hologram projector.

She kept forgetting that though Daniel wasn't an information specialist, he *was* a professional trained to use state-of-the-art military hardware. Given a little time and experimentation she might be able to get more out of the equipment than Daniel could, but he handled it smoothly for its intended purposes.

The *Princess Cecile* was the cigar-shaped corvette Adele had seen in flight only a few days earlier during the Founder's Day celebrations. It was moored in the center of the bayou, at a distance from the rows of generally larger ships along the shore.

A flat barge was tied to the main hatch. Many of the corvette's other hatches and ports gaped also. The scene reminded Adele of the way the *Aglaia* had looked before she was captured.

The aircar parked in the middle of the barge's deck could carry at least a dozen passengers. The car's gray-enameled sides were marked with Alliance crests and stenciled government motorpool legends.

"Set us down on the tender's stern and pray we don't swamp her," Daniel ordered. "Keep the fan speed up in case it does."

He looked at Adele and shook his head. "If *they'd* landed on one end or the other, we could center our weight and there'd be no problem."

"If wishes hooked fish," Hogg put in tartly, "then you and I wouldn't have ate so much dried food when we'd go off camping."

Daniel's servant wore a commando uniform that couldn't be said to fit him even after he'd done some rough-and-ready tailoring to the sleeves, trouser legs, and waistband. Nobody'd suggested that the uniform should go to somebody who was more nearly the right size and age, however.

Adele was just as glad of that. At least some of the sailors were good shots, and their courage was beyond question. In the present business, however, she trusted Hogg's reflexes as she did those of no other member of the party.

Hogg carried a stocked impeller for choice. At Daniel's orders, so did Lamsoe, Sun, and Dasi. Adele hadn't understood why until Hogg explained to the sailors.

Sub-machine guns were lighter, handier and fine at short range. The light pellets were next to useless against vehicles or targets a hundred yards away, however. The group didn't know what they'd be facing in the next few minutes, and Daniel's desire for a range of alternatives was worth the extra weight.

Gambier dropped the APC to the surface of the water, then bounced up onto the tender. The inevitable gush of spray soaked the car already there. The driver jumped into her cab, shaking her fist at the APC.

Daniel smiled faintly. "Whoever's here ahead of us complicates things," he said, "but we'll handle it."

Adele nodded crisply. "I didn't do a cull and sort for messages referring to the *Princess Cecile*," she said. "It's my fault."

The APC settled. The tender rocked uncomfortably but finally stabilized with a slight list. When Gambier was sure it wouldn't turn turtle, he shut down the engines.

"It was your fault that time is finite and that I was in a hurry?" Daniel said. "No, I really don't think it was."

He turned to face the enclosed troop compartment. "Same drill as before: Ms. Mundy does all the talking until I give orders to the contrary."

Adele saw Daniel's jaw muscles twitch in a familiar smile. "Or the shooting starts, all right? But we don't start it."

Adele stepped onto the tender's quivering deck. The car's driver had gotten out again; she wore an Alliance naval uniform. "You there!" Adele snapped in upper-class scorn. "Who told you to land in the middle of this site? What are you doing here, anyway?"

She heard Hogg murmur in pleased appreciation.

The driver swallowed a lungful of protests in sudden fear. Greenish *kift* juice dribbled down her cheek.

"Look, I'm just driving Commander Strachan and the inspectors," she said as she backed toward the cab again. "Look, I'll move it, all right?"

She closed the hatch behind her before Adele could have replied if she wanted to. "They'll be examining the ship to take her into Alliance service," Daniel murmured into Adele's right ear. "Probably three officers and aides, but nobody looking for trouble."

The aircar's fans howled; it slid sideways clumsily. Adele strode toward the corvette's hatch, trying to ignore the way the deck hopped beneath her soles. She hoped the idiot driver wouldn't manage to fall off the tender and bring a rush of people out into the open.

The *Princess Cecile* was much more cramped than the *Aglaia*. Two Kostroman sailors were in the entrance lobby, standing beside mops and buckets of soapy water. They stopped talking when they saw the "commandoes."

"Where are the inspectors?" Adele demanded. She heard footsteps and a mixture of voices approaching.

The sailors looked at one another. A group of people wearing Kostroman and Alliance officers' uniforms walked into the entranceway from the hall to the left.

"What's this?" said an Alliance officer.

"Leary!" a Kostroman officer cried. Adele recognized him as one of the plump young peacocks she'd met at the Admiral's Ball. His name was Candace. "What are you—"

Adele had her pistol out but down at her side. It wasn't a magic wand; you didn't point it for threat the way sailors behind her were doing with their weapons. "Don't move or I'll kill you!" she said, her eyes holding those of the officer from Pleasaunce.

Paunchy, in his thirties . . . his light ginger hair would fluff out like a halo when the pellet penetrated his cranial vault through the light bones at the back of his eye socket. She could see it—

Hogg stepped forward and made a quarter turn of his upper body. He planted the butt of his impeller in the pit of Candace's stomach. Candace fell to his knees, then spewed his dinner on the unscrubbed metal decking.

All around Adele Cinnabar sailors seized Kostroman and Alliance personnel alike, forcing them to their knees at gunpoint with shouted threats. Teams scrambled down the halls in both directions from the entrance alcove. A sub-machine gun fired, a needlessly long burst that sent bits of pellet and chips from the walls sparkling all the way back into the entrance. Someone screamed curses in a Cinnabar accent.

"Sir, they've locked the power room!" a voice cried.

"The bridge is secured!" another voice called.

The Alliance officer's nametag read Strachan in black letters on a gold field. He hadn't moved except to close his mouth since Adele spoke. Two sailors caught Strachan by the elbows, kicked his knees forward, and began strapping his wrists behind his back with cargo tape. He didn't resist, but his eyes never left Adele's.

The vessel shuddered as a heavy door slid to a stop. Daniel returned to the entrance alcove from the left; from the bridge, Adele supposed. "That was the power room containment bulkhead," he said with a scowl. "There's no override from the bridge."

He glanced around. A dozen captives lay on the deck, trussed like hens for market.

Hogg returned from the tender and gave Daniel a thumbs up. "We've got an aircar now too, sir," the servant announced. "We're coming up in the world."

Daniel's usual grin replaced the scowl. "Well," he said, "we can't burn through the containment bulkhead even with the plasma cannon, so I guess we'll have to talk some Kostroman sailors out of the power room."

"I guess we will," said Adele Mundy as she pocketed her pistol.

"Look, Leary . . ." Candace said. The gray sheen of his face made him look like a death mask of his normally handsome self. His seat was swiveled to face out from the Attack Console.

Candace rubbed his forehead and went on, "I'm sorry I ever met you! Are you trying to get me killed? First you come to my house, my *house* for God's sake! And now you think I'm going to help you and a gang of pirates steal a ship? You must be out of your mind!"

Daniel sighed. He'd thought he could bring Candace around if he took the Kostroman to the bridge. There were no open threats—though Hogg was nearby, trimming his fingernails with a knife as he pretended to watch Adele at one of the bridge consoles. The captured Alliance officers were in the wardroom, nearby but out of sight. All that was happening was that Leary and Candace, friends from different planets, were talking over a mutual problem.

Candace didn't see it that way. Well, Daniel hadn't really expected he would; but neither did Daniel see any other practical way of getting the Kostromans in the power room to surrender. Adele was sure that they couldn't get a message out, but Daniel and his Cinnabar crew couldn't lift the *Princess Cecile* with an unknown number of hostile sailors in charge of her power room.

At the moment the vessel was running on standby power from the auxiliary power unit in a bow compartment. The APU's output wasn't enough to operate the plasma motors, much less the antimatter conversion system of the High Drive.

"Leary," Candace said, speaking with the desperate earnestness of a man in fear of his life, "I'm neutral in this, just like I told you before. I don't wish you any harm, but the Alliance of Free Stars is in *power* now, there's no two ways about it."

Daniel sat on a fold-down jumpseat on one edge of the console. Candace tried to rotate his seat to face away from Daniel. Hogg held the chair where it was.

Candace acted like a kid hiding his head under the blanket to keep the bogeyman from finding him, Daniel thought. Cowardice like that in a man, let alone a fellow naval officer, turned Daniel's stomach.

"You've got to leave me out of whatever you're doing," Candace said. "They'll *kill* me!"

"Sir?" said Hogg as he looked down at the Kostroman in disgust equal to Daniel's own. "It sounds to me like the problem is he's more afraid of what the Alliance is going to do to him than he is of us. Let me have him for a couple minutes and he won't think that anymore."

Adele turned her head toward the three men without expression.

"No need for anybody else to watch," Hogg added in slight embarrassment. "I'll take him down to the forward magazine."

Candace hid his face in his hands. He was shaking. It suddenly struck Daniel that the Kostroman's fear wasn't really for his physical well-being but rather because he was being asked to make a decision. Candace was more afraid to act than he was to die.

Daniel stood. He smiled at Hogg and Adele. "No," he said. "Benno here's a friend of mine and I don't want anybody to hurt him."

He paused to let Candace relax slightly, then continued, "The Alliance officers he was squiring about the ship aren't friends of mine, though. Remember how we killed those first two commandoes to get the others to talk, Lt. Mundy? Go next door and do the same thing to Commander Strachan and his staff, one at a time."

He paused. "Until Benno decides to help us."

Adele rose from the commo officer's console, still without expression. "Take your sub-machine gun," Daniel said, nodding toward the weapon she'd left hanging from the back of her seat.

"Yes," Adele said. "That's the better choice for this purpose."

Candace stared at the three Cinnabars in horrified amazement. Daniel wasn't sure that the Kostroman was really taking in what was going on.

"Look, sir," said Hogg. He looked at least as concerned as Candace did. Hogg had been unconscious when Daniel and Adele put on their charade with the commandoes, so he thought this was real. "This is, you know, more up my alley. I'll take care of it."

"No," said Adele, "I will. I haven't killed anyone for a few days."

She looked critically at the Alliance sub-machine gun, then threw the lever on the back of the receiver to charge it. The mechanical *clack* within the weapon sounded like a dry chuckle.

She looked at Candace and said, "You'd best hope you don't fall into the hands of the Alliance after I've killed the six officers in your charge. The head of the operation is a man named Markos, from the Fifth Bureau. He's not a gentleman. The very best you can hope for is that you'll be quickly executed."

She smiled. Even Daniel felt his stomach clench to see the expression. Adele walked out of the bridge, holding the submachine gun in her right hand with the muzzle safely raised.

"Candace, I'm sorry as I can be," said Daniel, shaking his head, "but I need you to talk your people out of the power room. I've got nothing against you or them—I'll let you all go free before we lift ship. But if any of those Alliance officers die, God himself couldn't save you if you get into Markos's hands."

He wondered if Markos was a real person whose name Adele had gotten from signals intelligence or if she'd simply invented the name. When she was doing her sinister act, she was scarier than Hogg with a drawn knife—and Hogg wasn't acting.

"Leary—" Candace pleaded.

"Get out of the way," Adele's voice ordered from the wardroom. Her words clear and utterly calm. The bridge and wardroom hatches were both open. The noise of ratings inspecting and readying the vessel for space wasn't loud enough to dull Adele's perfect enunciation.

There was a mixed gabble of protest in Alliance accents. The examination team was a commander and two lieutenant commanders, with three midshipmen as aides. Daniel wondered if any of them had been present when Admiral Lasowski was murdered.

The sub-machine gun fired a short burst. Pellets disintegrated and spalled bits off the decking. A spark danced into the corridor to hiss on the lip of the bridge hatch. Alliance voices rose in screams.

There was a second burst.

The prisoners lay on the deck of the wardroom with their wrists and ankles taped. Daniel hadn't decided what to do with them; they were simply out of the way for the moment.

He'd expected Adele to shoot into the couch or one of the wardroom chairs, but from the terrified cries she must be putting each burst into the deck within an inch or two of a prisoner's ear. The carpet was glass fiber and nonflammable, but the stench of smoldering human hair indicated where some of the sparks were landing.

"Oh God oh God oh God!" Candace said. He'd squeezed his palms over his ears, but he still couldn't shut out the screams from the wardroom. "Stop it! Stop it!"

"Cease fire!" Daniel cried. He returned his attention to Candace.

Quietly he resumed, "Now, I hope that means you're ready to help us, Benno. Because if you're not . . ."

Adele walked back onto the bridge. Behind her a rating clanged shut the wardroom hatch, smothering the prisoners' voices. The muzzle of her sub-machine gun glowed; heat waves shimmered in the air above the barrel shroud.

"I'll talk to them," Candace said. He wiped tears from his eyes, then lowered his hands and faced Daniel with an unexpected degree of dignity. "I'll say anything you please. And I don't care what you do then. You're all animals!"

Adele draped the sling of her sub-machine gun over the seatback again. She looked at her right wrist. The skin was smudged with a black residue: metal from the pellets' driving skirts, vaporized by the flux and redeposited on the shooter's skin.

Candace turned his seat. He stabbed a button on the left wing of his console and said, "Bridge to power room. This is Lieutenant Candace. Whoever's in charge of the power room, report now."

Daniel shifted position slightly so that he could look over the Kostroman's shoulder at the communicator's holographic display. That wasn't much help because though the display came alive, somebody had flung a shirt over the power room's imaging pickup.

"Sir, what's going on?" a male voice said. The words were a plea, not a demand.

Daniel nodded toward the console's pickup and gave it a pleasant smile. The ratings in the power room could see him even if he couldn't see them, so it was important to project an aura of friendly calm.

"Gershon?" Candace said. "It's all right. We've been captured by the Cinnabar navy but I know the officer in charge. Everything will be all right so long as you open the power room with no trouble. They, they're . . . It's really very important that you surrender right away, Gershon."

He swallowed. "Really very important."

A last tear dropped from Candace's chin to the sill of the console. His hands were folded in his lap, but they were still shaking.

"Sir, what'll happen to us if we raise the containment bulkhead?" Gershon's voice asked. "Are they, you know . . . ?"

"You'll be confined aboard the *Princess Cecile* until just before we're ready to leave Kostroma, Gershon," Daniel said mildly. He rested his right forearm on top of the console in order to look even more relaxed than his voice projected. "Then we'll let you and all those with you go."

As a smiling afterthought he added, "Or you can join us, if you like. The Republic of Cinnabar Navy can always use brisk fellows who know how to act in a crisis."

"Christ help us," Gershon muttered miserably. The shirt slipped away from the pickup. The bald, gray-bearded Kostroman at the power room communicator looked as though he'd just volunteered to jump into vacuum.

"Open the bulkhead, Carney," he ordered. He pulled his shirt on to cover his scarred torso. A worm gear began to whine, hauling back the massive barrier intended to prevent a fusion bottle ruptured during combat from venting its contents through the entire vessel.

"We may as well give up," said Gershon. He was speaking toward Daniel, not Candace in the foreground. "We haven't got any rations or even water in here."

"You won't be sorry, I assure you," Daniel said. Commando-garbed Cinnabar ratings poured into the power room behind Gershon. They were securing the Kostromans without any serious roughness so far as Daniel could tell.

"Damn right," said Hogg, moving into the pickup's field for the first time. "And if you're smart, you'll sign up with Mr. Leary. You'll like serving under a real officer for a change."

Adele stood in the hatchway of the APC, waiting for Daniel to take his restraining hand off the coaming. She was so irritated that she'd have driven away while he was still talking, but Barnes was more respectful of his lieutenant.

The Alliance aircar approached the tender in a trough of spray, returning from the *Aglaia* with another load of sailors. Gambier was driving, but a Kostroman—Warrant Officer Gershon, the man who'd closed down the power room during the assault—sat beside him to provide an authentically non-Cinnabar voice for Tarnhelm Control.

"Look, Adele," Daniel said, raising his voice to be heard over the car's fans. "I think I'd better come along after all. It isn't proper for a civilian to be in charge of this. Freeing RCN officers is RCN business, and—"

"Mr. Leary," Adele said in a tone of very genuine cold anger, "in your company I have taken part in looting naval warehouses and in capturing not one but two naval vessels. There is no one in our mutual enterprise who knows the Elector's Palace as well as I do, nor whose accent can pass for that of an Alliance citizen. Your presence is necessary to ready the *Princess Cecile* for our escape. The twelve of us—"

She nodded toward Hogg and the ten sailors under Woetjans already within the vehicle. They and Adele wore commando uniforms.

"—can deal with the matter of the *Aglaia*'s officers just as readily as we could if your presence made our number thirteen."

She wrinkled her nose dismissively. "I don't object to you coming on grounds of superstition," she said, "merely because it would be stupid."

The aircar landed, rocking the tender despite the APC's centered mass. Gambier idled the fans and the noise level dropped.

"Sir?" said Hogg. "Have this bitch of a wog ship ready to lift when we get back, all right? Because sure as shit, *we're* going to be ready."

"Too fucking true," agreed Woetjans.

"Yes," said Daniel. "All right."

The car was disgorging its load of sailors. "Hold for me, Gambier," Daniel called. "I need to prepare the *Aglaia* for when we lift."

He looked at Adele and smiled wistfully. "Odd that it's so much easier to do something dangerous than to ask friends to do so, isn't it? Good luck. And Hogg?"

"Yessir?" the servant called. Adele had already started to pull the hatch to.

"Ms. Mundy has all the skills desirable in an affair of this nature," Daniel said. "She does not have experience, however. Don't let anything happen to her."

"On my honor, sir!" Hogg shouted as Adele clanged the hatch angrily closed.

Barnes skidded the armored personnel carrier away from the tender. Adele's stomach churned as they dropped to the water, then rose.

She wondered how many officers really thought it was easier to take risks than to order others to do so. If Daniel was an example, perhaps all the good ones did.

The *Aglaia*'s tactical operations center was an armored citadel at the opposite end of Deck E from the bridge. All the sensor inputs were routed here as well as to the bridge, through separate trunks.

Normally during battle the first lieutenant would be in charge of the TOC, while the captain commanded from the bridge and the Chief Missileer, a warrant officer, oversaw the missile launchers themselves. The weapons stations were entirely automated, but things go wrong with machinery even when nobody's shooting at you.

Daniel, in the TOC with the missileer, said, "To create a diversion when we lift to orbit, Chief Baylor, we're going to launch the *Aglaia*'s missiles on radio command while she's here in harbor. I'll deal with the software prohibitions, but I want you and your crew to remove the mechanical interlocks. There can't be any slip-ups."

"Bloody hell!" said Chief Baylor. His small, foxy face tightened with wrinkles. "Launch in an atmosphere? It'll . . ."

Daniel hadn't had much to do with the missileer on the *Aglaia*'s voyage out; Baylor kept to himself and his weapons, polishing the missiles' hulls and performing daily diagnostics on the launch and in-flight control systems. The other officers thought Baylor was strange, but he didn't cause trouble and he pulled his nonspecialist duties like anchor watch commander without objection.

A communications vessel was probably the perfect berth for a man like Chief Baylor. There was only a vanishingly low chance that the *Aglaia* would have to fire any of his beloved missiles—

But if she did, her crew could be certain the missiles would function perfectly.

"Yes," said Daniel harshly. "Launching in an atmosphere will certainly destroy the *Aglaia*. Depriving the Alliance of this valuable prize is a secondary reason for what we're about to do."

Missiles were miniature spaceships which had only High Drive for propulsion. High velocities were a requirement of interstellar travel, even when those velocities were multiplied by judicious use of bubble universes whose physical constants differed from those of the sidereal universe.

The High Drive was the most efficient way to boost a vessel to such velocities, but a certain amount of antimatter inevitably escaped the conversion process and was voided in the exhaust. When this happened in an atmosphere, antimatter and matter destroyed each other in a burst of pure energy just beyond the nozzle and wrecked everything in the vicinity.

Anti-ship missiles depended on kinetic energy and had no explosive warhead. Even a thermonuclear weapon would have been pointless in an object travelling at .6 *c.* Lack of atmospheric capability wasn't a handicap to the missiles because at those speeds, air was a solid barrier anyway.

Which didn't mean being hit by a just-launched thirty-ton missile was a love tap, however.

Baylor shook his head disconsolately. "Yessir," he said. "I've got my crew on alert, like you said, but I sure didn't figure you'd be asking us to do this."

The missileer's expression was similar to that Abraham must have worn when God ordered him to sacrifice his son. "I hate it, sir," he said simply. "I've served on a lot of ships in thirty-seven years, and this is the best of 'em. But we'll carry out orders."

Daniel nodded cold approval. "Make it so," he said. As Baylor turned to leave him alone in the TOC, Daniel said, "Chief?"

Baylor looked over his shoulder, expressionless.

"A ship is a tool," Daniel said. "It's all right to love a ship, but sometimes a tool has to be used, even if that means using it up."

He thought about the APC that was probably landing at the rear of the Elector's Palace about now. "Humans aren't tools," Daniel added. "But sometimes you have to use them up too. That's true for everybody who's taken the oath."

And for at least one librarian who hadn't.

The sides of the APC's troop compartment were lowered to give the big vehicle a less threatening appearance. Adele had examined the access restrictions for the palace. As she directed, Barnes idled them at surface level to the rear gate of the gardens instead of trying to overfly the wall and land close to the building.

The Alliance command had placed six posts of hypervelocity missiles on the palace roof and grounds to deal with vehicles which tried to evade the mandated entry checks. Properly designed layered armor could resist plasma weapons, perhaps for long enough to land a load of troops, but for defenders who didn't care about backblast, 500 grams of tungsten monocrystal moving at 5 kilometers per second was a good way to drill through anything short of a granite mountain.

The anti-vehicle batteries functioned automatically, irrespective of the target's Identification Friend or Foe signal. Adele had edited the control software to exempt their captured APC from the automatic defenses, but this wasn't the time to inform the Alliance forces of the fact.

Lamsoe was in the cupola. He and Barnes would stay with the vehicle while Adele led Hogg and nine sailors to the subbasement where the *Aglaia*'s officers were held along with other important prisoners.

Woetjans eyed the guard post. A heavily laden surface truck was ahead of the APC. The guards had lifted the bed's canvas cover and were checking individual crates of bottled liquor.

"These guys are regular army, not commandoes," the petty officer whispered in Adele's ear. "We commandoes think we're hot shit compared to them, you see?"

She growled a chuckle. "None of 'em are worth a fuck compared to the RCN, of course," she added. "But it's going to be a lot trickier than it would be if the wogs was still in charge."

The truck moved on. Barnes pulled forward. The sailors tried to look relaxed, with more success than Adele would have expected.

Adele had no particular feeling. She'd found if she viewed her present activities as information searches—which in a manner of speaking they were, data in the form of three Cinnabar naval officers—she could maintain the detached skill which was the best hope for success. If she thought of herself as responsible for the lives of these sailors and the officers they came to rescue, she wouldn't know how to behave.

The gardens were brightly illuminated from ten-meter pylons among the trampled plantings. The prisoner pen had been dismantled, but the wire lay in untidy bales along the north wall.

"What're you guys doing here?" asked the head of the guard detail to Barnes in the cab.

Adele leaned forward from the troop compartment and said, "The password is Nike. Countersign?"

The Alliance guards carried stocked impellers. An air cushion vehicle squatted behind a stone planter, covering the entrance with an automatic impeller in a small turret. The soldier watching from the turret hatch looked bored, but his weapon tracked the APC as it slid forward.

The detail commander walked back to face Adele directly. The compartment's deck gave her a height advantage.

"I said what're you guys doing here?" the guard said in a rising voice. "This is our operation now."

Woetjans spit onto the ground. She missed the guard's foot by several inches.

"All you have to say to me, soldier . . ." Adele said. She looked at the guard as though she wanted to wipe him off the sole of her boot. "Is the countersign. And if you don't give it, you'll see just who's in charge."

The guard scowled. The other troops in the detail stood by the gatekeeper's kiosk. Two of them hitched up their equipment belts and walked closer to the APC. So far as Adele could see, there were no Kostromans present.

"Vinceremos!" the detail commander snapped. He stepped away from the vehicle. "Have you noticed," he called loudly in the direction of his personnel, "how commando pukes wear helmets smarter'n they are?"

"Drive on," Adele ordered.

Woetjans pumped her middle finger in the direction of the Alliance soldiers as the APC waddled forward. The vehicle was sluggish because Barnes was keeping the speed down. The gardens were full of parked vehicles, and the detachment couldn't afford a collision.

Though Barnes crawled up the drive, Adele had the uneasy feeling that she had stepped onto a patch of glare ice. The APC's bow swung very slowly toward the left. They continued forward but the vehicle's axis no longer aligned with its direction of movement.

"He's pretty good," Hogg muttered critically. "He's driven boats as big as this bitch before, so he knows where the back and sides are. But he's not allowing for how much the armor weighs. He needs to correct quicker and not use so much fucking yoke when he does."

Woetjans looked worriedly from Adele to the cab. Ahead, a luxurious aircar stuck out a foot from the line of parked vehicles. The APC's rear fender would rip the car's side off in the next moment.

Barnes dropped his right skid to the pavement. It shrieked in a shower of sparks, then lifted again. The contact had braked their drift and straightened the course.

"He'll do," Adele said. She hadn't been going to let Woetjans shout at the driver anyway. Trying to directly control the work of somebody who's already over his head couldn't possibly have a good result.

"Pull in here," Woetjans called to the driver. "Onto the hedge. We've got the weight and it won't scratch our finish."

The petty officer looked at Adele. "If that's all right, sir?"

"Yes," said Adele. She hadn't thought of herself as being in real command of the undertaking, but that was how the sailors viewed her. She had to keep reminding herself to make decisions with crisp authority.

The hedged squares where Adele had met Markos were battered, but civilian vehicles weren't massive enough to drive through the remains of the bushes. As Woetjans had noted, the APC was. Perhaps it was a good omen that the detachment was able to park close to where they'd be escaping from the sub-surface levels.

But if you believed that, you could just as easily believe that Fate was giving with one hand in order to snatch the gift back with the other. Best trust to courage, discipline, and good marksmanship.

The APC shuddered as Barnes plowed the hedgerow with his side panel, then settled. When the driver cut the fans to idle, his own sigh of relief was audible over the sounds of the restive vehicle.

"Let's go," Woetjans said quietly. "Remember, company manners."

The detachment stepped down from the compartment in two ranks. Adele wiped her palms on her trouser legs. She'd thought she was perfectly calm.

Adele led the way up the ramp with Hogg at her side; Woetjans was one of the pair bringing up the rear. The Cinnabar sailors couldn't march in step and Adele didn't know what a military pace *was*, but Daniel assured her that they'd look out of place if they moved like parade-ground troops while wearing commando uniforms.

Despite the hour, lights were on all over the palace. The only time that was likely to have been true in the past was when the Elector was giving a party.

Adele saw the Kostromans for the first time since she'd entered the palace grounds: a group of low-ranking clerks, looking haggard and frightened as they left the building. She knew from her signals intelligence that the Alliance command was determined to take over every aspect of Kostroman life as soon as possible, but Kostroman bureaucrats were still necessary to the process. Their new masters were working them within an inch of their lives.

Or a step beyond. One of the messages Adele had skimmed was an order for the execution of a clerk who'd upset a glass of wine over a stack of account books while eating supper at his desk. The official charge was "treason against the Alliance of Free Stars." As the member of the Alliance military government had explained in her covering memo, the real purpose was to encourage other clerks to be more careful.

They entered the rear porch, covered by the overhang of the second and third stories. There was another guardpost, this time manned by troops whose rigid armor and opaque faceshields made them look like statues with only a rough resemblance to humans. Plasma cannon threatened from behind two semicircles of sandbags. Between the gun nests stood another soldier with an electronic reader.

Adele handed over the routing card she'd taken from the helmet of the commando lieutenant, a programmable chip in a rectangular polymer matrix. It had carried the commandoes' orders in electronic form that could be read on the helmet visors of every member of the unit so that complex operations could be executed without communications errors.

The faceless guard inserted the card in his reader. Adele had reprogrammed it so that it showed only a destination—the Elector's Palace—and reserved all other information under the highest security level of Blue Chrome operations.

The guard looked at the projected data, then returned the card to Adele and stepped out of the way. "Proceed," he said.

Or was it, "she said"? The voice was an electronic synthesis, just as were all sensory inputs the guard received. What sort of person could willingly live and function in a prison so strait that it touched their skin at every point?

But then, there were people who probably thought work in a library was a sentence to Hell. The universe had room for all sorts; though God knew, present events proved that many people weren't willing to leave it at that.

Adele turned left with the sailors sauntering behind her. Strip lights glued to the ceilings brightened the main corridor. People, two or three in a clot, stood talking in hushed voices outside the offices. Inside were Kostromans at tables made from shelving laid over furniture and stacked with paperwork, some of it from moldy boxes that must have come up from storage in the basement.

Each room had an Alliance overseer who looked tired but very much in command. The Alliance must have moved in a civilian administration as large as or larger than the invasion's military component.

Adele glanced to left and right in cold appraisal at those she passed. Bureaucrats, even Alliance personnel, avoided her gaze as she passed to the back stairs. No civilian wanted to know why a squad of commandoes had been summoned here.

Because of the bright illumination she noticed the corridor's murals for the first time. They showed scenes of Kostroman life during centuries past. The backgrounds were so varied that they must be of specific different islands. Fishermen cast hand lines from a sailing vessel; a farm family picked citrus fruit; a starship lifted from the water as a crowd cheered.

The artist had been skillful, but grime and the band rubbed by shoulders of those passing in the hall had reduced them to a shadow of what they must have been. Adele thought of her library. Was it perhaps enough out of the way that the palace's new masters had spared it, or had the books been treated with the same brutal unconcern that had tossed antique furniture from the windows of reception rooms to clear them for office space?

She should be worrying about humans, not books; but the books and their probable fate filled her mind anyway. She smiled at herself with wry humor.

The single soldier on guard at the narrow staircase down straightened when she saw a detachment of commandoes coming toward her. She carried a sub-machine gun and to Adele looked very young.

"Out of the way," Adele said with a curt nod. The Alliance soldier jumped sideways, knocking her weapon against the wall, pitting the ancient plaster.

Adele pulled open the door and led her detachment down the stairs in single file. Lighting had been improved even here: battery-powered lamps were stuck to the wall at each landing.

She hadn't expected the guard; there'd been no reference to a post at the stairhead in the electronic media Adele had examined.

It would have been a mistake to try to explain what the detachment was doing, however. The guard must have been placed by someone of relatively low rank, so she was therefore best ignored by commandoes claiming to operate on the instructions of Blue Chrome Command.

Blue Chrome Command was Markos. Adele wondered if that would amuse him. He hadn't seemed a man with a sense of humor.

Adele smiled faintly. She was finding more humor in life herself since she became a Cinnabar pirate.

The door to the basement level was open. A guard stood there as well. He turned from watching workmen installing power cables to stare as the detachment trooped past down the stairs. Adele gave him a hard glance.

The subbasement was well lit also, but that was a doubtful virtue in a region so decayed. The brick flooring rippled like the face of the sea—a useful simile, because at least half of the surface was under water. The ceiling arches dripped condensate, and an apparent spring stirred one pool clear of the pale algae that scummed the others.

A pump rumbled disconsolately, and the generator at the far end of the building vibrated at a higher frequency. Workmen had drilled fresh holes through the ceiling to pass power lines to the upper stories. The air danced with brick dust.

Adele approved of the additional wiring in principle. The execution of the work was simple butchery, however. One might as well shear a book down on the upper and lower edges so that it fit your new shelving.

Her detachment had returned to double file; the only sound they made was the splash of boots in the foul water. The bays filled with the detritus of past generations looked like the wrack of a terrible storm. To Adele it was a sad reminder of the ephemeral nature of human civilization; but then, she saw most things that way. Hogg and the sailors probably had a different viewpoint.

The pumps were in four brick alcoves jutting from the lengthwise exterior walls, arranged in an X pattern with the outside entrance between the pair on the north side. The pumps were huge cylinders sunk beneath floor level and venting through ceramic pipes half a meter in diameter. They had more than sufficient capacity to keep the subbasement dry.

Only the southwestern pump still worked, and a grumble from

it suggested not all was well with that one either. As Adele passed
between the eastern pair of pumps, she glanced through the arch
to her right. Workmen had recently removed the end cap of the
big electric drive motor. The Alliance planned to put this portion of its house in order also.

The broad outside stairs were a continuation of the light well
that provided natural illumination for the basement level. The sliding
doors that could offer twenty feet of width for large objects—
the pumps and the fusion generator were obvious examples—were
closed and barred, but the pedestrian door set in one of the larger
panels stood ajar.

The guard post covering this entrance was outside and up a
level, at the basement landing. Through the door Adele heard a
jig, distorted by reverberation in the stone-lined masonry pit of
the light well. The soldiers were playing music that had been popu-
lar when Adele was on the staff of the Bryce Academy.

She'd never had a taste for music and she doubted that a
connoisseur would have found the jig to have been of any particular merit, but it took her back to a time that was now forever past for her. She regretted its loss, as surely as she regretted
the loss of her childhood.

The music shut off in mid-chord. Well, so had that stage of
her life.

The fusion generator was in a masonry room on the western
end of the subbasement. According to architectural files, the original
plan had been to enclose the generator in all directions but one,
a curtain wall to the west. That way if the Tokamak failed it would
vent its plasma harmlessly into the open air.

Later Electors had added to the initial structure. The ionized
plume would now envelop the west wing and everyone in it, but
Adele had found no evidence in the records that this was viewed
as a problem. Fusion bottles rarely failed; and if this one did, well,
the west wing was given over entirely to servants' quarters and
the offices of low-ranking clerks.

Alliance officials had used the three bays in the northwest corner
of the subbasement as a high-security prison. The wall of the
generator room formed the south side, and a mesh of barbed wire
woven on a steel frame closed the open end.

Twenty Kostroman citizens—Walter III and members of his
immediate family—shared two bays of the makeshift prison. The

Aglaia's five officers were in the remaining one, brightly illuminated by floodlights in the vaulted ceiling outside the enclosure.

The prisoners had no privacy and no chance of escape, but Adele
saw as she approached that the twelve Alliance soldiers on duty
were a great deal less than alert. She and her detachment made
no attempt to conceal themselves, but they were still within twenty
yards of the post when a guard looked up, realized the splashing footsteps weren't condensate dripping after all, and shouted
in surprise.

Guards jumped to their feet and zipped their uniform tunics
closed. They'd appropriated furniture from the upper levels. The
luxurious chairs, couches, and tables made a dissonant tableau
among the utter squalor.

"Who's the officer in charge?" Adele demanded. She didn't raise
her voice, but the tinge of scorn in her voice was proper either for
the lieutenant she pretended to be or the craftsman she truly was.

A lanky soldier, the oldest in the squad by several years, stepped
forward. Instead of identifying himself he said, "Sir, this is a
restricted area."

He tried to sound forceful and threatening. His act wasn't nearly
as good as Adele's.

"Yes," she said, "it is." She handed him the routing card. The
codes Adele had implanted in the chip would direct the guards
to turn over the five Cinnabar officers to the detachment of commandoes.

The chip wouldn't explain why: that was beyond the guards'
need to know. The guards would have been sure something was
wrong if Adele had included unnecessary information.

Some of the prisoners moved forward, drawn by hope of
something to punctuate the boredom. The individuals weren't iden-
tifiable until they almost touched the wire mesh. Light glinting
from the steel threw a haze over those beyond it.

Walter Hajas was in the middle bay. Captain Le Golif, whom
Adele had seen during the Founder's Day Banquet, stood grim-
faced with his four juniors. She didn't think either man would
recognize her.

The sailors had bunched slightly when Adele and Hogg stopped.
Woetjans suddenly pushed through her subordinates, put her lips
to Adele's ear, and whispered tautly, "Sir! Two guys come down
the side stairs and they're behind us!"

"You there!" someone called. The subbasement was so huge and multi-bayed that the words, though shouted, didn't seem loud. "What's going on here?"

Adele recognized the voice.

"Kill them!" she shouted, reaching for her pocket.

Hogg carried his impeller slung under his right arm with the muzzle forward. His right hand had ridden lightly on the grip from the moment he left the *Princess Cecile* on this mission. The guard commander's mouth gaped as Hogg's slug punched him mid-chest before Adele could complete the second word of her warning.

The soldiers were too startled to react. Hogg killed three of them standing before the rest of the survivors threw themeselves toward cover. Brick shattered and a Kostroman prisoner doubled up with a cry: an impeller slug didn't stop when it hit its intended target.

The sailors had fast reflexes but they weren't trained killers. Only Dasi fired at the two figures who dived into the nearest pump alcove. He missed, though his impeller blasted a head-sized divot in the brick wall.

Adele didn't bother to shoot. The guards weren't worth her concern, and she couldn't get a clear shot past the members of her detachment before the real targets were under cover.

The voice had been that of Markos. He and his aide had decided to see the prisoners without giving electronic warning.

A volley of sub-machine gun pellets blew powder from the north wall and stuffing from the furniture. The sailors were trying to copy Hogg now that they understood what was required, but the surviving guards were mostly safe in a side bay.

A guard fired his sub-machine gun. Pellets slapped and scarred pillars on the other side of the vault, but the shooter couldn't hit the Cinnabars for the same reason they couldn't hit him and his fellows: at the present angle a three-foot-thick brick wall was in the way.

Hogg shouldered his impeller with more deliberation than he'd shown previously and fired one round through the seat of a red plush divan. The guard hiding there leaped up with a scream, then collapsed. The divan broke beneath her. The slug had smashed the frame on its way to her chest.

Civilian prisoners were screaming and throwing themselves into the back of their cells. Captain Le Golif pointed toward Adele and shouted, "Run for it! You'll be killed if you try to get us now!"

He was right in one sense: at least six of the guards were alive and armed. The open front of their bay was only twenty feet from the mesh barrier enclosing the *Aglaia*'s officers.

The Alliance soldiers were shocked and frightened, but they were still capable of pulling a trigger. With a sub-machine gun, that's all it would take to chop to mincemeat anybody trying to break open the prisoner cage.

Adele had the pistol in her left hand. Her right elbow held the burdensome sub-machine gun to her side to keep it from flopping. For a moment, only her head and eyes moved.

Le Golif was *half* right. Adele and her sailors couldn't run, either, except past the pump alcove where Markos and his aide had taken refuge. Ruthless didn't necessarily mean skillful, but Adele didn't doubt that the pale sociopath could knock over human targets just as quickly as they appeared before her.

A sub-machine gun fired in the alcove. The burst wasn't directed toward the opening. Brick shattered and a few pellets rang on the steel pump housing.

"Sun, Polin, Hafard!" Woetjans roared. Like Adele, the petty officer had seen that there was no way out for the detachment except past Markos. "On the count of three, with me."

She pointed toward the front arch with her left index finger; the sub-machine gun was in her right hand, the stock extended to the crook of her elbow. The sailors she'd named were, like her, among the majority carrying sub-machine guns rather than impellers.

"One—"

A second burst within the alcove. The impacts sounded as though someone had thrown a case of glassware against the wall. A single bit of metal ricocheted through the arch, trailing a corkscrew of smoke.

"Stop!" Adele shouted. "Stop, she'll kill you all!"

Woetjans turned with an expression combining surprise and frustration. "Sir!" she pleaded. "There's no—"

Hogg pointed his impeller at the side of the alcove. "Dasi and Koop," he said. Those three—and Lamsoe, back in the cupola of the APC—carried stocked impellers. "It's just fucking brick after all. On the count, one, two, thr—"

The impellers fired a ragged volley. The slugs were aimed a few inches above the base course. Each impact blasted out thirty or more pounds of pulverized brick.

Adele turned away and coughed heavily. Blood gummed her right eyebrow. She threw an arm across her face, knowing she'd have been too late to save her eye if the thumbnail-sized chip had hit an inch lower.

Size was a great advantage in handling an impeller's powerful recoil. Dasi was a huge man and Koop was well above average. Hogg was the lightest by fifty pounds, but his impeller was back on target an instant before those of the two sailors.

As Adele turned, a guard stuck his head and the barrel of his sub-machine gun around the corner of the bay in which he'd taken refuge. Adele shot him, then shot him again in the ribs.

He'd leaped like a pithed frog when her first pellet blew a hole above his right eye. So long as the target was moving, she had to assume it was a danger to her and her detachment. She'd pay for what she did tonight in dreams or in Hell, but no one would ever say that Adele Mundy had skimped a task because of what it would have cost her.

The dead man thrashed in the pool of his own spreading blood. None of his fellows would follow his example in the next minute or two. Adele remembered the helmet visor. She pulled it down and returned to what Hogg and the sailors were doing.

Their impellers slapped. The sound of slugs smashing bricks was sharper yet, and echoes turned rapid fire into the rattle of automatic weapons. Adele guessed each man had fired about six rounds when a long section of wall fell into the alcove with a roar louder even than the gunfire.

The other sailors emptied the magazines of their sub-machine guns into the spreading dust cloud. Compared to the *crash* of the impellers, the lighter weapons sounded like the buzzing of insects.

"Cease fire!" Woetjans screamed. She charged with her empty weapon raised to use as a bludgeon. Adele, for reasons she couldn't possibly have articulated, was with the half-dozen sailors who followed the petty officer.

The commando helmet had nose filters Adele hadn't known about; the air she breathed was close but not chokingly full of peach-colored dust.

Bricks had collapsed into the drainage sump, burying Markos's aide there. Her right hand stuck out of the rubble. It held a pistol, not the sub-machine gun Adele knew the woman usually carried.

The output pipe was shattered just above the pump casing. The sub-machine gun lay on the floor beneath it. Markos's right foot, flailing wildly to find purchase to thrust him higher, stuck out of the hole he'd hammered through the ceramic pipe with sub-machine gun pellets.

"There!" Adele said. She aimed but didn't shoot because too many sailors were moving in the dust cloud.

Woetjans followed the line of Adele's pistol. She jumped to the motor housing and grabbed the spy's ankle. When Woetjans pulled, Markos slid out of the pipe. He was covered with ancient slime and his face bore a look of bestial rage. Woetjans hit him in the middle of the forehead with her gun butt.

"Bring him as a hostage!" Adele said, backing out of the ruined alcove. She lifted her visor because it made her feel trapped. Bricks continued to dribble from the top of the opening as gravity overcame the grip of old mortar.

"Mistress, we'll have to shoot our way out," Hogg said from beside her. "They may not have heard us upstairs, I'll hope they didn't, but they'll sure hell know something's going on when we turn up looking like we do."

"Oh," said Adele, considering a point she should have seen for herself. The brick dust had started to settle; a great deal of it had settled on the skin and uniforms of the Cinnabar detachment. Sailors who'd dived for the floor when the shooting started were blotched with muck and algae besides. As soon as they appeared in public, there'd be questions that would inevitably lead to shots.

Hogg was right. If there was going to be shooting, it was best for the Cinnabars to start it.

Woetjans tossed Markos to the floor beside Adele; a sailor quickly bound the spy's hands behind his back, using a belt stripped from a dead guard. Adele hadn't heard any order pass. The sailor simply understood and executed the task.

Adele felt her face quiver with the beginning of a hysterical laugh. *Why couldn't Kostroma produce library assistants of that quality?* She forced her cheeks into a frozen rictus until the fit passed.

"If it's all right to use the helmet commo now I can set things up with Barnes and Lamsoe," Woetjans said. "Unless you want to . . . ?"

A surviving guard fired a short burst from the bay where he and his fellows remained. A sailor fired back. Neither hit or could possibly hit anything but brick.

"Get out!" Captain Le Golif repeated.

He stood behind the wire, feet slightly spread. His arms were behind his back as though he were reviewing a parade. Pride in Cinnabar made Adele flush, despite the cold awareness that the men who cut her little sister's throat might have been personally brave as well.

Adele hadn't *seen* an armored personnel carrier until a week before. Among other things she had no idea of what might be the rate and duration of fire of the heavy weapons involved.

"No, you have a much better appreciation of the factors," she said.

The petty officer glanced down at Markos. "And you want him along?" she said without emphasis.

"Yes," Adele said. "I do."

Markos was useless as a hostage: trying to negotiate their exit from Kostroma would simply alert the Alliance command to their presence. The detachment might escape in a rush; if the Alliance had time to set up, every Cinnabar on the planet would die or be captured.

Adele had called Markos a hostage because the only other alternatives were to kill him in cold blood, or to let him live. She'd meant it when she said she wouldn't be party to a cold-blooded execution.

But she'd pull the trigger herself if it was that or setting free the monster she knew Markos was.

"Message received," Daniel said, speaking into the integral microphone at his console in the *Aglaia's* tactical operations center. Domenico was in charge at the *Princess Cecile*. He'd used his initiative—against Daniel's orders for communications silence—to relay the warning from the detachment in the Elector's Palace. "We're on the way. Leary out."

Chief Baylor looked at Daniel with concern. The missileer had just arrived to report his team was done with the starboard installations, Missile Tubes One and Three, but that there'd been damage to the port-side handling controls when the *Aglaia* was captured. It'd take an hour to clear, and the Cinnabars hadn't had an hour even before the wheels came off for the palace detachment.

Daniel keyed the general communicator. "All personnel to the main hatch and begin loading," he said calmly. "Bridge out."

He'd hoped to make the final transfer from the *Aglaia* to the *Princess Cecile* in two stages, but the car could carry the nineteen Cinnabars so long as Gambier stayed low and used surface effect. That was an easy problem. If Daniel'd thought it would have helped the palace detachment, he'd have swum to the Navy Pool pulling the missile crew on a raft.

Chief Baylor didn't leave the TOC. Daniel felt a surge of rage—did the man think orders weren't meant for him?—but suppressed it instantly. Baylor didn't need to guide his people to the main hatch. Daniel was jumpy because he held himself responsible for allowing the palace detachment to take a vain risk.

He touched the switch opening the hatch of Hold Two, then keyed the general communicator, audio only. Video required more bandwidth than might be available during combat. Trained naval personnel ought to have their eyes on their tasks anyway.

"You're free to go," Daniel announced to the former Alliance guard detachment. They'd be jumping up in their prison as light entered through the opening hatch. "We've left an inflatable liferaft tied to the mooring pontoon for you. I strongly recommend that you use it to get away from the *Aglaia* as fast as you can. Bridge out."

Daniel swung out of his seat and headed for the door. Baylor followed in his wake, frowning again. It was a familiar expression on the little man's face.

"We might've left them where they are," Baylor said over the clash of his boots and Daniel's on the metal stair treads. "Though I don't guess a bunch of groundhogs're going to reprogram the targeting computer in the time they'll have to try."

"I don't guess they are," Daniel agreed, feeling his irritation rise again.

As Baylor said, the Alliance personnel were from the ground forces rather than the navy. If they even knew where the TOC was, the chance they could reset the programmed sequence was less than the possibility of them flapping their arms and flying to the *Princess Cecile* ahead of the aircar.

Besides, leaving the prisoners locked in the *Aglaia* was a sentence of death by fire or suffocation. Daniel didn't hate anybody that much. He hoped he'd *never* hate anybody that much.

He hit the Deck C landing and sprinted down the corridor toward the hatch. The Chief Missileer ran at his side.

"It sounds like Woetjans is really in the middle of it," Baylor said. He talked out of nervousness. Also, he was displacing his fear rather than acknowledging that his real concern was the certain doom of the *Aglaia* and his beloved missiles with it.

A rating stood in the main hatch with a sub-machine gun. When the officers reached the concourse he shouted, "Here they come!" over his shoulder to the aircar quivering in dynamic balance on the pontoon.

"They're professionals," Daniel said to Baylor. He was out of the *Aglaid*'s hatch for the last time, into warm salt air and a sky not far short of dawn. He crossed the catwalk and paused, gesturing Baylor and the rating into the vehicle ahead of him.

They were professionals, Adele and Hogg as surely as the *Aglaid*'s crewmen. They would do the best they could under the circumstances.

And by God! so would Daniel Leary and the contingent directly under him.

"Remember," said Woetjans to the detachment, "shoot anything you please but *don't* shoot the fucking APC, right? And keep moving but help your buddies. We don't leave nobody behind even if their head's blown off. Ready?"

The general murmur of assent sounded to Adele like feeding time in a bear garden. She smiled faintly. Everyone in the immediate area would shortly prefer that a pack of bears had rushed up from the depths of the Elector's Palace.

Woetjans keyed her helmet. "Barnes, get moving," she said.

Two clicks on Adele's helmet intercom signaled wordless agreement. The APC was going into action two high levels above the poised detachment.

"Remember," Woetjans said. She sounded peevish, like an adult trying to control unruly children. "*I* fire the first shot."

She nodded to Dasi and Koop; the big sailors put their whole strength into sliding the equipment door sideways so that the detachment could exit as a group rather than dribbling one at a time through the pedestrian doorway.

The door's rattle drew the attention of the entire detachment on the landing twenty feet above. The Alliance troops stared in amazement at the squad of commandoes starting up the broad stairs toward them.

Woetjans was on the left end; Adele was beside the bosun's mate, holding only her pistol, and Hogg was to Adele's right with her sub-machine gun in his hands and the impeller slung across his back. Three more sailors completed the first rank; Dasi and Koop fell in behind with the two men supporting Markos by the elbows.

"Buddha!" cried an Alliance soldier. He pointed toward Markos, pinioned and groggy. "They've got—"

Faces—angry, surprised; none of them frightened, not yet, because they didn't have time. They were lighted from above by a glaring fixture the Alliance had bolted to the wall. Ten soldiers, perhaps a dozen.

Woetjans may have squeezed her trigger first, but Adele doubted there'd been a heartbeat between any of the five weapons firing. Only Hogg of the five shooters failed to empty the 300-round magazine of his sub-machine gun. The guard detachment melted like frost in a torrent.

Adele ran up the stairs. A mist of dust and blood pulsed in the floodlight. She didn't know why she was shouting. Her foot slipped and she *did* know why, but she didn't look down to make sure.

Gunfire and screams echoed in her mind. A soldier lay on the landing, pounding the bricks with his remaining hand. Hogg finished him as he passed; probably a waste of ammunition, but because it was Hogg only three or four rounds.

An Alliance official looked over the carved stone coping of the light well. Adele shot him. His peaked hat flew off and his face jerked back with a red smear where his forehead had been.

Adele was winded already, gasping to breathe brick dust but wishing that dry smell could mask the stench of bodies sawn inside out by hypervelocity pellets. She thrust her hand against the wall where the stairs switched back. The surface was cratered and sticky.

Powerful drive fans howled. A bolt of plasma ripped overhead, dimming the banks of light and setting off a bloom of ionized fire that must have been one of the Alliance gun nests in the entryway.

Barnes and Lamsoe were doing their part, all of them were doing their part. Nothing else mattered now.

Adele tripped. A sailor caught her. They were at the top of the staircase. The APC turned on its axis in front of them, bunting civilian vehicles into crumpled ruin. The right side panel was raised but the left one was still locked down so that the detachment could leap aboard.

Adele stopped. She fired, aiming at white blurs that were faces. Plasma lit the sky. This time the plume carried with it the skirt of the gun vehicle at the garden entrance, devouring the flexible fabric in orange flames that were a shadow in the iridescence.

Any blur, any face, any soul within them if men have souls.

Woetjans caught Adele around the waist and leaped into the troop compartment. The APC lifted on the full screaming thrust of its fans.

Adele twisted on the hard deck. Hands gripped her to keep her from sliding out of the vehicle. She slid a fresh magazine into the butt of her glowing pistol, and the victims in her mind shrieked louder than the fans.

Daniel fiddled at the *Princess Cecile*'s command console, trying to get the adjustable seat positioned properly for him. The controls were reversed from those on similar Cinnabar equipment; he kept getting a hump in the upholstery where he wanted a dip and vice versa.

The ship's systems were live: the telltales were green or amber, with the only red warnings those for the open main hatch and the enabled armament switches. The *Princess Cecile* was fully crewed with some of the most experienced ratings in the RCN. There was only one commissioned officer, but that wasn't unheard of for a vessel as small as a corvette.

The single officer shouldn't have been a junior lieutenant on his first cruise, but that wasn't a problem that Daniel could find it in his heart to really regret.

Lt. Daniel Leary, Officer Commanding the RCS *Princess Cecile*. That was a fact forever now, even if he died in the next ten minutes or the RCN cashiered him after he reached Cinnabar.

Dying in the next ten minutes was actually quite probable, because the *Bremse*, an Alliance cruiser/minelayer, was in orbit over Kostroma.

Daniel's main display was a Plot-Position Indicator for the region above the planet to an altitude of 100,000 miles; near space by interstellar standards, but if the *Princess Cecile* could get through it alive she'd have a very good chance of making it the rest of the way home. The Commonwealth of Kostroma's automatic defense system hadn't been a joke, not quite, but the Alliance had come prepared to update the defensive constellation to a level of protection comparable to that over Pleasaunce.

Alliance cruiser/minelayers were built on the hulls of large light cruisers, but their large magazines were configured to accept either missiles or thermonuclear mines like the ones the *Bremse* was deploying now above Kostroma. The ships were fast because their mines could interdict hostile planets as well as defend friendly ones; and even though the *Bremse* would be heavily loaded with mines, Daniel was sure she could out-slug a Kostroman corvette by a considerable margin.

The options available to the *Princess Cecile* were guile or incredibly good luck. And disaster, of course. Disaster was far the most probable option.

"The Mundy section is beginning extraction," said Domenico from the console to Daniel's right. That was normally the navigator's position, but Daniel had put the bosun there for now because he needed someone trustworthy handling communications.

Navigation and attack were Daniel's own responsibilities until he handed the *Princess Cecile* over to somebody better qualified. He switched the main display to an attack screen which echoed data from the *Aglaia's* sensors. The PPI shrank to a holographic fifty-millimeter cube, one of a series of similar displays at the upper edge of the projection volume.

"Understood," Daniel said. He tried to keep the gleeful excitement out of his voice. He didn't want the crew to think he was insane. . . . "Alert the ship."

Domenico passed the report over the general communicator in a rasping tone with as little emotion as he'd have put into a drinks order. These were good people, and they were depending on Daniel Leary.

"Holy shit!" said Dorfman. She'd been gunner's mate aboard the *Aglaia*—a communications vessel didn't rate a warrant gunner— and was seated at the remaining bridge console with responsibility for the corvette's defenses. "All the missile batteries at the palace just fired!"

"Yes," said Daniel as he transmitted preprogrammed commands to the *Aglaia*. "We're fortunate to have a communications officer of Ms. Mundy's skill. She said she'd trip the automatic defenses to create a diversion as they departed the target area."

Daniel pressed the red Execute switch with the full weight of his thumb. "And now," he added with satisfaction, "we're going to create a diversion of our own."

Fifty feet below the APC, a line rippled through three blocks of housing in the center of the city. Buildings crumbled. A pall of dust spread up and outward. Where the hypervelocity rockets hit something harder than brick an occasional spark flew into the night, but the flames growing slowly in the projectiles' wake were for the moment unimpressive.

Adele stared in horrified amazement. She'd had no idea that the rockets would penetrate so far. All she'd intended was to add to the confusion by destroying vehicles parked in the palace gardens.

"It is very important that you preserve my life," said Markos. "Your superiors will punish you severely if anything happens to the information I bring them about my nation's intelligence operations."

Adele turned. Sailors stared in disbelief at the hostage, still bound, who sat upright in the middle of the compartment.

"That woman is a spy," Markos said, nodding toward Adele with a malevolent expression. "Her real name is Adele Mundy. She was recruited on Bryce."

"Why you lying *bastard*," Woetjans said. She punched Markos in the face. He fell against Dasi. The sailor knocked him upright again with an elbow.

"I do not lie," Markos said, dripping blood from a cut lip. "There's proof of what I say in the data unit that looks like a communicator on my belt. I'll give your superiors the key to the information inside as soon as they guarantee my safety."

He turned his gaze on Adele again. "She's a spy," he repeated. "She provided the information that permitted us to capture the palace and your ship so easily."

Adele was detached. It was as though she were listening to the history of an alternate reality in which events transpired in a fashion slightly skewed from those in which she had participated.

But only slightly skewed: the reality would be enough to hang her. She thought of the Three Circles Conspiracy and the Cinnabar traitors betrayed in turn by their Alliance paymaster.

Adele Mundy didn't belong in this world; or any, she supposed. She'd briefly thought otherwise, but she'd been wrong.

She smiled. A sailor swore under his breath.

"That's a lie, right, sir?" Dasi said. He was pleading. "It's all bullshit that he's talking!"

The APC was over water now. To the north behind them, fires burned in Kostroma City and weapons fired at nothing.

Adele continued to smile. There was no way out. She could lie, but the sailors wouldn't forget Markos's words. She was quite certain evidence would be found to implicate her. Markos would have arranged that, so that if she balked at some demand he could threaten her with exposure to the Cinnabar authorities.

As he was exposing her now, to save himself and punish her with the same stroke.

The sailors stared at Adele in stricken horror. They'd seen her shoot. But she couldn't fly an armored personnel carrier, and she couldn't kill the sailors who'd risked their lives for her and with her in the past. The only family she'd known since the proscriptions; and in a real sense, the only family she'd ever known.

"I'll handle this," said Hogg. He raised the flap of Markos's jacket and unclipped the belt communicator.

"Be careful," the spy warned. "If you try to retrieve the data without the codes you'll destroy it instead. But I will tell all to the proper authorities."

He sneered at Adele in bloodthirsty triumph. His lips and left cheek were swollen from Woetjans's blow.

Hogg weighed the false communicator in the hand that didn't hold a sub-machine gun. "You know," he said conversationally, "the master wouldn't believe a word of this. He's a honest sort himself, my master Daniel, and he thinks the whole world's like him. But there's a lot of people back on Cinnabar who *would* believe it."

He grinned at Adele. "Right, mistress?" he said.

"Yes," said Adele.

Hogg shot Markos in the temple. The spy's head jerked sideways, losing definition as hydrostatic shock violently expanded his brain tissue.

Hogg thrust his right leg straight, shoving the corpse out the open side of the APC. He tossed the communicator after Markos. He fired a burst from his sub-machine gun as the little object spun off in the vehicle's wake.

"Missed," Hogg said. "When my eyes was better I'd have blown it to shit in the air, but I guess we'll have to trust salt water to do the job."

He looked around the troop compartment. Everyone was staring at him. "What the fuck's going on?" Barnes demanded plaintively from the front cab.

"It's like this," Hogg said to the sailors. "The master told me to take care of Ms. Mundy, there."

He nodded to Adele. The sub-machine gun was still in his right hand, pointed toward empty night sky through the open side of the vehicle.

"Giving her to this guy and his sort—and they're all the same sort, I don't give a fuck what color uniform they wear," Hogg continued. "That wouldn't be doing my job. Besides, you can't trust *them* even if they do happen to tell the truth."

"Too fucking right," said Woetjans. To Adele in a respectful voice she went on, "You got a bad burn on your hand there, sir. Better be sure to get it looked at the next time you get a chance."

Adele looked at the throbbing blisters on the thumb, web, and index finger of her left hand, her gun hand. She held her hand out to Woetjans.

"Yes," she said. "Perhaps you'd do it now. I believe we have a few minutes before we reach Lieutenant Leary and our new vessel."

"The APC's approaching at speed!" Domenico said. The bosun's console displayed the region centered on the Navy Pool at a scale small enough to include Kostroma City miles to the north.

"Direct the crew to their stations, Mr. Domenico," Daniel ordered without looking around. "Ms. Mundy takes over the commo desk, and you head up the emergency team until we're out of the system and in one piece."

A computer-generated model of the *Aglaia* was at the center of Daniel's display; the remainder of the imagery was that gathered by the *Aglaid's* sensors and transmitted to the *Princess Cecile*.

The *Aglaia* launched missiles across the Floating Harbor.

The first round lifted at a flat angle from a bath of steam and plasma. The harbor surged as though it'd been bombed. Nearby pontoons rocked violently, breaking their tethers and grinding against one another like blunt concrete teeth.

The second missile exited with less immediate disruption because

its predecessor had blown a hard vacuum in the sea about the
Aglaia's flank; water pressure hadn't had time to fill the man-made
event. The missile trailed a corkscrewed line of fire as bright as
the sun's corona, matter and anti-matter annihilating one another
in its wake.

Anti-ship missiles were intended for use over stellar distances.
Even accelerating at 12 gravities, the first round was only trav-
elling at 800 feet per second when it nosed over toward the
Alliance destroyer moored a dozen berths away in the Floating
Harbor. The ball from a flintlock musket moved faster than that.

But the missile weighed thirty tons.

It hit the destroyer on the upper curve of the hull, a third of
the way back from the bow. Heavy plating crumpled. The warship rolled 90 degrees on its axis, then rolled back and gulped
water through its open hatches. Steam and smoke from electrical
fires swelled about the injured vessel.

The missile ricocheted skyward as a point of light. It swelled
as it mounted toward orbit because its drive devoured ever more
of the missile's own fabric as it rose. A rainbow bubble marked
the final dissolution.

The second missile was intended for another destroyer, but the
guidance system was marginal at such short range and might have
been damaged by the previous round. It hit the harbor's surface
short of its target and bounced out of the spray at an angle flattened by friction with the water. It cleared the destroyer by what
looked to Daniel like less thickness than you'd use to shim a
bearing.

The missile was beginning to tumble when it collided three
berths distant with a big transport that had arrived with a battalion of Alliance troops. For a fraction of a second the two merged
like a log and a giant buzzsaw; then anti-matter from one or the
other turned the immediate area, tens of thousands of tons of metal
and sea water and flesh, into a plume of light.

Daniel split his main display between the PPI and an attack screen.
The remote targeting screen shrank to a cube of vivid light in a
corner. At its center, the *Aglaia* was sinking, gutted by her own
missiles.

The *Bremse* orbited twenty-nine thousand miles above Kostroma's
surface. She was in the sky above Kostroma City now; on the PPI
a point moved away from the blue icon that was the Alliance

cruiser—another mine, making the present total 131 according to the sidebar at the edge of the display.

Daniel keyed the guard frequency, the universal emergency channel, and cried, "Commonwealth ship *Princess Cecile* to all vessels, emergency, emergency! Ships are blowing up in the Floating Harbor! Do not land in the Floating Harbor! All vessels on the planetary surface, lift at once to escape the explosions!"

The *Aglaia* had managed to launch a second pair of missiles. If ships had souls . . .

But humans do have souls, and humans who depended on Daniel Leary would die unless he focused on the next step of the road to safety. He opened his mouth to blurt another dollop of simulated panic to justify the *Princess Cecile* lifting. Before he could speak, a voice from the console demanded in a guttural accent, "AFS *Bremse* to *Princess Cecile*. What is going on down there? Over."

"Emergency!" Daniel repeated. He heard a bustle beside him, figures moving at the right-hand console. "Ships are blowing up, *Bremse*! We must lift to save ourselves. All ships on the surface must lift!"

"*Bremse* to *Princess*," the harsh voice spat back. "Negative on lifting, *Princess Cecile*. Stay where you are and provide a full imagery link on commo channel twelve, no encryption. Over."

"Emer—" Daniel said. An amber bar slashed across the green telltale on his display, indicating that the channel was locked to him. He turned his head in surprise.

Adele sat at the console to his right. Her uniform was splotched with blood, brick dust, and substances Daniel couldn't even hazard a guess at.

He'd thought his own was the master unit and couldn't be overridden. That wasn't true, at least with Adele working in the same system.

"*Princess Cecile* to *Bremse*," Adele said. Her voice was perfectly calm. Anyone who'd had experience with people reacting to crises would assume she was in shock. "We are transmitting data now as we lift off. I repeat—"

She pointed a bandaged left hand to Daniel. He nodded; he was already initiating take-off sequence. Domenico had sealed the *Princess Cecile* as soon as the palace detachment boarded, so it was just a matter of bringing up pressure to the plasma motor feeds and unlocking the outriggers so they could be brought in as soon as the vessel left the water.

"—we are lifting off for safety. *Princess Cecile* out."

The motors rumbled beneath them. The *Princess Cecile* shuddered on a bubble of steam and plasma, then began to rise. She was shorter than the *Aglaia* and therefore wobbled at a higher frequency as she found her balance, but she was a lot steadier than Daniel had expected.

He grinned at Adele, then settled into his seat. His fingers moved across the console's keyboard as he set up the next step on the corvette's targeting display.

One step at a time, until they got home or went off the end of the final cliff.

Adele coughed wrackingly, doubling over in her seat to bring up orange phlegm. Her first thought was that she'd had a lung hemorrhage, but the color came from the brick dust she'd breathed as they shot their way out of the palace. It and the ozone generated by electromotive weapons were irritants, but she didn't think either of them would kill her.

She wiped the sputum on her sleeve and went back to work. The fabric couldn't be much filthier than before anyway.

Starships weren't stressed for high acceleration. The *Princess Cecile* lifted at less than 2 gravities, making flesh a burden but nothing worse. Sailors moved about, albeit a little slower than they had in Adele's library; and as for Adele, she noted with a cold smirk that many of her plumper contemporaries carried as much weight every day of their lives.

Daniel, instead of using the ship's communication system, turned his head to say, "Adele? The *Bremse* up there's laying a defensive array. Can you find the command node so we can destroy it?"

Adele put down her wands. "The constellation hasn't yet been activated, but I'm changing our identification codes to mimic those of the *Goetz von Berlichingen*. That way we'll be safe if they switch it on."

"Yes, but can you spot the command node?" Daniel said. "We can destroy it with cannon or even a missile if you can just locate it."

Adele heard in his tone the ingrained irritation of a male trying to get information from a female too dense to understand a simple question. She didn't say: "Yes, if you're stupid enough to want to commit suicide that way I can help you do it."

Instead Adele said, "If the command node is destroyed each unit of the constellation will react to any ship within range except the *Bremse*. The command node is—"

She twitched a control wand without taking her eyes away from Daniel. An object on Daniel's visual display changed from an icon distinguished only by number to a pulsing ball as red as murder.

"—here."

"Ah," said Daniel. His face was blank as he assimilated what he'd been told: *all* the things he'd just been told, including the fact that he'd acted like a fool. "Adele—Ms. Mundy. My concern isn't so much for our own safety from the defenses, as for the safety of the Cinnabar force that retakes Kostroma."

His expression was momentarily that of an older man and a very hard one. "As one most certainly will."

He swallowed, settling into a calmer state. "Is there a way we can disable the constellation before we leave the system? Even if it means risk for us. Though not suicide, if you please, not at this point."

Adele's subconscious responded with a surge of pleasure to Daniel's engaging grin. She'd frequently called people fools to their faces. She didn't recall ever before meeting someone who analyzed the criticism, then accepted it because it was valid. Certainly no men had done so in the past.

"If you can put me aboard the node," Adele said, "I can disable it. I can make it change sides, if I've the time."

"*Bremse* to Kostroman vessel *Princess Cecile*," growled the communicator. "Orbit at thirty thousand kilometers. Do not leave that assigned level or we'll destroy you. Over."

A different officer was handling the *Bremse*'s communications now. This one was female and had an upper-class Pleasaunce accent. Senior personnel had been recalled to duty when chaos broke out in Kostroma City.

Daniel bobbed his head as he considered. "Tell them we acknowledge but we're having trouble with our reaction mass shutoffs," he said.

He waggled a finger toward his console. The four quadrants of the main display were now split into separate screens which he kept in the corner of his eye. "Actually, the fuel feed's about the only part of the drive system that seems to be working to spec. Three of the plasma nozzles should have been replaced a couple maintenance cycles ago."

"*Princess Cecile* to *Bremse*," Adele said. "We acknowledge your orders. We'll orbit at thirty thousand kilometers as soon as we've repaired the reaction mass shutoffs. *Princess Cecile* over."

The *Bremse* was laying a defensive array at 44K kilometers above Kostroma's surface, geosynchronous level. Adele didn't doubt that the cruiser was willing to destroy a Kostroman vessel that disobeyed its orders, but there were other things going on that might well seem more pressing to the Alliance officers.

Killing a ship was a complicated business. Very different from squeezing a trigger and seeing a face swell, eyes bulging and the first spray of blood from the nostrils . . .

"*Bremse* to *Princess Cecile!*" the communicator said. "You'd better stabilize where we tell you, you wog morons, or you'll be lucky if enough of you gets home that your families can breathe you! *Bremse* out."

Daniel's expression was one that Adele wouldn't have liked to see had she thought it was directed at her. "The node is big enough to board?" he asked. His left hand on the keyboard was making corrections to the targeting display.

"Big enough for a dozen technicians at once," Adele said. "I've checked the design drawings. There'll be a programming crew aboard it at least until the whole array is deployed. A boat can take me there using the codes that the shuttles for the work crews use."

"How big a party do you want?" Daniel asked. "We don't have combat suits, though."

Adele sniffed. "There'll be three or four Alliance programmers," she said. "Give me somebody to drive the boat and another sailor or two to keep the programmers out of my way."

Daniel nodded. His finger touched the general call button. "Woetjans, Barnes, Dasi, and Lamsoe to the bridge," he said, his voice syncopating itself through speakers in every compartment.

Adele noticed distortion. The *Princess Cecile*, though clean and fit-looking, wasn't as tight a collection of systems as it might have been if its present crew—communications officer included—had longer to work on the vessel.

"And the *Bremse*?" Daniel asked. "Can you . . . ?"

"I doubt it," Adele said. "As a safety feature there's a lockout chip common to the *Bremse* and every mine of the constellation. It's an infinite non-repeating sequence, not a code I can break. The system won't even permit me in the node to command a mine to attack the *Bremse* so long as the lockout's in place."

The four sailors came at a shambling run. The weight of continued acceleration showed in the taut lines of their faces, but not in the speed of their arrival. Woetjans didn't even look strained.

"You're to take Ms. Mundy in the cutter to track Kay-Kay One-Four-Three-Oh," Daniel said with perfect enunciation and economy. "That's the command node of the defensive constellation under construction. There'll be Alliance personnel aboard, but they shouldn't expect trouble. In any case, you'll protect Ms. Mundy and provide her with any assistance she requires. Do you understand?"

Woetjans grinned broadly. "Yes *sir*," she said.

"You'll launch when we're opposite the planet from the *Bremse*," Daniel said to the bosun's mate. "That's about seven minutes, so don't waste time."

Adele raised herself from her seat, trying not to stagger under the strain of her added mass. Without comment Barnes and Dasi stuck hands under her elbows and lifted her with easy grace.

Lamsoe murmured, "Proud to be chosen, mistress. There's always something happening where you are."

"It's an occupational hazard for librarians," Adele said with a feeling of amusement that surprised her.

They started down the corridor to one of the circular stair towers. The sailors continued to carry Adele though she dabbed her feet to the deck in stubborn determination not to seem completely helpless.

"Baylor to the bridge," the general call ordered in Daniel's voice.

"I've never worn an atmosphere suit," Adele warned. "I'll need help putting it on."

She'd need help with more than that, and she'd need luck as well. Thus far she'd had both.

And the greatest luck in Adele Mundy's life was that now for the first time she *did* have help.

Chief Baylor entered the bridge. He'd barked his left knuckles, his right arm to the elbow was a black smear of congealed lubricant; and his expression was furious enough to face down a fox terrier.

"Sir," he said, "I've got fucking work to do so I'd really appreciate you getting to the fucking point!"

"You've become Attack Officer," Daniel said calmly. "That's your console."

He pointed to the navigator's console, empty since Adele's departure. "I've programmed the first two missiles but you'll launch any others. There are others, I hope?"

"Oh," said the warrant officer. "I—"

Baylor seated himself. He typed with the power of somebody driving nails expertly: far harder than necessary for the job but absolutely precise. The PPI switched to a targeting screen, similar in gross essentials but vastly different in detail and the keyboard functions associated with it.

"Well, not so very different from ours," he said with something short of approval.

Baylor looked back at Daniel. "Sir," he said, "we've got ten missiles aboard, all of them in the ready magazines now and I think they'll at least launch. Those wog cretins just let them sit in the grease they got them in from the factory. I swear! They're Pleasaunce built, though, and they seem to power up all right."

He shook his head. "They're low-acceleration models. Seven gee max. I wish to God we could've transferred some of my babies from the *Aglaia* before, before . . ."

The *Princess Cecile* was over Kostroma City at this point in its orbit. A quadrant of Daniel's display showed an enlarged view of the scene below. Dawn had broken over the capital, but fires blazed beneath trails of smoke. Explosions flashed in the Floating Harbor.

A warship on the surface fired plasma cannon in quick, nervous flickers. So far as Daniel knew there was no real enemy for the bolts to engage.

"Yes," Daniel said. "I regret that too."

If *he'd* been wishing for things, he'd have started some distance beyond a chance to transfer missiles between ships. That was an all-day job and they didn't have the heavy equipment to carry it out besides. He knew, though, that Baylor was mourning the loss of what were "his babies" in every sense but the biological.

Baylor gave him a faint, thankful smile. "I guess worse things happen in wartime, sir," he said. He reached for the commo key as he added, "I'll put Massimo in charge at the tubes. She's a good man. I got a good team."

Message traffic was passing from the *Bremse* to the ground at an increasing level of frustration, and from the ground to the *Bremse* with frequent contradictions caused by a complete collapse of the civilian communications net. Since the Alliance forces hadn't yet built an alternative net, commo was unit to unit rather than through a multilateral system which could analyze the data from all points simultaneously.

Locking bolts withdrew with a clang. The cutter spurted clear of the hold. The *Princess Cecile* shuddered in reaction. Bolts rang again to reseal the corvette.

Daniel wondered if the confusion in Kostroma City was a result of something Adele had done but hadn't bothered to mention, or if it was a chance result of the burgeoning disaster. People talked about the fog of war, but the truth was a much harsher thing. In war a fire swept across all sources of information. Equipment failed and humans, trying to balance dozens of competing crises, lost them all in crashing shards.

"I thought you'd be handling the Attack Board, sir," Baylor said. His hands were spread across the virtual keyboard. He faced the display with an expression as solidly determined as the nose of one of his beloved torpedoes.

Daniel looked at him. The missileer was setting up course data based on possible locations of target and tube. The courses would have to be refined when it came time to actually launch, but having a setup in the computer made that simpler by a matter of seconds or even minutes.

"If shooting starts, chief," Daniel said, "I'm going to have my hands full with the ship. If things go better than I expect, we'll just wait here for the cutter to return."

A particularly bright flash lit Daniel's display. When he turned to view the image directly the Floating Harbor was completely shrouded by steam. The fusion bottle of one of the moored vessels had failed catastrophically.

"They didn't do so bad, did they, sir?" Baylor said with a wistful smile, looking at the display over Daniel's shoulder. "My b— Our missiles from the *Aglaia*, I mean."

"No, chief," Daniel said. "They taught some wogs what it means to go up against Cinnabar."

He said the words to console the missileer, but as they came out Daniel felt his own pulse surge. It was childish and for that

matter uncivilized to feel this sort of murderous patriotism. That
didn't make the reaction any the less real.

The *Aglaia*'s missiles were of the twin thruster design with dual
antimatter conversion systems. They were the only type in first-
line use in either of the major navies.

Kostroma had purchased single-thruster missiles to equip its
warships. These were much cheaper, since the High Drive was
the system's only expensive component. Guidance was loaded
before launch. Complex sensors and terminal guidance equipment would have been a waste of money due to the high velocities involved and the fact that missiles were ballistic at normal
engagement ranges.

The *Princess Cecile*'s missiles were the same size and would reach
the same velocities as those of the *Aglaia*—or the *Bremse*—but they
did so at a leisurely rate by comparison. This was a particular
handicap at short ranges; and if it came to a fight with the Alliance
cruiser, it would be very short ranges indeed by the standards of
interstellar warships.

"What do you think our Alliance friend has to send us, chief?"
Daniel asked. "If it comes to that."

Baylor wrinkled his nose. "Four tubes only," he said. "The fire
director's the same type they fit in the *Krestovik* class with twice
the tubes, though, so they can keep rounds coming at ten-second
intervals as long as there's anything in the magazines."

He spread his small, muscular right hand above his keyboard
without touching it. "The magazines, though, that's a guess, but
carrying a full defensive constellation I'd guess thirty-six missiles.
Maybe thirty-eight if their missileer knows his business, and maybe
only twenty if some dickhead with a lot of braid thinks, 'They're
not coming to fight, so let's use the stowage for something useful like fancy rations.'"

Baylor cleared his throat in embarrassment. "Not meaning to
insult you, sir," he added.

"I wouldn't feel insulted even if I had a lot of braid, chief,"
Daniel said. "Which I most certainly do not."

"Thing is, sir," Baylor said, "they'll be high-acceleration types
and ours aren't. There's no getting around that."

"*Bremse* to unidentified vessel at thirty-nine thousand kilometers!" the communicator snarled. The Alliance cruiser had noticed
the cutter at last. Too bad, but Daniel had expected it. "Cut power

and identify yourself immediately or we'll destroy you. I repeat, identify yourself immediately! *Bremse* out!"

Daniel touched a console button whose protective cage he'd flipped back even before the *Princess Cecile* reached orbit. The vessel's general alarm, sets of three treble pulses, sounded in all compartments.

He lifted his finger from the button and said over the communicator, "General quarters. Prepare for action."

To Baylor Daniel added, "Well, chief, let's see what we can do with the present equipment, shall we?"

Covering a mind full of doubt with a tight smirk, Daniel stroked the firing toggle to launch the corvette's first pair of missiles.

"—repeat, identify yourself immediately or we'll destroy you!" said the voice from the communicator. "*Bremse* out!"

"You'll do wonders," Woetjans muttered reflectively, glaring at the cutter's minimal display. "Put us in the shadow of one of the mines they been dropping, Lamsoe. If you can, anyhow. I'd say put the command node between us, but we're too fucking far."

Here aboard the cutter, Adele had no feeling whatever for distances or even directions. Because of space restrictions the Plot-Position Indicator was projected on a concave combiner lens in front of Lamsoe, the pilot, rather than as three real dimensions in the air above the console. Adele wasn't even sure whether the cutter was one of the points on the curved display or if they were instead the center of the display's lower horizon.

She turned to Dasi, strapped into the fold-down seat beside her, and said, "Will they fire at us?" It didn't occur to her until after she spoke that the sailor might think she was frightened.

Dasi shrugged, though the loose-fitting atmosphere suit barely quivered. "They can try, but I don't guess they're going to do much across forty thousand miles. You know how plasma spreads."

The cutter had a single thruster. The deck quivered as the nozzle gimbaled around. When the thruster fired at its new heading Adele found herself hanging from the strap as the bulkhead tried to accelerate away from her. The plasma flow's high-frequency vibration made dust shimmer in the air.

Adele tried to settle herself. That was impossible while wearing an atmosphere suit. The suits were meant for transfer in vacuum, not work. They were awkward, uncomfortable constructions of rubberized fabric with stiffening hoops. One size fit all—in

Adele's case, fit very badly. The gauntlets separately clamped to the cuffs came in three sizes, though for Adele a pair marked SMALL wasn't.

The helmets were plastic castings shaped like the bottoms of test tubes, clear on the front and with round lenses like miniature portholes on either side. Aboard the cutter the Cinnabars wore the helmets open on the hinge at the back of the neck. They had no communication equipment, nor was the plastic clear enough for piloting a spacecraft.

"Think we're worth a missile?" Barnes wondered aloud. Neither of the men seemed concerned, either by the situation or by Adele's state of mind.

"A little tub like this?" Dasi scoffed. "No! Though she handles pretty good, don't she?"

"The captain's launching," Woetjans said. Adele couldn't place the emotion she heard in the petty officer's voice. "He's taking the cruiser away from us, I guess."

"God have mercy!" Lamsoe muttered over the plasma whine. "That big bastard'll eat them alive."

His fingers moved on his control keys. The flow cut abruptly. The thruster pivoted again, then resumed firing. In a tone of professional detachment Lamsoe went on, "One minute thirty to docking."

All four sailors stared at the display. Woetjans stood beside the control console, gripping attachments because she wasn't strapped in. Barnes and Dasi, facing one another in jump seats, leaned forward for a better view.

Adele could see the display past the pilot's shoulder, but it meant absolutely nothing to her. The full-sized console aboard the *Princess Cecile* had been simple to understand. When three dimensions were flattened to two, they became an alien world. It horrified her to realize that Barnes and Dasi, who (not to be unkind) between them might approximately equal her intelligence, watched with full appreciation the data which passed before her in a cascade of gibberish.

"Missed!" Dasi said. "Shit, they weren't even close!"

Barnes shook his close-cropped head in dismay. "Well, the captain's young," he said. "Not everybody's born to be an attack officer."

Woetjans turned toward them in fury. "How about shutting the fuck up, will you?" she said. "Did you ever think he just spit a couple missiles out in a hurry because our asses was in a sling?"

"That Alliance bastard didn't even maneuver," Dasi said in disappointment. "Missed 'em clean, and there's only ten missiles aboard."

"Eight now," Barnes agreed sadly.

Adele felt cold. If Woetjans was correct, it was an even more damning indictment of Lt. Daniel Leary that he hadn't used the available time to set up his initial attack on the cruiser/mine-layer. She couldn't believe that: she'd watched Daniel updating his launch sequence throughout the time they were on the bridge together.

No, Daniel wasn't slack. He just wasn't very good at that part of his job. He'd told her that his Uncle Stacey hadn't been a fighting officer for all his courage and skill in other aspects of spacefaring. Apparently Daniel had that part of the Bergen heritage as well.

It was unfortunate that they were all learning this in the middle of a battle. Though perhaps that didn't matter. The sailors obviously thought the battle was unwinnable to begin with.

"Docking!" Lamsoe warned. He lifted his hands from the controls and swung his helmet into place.

Automatic systems took control of this final portion of the journey. Adele felt the cutter rotate minusculely under the impulse of the maneuvering jets, steam rather than plasma. Even for the experts she assumed this Cinnabar crew were, the process of manual docking would be a maddening, time-consuming task.

She reached for her own helmet. The hinge was at the back of her neck so she couldn't see what she was doing. Dasi's big hand gently brushed hers away.

"Hunch a bit, mistress," the sailor said. Adele tried to obey but the edge of the helmet still grazed her forehead as it pivoted down over her head.

There was a click and a cool pressure as the helmet sealed. The oxygen bottle switched on. Simultaneously Adele felt the rasp of the cutter's docking mechanism interlocking with its mate on the command node's surface.

The sailors drifted in the weightless cabin. Heavy wrenches dangled from their belts. They couldn't carry real weapons because the programmers wouldn't open the airlock's inner hatch to an obvious threat, but burly sailors with wrenches should take command of the situation without difficulty.

Woetjans was opening the cutter's hatch. Adele tried to get up. She couldn't. Dasi—or was it Barnes?—reached down and released her safety strap.

The hatch released and pivoted inward. The gush of cabin air into vacuum would have carried Adele with it if Dasi—she was almost certain it was Dasi despite two distorting layers of faceshield—hadn't gripped her.

The node's airlock was three feet away, hard to see because of the flat lighting. Woetjans spun the wheel and pulled the lock open, using the cutter's hatch for purchase. She entered; the sailors launched themselves after her. Dasi and Barnes each held one of Adele's hands in the process, and Lamsoe clamped the outer lock shut behind them.

The chamber's interior was illuminated. Adele could tell that atmospheric pressure was building by the way the figures of her fellows filled out as air molecules began to scatter the light.

The sailors unlatched their helmets. Adele struggled with hers for a moment before Dasi did the job for her. The air was thin, frighteningly thin for a moment, but the sailors didn't seem to mind.

The hatch to the node's interior had a small window with a speaker plate directly beneath it. An eye showed through the window and the plate demanded, "What the hell are you doing here?" in a tinny voice.

"We're from the *Katlinburg*," Adele said in her Bryce accent. "She exploded in the harbor. Let us in."

"You don't belong here," the voice said in a mixture of anger and puzzlement.

"For God's sake, let us in!" Adele said. The *Katlinburg* was one of the Alliance transports; very possibly she had exploded by now. "We can discuss what we're doing here then!"

The eye vanished. For a long moment Adele was afraid that this was the end: the frightened programmers simply weren't going to let strangers into the command node.

The inner lock rang as bolts withdrew. The hatch pivoted into the station.

Four worried-looking technicians were in the node's central concourse. They were unarmed. From their dark complexions and hazel eyes they were natives of Willoughby, a world the Alliance had conquered less than five years earlier.

The technicians were probably political prisoners. At any rate the Alliance authorities obviously didn't trust them because there was also a detail of four uniformed soldiers with them on the command node.

The soldiers had sub-machine guns. They were pointed at the Cinnabars.

Daniel Leary sat at the command console of the *Princess Cecile*, as integral a part of the corvette as the sensor suite or the High Drive that responded to his touch.

He was braking at 1.8 gravities, the most strain he was willing to put on the corvette's structure. Even that was harder than he'd initially intended, since he knew the hull was modular and had been maintained by personnel with lower standards than the RCN would accept.

Daniel had been unjust to the *Princess Cecile*. Liftoff had proved the craft was as tight as a unit-built Cinnabar hull. Whatever else you said about Kostroma, they knew how to build starships here. The *Princess Cecile* would be a prized command in Cinnabar service, a handy little vessel whose crews would love her. All she needed was a once-over to make right a decade of neglect.

And of course she needed to survive to reach Cinnabar. Daniel wasn't concerned about that ultimate result now, because every thread of his being was focused on the actions that would make it possible.

Personnel shouted on the bridge and over the commo net. The crew wasn't worked up on this vessel, and because of the missing officers there was a degree of confusion that wouldn't normally have occurred with veterans like these.

A part of Daniel's mind was aware of what was going on around him, but the chaos touched only the surface. The core of him was the *Princess Cecile*, feeling her skin grow hotter as the *Bremse* lashed her with plasma cannon.

It was almost unheard of for a starship to use its secondary batteries as offensive weapons in space. Even now, though the *Bremse* and *Princess Cecile* were too close and slow for missiles to be really effective, the distance between vessels orbiting at different heights and orientations was beyond the range at which plasma cannon were a serious threat.

A sensor suite amidships degraded 13 percent at the stroke of the *Bremse*'s directed ions. For the moment Daniel ignored the problem. The *Princess Cecile*'s processors could compensate for the loss. If he needed greater precision, he'd rotate a replacement suite into place.

Conformal sensors in a ship's outer hull always suffered mechanical wear when a ship was in service. Alliance cannon had done nothing that a week cruising in the solar wind from Kostroma's Type O sun wouldn't have equaled.

Daniel's braking thrust meant the *Princess Cecile* in effect dived toward the planet, spiraling around Kostroma in an increasingly tight orbit. As the corvette approached the surface, Kostroma and the extended volume of the Kostroman atmosphere subtended a greater portion of the *Bremse*'s orbit.

The *Princess Cecile* passed into Kostroma's shadow. The *Bremse*'s cannonfire ceased; a better commander would have ended the vain process long before. Shooting at the *Princess Cecile* degraded the cruiser/minelayer's own sensors and eroded the bores of weapons meant for the *Bremse*'s defense.

Of course the *Bremse*'s captain probably didn't think he had much to fear from the *Princess Cecile*'s low-acceleration missiles. He might well be correct.

Chief Baylor launched a single round. Daniel's control inputs went to the Attack Board and were automatically figured into the launch commands. What the Attack Officer had to do was to calculate, with the help of his sensors and AI, where the target would be when his missile arrived.

This was a relatively simple—"relatively" being the key word—process when the vessels were at normal engagement speeds and ranges. A ship moving at a significant fraction of light speed, attacked by a missile at its terminal velocity of .6 c, had no time to maneuver.

Since the missile's course was based on sensor data that was several minutes old, the chances were very high that the target had done something in the interim that would cause the attack to fail. You didn't have to worry about the target reacting to your missile, however, except with point-blank slugs of ions in an attempt to decelerate the projectile by converting its substance to gas and forward thrust.

At these cislunar ranges, the target could see a missile in realtime from the instant of launch. The *Princess Cecile*'s low-acceleration weapons weren't a serious threat to the *Bremse* unless the cruiser/ minelayer's entire bridge crew was asleep; even then the automatic avoidance system, meant for maneuvering in the constricted space over a major harbor, would probably get them out of the way.

The *Bremse*'s missiles, though . . .

"Blue vessel is launching!" Dorfman said. Daniel was already aware of the dot separating from the icon highlighted blue, the traditional hostile designator in Cinnabar service. "Defensive batteries are live!"

Daniel released a control key, reducing the *Princess Cecile*'s thrust by a fraction. Three more dots appeared at ten-second intervals, the shortest period at which missiles could be launched without the exhaust of preceding weapons damaging those that followed.

The missiles accelerated at a full 12 Gees, but the corvette would be a thousand miles away when they reached the calculated impact point. The *Princess Cecile* handled beautifully, and with Daniel Leary at her controls she was safe until she was too close to Kostroma to continue maneuvering.

The trick wasn't merely to stay alive till then, however. Daniel was trying to pilot two vessels, his own and the *Bremse*. He was dragging the cruiser/minelayer behind him like a dog on a leash. If the corvette was *here*, the Alliance captain would strive to put his vessel *there*.

The process would continue in infinite sequence until there *was* a point Daniel had calculated before the *Princess Cecile* lifted from Kostroma; or until the *Princess Cecile* and her Cinnabar crew disintegrated in a gush of molten metal because her young captain had cut things a little too close.

"You're not authorized to be here," said the older female soldier who seemed to be in charge of the guard detail. "This place is top security!"

"We were just lifting off to launch a message cell," Adele said. "The ship blew up and damaged us, so we had to dock here. We need to contact the *Bremse* so they can send down aid to the surface."

She picked at the cuffs of her gauntlets. She couldn't see them clearly because of the way the sleeve ballooned, and she hadn't paid any attention to the method of closure when Woetjans sealed them for her.

"Somebody help me off with these damned gloves," Adele said peevishly. She held her hands out to Dasi, ignoring the guns pointed at her and her fellows. The node was weightless, but everyone aboard it was floating within thirty degrees of the hatch's alignment.

"How did you get here?" asked a technician; a man in his sixties, at least twice the age of the other Willoughbies. "Only the supply vessels are supposed to be able to dock without being destroyed by the defenses."

Willoughby was a center of electronic manufacturing and had provided a haven for disaffected Alliance citizens. The latter had been both a thorn in the side of Guarantor Porra and the key to the recent Alliance capture of the planet: feigned refugees had subverted Willoughby's automatic defense array when the Alliance fleet arrived.

"Of course we weren't destroyed!" Adele snapped as Dasi drew her gloves off. The sailors were keeping silent, waiting for her to tell them what to do. "We're the *Katlinburg*'s cutter, I told you."

Another Willoughby opened her mouth to speak. The senior technician shushed her with a quick gesture.

The technicians understood that friendly or not, the cutter shouldn't have been able to approach the command node without setting off the close-in defenses mounted on wands projecting from the node's hull. These would blast a hail of faceted tungsten pellets in the direction of any object that tried to approach without the proper codes. Only the cutters bringing supplies from the *Bremse* should have had those codes.

Dasi removed the right gauntlet and started on the other. The *Bremse* sent not only supplies but changes of guard: Adele could see that by the relatively good health of the soldiers compared to the sallow puffiness of the technicians.

The cruiser/minelayer maintained gravity by constant acceleration. Its High Drive used water molecules for conversion. A ship in station above Kostroma could replenish its tanks by dipping down to the surface for an hour every few days.

The command node was a satellite with only maneuvering jets. Those aboard her would feel the effects of weightlessness within days; the technicians had been in this high-technology prison for the full two weeks since the Alliance invasion.

"Paltes, call the ship and see what the fuck we're supposed to do about this," the Alliance non-com said. "You lot—"

She waggled her sub-machine gun toward the Cinnabars and drifted slightly back in reaction. Unlike the sailors, the Alliance guards weren't used to weightlessness.

"—get into the airlock again till they tell us what to do. I shouldn't have let you in."

Dasi removed the other gauntlet. He was between Adele and the guards. She reached into the pouch on her equipment belt with her left hand. "All right," she said calmly to the non-com, "but you're going to be in trouble—"

As Adele's hand came clear of the pouch, she shot the non-com through the bridge of the nose. Recoil—even the pistol's slight recoil—spun Adele sideways. She fired twice more as she rotated.

The guard whose right forearm Adele had shattered with a pellet meant for his upper chest jerked the trigger. His gun pointed toward the far wall. Pellets raked a programming alcove. Faint gray smoke drifted from holes punched in the structural plastic.

Adele bounced off the airlock. She turned desperately to see what was happening. Barnes and Dasi had the uninjured guard between them; Dasi was bending the man's gun arm over his knee to break it. Woetjans held the guard who'd fired by the throat with one hand as she hit him an unnecessary second time with the wrench in the other hand.

There was no need to worry about the non-com, nor for the soldier whose blood spurted one final time before his heart stopped for lack of fluid to pump. When a pellet hit the soft tissue of a human throat, the wound it tore looked more like a bomb crater.

Adele returned the pistol to her tool pouch. She pushed herself carefully toward a programming station. She reached a different alcove than the one she'd intended but that didn't matter, they were all the same.

Her leg, red with the globe of body fluids she'd brushed on the way, couldn't be allowed to matter either.

The *Princess Cecile*'s quartet of plasma cannon roared like a swarm of bees. They were four-inch high-output weapons with a hundred times the flux density of a thruster nozzle. The corvette's maneuvering jets fought to keep the vessel in alignment. Dorfman had his finger on the armament override, keeping the weapons on continuous fire even though he was burning their throats out.

There wasn't any point in saving the cannon for further use if the ship itself was a shower of meteors hitting the Kostroman atmosphere.

A space battle at these short ranges was a dance in which either party moved in conscious relation to her opponent. Computers determined the maneuvers; two battle computers given the same data would come to the same "best" result.

Daniel was poised over the controls. Before the battle started he'd directed the *Princess Cecile*'s AI to follow an extremely complex set of parameters. The corvette continued on a ballistic course for three long seconds despite the oncoming missiles. She *had* to hold the setting in order to lead the *Bremse* to where Daniel wanted the cruiser to be.

The parameters were beyond computation to a greater than 15 percent probability of success, but that was a much greater chance of survival than Daniel saw in any other course. Next time perhaps Fate would hand him a cruiser to hunt down some poor bastards in a second-class corvette.

He laughed, to the amazement of the other bridge personnel. An Alliance missile grazed the *Princess Cecile*.

The impact may not have been the missile itself but rather the ball of vaporized metal surrounding its ion-pitted head. It slapped the corvette, flexing the hull and shutting down all the vessel's electronics for a momentary self-check. The hull whipped three times more before it came to stasis, and even then nerves as trained as Daniel's could feel the tingle of harmonics which took longer to damp.

Emergency lighting went on; at least part of it did. That seemed to be an area where the Kostromans had skimped maintenance. Daniel's console came up again. A ship status display filled the main screen; the PPI had shrunk to a sidebar.

The *Princess Cecile* was tumbling faster than the maneuvering jets could handle. Daniel fed in thruster input more by feel than in response to his readouts.

They'd lost atmosphere and were losing more, but the leak wasn't serious and the rate was decreasing. There was severe damage to the port quarter between frames 79 and 92, but the inner hull wasn't penetrated and Daniel suspected, *felt*, that the outer hull might not be either. Plating had crumpled and the whipping had opened hull seams. That was where the air loss was occurring.

Domenico's emergency team had already started rerouting a severed data trunk amidships. Two ratings lugged a cannister of sealant up the bridge corridor and thrust the nozzle against a deck joint. The High Drive was running hot, but that was because the *Princess Cecile* was getting into the fringes of the Kostroman atmosphere. Have to make a decision soon, but first—

Daniel switched his display to the Attack Screen. The two missiles he'd launched at the start of the action were on it, heading back at terminal velocity.

Daniel had programmed the missiles to rotate three minutes into their flight, brake to stasis, and return to a target above Kostroma. The course reversal wasted fuel, but single-thruster missiles had the same conversion mass as their high-acceleration cousins and only half the rate of usage. Because of the additional distance this pair of projectiles had travelled, they were at .6 *c* when they crossed the point where the *Bremse* might have been and almost was.

Almost.

The missiles were a streak on the *Bremse*'s sensors. They passed within a mile of the cruiser/minelayer; one of them might have been closer yet.

The missiles hit the Kostroman atmosphere and mushroomed into fireballs that ignited the sky above an entire hemisphere. The same conversion of mass and velocity into thermal energy would have turned the *Bremse* into a ball of gas.

If.

Baylor's console was still out. The missileer had an access plate off and was shouting into a communicator he'd laid on the floor to free his hands as he worked. There was only one missile left in the corvette's magazines, so the temporary lack of an Attack Officer wasn't serious.

Dorfman still had his electronics, but the gunner's mate had already burned out his guntubes. That section of Daniel's status display was red and pulsing, warning of catastrophic failure if the weapons were used again.

Dorfman stabbed his keyboard with blunt fingers, removing the software interlocks that would prevent the guns from firing. A plasma cannon exploding when its barrel split would do damage to the ship, but not as much damage as a hit by an Alliance missile.

In their present condition the four guns would provide very little protection, but you do what you can. Everyone aboard the *Princess Cecile* was pulling his weight in the best tradition of the RCN.

Daniel replaced his Attack Screen with the Plot Position Indicator. The near misses had rattled the *Bremse*'s captain: the Alliance vessel was accelerating at over 2 gravities on a course skewed from any she'd been following to that point.

In a minute or two the Alliance commander would realize those missiles had been a one-off chance which the *Princess Cecile* couldn't repeat. The cruiser/minelayer would turn onto a following course and run down a quarry which could no longer use the planet as a shield.

Daniel rotated the corvette and increased thrust, climbing up from Kostroma's gravity well. They'd head out of the system for as long as they could. He felt his cheeks sag under acceleration. A 15 percent chance of success had really been pretty good, given the odds he and his crew were facing.

They had no chance at all now.

Adele ran the system architecture a third time, searching for the lockout that protected the *Bremse* from its own mines. She was sure that the safety device was a separate chip, not software within the main command and control unit.

She was sure of that, but she couldn't find any place within the design for the chip to reside. And the lockout *wasn't* in the software either!

The living guards were bound with wire and floating in the middle of the concourse. One had bandages on his arm and forehead; the other's broken limb was taped to his chest. The technicians from Willoughby were unharmed but as silent as the two drifting corpses.

The four Cinnabar sailors clustered around a programming alcove which they'd set to display the planetary environs. Adele glanced toward them out of frustration. She was doing something wrong. She hadn't been sure she could remove the lockout, but she hadn't expected any difficulty in locating it.

Woetjans looked grim in stark contrast to her ready cheerfulness as the cutter approached the control node. *All* the sailors looked grim.

"Mistress?" the petty officer said as she caught Adele's eye. "Is there anything we can do to help Mr. Leary? They're going for the high jump if we don't."

"If you can find the *damned* lockout chip that prevents the mines from engaging the ship that laid them, then we can do something," Adele said in a voice so savage that she wouldn't have recognized it herself.

"Mistress?" said the eldest of the programmers. "That's part of the sensor receiver, not the control system. It's in the third chassis slot and has a blue band across it."

"Where?" said Woetjans.

Another programmer turned to the console beside him. "This one!" he said.

The cover panel had quick-release fittings. The programmer was fumbling with them when Lamsoe, Barnes and Dasi arrived together. The sailors brushed him out of the way with as little concern as Woetjans showed for the floating corpse with which she collided on her way to the unit.

Lamsoe stuck his prybar beneath the edge of the cover. He twisted. The plate lifted enough for Barnes and Dasi to reach under it. The plate flew up, accompanied by fragments of broken fasteners.

Adele checked her own work. If the lockout was eliminated, she shouldn't have to do anything more. But because she was who she was, Adele entered the main database for a schematic of the sensor control system.

Woetjans reached over the shoulders of her subordinates. Her hand came up with a component from which the locking screws dangled, along with bits of chassis.

A relay clicked somewhere within Adele's console. Two icons vanished—one minusculely before the second—on the display the sailors had been watching.

Adele wouldn't have been sure what had happened if Woetjans and the others hadn't begun to cheer.

Daniel's first thought was that a fault in the system caused the change in the Plot Position Indicator. It was too good to be true.

He still switched to a direct imagery of the cruiser/minelayer and scrolled back five seconds before the event. There wasn't a great deal he could do that was *more* useful, after all.

The *Bremse* was a blunt-nosed cylinder of eighteen thousand tons or so loaded. Her present attitude toward the *Princess Cecile* was three-quarters on, so foreshortening made her look tubby. Had he wished Daniel could have rotated the image on his display to show the Alliance vessel's full 780-foot length, but he didn't need a schematic.

At the five-second mark the cruiser/minelayer expanded on a line intersecting the vessel's long axis. A sleet of atomic nuclei had just ripped through her at light speed.

Plasma weapons weren't effective against starships because the bolts lost definition in the vastness of astronomical distance. A charge that could be safely generated on one vessel was unlikely to harm a similar ship across tens of thousands of miles.

A mine was under no such restriction as to the size of the charge. Its external structure only had to survive the first microsecond of the thermonuclear explosion in its heart so that its magnetic lens could direct the force of the blast toward the target.

In practice, lens efficiency was on the order of 60 percent. Sixty percent of a 3-kiloton explosion, even attenuated somewhat by distance, was enough to gut a dreadnought.

It opened the *Bremse* like a bullet through a melon. The forty or so mines still undeployed in the cruiser/minelayer's hold went off in a series of low-order explosions that turned the wreck into a gas cloud, but that was an unnecessary refinement.

Daniel cut thrust to one gravity, then hit the alert button. "All hands!" he said. "All hands! The *Bremse* has blown up! I repeat, the cruiser chasing us is gone!"

He thought for a moment about the five hundred human lives lost with the starship. There was no triumph in the thought, but there was no pity either. They'd died in the service of their state as Daniel Leary expected someday to die in the service of Cinnabar. So be it.

Dorfman had stood to hug the rating who held the sealant cannister. Baylor's console was live again, but the missileer gaped instead at Daniel's display. By now the image was only a haze that would soon be indistinguishable from any other volume of cislunar space. Voices elsewhere cheered, but some shouted doubtful questions. Not everybody aboard the *Princess Cecile* could believe they were alive and likely to remain that way for the immediate future.

Come to think, if there was a heaven it would be a lot like this. At least for Daniel Leary . . .

Daniel switched back to the PPI. For what seemed forever he'd been focused on the relative location of three points: Kostroma, the *Princess Cecile*, and the *Bremse* pursuing her. The intricate dance had ended and Daniel's mind was suddenly as clean as that of a baby starting a new life. Now he had to bring the corvette into orbit, ideally in close alignment with the command node so that the personnel who'd saved his life could return to the *Princess Cecile*.

Domenico entered the bridge. He looked wary and exceptionally calm. He threw Daniel a salute that proved not all combat sailors were slack about ceremony and said, "Chief of Rig reporting for orders, sir!"

It was his way of asking, very professionally, if the emergency was over.

"Yes, it's real, Domenico," Daniel said. "Mind, let's not have a bulkhead blow out now that we think we're safe. We'll pick up Ms. Mundy's detachment, then see what shape the ship's in and—"

Domenico's face went stiff. "Sir, check your display!" he said.

Daniel turned. There were three new dots just within the present 15-light-second boundary of the PPI. As he watched, two more dots appeared. They were starships dropping out of sponge space and proceeding the remainder of the way toward Kostroma at maximum braking effort.

Daniel touched the attention signal and called, "General quarters!"

Four more dots joined the five recently added to the display. The nine ships couldn't be said to be in tight formation, but for vessels which had just left sponge space they were in remarkably good order. The admiral in charge must be pleased with her subordinates.

Because there was no question at all that this was a naval squadron, not some sort of merchant argosy returning to Kostroma.

The repair crews were back at work; apart from them, there was a hush over the *Princess Cecile*. Domenico leaned over Daniel's shoulder to peer more closely at the display. "Does that read Tec-Ay-En One-Four-One-Eight?" he asked.

The *Princess Cecile*'s PPI would assign an all-numerical designator to an icon if the object didn't provide one. Starships normally broadcast an alpha-numerical identification signal, however, the pennant number for naval vessels and a similar designator for merchantmen.

Daniel nodded. "Yes," he said. TAN1418 didn't meant anything to him.

"That's the *Rene Descartes*!" the bosun cried. "By Vishnu's dong, sir, I served on the old bitch for three years, I did! She was guard-ship over Harbor Three when we left Cinnabar, I swear to God!"

Daniel started to say, "Are you sure?" but caught the words just before they made him sound like a fool. He didn't know what else to say. Except—

He chimed for attention and announced, "All hands. I believe the vessels inbound are an RCN squadron, which will be very welcome. Continue repair work until further notice, but don't forget where your action stations are."

Daniel almost rang off, but a further thought struck him. "And fellow citizens?" he said. "Thank you. Your performance has been to the highest standards of the Republic of Cinnabar Navy."

There were cheers all over the ship. Daniel was choking. He knew he'd be replaced on the *Princess Cecile* as soon as the regular navy arrived, and he might never command another ship. But no captain, *ever*, would have a better crew than he did!

The icons on the PPI continued to re-form as the newcomers approached Kostroma. The last four were probably transports: they remained two light-seconds behind the leaders. The five warships were arrayed flower-fashion with the battleship in the center.

They'd noticed the *Princess Cecile* as well. Because Dorfman still had a gunnery display on his console, the interrogatory was routed to Daniel: "RCS Vessel *Rene Descartes*, Captain Lairden command-ing, carrying the flag of Rear Admiral Ingreit. Vessel signaling Are-Em Six-Nine-Three, please identify yourself. Over."

It took Daniel an instant to realize that he was RM693. He'd never had occasion to check the *Princess Cecile*'s pennant number.

He took a deep breath, then hit the general communicator switch as well as the intership hailing channel. What he was about to do was worthless braggadocio that was bound to irritate the senior officers on the other end of the line.

But he was going to do it anyway. He was a Leary of Bantry; and the crew, still for the moment *his* crew, would appreciate it.

"This is RCS *Princess Cecile*," he said, "Lieutenant Daniel Leary commanding. You are authorized to orbit within our automatic defense array."

He cleared his throat and went on, "Allow me to say that your squadron is a welcome addition to the RCN forces on station here. You'll be very useful in helping mop up the remaining unpleasantness on the ground. *Princess Cecile* out."

There was as much laughter as cheering in the corvette's compartments this time. "By Vishnu!" the bosun said in delight. "By Vishnu, sir!"

Daniel smiled faintly. He could imagine what Admiral Ingreit would say when he heard the message. On the other hand, he could imagine what Speaker Corder Leary might have said in similar circumstances. In that, at least, father and son were more alike than different.

Daniel switched to the channel dedicated to communication between the *Princess Cecile* and Adele's detachment. He'd better inform the command node promptly, or Admiral Ingreit was going to find his squadron in range of a hostile and demonstrably lethal defensive constellation.

BOOK FOUR

Twenty people sat at consoles around the walls of the outer room. Adele would have called them clerks if this had been a civilian setting. She didn't know what they were on a battleship.

"Come in, please," said the man seated at the desk of the small inner office. "And close the hatch behind you if you would."

Adele obeyed. She didn't like the feeling in the pit of her stomach, and she didn't think the problem was her return to gravity after six days weightless in the command node. Strictly speaking the *Rene Descartes* was under 1-gee acceleration, not real gravity, but the only difference Adele could tell was that the battleship had changed course twice in the hours since she'd come aboard.

"We've completed integrating the defense array your ships brought with the Alliance mines already in place," she said. "I'd like to return to the ground, now. I was told to see you about transportation."

The man seated on the other side of the desk was tall, very fit, and about thirty years old. He wore an officer's uniform, but there were no rank insignia on his collar or sleeves.

The man chuckled. "Yes," he said, "we'll talk about transportation in a moment." He stood and reached across the desk to offer his hand. "My name's Elphinstone. Please sit down, Ms. Mundy."

The walls of the office had large flat-plate displays that gave the impression of windows, though the scenes were different. A starscape spread behind the desk as if the room were open to vacuum. Adele found the effect disconcerting, which was very likely Elphinstone's intention.

His handshake was firm; a little too firm. Elphinstone was playing a variation of the childish game of trying to crush the other party's hand with his own. He was demonstrating how much stronger he was than the small woman, and by implication how completely the situation was under his control.

Adele imagined Elphinstone's eyes bulging to either side of the bullethole. She shook her head in violent self-disgust. The sailors had tried, but it was impossible to clean the control node well enough to get rid of the smell of rotting blood.

Elphinstone wasn't smiling now. He coughed, then gestured to the single chair in front of the desk and repeated, "Please sit down, mistress."

His composure returned as he settled into his own more comfortable chair. "It's quite an honor to meet you," he said. "You're the reason for our easy victory here on Kostroma, you know."

Adele looked at the wall showing Kostroma City from an apparent thousand feet in the air. Most of the fires were out by now. The Alliance forces on the ground had been willing to surrender when they realized they were trapped beneath a hostile fleet and automatic defensive array.

The Kostromans themselves had felt otherwise when they saw that Alliance personnel were suddenly at their mercy. Assassination was a staple of local culture; mercy toward one's enemies was not. From the reports Adele listened to in the control node, it seemed that folk wearing Zojira colors had been the quickest to turn on their former allies. They may have hoped their neighbors would forget what they'd been doing a few weeks before.

"I was part of a group," Adele said. "A group I'm very proud to have been a member of. And I've helped put the defensive array in shape, so now I'd like to be returned to the ground."

The technicians from the Cinnabar squadron were skilled, but they didn't know the Alliance system in detail and they didn't have Adele's ability to chart paths through the unfamiliar. She and the four programmers from Willoughby—volunteers, now that they'd been freed—remained in charge of the Alliance command node until the systems were fully merged: integrated to the standards of Adele Mundy.

"You're far too modest," Elphinstone said with a chuckle that made Adele think of a stream of oil. "Fortunately, you have friends to advertise your merits, so to speak. Otherwise—"

There was no change in his voice, but his hard, brown eyes glittered.

"—there'd be some problems with your background."

"My understanding," Adele said in a voice that was perfectly distinct and as flat as if synthesized, "was that an Edict of Reconciliation was passed nine years ago to reintegrate survivors of the Three Circles Conspiracy into Cinnabar society."

There was no point in pretending she didn't know what this *toad* was talking about. She'd known it was going to be this as soon as she'd entered his office.

The deck shifted as the *Rene Descartes* changed tack so that the constant thrust didn't send them out of the system. Adele felt the fluid in her inner ears spin queasily, though "down" remained the same direction.

A month ago she would have wanted to be sick. Now her mind was too busy thinking about where to place the pellet in the body of the man across the desk, and that was worse.

"As I say," Elphinstone said, "you have friends. Admiral Ingreit will use all his influence to clear up any remaining disabilities. And I—"

He laughed unctuously, a polite sound that Adele couldn't help contrasting with Daniel Leary's honest bellows.

"—know some people myself, you see." Elphinstone tented his hands and went on, "As a formality, though, we'd like you to sign a report showing that you were operating here under Admiral Ingreit's direction. This won't detract any from the credit you're due, I assure you."

Adele leaned back in her seat. Daniel might actually think this was funny. "What about Lieutenant Leary?" she asked.

"Ah, yes, Lieutenant Leary," Elphinstone said. "Yes, that's an interesting situation. There've already been questions asked in high places about how he managed to survive when all his superiors were killed in the fighting."

"They were executed in the Grand Salon of the Elector's Palace," Adele said in the voice she'd used ever since she entered this room, this *den*. "They were each shot once in the head except for the man who claimed to be from the Navy Office. I believe he was actually a spy. He was shot twice because he was twisting on the floor."

Elphinstone blinked. Adele wasn't sure whether it was her words

or their implications that had taken him aback. After a moment
he said, "Yes, I see. Ah."

He cleared his throat and continued in a colder tone that was
probably the one he found natural, "You see, mistress, Lieutenant
Leary is a headstrong young man who would cause a great deal
of trouble for himself and others if he were allowed to. That's
why it's important that your account of events be put on record
as soon as possible. Admiral Ingreit is very insistent on that point."

Adele stood. "I don't think the admiral would like my account,"
she said. "It would be accurate. Now that we've had our conversation, can you direct me to the person who can get me to the
ground? I don't like the atmosphere on this ship."

"Sit down, Ms. Mundy," Elphinstone snapped. "I don't think you
quite understand. There were exceptions to the Edict of Reconciliation and I'm very much afraid your name will turn out to be
one of them unless you see reason. Do you understand what I'm
telling you?"

Adele had started to reach for the door. She turned, thinking
of what Hogg had said about intelligence agents. She smiled faintly.

Elphinstone got up and walked around the desk to face her.
There was a wary look in his eyes, but his expression was as bland
as a data console.

"Either you help people who want to be your friends," he said,
"or you're executed as a traitor to the state. You really have no
choice."

Adele opened the door—the hatch, she supposed she should
call it on shipboard. Subordinates looked up from consoles, then
quickly looked down again.

"Are you telling me that a citizen of Cinnabar has no choice,
Mr. Elphinstone?" Adele said loudly enough to be heard far down
the corridor. "Are you saying that a Mundy of Chatsworth has
no choice?"

She slapped the startled man with her right hand. "This is
my choice!" she said. Her fingers stung as though she'd laid them
on a hot stove. Four discrete marks blazed red on Elphinstone's
cheek. "I can be contacted at the library in the Elector's Palace—*if* you can find a person of breeding to act for you in a
matter of honor!"

Adele strode through the outer office. No one spoke or tried
to stop her. She turned right for no reason except that there were

only two possibilities and she was too angry to attempt a rational choice.

She kept walking. She had no destination, but the adrenaline surging through her bloodstream had to be burned off somehow. Fight or flight . . .

"Mistress?" said a familiar voice. "Mistress Mundy?"

For the many minutes since she left Elphinstone's office, Adele's eyes had operated solely to keep her from walking into objects. She saw people and bulkheads with the same lack of distinction.

Her eyes and mind locked back into focus. She entered a large room with hatches along one wall—a docking bay like the one by which she'd arrived on the *Rene Descartes*. A number of sailors stood in groups, waiting for officers to return.

Woetjans had called to her. Barnes, Dasi, and a third *Aglaia* sailor whose name Adele didn't know were with the petty officer.

"Have you been keeping well, mistress?" Woetjans asked. "We heard you were working on the minefield still."

"I'm not all right now," Adele said. Her face hardened. "Can you take me to Kostroma City? I need . . ."

She paused. If the interview with Elphinstone had cost her the ability to speak precisely, then she'd lost more than her life.

She smiled. "I very much *want* to get off this ship," she said.

The petty officer had no readable expression for a moment. Then she said, "Yeah, sure."

She gestured her three subordinates toward the nearest hatch. "Saddle up," she said. "With luck we'll be back before the quartermaster wants to leave."

"He's going to be really pissed if we're not," said the sailor Adele didn't know by name.

Barnes knocked the man down.

In a furious tone that shocked Adele even more than the blow, Woetjans shouted, "Then I'll answer to him, won't I, Blessing? Your job's to carry out the orders *I* give you!"

Others in the docking bay watched the unexpected tableau, but no one moved to intervene. Dasi walked over to the hatch controls. "Yeah," he said. "And if you think you got problems with what just happened, Blessing, you better pray Mr. Leary don't learn you tried to give the lady a hard time. They'll probably make somebody else captain of the *Princess Cecile*, but until they do you'll think you died and went to Hell."

The hatch opened. It was the inner door of a large airlock holding a cutter. Woetjans gestured Adele through ahead of her.

Adele didn't speak. There was nothing more to say; and anyway, her throat was too choked by emotion.

Captain Kryshevski was an hour later leaving his office than he'd thought even remotely possible. Mistress O'Sullivan's establishment would be open till dawn, but the chances of getting a taxi at the back of the Elector's Palace weren't good.

Kryshevski could have a naval vehicle take him, but that would be impolitic at best. He might well meet other officers at the tables, but he'd be a fool to put his activities on record with those who weren't themselves implicated.

Nothing illegal about gambling, of course. Nothing illegal about gambling for very high stakes. But questions might be asked, and Captain Kryshevski didn't have a wealthy family to provide answers.

He returned the guards' salute and stepped into the street. To his relief, there was a jitney waiting with its diesel ticking over. The driver, an older man, hopped down from his seat and opened the door to the rear compartment. He looked to be a scoundrel, but he bowed and said, "Where to, master?" in a polite tone.

Kryshevski wasn't about to argue with what seemed better luck than he had any right to. Maybe it was an omen of the night's play. He got in and said quietly so that the guards wouldn't hear, "Stoneyard Street, beside the entrance to the gardens. You know where that is?"

"I sure do, master," the driver said. He closed the compartment and boarded again. The light vehicle rocked with his weight over the single front wheel.

The jitney was already pointed in the correct direction. They started, and the rhythm of the wheels on the hard pavers began to soothe Kryshevski's irritation at the problem that had held him in the office. It was *impossible* to find enough guard detachments from a squadron that hadn't been intended as an occupation force.

The jitney stopped. A middle-sized man opened the compartment door. Kryshevski fumbled for the latches of his briefcase, cursing himself for not carrying the pistol in a more accessible location. He relaxed slightly when he realized the man wore a Cinnabar naval uniform.

"This taxi's taken!" Kryshevski said.

"It's not exactly a taxi, Captain," the man said, "but I'd be more than happy to carry you to your destination."

The driver leaned over so that Kryshevski could see him through the open door. "I knew you'd want me to help the captain, Master Daniel," he said in what Kryshevski now recognized as a Cinnabar accent.

"You were quite right, Hogg," said the man. He stepped up into the compartment.

Kryshevski began to laugh. "Caught!" he said. "Caught for fair, by God! You're Lieutenant Leary and I've been dodging you all week!"

Daniel closed the door. Hogg drove off again, though very slowly. "If you have, sir," Daniel said, "I'm sure it's because you didn't know what I wanted to see you about."

Hogg had taught him early that the successful hunter didn't tramp through the forest looking for prey: he found a game trail and waited for his victim to walk down it for the last time.

Hogg had also taught him that a wire-loop snare was just as effective as a bullet and the hunter could sleep longer besides. Garroting the squadron's personnel officer wouldn't advance Daniel's case, but a time or two during the past frustrating week he'd imagined Captain Kryshevski with a black face and protruding tongue.

"Well, I'd like for that to be true, boy," Kryshevski said. He was handling the business like a gentleman of breeding rather than snarling in fury at the way he'd been trapped. "I guess I know now how you were able to give the Alliance such fits."

He chuckled again, shaking his head. His face sobered and he went on, "The *Princess Cecile*'ll put a small fortune in your prize account when the Navy Board buys her into service, as I'm sure they will; but you won't be breveted 'commanding' to take her back to Cinnabar. That'll go to a more senior lieutenant. And let's face it, boy, to a lieutenant who's got more interest than you do."

"Yes, sir," Daniel said. "I know that, and I wouldn't waste your time discussing the matter."

Interest was a reality of all walks of life, not just the RCN. You helped those who could help you. To object would be as silly as objecting to sex or to the necessity of breathing.

That didn't mean that senior officers found promotion opportunities for incompetents: no sane admiral wanted to be saddled with a band of protégés who were unable to carry out his orders effectively. It *did* mean that of two qualified persons, the one whose connections could most benefit the officer making the decision would get the promotion.

Daniel couldn't imagine living under a system in which the person making the decision didn't feel personally responsible for his choice. He wouldn't want to live in a world without interest. Unfortunately, until Daniel got enough reputation that some senior officer took him under a wing despite the possibility of Speaker Leary's wrath, he was very much without interest himself.

"I just wanted to see that the paperwork for my crew was processed correctly for distribution of the prize money," he said. "In particular I'd like to check on my first officer, Ms. Mundy, whom I breveted lieutenant from her former rank."

"You *what?*" said Kryshevski, dumbfounded.

"It's unusual for a junior lieutenant to grant brevet rank, I know," Daniel said calmly. "But as you're aware the Kostroma mission was an admiral's slot, and I was the senior officer surviving at the time I granted the commission. That Lieutenant Mundy was critical to the success of the operation is of course obvious after the fact."

"But good God, boy!" the captain said. "You can't brevet a civilian."

"Ms. Mundy had the rank of sergeant in the Officer Training Corps of her school," Daniel said. He had no idea of whether or not that was true, but it was likely enough for a Mundy of Chatsworth. "I think under the circumstances that should cover the legalities."

Kryshevski looked at him sharply. "'Under the circumstances,'" he repeated. "The circumstances being that you won't make a fuss about command of the *Princess Cecile* going to somebody else. That's what you're saying, isn't it?"

"I wouldn't want to put it that way, sir," said Daniel. "But you can assure Admiral Ingreit that I have no intention of objecting to his choice of officers for any ship under his command. The *Princess Cecile* included, of course."

"You are a smart little bugger, aren't you?" Kryshevski said. There was admiration in his tone. "Well, I guess I shouldn't wonder that Speaker Leary's son knows that politics is the art of the possible."

Daniel smiled without real humor. "The driver is my old servant," he said. "He taught me to play cards, among other things. And he certainly taught me not to overplay my hand."

"I'll see what I can do," Kryshevski said. "Between us, I don't think your friend needs to worry about her share. They'll rescind the grant on Cinnabar, but it'll be valid for the period in question."

He sighed. "There's a school of thought," he went on, looking toward the compartment's blank front panel, "that says an officer clever enough to capture a corvette is likely clever enough to command her. Especially when he's already been clever enough to destroy an Alliance cruiser."

"The *Bremse* was Ms. Mundy's doing, not mine," Daniel said quietly. "I was very lucky to have her under my command."

Kryshevski shook his head. "Speaker Leary's son and a Mundy of Chatsworth," he said. "He'll have kittens when he finds out, won't he?"

"I don't see my father very often these days, sir," Daniel said in what was for him a cold tone. "I don't think he has much opinion on naval matters, and my relations with Ms. Mundy are entirely a naval matter."

The jitney stopped. Hogg opened the door on Kryshevski's side.

Kryshevski paused. "It wouldn't be to your advantage if word that you met me got out," he said.

"I'm aware of that, sir," Daniel said. "I don't think there's any chance of that occurring."

Kryshevski stepped down. Hogg bowed to him and said, "There's some loose bricks on the right in the ceiling of the passageway to Ms. O'Sullivan's. You'd be wiser to chance the puddle on the left instead of getting brained trying to arrive with dry shoes."

Kryshevski handed Hogg a tip that made his eyebrows lift with pleasure. He was laughing as he entered the gateway.

When the footsteps didn't stop at the first door beyond the head of the stairs, Adele realized the visitor was coming for her. The man in the second room down the hallway worked nights, and the woman in the remaining room would only be returning at this hour if she had a client. The person coming was alone.

Adele took out her pistol and laid it on the desk at which she sat facing the door.

The knock was discreet. "Yes?" Adele said without getting up.

"My name is Sand, mistress," replied the voice of a woman with a cultured Cinnabar accent. "I'd be grateful for a few minutes of your time."

Adele considered the situation. She'd returned to the apartment she'd lived in before the coup because she had nowhere else to go. She still had nowhere to go.

"Come in," Adele said. She'd known someone would come. She'd expected more than one person, but she hadn't expected them quite so soon. "The door isn't locked."

The door opened. Sand was about sixty years old. She wore a long cloak and shoes that seemed unobtrusive unless you realized what they must have cost. She was heavy, though not quite what even Adele's lack of charity would call fat.

"I appreciate your seeing me," Sand said, sounding sincere. "I regret the hour, but I came as soon as I could."

"You came from Elphinstone," Adele said. Her lips smiled. "Let me rephrase that: Elphinstone works *for* you."

She didn't suggest her visitor sit down. The room's only chair was the one in which Adele herself sat anyway.

Sand laughed and seated herself on the edge of the low bed. "Commander Elphinstone most certainly does *not* work for me," she said. "He's a naval officer. Wonderful fellows in their place, naval officers. Rock-solid, straightforward people, crucial to the survival of the Republic. Unfortunately . . ."

She paused to throw back the wing of her cloak. The price of the suit she wore beneath it would have paid Adele's apartment rent for a year. Sand brought an ivory snuffbox out of an inside pocket, offered it to Adele, and put a pinch in the hollow of her left thumb.

"The trouble with naval officers," Sand continued, "is their confidence that the only way to an objective is through the direct application of force. Whereas civilians like you and me know—"

She snorted, pinching shut the opposite nostril, then sneezed violently. "Nothing like it to keep your head clear," she said in satisfaction.

Sand met Adele's eyes squarely. "Sometimes all you get from driving head-first into a situation is a headache, Ms. Mundy," she said. "Which is what that fool Elphinstone has caused for me. I'm hoping that you'll not let that prevent you from acting to your advantage and to that of the Republic."

"I'll give you the same answer I did him," Adele said coldly.

She felt silly to have the gun in plain sight, though it would be worse at this point to pocket it again. Sand didn't use force, and she was much more dangerous than those who did.

"If I asked the same question, I'm quite sure you would," Sand said. "And if you think I *would* ask the same question then I've misjudged your abilities of analysis."

Adele laughed and put the pistol away: an apology for being foolish, understood and accepted by Sand's nod of approval.

"It's obviously to my benefit to help you," Adele said. "I'll do so if I'm able to with honor. But you should be aware that my honor *is* engaged in this matter."

"Oh, no one has designs on your honor," Sand said good-humoredly. "And there's plenty of honor to go around in a victory as great as this one. Admiral Ingreit will get the formal thanks of the Senate for capturing Kostroma, and as for Lieutenant Daniel Leary, well, he'll be a nine-days' wonder, won't he? The last thing a wise senior officer would do is to seem to be blackening the name of the hero of so brilliant an exploit."

"Some people might not see it that way," Adele said.

Sand snorted. "Some people are fools," she said.

Her face, never particularly attractive, was suddenly that of a bulldog preparing to leap. "Let me assure you, mistress, that Admiral Ingreit is capable of taking good advice if it's put in a form he can understand. My delay in visiting you was because I thought it desirable to discuss matters with the admiral first."

Adele laughed. "I'd offer you a drink," she said, "but I don't have anything on hand. I don't have very much at all, to be honest, including the next week's rent."

Sand nodded without comment. "Have you seen Lieutenant Leary recently?" she asked.

Adele shook her head. "Not since shortly after the fleet arrived," she said. "I went to the command node to help with integration, and Daniel had his own duties. I believe he's still aboard the ship we captured, but I didn't care to bother him after I left the battleship."

She half-smiled. "I was afraid I might be contagious, you see."

Sand nodded again. She opened her belt purse and took from it a business card.

"I believe that a person with your natural abilities could be of enormous benefit to the Republic," she said. "What some would think of as—please forgive me—your disabilities are in fact extremely good cover for a person of undoubted loyalty to Cinnabar."

Adele's smile was more wry than bitter. "I don't think it would be difficult," she said, "to find those who doubt my loyalty."

Sand stood to place the business card on the desk. "I believe we've already discussed how easy it is to find fools, mistress," she said. "I try very hard not to be one of their number."

The front of the card read simply BERNIS SAND. Adele turned the card over and squeezed the diagonally opposite corners. A twelve-digit number appeared on the blank surface, then vanished when she released the pressure.

"When you're next on Cinnabar you might call there," Sand said. She stood and carefully returned the snuffbox to its pocket.

"Thank you for the suggestion, mistress," Adele said, "but I don't expect to be on Cinnabar in the foreseeable future. To be honest, I don't think I'll return to Cinnabar until I can do so aboard a naval vessel commanded by Mr. Leary."

She cleared her throat. She was profoundly embarrassed at what she was doing. The Mundys of Chatsworth were not a house that interested itself in trade, so it was bad enough to find herself bargaining. Further, she was boasting by putting a high price on herself when she was three florins from starvation; and she didn't know enough about the navy to be sure Sand could pay that price even if she chose to.

Adele smiled. Not for the first time she realized that some people would do more for others than they would do for themselves. That was perhaps as good a definition of friendship as one could find; and a definition of patriotism as well.

Sand laughed. "Goodness, you do have a low opinion of the way the navy's run," she said in a plummy voice. "Well, since you met Elphinstone this afternoon I can see why you would. I assure you that Admiral Ingreit is too sophisticated to be taken in by the rumors about Daniel Leary being on the outs with his father."

Adele blinked. The words were quite clear, not the jargon that had frequently confused her when she was around the sailors. But they made as little sense as, "You can breathe chlorine now."

"Yes, a politician as clever as Corder Leary knows how important the health of the navy is to the Republic," Sand continued. "And what better way to gauge that than through his own son? Especially if the boy sees all parts of the service that would have been hidden from a top-rank noble. The admiral and I were discussing that very subject at dinner tonight."

"Ah," said Adele. "I do see."

She stood and sidled out from behind the desk. "And I see that I owe you an apology, mistress."

She offered her hand. Sand shook it firmly and said, "No apology required, Ms. Mundy. You hadn't known me long enough for accurate analysis. I *have* studied you, however. I trust communication will be easier in the future."

Sand closed her cloak about her. "Good night, then, mistress," she said.

Adele cleared her throat again. "I think he's the sort of officer the RCN needs," she said. She noted with amusement that she'd used the sailor's term for the organization rather than calling it "the navy" as a civilian would have done. "That the Republic needs."

Sand looked at her. "As do I, Ms. Mundy," she said. "Otherwise our discussion tonight would have turned in different directions."

She closed the door behind her with a slow, firm pressure till it latched. The warped panel would have sprung open if Sand had slammed it.

Adele walked toward the harbor through bright sunlight. When Woetjans and Barnes brought her the invitation to board the *Princess Cecile* in orbit, they'd expected her to fly to the cutter in their airboat. She let them take most of her limited possessions, but not the personal data unit on her thigh; nor the pistol; nor herself.

Adele didn't bother to analyze why she'd refused. The sailors were surprised but as always respectful, and they were used to her surprising them.

She'd walked all the time she was Electoral Librarian, but not usually in daylight. Kostroma City's street life had returned with all its noisy vibrancy. There was still a tinge of smoke in the air, but the sound of construction work was even more general than it had been when Adele arrived.

In Kostroma City it was always "after the cataclysm." The Alliance invasion differed in scale but not in kind from the coups and fires and riots of the past, and the citizens were dealing with the aftermath in the familiar ways.

People had died. Some of the reconstruction was being done by families new to Kostroma, but the city found that a familiar pattern also.

A vendor was selling fish fried in dough from a cart. His customers blocked the pavement. A woman sat on the low coping of the canal in the middle of the boulevard, looking down the street. In skirting the crowd, Adele's leg touched the back of the seated woman's jacket.

"May I speak with you, mistress?" said the woman. Adele turned.

"My name is Tovera," said the woman.

She was Markos's aide.

A quartet of burly footmen preceded a jitney driving down the street. Adele didn't recognize their colors, puce and green. The lunch crowd squeezed toward the side to give them room.

"There's a courtyard a few doors down," Tovera said. The bruises on her face and exposed hands had faded to sepia and a sickly yellow. "It should be quieter. There's no one in the house now."

She stood, smiling faintly. The wince as she moved was almost imperceptible. "They were buried last week."

"I thought you were dead," Adele said.

That was half true. Adele had never considered the aide to be alive; or at least, a living human.

"Move it!" snarled one of the servants clearing a path for the jitney. He raised his baton, to prod or strike.

Tovera turned. "Don't even think about it," she said pleasantly.

The servant jerked back. "Well fuck you, then," he snarled, but in a muted voice. He stepped around the two women and pushed a pair of strangers against the lunch cart.

Adele took her hand out of her pocket. "Yes," she said. "Let's get out of the street."

The door had been opened with axes. A mythological frieze decorated the panel's bronze facing. Adele paused for a moment to finger a delicately molded satyr carrying off a nymph; both figures had been decapitated by the same stroke.

Adele couldn't feel sorrow for dead strangers; but the artwork which had shared their destruction made her face tremble to behold.

She walked through the littered hallway, following Tovera to the courtyard in back. A citrus tree was in bloom, and half the daffodils had survived being trampled.

Tovera seated herself on the bench built into the courtyard wall.

Adele sat on the opposite side, avoiding the pool of flaking blood which tiny insects were carrying away.

"I had a hand free," Tovera said. "I dug myself out brick by brick. It was easier after I uncovered my face and could see again."

"What do you want?" Adele said. She didn't think the aide intended to kill her, but she couldn't imagine any other purpose for this meeting.

"I told Markos you were too dangerous to use the way he tried to," Tovera said musingly. "He didn't believe me. He didn't think I could know anything about people."

She smiled. "But I knew you, Ms. Mundy."

"What do you *want*?" Adele repeated.

"I want to serve you," Tovera said. She was still smiling.

"Don't be absurd," Adele said. She stood up. "You're too dangerous to have around."

Her face hardened. "You're too dangerous to live, Tovera. Good day."

"Mistress!" the aide said. Adele paused on her way out of the garden and faced Tovera again.

"There's a piece of me missing," Tovera said. "Do you think I don't know that? I can watch other people, mistress. It's like running my fingers all around the edges of the hole, but that doesn't put the piece back."

She stood, walked a step closer, and knelt at Adele's feet. "Let me use you for the piece of me that isn't there," she whispered.

"Get up," Adele said. "For *God's* sake."

Tovera rose gracefully despite the pain Adele knew must twist every muscle. That the aide had survived the wall's collapse was perhaps less surprising than the fact she could still move.

"Markos had a goal," Tovera said softly. "He planned to be Guarantor of the Alliance some day. I didn't believe that, but it didn't matter. I would have died for him, mistress, because I don't have a goal: only the tasks somebody else sets me. And I think you understand that."

The implications of Tovera's smile were a black pit that tried to swallow Adele Mundy's soul. Adele's mind formed the words, "You're insane!" but she didn't say that because it wasn't true.

Tovera was correct: she was missing a piece. She was no more insane than Adele's pistol was. Either one would kill when instructed to, without compunction and without remorse.

Adele's mind said, "I'm *not* like you," but she didn't speak those words aloud either. Instead she said, "Why did you come to me, Tovera?"

The aide's face was still. She shrugged. "Because you know what I am," she said, "but you don't really care. Any more than you care how tall I am or that I'm a woman. That's just information to you."

For no conscious reason, Adele thought of the people she'd killed here on Kostroma. She didn't know their names. She didn't know the name of a single one of them, and nothing she could do would bring them back.

She couldn't breathe life into dead clay.

"Yes, all right, Tovera," Adele said. "I don't know if I'll be able to pay you, and I'm not even sure you can travel back to Cinnabar with me"—though she suspected Woetjans would stow the servant aboard even if Daniel unaccountably refused to take her formally—"but welcome to service with the Mundys of Chatsworth."

Adele smiled like an icicle. "Sadly decayed though I'm afraid the house is."

Daniel moved his hand in front of his companion's faceshield and gestured toward the blue magnificence of Kostroma "rising" beyond the stern of the *Princess Cecile*. "Isn't it a wonderful view, Adele?" he said. "Though I guess you saw it before when you boarded the command node."

Adele's voice, tinged with a dry humor audible despite the compression of the radio intercom, replied, "I had other things on my mind at the time. And these helmets actually allow one to see out."

She touched her faceshield. She now wore an RCN rigging suit, as did Daniel and most of the forty crewmen working on the corvette's hull and masts. A few ratings still had Kostroman rigging suits, bulkier and more difficult to put on and take off than their Cinnabar equivalents. Even so there was no comparison between this equipment, meant for work in vacuum, and the lightweight transfer suits which were worn only minutes at a time.

Hogg and Domenico were working in separate ways to replace the last Kostroman gear. Daniel suspected that meant the *Princess Cecile* would leave for Cinnabar with a complete double set of rigging suits. If nothing else they'd make useful material to trade with the complements of other ships in Harbor #3.

Daniel led Adele by the hand toward the repaired portion of the hull. He was familiar with the stiction-*release* of the magnetic soles each time his foot lifted, but his companion looked as though she'd blundered into a tar pool. Release—for one boot at a time— was automatic at a moderate level of upward pressure, but Daniel remembered how frustrating he'd found it the first time.

He was six years old, then, wearing a suit that must have been made for a midget as he walked the hull of an intrasystem transport with Uncle Stacey holding his hand. Now he was on his own starship, his own *command*, beneath the splendor of a distant world.

Of course it wouldn't be his command for very much longer. Well, perhaps some day. Fate had given Daniel Leary everything he'd hoped for as a boy: far planets and a starship command. Fate probably wouldn't take the planets away from him, and if he never again commanded, well . . .

He laughed. Adele turned within her rigid helmet to look at him.

"Just thinking that I should've been more careful about what I wished for," Daniel said musingly. "It's funny how things work out sometimes."

"Yes," Adele said. "It is."

Daniel again put a hand in front of Adele so that she'd see it, then pointed to the mast they were trudging past. Six riggers were raising and lowering it repeatedly to be sure it was properly installed. Lieutenant Mon, borrowed as an unassigned officer to help refit the *Princess Cecile*, was directing them.

"We replaced three of these as battle-damaged," Daniel explained. He and Adele were on a private channel, neither interfering with the work crews nor overheard by them. "If the parts' cost had been coming out of our own maintenance budget, there's probably only one I'd have bothered with changing. These spars came from transports caught in the Floating Harbor."

"They were prizes, then?" Adele said. "Do I have the term right?"

Daniel smiled faintly. "That's the word you mean," he said, "but in this case the ships themselves may not turn out to be prizes. The Kostroman vessels will probably be released to the original owners with a payment to the fleet that recaptured them. But after a victory like this everybody expects warship crews to bring their ships up to specification from what's lying around, so to speak."

He tapped the hull plating with a toe. "The frames here were fractured when the missile grazed us," he said. "A good thing I didn't know that or I'd have been afraid to reverse course under full power."

Adele turned and looked at him. She smiled.

"Yes, well," Daniel admitted in embarrassment. "I suppose I might have done pretty much the same thing but I'd have worried about it."

Adele smiled more broadly. He'd never before seen her show such obvious amusement.

"Well, I'd have worried when things calmed down some," he said in exasperation. "For pity's sake, woman, it's a figure of speech."

"It's a piece of nonsense," Adele said. "I've seen you when things go wrong, remember?"

"Yes, well," Daniel said, embarrassed now for a different reason. "There isn't time to think, but the civilians don't understand that. Sorry to have been treating you like a civilian."

His foot caressed the hull again. The rigid toe-cap had no feeling, but Daniel's touch was really spiritual rather than physical anyway.

"The *Princess Cecile* here was a dream to repair, you know," he said. Part of him was vaguely aware that his companion didn't know anything of the sort. "Back on Cinnabar the taste's all for unit-built hulls because they're stronger."

Daniel's toe rapped for emphasis. "And who can argue against that? you say. But there's not a corvette in RCN service that could have taken the blow we did *without* structural damage, and not a unit-built hull in the universe that could have been repaired so easily. We'd be talking about six months in Harbor Three, not a week in Kostroma with the work mostly done by the vessel's own crew!"

"I take your point," said Adele. He turned to look at her face to see if she was laughing at him again. She didn't appear to be; at least on the surface.

Sunlight winked from metal. Distances in vacuum were impossible to gauge accurately by eye, but there was little doubt that this sheen was from a cutter approaching the *Princess Cecile* with a message that couldn't be radioed.

Daniel had little doubt as to what the message was, either.

He sighed, then looked again at the great ball of Kostroma. He'd been granted so much that it would be churlish to complain that it wasn't more. Besides, a Leary of Bantry didn't whine.

"Shall we go inside?" he said quietly to Adele. "I believe that will be my relief, Lieutenant Enery, and as a matter of courtesy I'd like to receive her in person. Otherwise she might think I resented her promotion to command."

Daniel had vanished toward the bridge while Adele with the help of two sailors was still getting out of her vacuum suit. Tovera was still in Kostroma City, retrieving equipment "that you'll want, mistress," from some store of Markos's. Adele wondered if her new servant was any better at dealing with weightlessness and vacuum suits than she herself was.

The rigging crew had come inside through a remarkable number of airlocks. Apart from the twenty or so sailors still on the ground dealing with supplies and other final arrangements, the *Princess Cecile*'s entire crew was present.

"How many hatches are there?" Adele asked Lamsoe as he stowed her suit in careful alignment with a score of others in the locker.

"Six is all, mistress," he said. "Not really enough, either. It's not like we was a transport and could wait till next election before we got the rig adjusted."

He tugged her gently. A week in the command node hadn't significantly increased Adele's skill at moving in weightlessness. "Now if you'll come this way, we'll get you with Mr. Leary on the bridge."

"An officer from the flagship boarding!" said the general communicator. The latch of the main airlock clanked.

Lamsoe sprang the remaining twenty yards toward the bridge with Adele in tow. Other personnel, standing to attention while one hand anchored them, squeezed out of the way. Lamsoe's skill was such that they sailed down the corridor without touching a wall.

Daniel, wearing a white uniform with gold hussar knots across the bosom and a worm-track of gold braid down the trouser seam, was talking earnestly with Lt. Mon He'd changed into this resplendent full dress uniform while Adele was still struggling out of her vacuum suit. His eyes noted Adele but he was too involved to greet her.

Lamsoe handed her off to Hogg, who wrapped her hand around a stanchion with gentle pressure and then vanished into the wardroom. They were treating her like a sack of grain, but at least she was valuable grain.

A pair of unfamiliar officers wearing dress uniforms similar to Daniel's came up the corridor skillfully though without Lamsoe's panache. One was a woman in her mid-twenties; the other merely a boy, probably no more than fifteen.

They halted by gripping the hatch coaming and swung upright. The woman saluted Daniel. "Lieutenant Bara Enery reporting aboard, sir!" she said.

Daniel returned the salute. "Welcome aboard the *Princess Cecile*, Lieutenant Enery," he said. "I think you'll be pleased with what you find here."

He sounded not only friendly but mildly pleased. Adele had heard sailors muttering about "the bitch slotted to replace Mr. Leary." Daniel himself, the one time he'd mentioned Enery, referred to her as a very professional officer with a good head for astrogation.

"Before you read your orders, Lieutenant Enery," he said now, "may I present my officers?"

"Please do, captain," Enery said in an accent that marked her as a member of the best circles of Xenos. "But I should emphasize that I don't bring orders of any sort with me. My understanding is that a courier will be arriving from Admiral Ingreit in a few minutes, but I wanted to speak briefly to you before that event."

Daniel nodded as though the statement didn't surprise him. Adele kept her frown internal. She didn't doubt Ms. Sand's good intentions, nor that Sand would make good her hinted promise eventually; but a great deal depended on the intelligence of Admiral Ingreit. If Ingreit was the dunce his employment of Elphinstone implied to Adele, Sand's brilliantly indirect approach might pass right over the gold braid on the admiral's hat.

"This is my first officer, Ms. Mundy," Daniel said, gesturing with a cupped hand to Adele. "You will have heard of the way she captured the Alliance defensive array."

Enery nodded politely, but the youth beside her goggled at Adele. Adele gave him a cold smile. He'd probably been wondering what a worn-looking civilian was doing on the bridge to begin with.

"And this is Lieutenant Mon," Daniel continued. Mon wore a

loose-fitting service uniform. His formal wear had been aboard the *Aglaia* when she sank in the Floating Harbor. "He's been seconded to the *Princess Cecile* to take charge of repairs. Without his expertise there would be several weeks' work yet to complete."

"Courier from the flagship boarding!" the general communicator announced. A detail under a petty officer was on duty at the main hatch. Adele thought the voice was that of Dasi.

As if he hadn't heard, Daniel turned and said, "Mon, Ms. Mundy, I don't know whether you've met Lieutenant Enery. She's Admiral Ingreit's signals lieutenant at present, but I understand she's due for a posting that will use her considerable talents better."

"Mistress," Adele said, nodding acknowledgment.

Enery lifted her chin in the direction of the boy. Despite her good breeding, Enery was obviously embarrassed by Daniel's honest graciousness. "My nephew Piers," she said. "Admiral Collodi's grandson, you may know."

Which made Enery herself an admiral's niece. Not surprising, of course.

"As a matter of fact, Leary," Enery went on, "that's what I'd like to discuss with you. There's rumors going about and of course one doesn't like to take them seriously. But if I should be offered a command, I'd be honored if you'd become my first officer."

The sound of the hatch releasing rang through the *Princess Cecile*.

Enery raised her hand. "Now, don't misunderstand," she added. "If you'd prefer to have nothing more to do with, with any ship I happen to command, no one would blame you in the least. But I want you to know that I have the sincerest regard for your abilities."

Daniel swallowed. "Ms. Enery," he said, "I would be pleased to accept a line appointment under an officer of your abilities. Greatly pleased."

The courier was an officer wearing what she had heard Daniel call a 2nd Class uniform. That gave the corvette's crowded bridge a remarkable range of clothing styles. Adele wondered whether the same thought had caused the smile at the corners of Daniel's mouth.

The courier held a document tied with ribbons which had been sealed with wax. Enery reached for it.

"Excuse me," said the courier with irritation. "I have orders here for Lieutenant Daniel Leary."

"Good God almighty!" blurted a sailor in the corridor outside.

Enery went pale. She slid aside. Daniel took the document and broke the seal with a sideways flick of his index finger. He looked as though he'd been sandbagged. He read the text, then raised his eyes to meet the gaze of those around him.

"It is the Senate's pleasure," Daniel said in a trembling voice, "through the agency of its servants in the Navy Board, to appoint me to the command of the corvette *Princess Cecile* for the purpose of carrying her to Harbor Three on Cinnabar where she will be surveyed by a committee of naval assessors."

He lifted the document again. "So help me God," he said in a wondering voice.

Lieutenant Enery bowed. "Allow me to be the first to congratulate you, Captain Leary," she said in a choking voice. She had to wait for Daniel to recover enough to take her hand; then with her confused nephew in tow she propelled herself down the corridor to the main hatch.

Enery had behaved with a decency equal to Daniel's own, Adele thought. It was a pity that the crew couldn't hold their cheers until the embarrassed officer had left the corvette.

The crew had its orders; there was no reason for the captain to be on the bridge. One could tell a great deal from the command console about the way a ship was handling as it entered sponge space, but one could tell even more from just below the tip of a fully extended ninety-seven-foot mast.

Daniel very deliberately stretched the fingers of his left hand outward, feeling the crackling pressure of the universe against their tips.

Eighteen of the *Princess Cecile*'s twenty-four masts were extended in whole or in part. This first entry into sponge space was a test of both the ship and the way the crew handled her. Petty officers stood at the base of mast clumps to relay the bosun's semaphored orders and to judge the performance of the ratings carrying them out. There shouldn't be any problems, but better to learn while still in the Kostroma system than when unexpectedly confronted by an Alliance cruiser.

Squadron Logistics had granted the *Princess Cecile* five missiles for self-defense on the voyage to Cinnabar. Chief Baylor had two full magazines, twenty rounds, instead of the allotment. Several of the squadron's missileers had expended a few practice rounds on their books rather than by launching them through the tubes, and Daniel had taken an advance from his prize account. If there was a better way for a captain to spend money than in turning his command into an effective fighting unit, Daniel Leary hadn't heard of it.

Around him shimmered a golden light that only spacers saw: the wobbling glow of Casimir energy, visible only at the margins of reality. What looked like stars beyond the veil were not that nor even galaxies: each separate point was a universe in itself, as complete as the sidereal universe from which the *Princess Cecile* was even now edging.

A hydraulic semaphore spread its arms. A rating in the bow cluster made a manual adjustment, and the tip of a mast near Daniel cocked forward thirty degrees from the topmost joint.

The *Princess Cecile*, driven by the greater pressure of Casimir energy on one aspect of the ship than on the other, slid fully into the gap between universes. Her captain, Lieutenant Daniel Leary, reveled in his first command.

The light of all existence flared about him.